Saro

SARO

by

Nikę Campbell

Narrative
Landscape
Press

Copyright © 2022 by Nikę Campbell

The right of Nikę Campbell to be identified as the author
of this work has been asserted by her in accordance
with the copyright laws.

All rights reserved.
No part of this publication may be reproduced, transmitted,
or stored in a retrieval system, in any form or by any means,
without permission in writing from the copyright holder.

ISBN: 978-978-59204-7-5

Published in Nigeria in 2022 by Narrative Landscape Press
9, Odunlami Street, Anthony Village, Lagos, Nigeria
07014522083, 09090554406 – 7
contact@narrativelandscape.com
www.narrativelandscape.com

A catalogue record for this book is available from
the National Library of Nigeria.

Cover Design and Text Layout by Ayebabeledaipre Sokari

Dedication

For my ancestors, your tears and toil were not in vain.
For my children and generations after, always remember you came from greatness.

NEGROLAND and GUINEA.

with the European Settlements, Explaining what belongs to England, Holland, Denmark &c.

By H. Moll Geographer.

E. Stands for English
D. for Dutch

Figure 1: Map of West Africa with slave trade routes from Marina to Freetown
Figure 2: Alade Okikilu Family Tree

PART I: OṢIWOOLU

Abẹokuta and Èkó
Southwestern Nigeria
Circa 1836

Ẹgba ko l'olu, gbogbo wọn ni nṣe bi Ọba

The Ẹgba do not have a Chief for they all behave like Kings

– Ẹgba Proverb

Chapter One

The Storming
Palace, Ake, Abeokuta
Circa 1836

*D**awn broke over the river* as the three girls walked to the bank with empty pots. It was typical for more of their mates to be racing to the river by now, but the air was thick with silence and that did not sit well with one of the girls.

"Is today not our bath day? How come no one else is here?"

The other two shrugged and bent to splash water on their faces.

Idowu, the curious one, looked around, her frown deepening when her eyes settled on the bush behind them. It moved and stopped. She rubbed her eyes to make sure it wasn't her imagination. She called to her friends, but they were already halfway into their gossip about one of the royal guards. Her fingers shook as she placed her pot on the ground and moved towards the bush. She bit her lower lip in trepidation, but her feet, with a mind of their own, drew her closer as the bush began to move again.

"Stupid boys! Are you spying on us again?"

The leaves shook vigorously, drawing the attention of the other girls. They ran towards her, demanding to know what was going on.

The voice was raspy, but they could decipher the words.

"The west winds will bring the four."

The girls gasped but rather than run, they edged towards what could be their death. A clearing appeared behind the bush, and a few feet further, a petite woman lay drenched in water. Her wrapper was still firmly tied to her chest, but her head wrap was by her head. She repeated the phrase. They inched closer to stare. Her pupils had disappeared and all they could see were the whites of her eyes.

"Look at her eyes! Why do they look like that?"

"Shh! Be quiet. Don't you know who this is?" Idowu asked with the impatience one would have with a child.

The other two looked at each other and shrugged. Idowu sighed and knelt beside the woman.

"It is the queen mother, Wuraola. Do you not know she is the reader of hearts and seer of the unseen? We are trespassing. We must leave her to commune with the spirits."

The woman jerked and her pupils rolled back into place. She sat up and sent the other two girls running like they had seen an apparition.

Idowu lowered her head in greeting. "Welcome back, Maami."

Wuraola sized the girl up. Satisfied, she took her hand and squeezed. "We must hurry. They come to take the throne while my son is away. We must hurry."

The palace in Ake was agog with activity when Wuraola and Idowu arrived an hour later. They squeezed through the crowd that had gathered at the entrance.

"Make way for the Queen Mother!" Idowu shouted, over screams of "treason". The royal guards were no longer at their posts at the pillars. In their place were masked, strange men barricading the entrance with their bodies. Their blood-streaked machetes were splayed across their broad heaving chests, enough warning for anyone who dared to cross the line.

Wuraola leapt towards them. The noise stopped and all eyes turned to the battle about to ensue.

"It is only a mouse who comes out to play when the master is away. Who sent you?"

A man stepped forward, white powder encircled his eye. Both eyes spat hate. "We know who you are, Queen Mother, and we are ready for you. And so is he!" He pointed at the palace. "He is waiting."

He ordered the militia to let Wuraola pass through. When Idowu followed, they blocked her way.

Wuraola said without turning, "She is with me."

The men looked to their leader.

"Let her in."

Idowu ran towards Wuraola. She took her hand, and they entered the courtyard together.

Chapter Two

Uneasy Lies the Head
Marina, Èkó, Southwestern Nigeria.
Three Days Before
Circa 1836

It was an unusually hot afternoon when Marina received royal visitors from Ẹgba Kingdom. Pedestrians, most of them traders, heavy-laden with wares on their heads, pushed towards them in excitement.

Men dressed in white cotton buba and kafo surrounded the young king and queen. A white beaded crown adorned Ṣiwoolu's head, and large coral beads graced his neck and agbada – a hand-woven flowing attire that skimmed his ankles. The edges of his kembe, trousers worn mostly by the wealthy and whipped in an intricate spiral maroon design, peeked beneath the agbada. Though the people clamoured for his attention with cries of "Kabiyesi!", he looked through them, lost in his thoughts.

When the people's curious eyes found the petite woman beside him, they fell on their knees before her. Dotunu's ebony skin, washed daily with black soap and rubbed religiously with shea butter, glowed. She exuded an aura that drew them in, and the four red and white marks painted on her forehead, held them in a trance. The infinity gold chain, a gift from her father, glowing on her collar bone was paired with double coral beads around her neck

– another gift from her father. Her accessories flattered her maroon and gold-striped buba that accentuated her voluptuous figure. Her stomach protruded with the baby growing within her, and with every step she took, the beads around her ankles jiggled.

"Olowo ori mi."

Dotunu's endearment brought Şiwoolu back to the present. The beads decorating his crown swung slowly when he looked down into his wife's warm brown eyes.

He smiled. "Are you tired? Do you want to rest?"

She shook her head, her dangling coral earrings touching her slender neck. "I am well," she said, rubbing her growing belly. "We have enjoyed the company of your friend, Sunmonu, for two days now. It is time we ventured out on our own."

"You are right. It is indeed a beautiful day to be out."

Şiwoolu took a deep breath. This was not his first time in Èkó. He had visited once with Ọgbẹni Dele, his mentor and a prosperous commercial trader from his village, Iporo Ake, before he became king – after his father, Alade, was killed.

A passer-by grabbed Dotunu's hand and fell to her knees.

"A blessing, Olori!"

It was an elderly woman paying homage. Her bushy brows arched as she looked up into Dotunu's face.

"Step back!" Olatunde, the head of the royal body-guards commanded in a deep threatening tone. A wall of bodies formed around him as he struck a white tasselled staff into the ground and grabbed the woman's shoulder from behind.

She turned and gasped, eyes fixed on the tall, muscular man who towered over her. His nostrils flared as he examined her. He had the same effect on everyone he encountered. When Şiwoolu brought him to Iporo Ake from Èkó two harvest seasons ago, the villagers would follow him around, marvelling at his physique. He was as tall as their thatched-roof huts, his arms, triple the width of a hoe's handle. He made the young maidens swoon when he walked by, many commenting on the clay colour of his skin. His nose was long and pointed, and the village children lingered past their bedtime as he entertained them under the stars. They were most excited when he licked the tip of his nose and juggled three coconuts in the air. His long legs could cover acres of farmland quicker than anyone and he was most handy with the sword – the very reason Şiwoolu employed him.

"Stop!" Dotunu shouted as she flung his arm away. "She's just an old woman. More importantly, can you not see that she is one of us?"

All eyes fell on the abaja òró – three perpendicular lines, each about three inches long – etched into each cheek of the woman's face. She reminded Şiwoolu of his mother, Wuraola, who had the same markings.

"Mama, please get up!" He leaned forward to help her to her feet. Olatunde apologised softly. He turned around sharply and motioned to the seven guards that had surrounded him to join the other eight a few feet ahead of them, ready to spring at his orders.

Dotunu pulled the old woman into her arms.

"Thank you, my daughter, thank you. Kabiyesi! Allow me to greet you the proper way."

She began to bend her knee but Şiwoolu grabbed her arm and pulled her up again. "No, Mama! Let us move to the side of the street."

He pointed to an orange tree a few feet away from the onlookers, where a woman with a child strapped to her back stood with a large tray of African star apples perched on her head. When she noticed the entourage walking towards her, she knelt before Şiwoolu and mumbled a greeting.

"Leave!" Olatunde shouted as he marched towards the kneeling woman.

She yelled and ran towards the crowd, her tray falling to the ground.

"Why does Olatunde behave like this? Have I not warned him several times to let people be?" Dotunu asked in an exasperated tone.

Şiwoolu's hands splayed over her arm. "Dotunu, don't upset yourself. You know why Olatunde does this. Remember the child you carry."

"Kabiyesi is right," the old woman said. She nodded and looked from one to the other. "What brings you to Èkó?" she asked, looking at Dotunu, who had moved to lean against the trunk of the tree.

"We're here for some rest and to see a friend. What brings you here?" Şiwoolu asked, one eye on Dotunu.

"My son moved here to trade. He works with a rich madam. He is my only child, so I followed him."

"Ah, a parakoyi, is he? I was also in training to be trader before this." Şiwoolu pointed to his crown and beads.

The old woman shook her head sadly. "I wish. At least that would be respectable." She paused, stretched her lips in what she hoped was a smile and said, "Your father, Alade Okikilu, what a brave man he was! Deliverer of our people. He will never be forgotten."

She held out her hand towards Şiwoolu. He took it and squeezed lightly.

"Thank you."

She walked towards Dotunu. "Where is your first son, the one that came not long after you married?"

Dotunu's even white teeth appeared briefly. "He is at our friend's house with Ireti, my care giver."

"Ah! The little prince!" She clapped her hands to her chest. "We were so happy when the people chose you to take your father's place after his untimely passing."

"It was ordained by the gods," Dotunu said with conviction. "Mama, tell me, how is Èkó? How long have you been here?" Her eyes twinkled with excitement as she gestured with her hands.

"My daughter, Èkó is not like our cluster of villages in Abeokuta o! These people have gone far and seen a lot. Have you been to the docks yet?"

Dotunu turned to Şiwoolu, her eyebrows arched. "What is that, olowo ori mi?"

He smiled, watching the emotions cross her face – curiosity, awe, and almost impatience at her lack of knowledge.

"It's where the ships land when they arrive at the shore," he said softly.

"Oh, the place Sunmonu told us to visit! 'A must! You

must go today! By noon!'" Dotunu mimicked Şiwoolu's bosom friend in a high-strung voice. It was followed closely, like thunder after lightning, by a hard laugh. Şiwoolu, remembering how adamant his friend had been, joined in.

As their laughter faded, the old woman nodded and smiled. "It is indeed a wonder. How the white man can live on that moving house for so many moons, I don't know!"

Her right hand went up in the air and she snapped her fingers. A small object dropped and rolled to the ground beside Dotunu's henna-tipped toenails.

"Let me help you, Mama." Dotunu bent before either the old woman or Şiwoolu could stop her. She moaned, grabbing her abdomen.

"Dotunu!" Şiwoolu grabbed her shoulders first. She stayed close to the ground, unmoving.

The old woman fell to the ground beside her, bushy brows knotted with worry. "Are you alright?"

Dotunu managed a short laugh, grabbed Şiwoolu's hand, and rose. The old woman picked up the elusive ring.

"This child continues to speak to me with kicks and tumbles. He is so different from his brother," Dotunu said.

The old woman smiled and looked at Şiwoolu with questioning eyes as he steadied Dotunu.

"She insists that it is another boy. She says he's..."

"In my dreams," Dotunu finished for him as she often did.

They glanced at each other and laughed. Şiwoolu's hand found its way to his child nestled within her and rubbed. He was rewarded with a kick. Dotunu chuckled as she placed her hand over his and looked at the old woman.

"Where our first son is calm, this one will take life by force. But both will be loving, just like their father."

If the old woman smiled any wider, her face would split in half.

"Our people are proud of both of you, so young and yet so wise." She stretched out her hand to Şiwoolu. "Here, for both of you to remember me by."

He looked down at the ring she held between her fingertips. "We can't take this, Mama."

Dotunu leaned closer. She shook her head upon seeing the object.

"Ah! No, Mama, we can't. It looks like a family heirloom."

The ring, now nestled in the palm of her hand, flashed as the old woman moved closer with it. Her mouth was turned down. Her eyes travelled to Olatunde and the guards who watched her every move.

"I was unable to attend your wedding, so here is my gift," she said.

Şiwoolu and Dotunu glanced at each other.

"Take it!" She pressed the ring into Şiwoolu's palm and pouted. "It's stayed in my family for this long for a purpose. Now it is time I gave it to someone else to bring them the same good fortune it has brought us."

"We cannot..." Dotunu protested.

"Better with you than with the wolves," she pushed the ring down the length of Siwoolu's middle finger. He raised his hand to examine it. It would have been a simple gold band but for the scalloped edges.

Dotunu and Şiwoolu glanced at each other. To refuse

a gift from an elder was an insult. The old woman smiled when they seemed to acquiesce and Şiwoolu thanked her.

A thin and wild sound reached their ears. It sounded like a crying child. Dotunu grabbed Şiwoolu's hand, searching for the sound as it got louder and closer. Olatunde and the guards circled the three, hands disappearing under their buba. Şiwoolu refrained from chuckling, his lips close to Dotunu's ears.

"It is fine, dear wife. It is just a horse."

Olatunde glanced at Şiwoolu with a stony face. He turned and called to the guards to step back. They made an opening for the royal couple to see. The sound of hooves hitting the ground grew louder as the horses advanced steadily towards them. The first horse was pure white. A whiff of its breath announced its last meal of grass. The tip of a black boot projected through an iron entrapment dangling from the side of the animal. The rider was dressed in an attire like a white şokoto and buba; the sleeves were as wide as those of Dotunu's buba. They stopped at his wrists, fastened with three small, round buttons. A black hat covered the top half of the face of a white man. A second man on a black horse rode up behind him. Dotunu pointed.

"Where did *he* learn to do that?"

The dark-skinned man was dressed just like the one before him but without the hat. His head was shaved clean and shiny. His white shirt with billowing sleeves was open almost to the waist, revealing thick, black, curly hair. His horse stopped beside Şiwoolu and Dotunu. His eyes roamed the crowd that had formed before he lowered his head to look at Dotunu. Şiwoolu saw the man's eyes when he finally looked at him as though he were an afterthought. They were grey. They reminded him of the colour of clouds heavy with rain.

"Sigmund!" The white man shouted.

The dark-skinned man with the strange eyes turned and shouted something back in a foreign tongue. Pulling on the rope tied to the animal's neck, he spit on the ground before riding away behind the white man.

"Kabiyesi!" Olatunde thundered as he and the guards pulled out their swords. The crowd shouted and fled.

"What were you waiting for, Olatunde?!" Şiwoolu's voice shook with anger as he pulled Dotunu's shivering body close.

Olatunde and his men fell to the ground. "Forgive us, Kabiyesi. For a moment, I thought you were already acquainted. It wasn't until I saw him spit—"

"Silence!" Şiwoolu's deep voice rattled with anger.

"Olowo ori mi, please. We draw attention to ourselves!" Dotunu whispered into the crook of his neck.

Şiwoolu pulled her closer. "We must go. This excitement is too much for the queen." He looked sideways at the elderly woman. "Thank you for the gift, Mama. Until we meet again."

The sun was setting when they returned to Sunmonu's house. The structure was hard to miss. It was the only one on a street of identical mud buildings that had arched wooden windows and a turquoise-painted door. The walls were a deep yellow and the corrugated roof, a rusty red. When Dotunu set eyes on it the day they arrived, she had giggled and requested that Şiwoolu commission the artisans to paint their own newly constructed palace the same colour.

The street was deserted; most households were in their backyards preparing dinner. Two figures were seated on the elevated square stone leading to the front door as they approached. A lanky frame, previously curved around a sleeping child, straightened.

"Ireti! Why are you sitting outside with the prince?" Olatunde shouted, running towards them.

Dotunu pulled up the wrapper that had enveloped her legs and hurried to them. Şiwoolu stretched out his hand to stop her, but she was faster. "Dotunu," he called out. "Take it easy, Olatunde can handle this."

The bodyguards stood on either side of the couple as their leader lifted the little boy of just over a harvest season from the prepubescent girl's lap. Ireti held the edge of the stone and stood up slowly. Her breathing was short and heavy as her eyes darted from Şiwoolu and Dotunu to the bodyguards and back again. Her cheeks, lined with faint diagonal marks on either side, were sucked in. She picked up a cloth bundle at her feet.

"Why are you dressed for a journey, Ireti? Why have you taken your belongings?" Dotunu asked, her words slow and her voice rising in anger.

Şiwoolu wrapped his hand around Dotunu's elbow and walked up the stairs with her until they were both looking down at their ward. Ireti fell into Dotunu's arms and buried her head in her bosom. Şiwoolu stepped back and gestured to the guards to disperse.

"Take the prince inside," he said to Olatunde.

When they left, he turned around to watch the two. Ireti gesticulated wildly, making incoherent noises.

"Ireti, slow down, I can't understand you," Dotunu said with a frown.

She stamped her feet, frustrated at her inability to speak. Şiwoolu watched the scene he was all too familiar with.

Dotunu pushed Ireti's hands down to her sides and wrapped her arms around her. Ireti became quiet. She trembled as Dotunu pulled her closer. "Someone has frightened her."

"Who? There was no one in this house when we left. Remember that Sunmonu said he had to meet a trader for some goods."

Dotunu turned back to stare at the child, her face contorted with fear. It was the same look she had when she first arrived at her home with Dotunu's father many harvest seasons ago.

"She wants us to leave now."

Şiwoolu sighed. "Why? What happened?"

He moved closer and touched Ireti's hands – wrapped around Dotunu's neck – for a moment. She began to whimper but did not budge.

"Just talk to her. She can hear you, you know that," Dotunu said. She whispered into Ireti's ear until she was quiet.

"Ireti, are you listening?" he asked.

She looked up at him with incredulous eyes and nodded.

"What happened when we were gone?"

She raised her hand and pointed at him, and then held up three fingers.

"Me? Three?"

She nodded and pointed to herself.

"You?"

She nodded, turned around and pointed towards the back of the house. Slowly, she crouched by Dotunu's feet with her hand over one ear.

"You were listening to three of me?"

Ireti shook her head and stamped her feet. Şiwoolu frowned.

"I don't understand! Dotunu, I have told you times without number to let us get a real servant for our son, but you insist it must be Ireti. Why? Is there something you're not telling me?"

Dotunu pulled Ireti up and walked her to the closed door. "Go in, please. I'll come to you in a moment. No! You have to go in. You can't stay here all night!"

They communicated for a few more seconds – words on Dotunu's part and gestures from Ireti. Eventually, Ireti conceded and went in. When Dotunu turned around, her eyes sparked with anger.

"I told you what she went through before she came to stay with my family, and I asked you when you wanted to marry me if you would accept her, if you would take what was mine as yours. Did you not agree?"

Şiwoolu nodded and opened his mouth to speak.

"Will you allow me to finish?"

"Continue."

"Ireti has endured a hard life though she has only seen eleven, maybe twelve harvest seasons. I can only tell you how she spent five of those. The rest she keeps buried in her head and heart. Experiences one should not endure at any age."

Şiwoolu took her hand but Dotunu pulled away, her eyes filling with tears. "She does not lie. She's afraid, and we must find out why."

He drew her close. "All right, Dotunu. Please, no tears. I'm sorry I upset you. No more speaking evil about Ireti. I know she means so much to you."

She wiped her eyes with her fingertips but said nothing.

"I will speak with Sunmonu once he gets back," he said.

"You will?"

"I give you my word, Olori."

She raised her head and stared into his eyes, embers of her rage still burning. "I believe you, Oşiwoolu. Let us go in."

The street was dark, but that was no problem for Sunmonu, for even with eyes closed, he could find his way home. How could he not? Much sweat and blood had been shed to ensure that his house stood out from all the others on the street owned by Èkó's new elite. He belched, wishing that for once, his large consumption of alcoholic beverages would bury the memories that lingered. He pushed open the front door with one hand, cradled an uncorked bottle close to his chest with the other and staggered past the first doorway in the hall, propelled by an internal force beyond his control. He stopped by the second door and turned – he could smell the shea butter Dotunu rubbed on her ebony skin and the coconut oil she massaged into her scalp. He touched the door handle.

"Ewé? Is that you?" Şiwoolu's deep voice cut through the silence and Sunmonu's wandering thoughts. He released his hand on the handle as though it burned a hole in his palms and walked back to the first door.

Olatunde's eyes met his in the dull light of the oil lamp as he opened it. The lamp, he often proudly told his guests, was a gift from the North. It sat on an overturned mortar a few feet from Şiwoolu. There were many strange objects in Sunmonu's private chambers. His travels beyond the shores of Marina were evident in the prayer rug rolled up in the corner of the room, a gift from the ruler of the northern region of Marrakesh, and the wooden tambourine leaning against the back of the door, an exchange for woven raffia mats with the white traders. The floating fragrance from the burning incense next to the lamp was another gift from a trader he had met on his travel to the eastern regions of the world.

Şiwoolu sat up on the wooden stool. From the impatient look on his face, he had been sitting for some time. His head was empty of the crown he had worn all day; it now nestled in a box in the room where his wife, son, and ward slept.

Sunmonu could see why his friend was popular with everyone, subjects and kings alike. He was muscular and taller than anyone Sunmonu knew – except Olatunde, who sat by the king's feet. His eyes, which never missed much, drew people in. They were warm, almost dancing with laughter, and always made the recipients of his gaze feel like they were truly being seen.

"Welcome, Ewé. Olatunde, you can leave us."

Olatunde rose. Sunmonu gripped the bottle in his hand as the giant of a man walked past him and closed the door. His agbada swept the floor as he sauntered towards the mortar, placed the oil lamp on the floor and sat down.

"I have told you to stop calling me a leaf, Şiwoolu! These are new times, and old things are behind us."

Sunmonu's nickname suited him well: he was as light as a leaf, a small man who had limbs like sticks and was as nimble as a cat.

Şiwoolu shrank back and covered his nose as an odour emanated from Sunmonu.

"Ewé, what is that smell?"

Sunmonu lowered his balding head and smelled his clothes, then he looked at Şiwoolu with narrowed eyes. "What smell, my brother?"

Şiwoolu rose and moved close. He covered his nose again. "That smell!"

Sunmonu's eyes laughed before his mouth did. "You must be referring to the drink I just had with my new clients. It's called scotch. Here!" He pulled the cork off the bottle and pushed it into his companion's chest. "Sit! Don't let it drop."

Şiwoolu looked down at the bottle and the same pungent smell hit him. He coughed and pushed it back into Sunmonu's hands before seating opposite him.

Sunmonu laughed and slapped his thigh. "Coward! Your size always deceived everyone but me!"

"Ewé, I am just cautious."

Sunmonu laughed again. A child's cry rang out. "Oh, I'm sorry, I forgot for a second that you are no longer a bachelor."

Şiwoolu smiled.

Sunmonu raised a finger. "But remember, I saw Dotunu first!"

Şiwoolu shook his head. "No, you did not. You keep saying this, but in truth you remember that she and her father came to see my father long before—" He paused and looked towards the door.

"Before we used to spy on her and the other maidens when they bathed in the Ogun River. Do you mean to tell me you haven't told your wife?" Sunmonu covered his mouth and chuckled.

Şiwoolu shook his head in exasperation. "Will you ever change?"

"Not likely. Drink!" Sunmonu pushed it into his hands.

"So that I'll become drunk like you? No, let one of us remain level-headed." He placed the bottle on the floor, close to his feet.

Sunmonu shrugged and dug into the pocket of his kembe. "Look at this one. It came with the scotch." He held the thick, round object in between his slender fingers. "It's a cigar."

"Sikar?" Şiwoolu asked hesitantly.

Sunmonu shook his head. "I said 'cigar'!" He put it to his lips. "You smoke it like this." He took it out and pretended to blow out air. "I would have lit it, but the smell may wake Olori and your mute."

Şiwoolu shook a finger at him. "You must stop that, Sunmonu! You know not to say that in Olori's hearing. That girl means more to her than, I dare say, Şomide and the child she carries."

Sunmonu snapped his fingers. "Yes! Thank the gods you said what has been on the tip of my tongue since you arrived." He leaned towards Şiwoolu. "What is really between that mute and your wife?"

Şiwoolu shook his head. "The more important question is why Ireti was scared to death when we arrived this evening. Something happened here, Sunmonu."

Sunmonu scratched his head. "Here? But I was not home."

"She pointed to the backyard, too scared to even venture there."

Sunmonu sprang up. "The backyard?" He wiped his face. "Nothing's there, just my storage room where I keep my goods, my unsold items."

The light flickered as Sunmonu moved his hand to scratch his head once more. He took off his agbada, revealing his buba and kembe which covered three-quarters of his legs. Şiwoolu looked down at his left leg, shorter by half an inch than the right one. The foot was twisted downward and inward from birth, and from afar, it resembled a malnourished, twisted tuber of yam. He was teased about it from a young age. Catching a glimpse of it reminded him why his friend wore the full regalia of his own volition, unlike he, who by tradition had to do so.

"Are you retiring to bed already?" Şiwoolu asked.

"No, not at all," Sunmonu replied, his words slurring.

"Drink your scotch and let us talk. You know that tomorrow we must return home."

Sunmonu unscrewed the top of the bottle and raised it to his lips. Şiwoolu waited for him to wipe the side of his mouth.

"Did you go to the docks at the Marina like I told you? You didn't, did you? You must go tomorrow!" Sunmonu said as he sliced the air with his right hand and dropped it with a flop by his side.

Şiwoolu chuckled. "Ewé! One would think you had a lot to gain from us visiting. Is there gold to be found there?"

Sunmonu raised his hand. "More than gold, King! You will see splendours beyond your wildest imagination! If it were not for that meeting with my new customer, I would have taken you. But don't worry, I will meet you there tomorrow before noon, since you must make the journey home to Abeokuta."

"All right," Şiwoolu acquiesced. "We should have more time since we already paid our respects to the king of Lagos, Ọba Ajosun, on our way here."

"As you should. Ọba Ajosun is a good king. His new wife has been a good influence on him."

Şiwoolu shook his head in wonder at this new version of his friend. Not only had his dressing and stance changed, but he had also established strong ties with royalty in Èkó.

"Ewé, my dear friend! So you know Olori Tinubu? Your travels have made a new man out of you. Such new confidence you have! Not like the old days, *ehn?*"

Sunmonu threw his head back and laughed. Then he sat on the floor, his beige-coloured agbada blending with the surface beneath him. "Ah, the old days. No titles, no frills," he said.

Şiwoolu sighed, his face transforming into one of longing. "We were just young men trying to become commercial traders. At least you succeeded, Ewé."

Sunmonu looked up at him with a grim face. "Things are tough out there. Èkó is not as easy as it looks. We all have to make sacrifices."

Siwoolu's forehead wrinkled. "Sacrifices? What do you mean?"

A short silence was broken by Sunmonu's snore. Şiwoolu waved a hand in front of his face and he opened his half-closed eyes.

"Never mind me, I think I am drunk," he drawled. Lifting his head, he continued: "Tell me about home again. I miss home!"

"What do you want me to tell you?" asked Şiwoolu.

"About our growing up and our life back then. Tell me about your father and your last journey with him. You know he was like a father to me too. Tell me." He grabbed Şiwoolu's ankle and shook it.

"All right! Just let me go," Şiwoolu said, and chuckled. He took a deep breath as the memories of his father washed over him like a flood. He was grateful for the dim light of the lamp that masked the tears that started to trickle down his cheeks, just as Sunmonu snored loudly on the floor. The memories of the trip he took with his father came flooding back. Unknown to both, it would be the turning point of their lives.

Chapter Three

Welcome and Farewell
Iporo Village
Circa 1834

Şiwoolu made his way across the family compound to his father's hut a day before another journey. His sole mission was to inform him of his plans to travel in a few days with Ọgbẹni Dele and his bosom friend, Sunmonu, to buy and sell merchandise and produce in the surrounding villages.

Alade coughed when he entered. He was sitting on the raffia mat, his feet spread apart. The left one that bothered him had his walking stick lodged under the back of his leg. Firewood crackled and sparkled in the corner.

"Baami, you still have this cough? Didn't you drink the agbo Maami made for you?

Şiwoolu prostrated before his father. When he felt his hand pat his back, he rose and sat by his side. Alade's bushy grey brows formed a line as they looked down at him. Şiwoolu still towered over him sitting down.

"Şiwoolu, I am still your father. If I choose to take or not take that thing your mother calls medicinal herbs, that is my business."

They stared at each other for a few seconds and burst into laughter. When he began to cough, Şiwoolu begged him to stop.

"Baami, I don't blame you. Maami's agbo is the worst I've ever tasted. Do you want me to get some from the neighbour? Hers goes down well."

He began to rise, but his father held him back. Alade pushed back his abeti aja, a fixture on his head for as long as Şiwoolu could remember. His snow-white hair peeked from under it. He straightened the cap and repositioned his left leg.

"I want you to accompany me to the meeting this time."

Şiwoolu's heartbeat quickened. He searched Alade's face for an explanation.

"Son, it is time you learn who and what makes up the backbone of our kingdom."

"You mean I will once again see the mighty Şodękę, another leader of the rebellion that freed us from the tyranny of the Alaafin?"

Alade nodded.

"Yes, my good friend Şodękę. We fought side by side in that war that liberated us from the Oyo slavers!"

Şiwoolu looked at the floor, debating whether to voice his thoughts.

"Why now, Baami?" he asked, looking up. Alade's knowing eyes told him that he had been anticipating it.

A small figure entered. Wuraola's plump face was illuminated by the light from the fireplace. She was not as old as Alade. She approached them, stooping slightly, hands behind her back.

"My husbands, what will you have me make to keep the hunger away until supper?" The abaja oro decorating her two cheeks rose as her eyes fell on Şiwoolu. "I have ipekere, fresh one from Iya Oloja, or is it kokoro you want? I just made some."

Alade sighed and Şiwoolu laughed.

"Maami, you know I stopped by you just before I came in here and you offered me the very same snacks. I am trying to keep fit, remember?"

Alade hit his stomach playfully. "You hear that, Iya Şiwoolu? Your son has become a man. Stop pampering him like a child. Let him be!"

Wuraola crouched slowly, a few feet away from them. Her threaded hair was stacked up on her head like swords. "Şiwoolu came of age five harvest seasons ago. Why didn't you take him then? Why now, as he has asked?"

Alade grunted. "Woman, nothing ever bypasses you, does it?"

She nodded and sat beside him. "You know very well I was listening by the doorway, baale mi."

Alade shook his head, though a smile played at the corners of his mouth.

"With your experience as a soldier, you should have known this!" she laughed.

Alade was one of the leaders of the Ologuns, the freedom fighters responsible for liberating the Egba people from the Oyo Empire. With his band of equally ferocious fighters, they led the people from the Maye's camp to settle in the rocky terrain, far from the thieving hands of the Alaafin, King of the Oyo Empire. He often travelled to meet with the council of war chiefs, the ologuns. His reputation brought prestige to Iporo Ake village and the whole of Egba Kingdom.

"Why now, Baami?" Şiwoolu asked again, his voice

breaking the eye contact between the two. He was used to doing this since childhood. They had eyes only for each other.

Alade sat up and nodded. "If you didn't ask, I would have questioned it." He paused and looked at Wuraola again. "The ruling council has called a meeting. It seems there is some news that will affect us."

Wuraola sighed.

"I was told to bring Şiwoolu to bear witness."

She studied her husband for a few seconds.

"That is all I can say," Alade said, looking away.

"All right," she said and began to rise.

Şiwoolu grabbed her arm when she lost her balance.

"Always at attention," she said, patting his arm. "Let me at least prepare something for your trip. It is a day or so on foot, and you will need your energy."

"E kuro le!" A young voice called from outside.

Wuraola shook her head. "Sunmonu! Were you not here a few hours ago? Do you even stay at home to help your mother?"

Sunmonu entered, half-dressed in a kembe, his skinny chest heaving. He prostrated.

"Maami, Baami, I hope I find you well."

Alade nodded and smiled.

"I hope you are taking care of your mother. You are the man of the house now."

Sunmonu rose and pushed out his chest. "Yes, I am after all son of Ademola, of the Jibodu ruling house. That's why I am very excited about this trip we are taking with Ọgbẹni Dele tomorrow."

Şiwoolu's head lowered to the floor. Sunmonu looked from father to son.

"Is something wrong? Are you not going again? His voice quivered with trepidation.

Wuraola looked at the two friends before her eyes rested on Şiwoolu. "I will leave you to prepare dinner."

Sunmonu grabbed Şiwoolu's shoulder and looked up at him when she left.

"Are *we* not going anymore? You know it is our final task before becoming full-fledged parakoyis."

Şiwoolu raised his head and shook it. "I must go with Baami somewhere tomorrow."

"Şiwoolu!" Alade shouted in the background. The fire crackled again. Şiwoolu went to his side and knelt.

Sunmonu mumbled an excuse and walked out of the hut.

"It is your decision, but why didn't you tell me you had another trip planned?"

Şiwoolu remained quiet.

"I know you have been looking forward to this trip."

"Yes, Baami."

Alade nodded. "If you choose to come with me, make sure you are ready to leave at the break of dawn."

Şiwoolu got up, in a hurry to escape his father's brooding gaze.

A full day of walking through neighbouring villages and the Ęgba forest brought Şiwoolu and Alade to Olumo Rock. He knew they had reached their destination when he smelled the smoke, and in the distance saw the thick dark smog floating above the trees.

"We have arrived," Alade said, as though voicing it would make it more real. Şiwoolu stood beside him transfixed. Alade tapped his walking stick against the rocks leading downward towards the glowing, orange light. "Follow me," he added, swinging his stick beside his left leg as he descended onto the first rock towards the shadows below.

They heard faint echoes morphing into a song that they both knew by heart, one that made Şiwoolu's head swell as though they were chanting his oriki. It was the anthem of their tribe.

> *Lori oke o'un pẹtẹlẹ*
> *Nibẹ l'agbe bi mi o*
> *Nibẹ l'agbe to mi d'agba oo*
> *Ilẹ ominira*
>
> *Emi o f'Abẹokuta ş'ogo*
> *N o duro, l'ori olumọ*
> *Maa yo l'oruko Egba ooo*
> *Emi ọmọ Lişabi*
>
> *Maa yo, maa yo, maa yo o;*
> *l'ori olumọ;*
> *Maa yo, maa yo, maa yo o;*
> *l'ori olumọ*

Abeokuta Ilu Egba
N' oni gbagbe rẹ
N' o gbe o leke okan mi
B'ilu odo Oya

Emi o maa yo l'ori Olumo
Emi o s'ogo yi l'okan mi
Wipe ilu olokiki ooo
L'awa Egba ngbe

Maa yo, maa yo, maa yo o;
l'ori olumọ;
Maa yo, maa yo, maa yo o;
l'ori olumọ

As they got closer to the ground, the song grew louder, and the shadows became men. When they reached the bottom of the rocks, they saw hundreds of them dressed in war attire. Their charms and cowries jingled, beating against their buba as they lifted their clenched fists in the air. Şiwoolu sucked in his breath when he saw a woman dressed in white, cowries dangling from her neck, wrists, and legs, shouting as ferociously as her male counterparts. A man stood in the centre of the circle, close to a large bonfire. He stamped his feet on the ground, his chest heaving rapidly. His eyes lit up when they fell on Alade.

"Ah, my brother and comrade has arrived! The soon-to-be! Make way!" the man announced.

Şiwoolu recognised his voice and tried to recall where he had heard it before, but there was no time to reflect because he noticed the men bowing in reverence as his father walked past them.

"Ẹgba ko l'olu, gbogbo won ni nṣe bi Ọba!" his father shouted aloud, lifting his hands in greeting, and the men replied in a chorus that echoed into the dark sky and laughed. "Indeed, we the Ẹgba people will no longer bow to anyone. We are all kings!" Alade repeated. Then he and the man embraced.

Curious, Ṣiwoolu stepped closer to stare at the other man and exhaled. He could never forget the face of the man who had fought side by side with his father in the battle against the Ọyọ Empire. His eyes were as sharp as a hawk's, they latched on to his face as he stepped away from Alade.

"So he came after all," he said

Alade smiled. "Ṣodẹkẹ, you sound surprised. I knew he would. He is my son after all, not a bastard."

The men grunted in agreement.

Ṣiwoolu turned to his father, taken aback by his comment. Alade's flippant comment the day before, to meet him at daybreak if he chose, had masked his confidence that Ṣiwoolu would accompany him.

"You are welcome, Oṣiwoolu, son of Alade of the house of Okikilu, the deliverer of our people," Ṣodẹkẹ said.

Alade held up his hand. "No! I am not the deliverer of our people! We all had a hand in delivering ourselves from our enemies. Ṣodẹkẹ, you have done a lot for us, not to talk of Lamodi."

A war cry broke out in the crowd and Ṣodẹkẹ joined in. Men, camouflaged by leaves, jumped out of tree branches and from behind rocks and began a war dance. The collective stomping of feet made the earth tremble, and their loud voices carried into the still air. Şiwoolu did not know when he began to stamp his feet, hitting the ground hard like the other men and blending with the bodies and rattling from the cowries on their ankles and clothing. Sweat poured like water down his body. He had no control over his feet, even when they began to hurt; it was as if he was under a spell. But it was the sound of Şodękę's booming voice, filled with raw power, calling out the names of the four regions that comprised the Ęgba kingdom, which brought everyone to order.

"Ęgba Alake! Ęgba Oke Ǫna! Ęgba Owu! Ęgba Gbagura!"

Bodies stilled and the earth beneath their feet was relieved.

"Sit!"

Şiwoolu obeyed like everyone else. A one-eyed man sat beside him on a rock. He noticed his father scanning the crowd in search of him from where he stood at the forefront. Şiwoolu waved to him and he began to walk towards him. But Şodękę touched his shoulder and he stopped.

"Brother, this announcement is about the future of the Ęgba kingdom. Please, stand by me." Şodękę looked at the crowd. "Our time in this new land has not been long – this place we now call Abeokuta: under the rock, our place of refuge."

The men murmured, but stopped when Şodękę began to pace the crowd, leaving Alade to stand alone.

"It is true, as our commander said, that we do not have a chief, for we are all kings. I remember when we once had a king – Alake Okikilu, kin to Alade and me – before he was cut down in the Agbaje war." Ṣodẹkẹ paused and sighed. "But there comes a time when we must awaken to the realities of this new world."

Alade looked at him, confusion written on his face. Even Ṣiwoolu could tell what Ṣodẹkẹ was about to say.

"In deliberation with the ogboni council," Ṣodẹkẹ nodded at the six men dressed in flowing aṣo oke sweeping the ground and seated in the front row, "we have decided that it is time to select our next king – Alake of Ẹgba kingdom – from the families of the four houses that rule the many villages that make up the kingdom. They are families comprised of the founders and fighters of the Ẹgba people, the same ones who led our migration out of the Maye camp in the Oyo Empire and set up settlements for our people here in Abeokuta."

The fire crackled as all held their breath. Ṣodẹkẹ turned to Alade and said, "As kinsman and representative of the Okikilu Ruling House, I nominate Alade Okikilu."

Jubilant cries erupted from the crowd, but Alade stopped them by tapping his cane on the ground loud enough for everyone to hear its echo before he faced Ṣodẹkẹ. He looked stupefied, his brows furrowing.

"Why me? There are other men just as deserving of this. Did you consider Abiodun, our kinsman who also resides in my village in Iporo Ake? Or even yourself?" he asked.

Ṣodẹkẹ smiled. "Abiodun said you would say that when we, and our entire village, decided to nominate you."

"Abiodun said that?' Alade asked. His voice carried

doubt. The men laughed at his humility, and when he heard this, he knew he had no choice but to accept. The shadow of a smile played on his lips, and Ṣodẹkẹ placed his hand on his shoulder in solidarity.

"You cannot reject this, Alade. The Okikilu Ruling House has spoken!" he said. Then Ṣodẹkẹ began to announce the three other ruling houses – Jibodu, Larun-Okukenu, and Lupo Mosuluka – and the families that made up each house. Everyone fell silent, then they began to whisper amongst themselves.

The woman Ṣiwoolu had noticed earlier sprang to her feet. She had beads on the tips of her plaited hair, which framed her round face. Whispers of "Mojiren," travelled through the crowd and filled Ṣiwoolu's ears. At last, he had come face-to-face with the woman that had fought alongside his father and the Egba army.

"We pick the Okikilu Ruling House, and Alade of the house of Okikilu, as our Alake."

Alade's eyes widened. "Is this true?' he murmured, looking from one face to another in the crowd as they dropped their gaze and prostrated, exclaiming in unison: "Kabiyesi o!"

Alade was quiet.

"The gods have spoken and so have our people!" Ṣodẹkẹ cried out from his position on the ground. The crowd remained motionless, waiting for his command. "You must release us to stand," Ṣodẹkẹ said, looking up at Alade.

He looked around in a daze. It was the first time Ṣiwoolu had ever seen him uncertain about anything. He wanted to run to him, to reassure him, but Alade's expression suddenly changed, and a determined look arose on his face.

"Rise, my people!" he thundered.

The men began to stand and move towards him, eager to pay homage to the new king.

"Where is my son? Where is Şiwoolu?"

"Şiwoolu!" The crowd joined in the search.

Şiwoolu could not move his legs. He yelled, but it was a whisper compared to the frenzy around him. He felt the one-eyed man beside him push him forward and shout: "He is here!"

The crowd helped him wade through, nudging and pushing until he stood beside his father who grabbed his shoulders and drew him close.

"Should I ever forget, son," he shouted into his ear, "remind me that one does not enter into the water and then run from the cold."

Şiwoolu smiled and grabbed him by the shoulder, his heart bursting with pride as the crowd chanted: "Kabiyesi o, Alade Okikilu!"

The news that Alade had been selected king arrived in Iporo hours before Şiwoolu and Alade did. They were met by jubilant villagers and drummers serenading them.

"Kabiyesi o!"

The crowd fell to the ground behind him. A lone figure stood at the back. Wuraola walked towards them.

"Alade?" She held out her hand when she was close. Alade grasped it and she sank to her feet.

He grabbed her shoulders and pulled her up. They gazed at each other for moments and then hugged. She stepped back and touched Şiwoolu's arm.

"Ọmọ Alade Okikilu, ọmọ kabiyesi ilu Ẹgba! Well done!" She chanted her son's oriki, causing him to feel proud once more. Alade looked around at the multitude still prostrated on the ground.

"Get up my people. We are one, get up!"

They began to rise and talk excitedly.

"We must prepare for the coronation, Kabiyesi!"

"Yes!" The crowd agreed.

"The whole of Ẹgba Land will be in attendance, we must be ready!" Another voice said.

A body rose slowly. "If I may get up, Kabiyesi?" the voice was frail. Alade followed the sound that came from the middle of the throng.

"Abiodun? Please get up!"

The older man rose with the help of his walking stick, beaming with pride. He turned to the villagers. "This is a great day for our village. Our son, our brother, our father, will be the first king of Ẹgba kingdom. Let us celebrate. Bring out the items we have!"

The people began, coming forward bearing baskets of food items. Some brought live goats, chicken, and freshly roasted bush meat still on skewers. They bowed before the three and placed their gifts before them. By the time the last person placed his gift, there were baskets of farm produce and sacks of grain that would fill six huts and overflow. Alade's eyes were glassy when Wuraola glanced at him. She nodded, squared her shoulders and spoke.

"We are grateful for your support. We are even more thankful that we are blessed with people like you. Please take back your food for which you have toiled for a full harvest season."

The people grumbled and refused.

"Please!" Her pleas fell on deaf ears. Then Sunmonu's mother came forward and picked up her contribution – others followed. Şiwoolu and his parents followed the departing crowd. As they drew near to their compound, they looked at each other. The gifts and their bearers were already waiting in the compound. Sunmonu's mother stepped forward, her petite self hunched over a tray filled with tubers of yam.

"This is from my family, Kabiyesi and Olori. I will begin to boil and pound them for your dinner." She smiled and headed towards the back of Wuraola's hut, where she cooked. The other women followed with their produce. Wuraola followed them, instructions rolling off her tongue. The men walked up to Alade with gourds of palm wine.

The crowd was still there at midnight. By then, the produce had disappeared into pots and the compound been transformed into a place of celebration and feasting. Alade watched from the bench, where he sat with Abiodun and a few of the village elders. They spoke quietly amongst themselves. He waved away all the food placed before him. Şiwoolu, surrounded by his mates in front of his own hut, stole looks at his father, unsurprised. Wuraola was the only one he would allow to make his food. He had once told him, "Şiwoolu, it is a wise man who eats only the food his wife gives him. All lizards lie flat on their stomach, it is difficult to determine which has a stomach ache. Nobody really knows the heart of man."

From Şiwoolu's vantage angle, he could tell his father was still in a daze. Wuraola whizzed through the crowd and spoke into Alade's ears. She finally convinced him to eat something and left to prepare pounded yam.

Şiwoolu watched as his father waited for Wuraola to bring the delicacy as the crowd thinned. When he could no longer stomach watching him suffer while Abiodun swallowed another ball of lafu by his side, he walked up to him.

"Should I go in search of Maami?

Alade smiled. "Yes, but first, give me some of the garri and fried meat your mother keeps in her hut. I cannot wait so long for the lafu I asked your mother for."

Şiwoolu went to his mother's hut where she stored the foodstuff. He paused at the doorway, where he saw the heap of sacks filled with foodstuff the women had transported from the backyard. It was a challenge to determine what was new and what his mother had stored before the overflow. He searched, pushed, and cut through the woven sacks, but there was no garri. When sweat began to trickle down his temples, he gave up and turned around to leave. His foot brushed against a medium-sized bag leaning against the wall next to the doorway. It was barely discernible in the dark corner. He undid the knot at the top. The smell of freshly made garri hit him. He rummaged through the hut, found a calabash, filled it halfway with garri and poured some water in. When he returned with the soaked garri, the bench was empty. Alade had retired to his hut, and his friends and kin had done the same.

He smiled when Şiwoolu handed the calabash to him.

"I could not find the fried meat. Do you want some groundnut?"

"If you can find some. It will go down well with this."

Alade leaned forward to drink from the calabash.

"Baami, don't finish this garri before I get back o!" he chuckled.

"Hurry then."

Şiwoolu followed the sound of voices coming from the back of Wuraola's hut. She was talking softly to two women.

"Şiwoolu, what brings you here? I thought you were already asleep."

"I want some fried meat and groundnut for Baami and I."

She raised her brow. "What for? I have made your father's food." She pointed at the tray not far from where they stood. Steam drifted from the mound in a bowl.

"The hunger was much, Maami. He could not wait. We are just about to drink the garri."

She grabbed his arm. "Which garri? All our garri is right there. I had the sacks brought out here." She pointed to the woven bags under the tree. The ones to the left are from the villages, the ones to the right, I bought myself."

"I found the sack of garri in your hut, Maami, just next to the door to—"

She tightened her grip. "I do not take things from people that do not hand them directly to me. You know that!"

Şiwoolu broke out in a sweat.

"Has your father started eating?"

"Yes, but—"

She took to her heels towards Alade's hut. Şiwoolu ran after her but could not catch up. Her feet flew across the emptied compound to Alade's hut. When Şiwoolu entered, the light from the firewood flickered. The room was almost in complete darkness. Wuraola was shaking Alade who was slumped against the wall.

"Ọkọ mi? Alade!"

Alade fell forward into her arms. His eyes were open but unseeing. A frothy substance dribbled down the side of his mouth. Şiwoolu fell to his knees beside him, screaming his name.

"Alade? Did you eat the garri?" Wuraola screamed as she shook him. "Where is it?" she turned to Şiwoolu.

He pointed at the upturned bowl on the floor, the mixture of garri and water, a puddle at his father's feet.

"No! Where did you get it from, the garri?" She screamed, holding on to Alade. Şiwoolu ran to get the sack of garri and brought it to her.

"Pour it out, everything!" She screamed again, tears streaming down her ashen face. In seconds, the white granules were covered with blackened ones. Şiwoolu shouted as he fell backwards to the ground.

Wuraola wailed, "They have killed your father! They have killed your father!"

Sobs filled Şiwoolu's throat as he clung to Alade's lifeless body.

Alade's death crippled Iporo and Egba kingdom. Initial disbelief at his assassination morphed into anger and a call for war. The people pointed fingers at the Oyo empire. It could only be them, they argued. They did not want to see them appoint a leader that would legitimise their statehood. The ruling council met round the clock and sent emissaries out to calm the people from village to village, but nothing seemed to work. It wasn't until Wuraola sent out a plea through the town criers, telling them that Alade would have wanted peace and they needed to respect his memory, that the brewing storm was calmed.

The burial rites were performed two weeks after Alade's death and the farewell celebration, which Wuraola insisted on, lasted into the late hours of the night. Most people were still asleep as Şiwoolu stole away from home in the early hours of the morning.

"Where are you going, Şiwoolu?"

Sunmonu stepped out of the shadows just as Şiwoolu stole past the tree trunk that had fallen across the path leading to the forest. Şiwoolu eyed his friend in defiance.

"And what are you doing up so early, Sunmonu? Did you sleep at all?" He hung a cloth bundle over his shoulder.

Sunmonu's eyes bulged in disbelief. "You're leaving?"

"Shh!" Şiwoolu sprang forward and placed his hand over his friend's mouth. Sunmonu's eyes were as round as the tangerines his mother sold at the Tuesday market. "Don't shout when I take my hand off, do you hear me?"

He nodded and Şiwoolu did. Sunmonu's mouth fell open.

"I must go, Sunmonu. This place suffocates me." He opened his mouth to say more, but the words failed to come.

Sunmonu's face instantly contorted into anger and sadness. "So you flee?"

Şiwoolu turned and began to walk into the trees. Sunmonu watched him. Şiwoolu stopped when his foot was an inch away from the forest.

"Please stop by occasionally to make sure my mother is all right," he said without looking back.

Sunmonu whispered his name as he merged with the night.

Şiwoolu walked for days through the forest, drinking from the streams and sleeping under moss-covered rocks. The nights offered privacy to cry and mourn his father. During the day, every step took him farther away from the place where everyone knew him as the son of the great warrior, Alade Okikilu. After what happened, he would forever be known as the one who had killed his father with poisoned garri.

He became light-headed, but he swore not to bow to the weak yearnings of his body. He could no longer keep count of the days of his self-exile in the forest. His feet throbbed from cuts inflicted by sharp thorns. His mouth was parched from thirst. The streams he had easily found with his father on their recent journey eluded him. Foxes howled at him, and deer were not in sight. A snake slithered past him and hissed threateningly. He wished it would bite him and take him out of his misery. He began to imagine things: the shadow of a man hiding behind tree trunks, whistling, like people communicating with each other. He cried out to the shadow to show himself, but there was no response. He tightened his grip on the hilt of his sword; the training he had been forced to learn from his father coming to his mind. For hours, he could not shake the feeling that people were trailing him.

It was nightfall when he decided to succumb to his cravings and rest. He was roasting a rabbit when he heard feet crunch on dead leaves. The hairs stood up on the back of his neck. This was not his first time hearing them, but this was the closest they had been. He tightened the grip on the dagger strapped to his waist under his kembe, feigning ignorance by singing softly as he awaited the intruder. He did not have to wait for long. When the sound came, he turned around and plunged the dagger into the shadow that had been following him for days. It cut deep into the neck of the stranger. The surprised look on his face would be Şiwoolu's waking companion for the rest of his life.

"Forgive me, king-elect," the dying man murmured, slumping against Şiwoolu and breathing his last.

"What did you say? Who sent you?" Şiwoolu screamed and shook him as he grew still. His hands shook as he laid him on the ground. Had he killed a village hunter by mistake? His heart sank. The man's head was clean-shaven. He leaned close to study his face; it was unmarked, which could only mean that he was not from this region. His clothes were the same hunters wore – dark coloured buba and kembe covered in leaves – but his words made him question this. What was he forgiving him for? When he searched his clothing and found nothing, he got up to find a place to bury the body, but it would be difficult with the small bonfire he had made with branches and leaves. He decided to wait until dawn. He closed the eyes of the corpse and lay down to sleep. In the darkness, a slight figure watched and hummed a song.

After Şiwoolu buried the corpse in a shallow grave he dug with his hands, he found his way towards the water he heard flowing close by. He could finally admit to himself that he had lost his way. The sound of splashing water grew louder as he neared what he imagined was a stream. The splashing stopped and he waited. Then he heard singing. The female voice was light and sprightly. A splatter and then another followed, as though she was dancing along with her singing. It was an unfamiliar song. She spoke the same dialect as him, but there was something almost magical in the way she formed the words and spoke them. He moved closer, holding onto the tree branches until he saw her through the space between two trees. A small, dying bonfire burned close to her. She was drenched from head to toe, the wrapper tied across her chest plastered to her body. Something glimmered around her neck as she turned close to the fire. She was petite, but curvaceous. Her hips swayed to the song she sang. She threw her hands out, fingers spread above her head. Her hair was plaited up into şuku, a style mainly worn by oloris, and interlaced with white beads. The same beads beat against her ankles. Her dainty feet threw up mud as she stepped in a synchronised fashion. She giggled and continued singing, bowing in the direction of the north and east.

When she turned to do the same in the south, she gasped and stood erect. She was just as he had pictured when he imagined they would be alone. The several seasons that he and Sunmonu had spied on the maidens at the stream had given him ample time to do so.

"How dare you watch as I pay homage to orisha oko! Who are you and how long have you been standing there?" Her voice did not falter as she walked up to Şiwoolu.

Holding up his hands, Şiwoolu stepped forward. "I am sorry for alarming you like this. I mean you no harm."

Her eyes widened when she saw his bundle.

"I am a traveller."

"Headed where?"

"Anywhere the earth allows me to tread."

Şiwoolu was pulled in by her eyes. He stepped closer and took in the thick, gold chain around her neck.

"Hmm...what is your name?" She asked, eyes latching on to his coral beads, the only thing of his father's he had taken.

"It does not matter what my name is."

Her brows rose. "How can you say that? Your name means everything!" She stomped her foot on the wet ground, spraying mud on his feet. He could care less. His eyes moved to her forehead marked with four short red and white lines. Her pouting lips held his eyes captive.

"Then what is yours?"

She smiled and wagged her finger at him. "You think

you are smart. Anyway, I am Dotunu, daughter of Elemere Keşi"

Everyone knew her father. Şiwoolu looked around. There were no signs that anyone was with her.

"Why are you here by yourself? You are the daughter of a titled man. Why would any father allow his beautiful daughter out of his sight at this ungodly hour and in the forest?"

She smiled. "Do not use flattery to distract me. I asked what your name is."

"That was not flattery. It's the truth. I—"

"Shh!" She covered his mouth with her hand and looked around. Nothing moved in the trees.

Şiwoolu pulled her hand off.

"We're being watched," she whispered and stepped sideways, hands on her waist. "Stop hiding and come out!"

For a moment everything was still, then a branch moved and trees rustled. Men camouflaged in leaves and charcoal emerged. One called Şiwoolu. He squinted and took a step closer.

"Şodękę?"

It was him, he recognised other council men from the burial.

"Şiwoolu, son of Alade Okikilu. Your kingdom calls you back home." Şodękę touched his chest. "The Council has selected you king of the Ęgba kingdom." He turned to Dotunu and smiled. "Thank you for keeping him safe."

Şiwoolu demanded to know what he meant by thanking Dotunu, but the men pulled him away, though, not quickly enough to stop him from catching the slight smile on Dotunu's lips. He realise she had pretended to not know him, just as he had her. That was when he vowed in his heart to make her his wife.

Chapter Four

Enticement
Marina, Èkó
Circa 1836
Two Days Before

Bare-chested men in rolled-up trousers rushed past the royal entourage, announcing that the ships had docked overnight. The king and queen were headed to the harbour to see those ships. It was the only thing that Şiwoolu knew would make Dotunu happy after the night before. He glanced at her often as they walked. Dotunu showed her displeasure in ways not easily discernible to others – it was in the tilt of her head to the side, the soft sigh that escaped her lips, and the light wrinkle in the corner of her right eye.

Tied snugly to Ireti's back, Şomide mumbled in his sleep. Şiwoolu reached over and patted his back. He leaned towards Dotunu, his hand sliding down her back and rubbing slowly. "I'm sorry," he whispered. Her eyelids twitched but she was quiet. He leaned closer until his lips pressed against her left ear. "I'm sorry. I didn't know he would leave so early."

Dotunu sighed and stared at the eight guards before them as they navigated their way through the crowd. Behind them, Olatunde and seven other guards, four of whom carried their wooden travel boxes, walked in silence.

Şiwoolu assured himself that he had done what he could by visiting the lone mud hut in Sunmonu's backyard before they left. He had woken up to find his friend gone, leaving a message with one of Şiwoolu's bodyguards to meet at the harbour later. Dotunu had sworn that she would not leave until Ireti's fears were assuaged and they had gotten to the bottom of the matter. The young girl had refused to step foot in the backyard, nor would she let Dotunu leave her side. They stood at the back door and directed the guards.

"It is there! Ireti says that is where she saw three men!" Dotunu's voice was strong and determined. Ireti pointed towards the bushes, making high-pitched sounds until the guards came upon something. Şiwoolu arrived when they started to pull back branches and leaves covering the roof of a building about six feet high.

Olatunde pointed to two guards. "Hurry up! You're wasting the king's time!"

They lowered their cutlasses and began to cut down the branches before them. A doorway appeared. A large metal lock stopped their advancement and a guard lifted his sword to break it.

"Wait!" Şiwoolu pulled up his agbada and stepped over the debris. "Don't destroy the door."

Olatunde moved closer. He fiddled with the metal lock and frowned. "What would you have us do, Your Highness?"

A guttural sound came from the house. Şiwoolu turned around in time to see Ireti turn and run towards the street.

"Ireti! Ireti!" Dotunu screamed.

Şiwoolu snapped his fingers and four guards ran after her.

"Your Highness, I await your command," Olatunde said, eyes fixed on the beaten, wood-framed door.

Şiwoolu stepped closer until he stood inches from the door. Olatunde held two of his fingers over his nose. "Do you smell that, Your Highness?"

Şiwoolu was in the process of shaking his head when his nose sniffed it out. "It smells like urine and ... vomit." He stepped back and swept the building afresh with his eyes. "What is this place?"

They stood in silence and then Dotunu's voice reached them.

"What is inside?"

Olatunde looked to Şiwoolu, who stood brooding before turning to his trusted bodyguard and friend. Olatunde's eyes had taken on a fiery look.

"This is not my kingdom to do as I please. Let us rest in the fact that we have surveyed the area," Şiwoolu concluded.

Olatunde's nostrils flared. He nodded to the guards, and they placed their swords by their sides. Şiwoolu glanced back at the house. Dotunu stood with arms crossed above her bulging stomach, waiting. He sighed and waved the guards away from the building, knowing full well that he would have to appease Dotunu sooner than later. The quick stop at the harbour before the journey home would be a start.

At present, Olatunde paused in his steps and cursed under his breath.

Şiwoolu stopped. "What is it?"

"It may have been two harvest seasons since I left this city, but I can still recognise the leading slave trader of the western coast, Joaquim Almeida." Olatunde would know, having lived in Èkó for many harvest seasons, after his Mahi slave master freed him. Şiwoolu watched as sweat formed on Olatunde's forehead, although the weather wasn't hot. His eyes were trained on a slender man in a top hat and three-piece outfit who sauntered past them with four others dressed alike. They tipped their hats to them and melted into the crowd.

"These returnees, visitors, vagabonds, whatever you choose to call them – ignore them!" The voice belonged to a stocky man, who, having caught their attention, pushed his foot off the rickshaw he had been leaning against. He wore a lightweight round hat tipped downwards, shielding his eyes. A thick moustache covered his upper lip and a red cloth was tied around his neck.

He was referring to the men the entourage had encountered. Smiling, he walked towards them. Olatunde ordered him to stop. He raised his hands and stepped back; his body hidden from Şiwoolu's view by the guards.

"My apologies. Aren't you the new king of Ẹgba kingdom?" he asked, his dark eyes appearing over a guard's shoulder.

Olatunde glanced sharply at Şiwoolu, who gestured to let the man through. He was a few inches taller than Dotunu, well-built and muscular. His outfit resembled a buba, but the sleeves stopped at his sculpted upper arms, and his kembe-like trousers were rolled up to his calves like the dockworkers who had sped past them, exposing stumpy legs and sandaled feet. As he bowed his head, his narrow necktie revealed his bulging veins. He smiled again, revealing yellow teeth under his moustache. A sound escaped Dotunu, and she quickly placed her hand over her mouth. Şiwoolu felt the beginning of a smile on his lips before he could stop it. He was glad for this man's comical relief.

"Your Highness, you seem surprised that I know you? Your name has travelled far and wide, and I recognise your staff." He pointed at the staff in Olatunde's hand and stepped closer.

Olatunde stamped the staff on the ground, rattling the white tassels. The man held out his palms. They were worn and wrinkled.

"I am sorry for being forward. But when I saw Olori," he bent his head towards Dotunu, "I could not but speak. Such beauty. It brought back memories of your union."

"You were in Ake for our union?" Dotunu asked.

He was a foreigner. His face was devoid of any markings that would have helped determine his homeland. He pushed back his hat and his smile matched Dotunu's.

"I was. My travels took me there," he said, hastily glancing at Şiwoolu before turning his attention back to Dotunu.

"Your travels? What is your occupation?" Şiwoolu asked, his eyes following the man's moving hands as he talked.

"I trade in palm oil and—"

"Palm oil? We don't grow that in—"

"I know, I travel through Abeokuta to the farmers I trade—"

"Do not interrupt the king when he is talking!"

Olatunde's voice thundered as he stamped the staff on the ground again.

The man raised his hands again. "I am sorry. May I introduce myself?" Şiwoolu nodded.

He bowed again. "Oriade, son of Şolana of Iperu, Ijẹbu Remọ."

"Ipẹru, Ijẹbu Rẹmọ. That is not far from us," Şiwoolu said as he nodded. "How long ago did you relocate to these parts?"

Oriade's eyes lowered for a few seconds before returning Şiwoolu's gaze. "Too long. I'm afraid Èkó has swallowed me up as it does every visitor." He chuckled. Turning to Dotunu, he bowed his head. "As beautiful as ever, my queen."

"Thank you, Oriade, son of Şolana of Ipẹru, Ijẹbu Rẹmọ. We must see you again. Maybe when next we visit," Dotunu smiled from ear to ear, not because she wasn't complimented often, but because, like the old woman from the day before, she had felt the warmth of his greeting.

"Yes, we must see again." Oriade raised his head and smiled back.

Şiwoolu felt Dotunu's hand on his back and looked down. She was pointing ahead. "Look! I think the ship people are coming down!" She pulled his hand and made for the ship. The white patches floating in the sky became yards of white cloth above the ship, tied to five thick pieces of wood. Deep male voices called out to each other in a foreign tongue. A long, wide plank fell, hitting the water and sand on the shore.

"That must be the new ship we've been hearing about

for a while now, the one going to the new world," Oriade said behind them.

Şiwoolu looked at him. "The new world? Where is that?"

Oriade's eyes danced about as he licked his lips and prepared to respond. Şiwoolu beckoned with his hand, and the scalloped ring the old woman had given him the day before flashed in the morning sun. The man scurried through the guards and stood beside him. His eyes followed Şiwoolu's hand as it lowered to his side.

"Oriade?" Şiwoolu prompted him to speak.

He blinked and blurted a reply. "It is where the white men, the new settlers, now reside. I hear there are vast fields for cultivation." His voice trailed off as he looked towards the sky.

"Let us walk closer then, to see more of these new settlers. Olatunde!" Şiwoolu called. The guard stood to attention and called to the others. Şiwoolu walked ahead of Oriade.

"If I may, my king?" Oriade asked, grasping Şiwoolu's hand. Şiwoolu looked down and he released it.

"My apologies, Your Highness. Allow me to escort you," Oriade suggested. "I can see you are interested in examining the ship, and I have a few stories to entertain you on the way."

Şiwoolu looked towards the man's rickshaw several feet away, its top covered with a cloth. "Are you not working today?"

Oriade chuckled. "I work early. Sometimes I finish before the crack of dawn. My customers are early risers, just like me. The rest of the day is mine to do with as I please."

Şiwoolu's eyes shifted from Olatunde's to Oriade's as he answered. "My guards come with me."

"Of course." Oriade ran to get his rickshaw, calling for them to follow him. When they were behind him, he began to whistle a tune that was not lost on Şiwoolu and Dotunu. She laughed softly, nudged Şiwoolu with her elbow, and asked, "Has Oriade forgotten for a moment that he is not Ẹgba and that our fathers defeated his people not too long ago?"

It was the song every Ẹgba knew by heart: the same song Şiwoolu's father and the Ẹgba soldiers sang when they were fighting three enemies at once – the people of Dahomey, the Ẹba-Idan of the Ọyọ Empire and the Ijẹbu.

> *Idahomi npa budọ si Oke Ata*
> *Ibadan npa budọ tirẹ si Atadi*
> *Ijebu npa budọ tire si Oke Owiwi*
> *A mọ budọ awọn mẹtẹta yi na*
> *Tani mo budọ Ọlọrun?*

"I hope he's aware that we won," Dotunu whispered.

"His enthusiastic whistling suggests otherwise. His sojourn in these lands must have distorted his memories," Şiwoolu whispered back. Oriade turned to face them and smiled.

"Just a little walk up that sandy hill, Your Highnesses," he shouted.

Olatunde motioned him to continue. Dotunu walked

faster, a few steps ahead of Şiwoolu. Tasting salt on his tongue, he called out to her as a seagull flew overhead, drowning out his voice. He took longer strides and grabbed her arm.

"Careful," he said, helping her along the small sand hill. She called to Ireti to hurry up. Şomide, hearing his mother's voice, flung out his arms as Ireti got closer.

"My son, come here! You're getting too big for your mother to carry for too long." Şiwoolu picked up Şomide from the unravelling folds of wrapper and oja on Ireti's back. The child looked up at Şiwoolu and grinned. He was the spitting image of Alade, his chubby baby legs swung towards his father's hip, touched it, and swung away again. Şiwoolu smiled as he recalled his last travel with his father through the Ẹgba Forest to the meeting under the rocks; the meeting that had changed their destinies forever.

Şomide looked ahead, fascinated by the view before him. Men of all colours and sizes poured out of the canoes that came to shore from the ships. Şiwoolu pulled Dotunu closer as they came towards the entourage. One brushed past him, his skin the colour of cocoa, his eyes the colour of dark grass. He nodded and smiled. His front tooth was broken. He said something out loud and bent slightly when he saw Dotunu. Dotunu smiled.

"Ẹ karọ!" She bid him good morning.

He stood in the same spot, bowed his head again to Dotunu and said, "Bom dia."

"Bom dia?" Dotunu asked.

He nodded, and she nodded back. They laughed. His eyes lit up when he looked at Şomide.

"Seu filho?"

"*Se* what?" Olatunde asked. "Move back!" He waved him backward.

The man's face fell, but he obeyed. Oriade called to the group to follow him, and the man's eyes widened when Dotunu waved and pointed to the ships ahead. He motioned to her stomach and shook his head.

"Go!" Olatunde shouted and pushed him back again. The man held up his hands, said a few more words slowly, and shook his head again.

"Wait. Can he not speak the white man's tongue that you understand, Olatunde? Ask him," Şiwoolu said.

Olatunde shoved the staff into the sand and turned to the man. His voice was loud and clear as he asked him, "Do you speak English?"

The man shook his head and said something emphatically as he pointed towards the ships. Ireti made a sound beside Dotunu.

"What? I don't understand him, Ireti," Dotunu said, chuckling. "Don't worry. We are only looking from here, nothing more."

"Your Highness, he speaks another language," Olatunde said with finality.

"Well, take him out of our path so we can go about our business."

Olatunde gestured for the man to walk away.

"He is just being nice, olowo ori mi. Be kind to him," Dotunu said softly as he was escorted away by two guards. The others hedged them in on all sides as more men trudged past, carrying crates and ropes. Unlike the man who had spoken to them, these men avoided looking at their faces.

"I must show you this new ship that has come from the new world, Your Highnesses!" Oriade shouted, pointing ahead.

Olatunde looked about. "Where is your..." He waved his hand back and forth.

"My rickshaw? Oh, I hid it in the sand. I have no need for it anymore."

"Lead the way, then!" Olatunde said curtly. Oriade waited for the two guards to rejoin the entourage, then continued. They walked closer to the ships.

"Your Highnesses, there it is. The one with the large sails flying high. No, not that one. The one behind it. The merchants have come to trade for seeds to plant in the new world."

The grandest of the lot was a little farther out in the water. It was much bigger than the one from which the men in the canoes had come.

"In the new world? Will they survive in that climate?" Şiwoolu asked, surprised.

"Yes, they have the same climate, it is just as hot. You would be surprised at the similarities."

"Have you been there?" Dotunu asked.

Oriade paused, pulled off his necktie and wiped his sweaty face. "Eh, no. I have only heard tales from those who have. Come with me."

He resumed walking. The steady stream of men disembarking from the ships had ebbed.

Oriade pointed to the ship, which cast a shadow over

them. It was something to behold: the five white sails flew majestically and painted on the hull in red were thick horizontal and vertical lines.

"That first ship we saw is called a caravel, made by the Portuguese. The man speaking to you came from that ship," Oriade said.

"Where do they come from, these Portuguese?" Şiwoolu asked, just as Şomide began to squirm in his arms. Ireti held out her hands for him and Şiwoolu handed him to her.

"Stay close, Ireti!" Dotunu shouted.

Ireti turned and nodded. She set Şomide down on the sand and he giggled as his toes disappeared in it. She pushed her feet into the sand too and fell to her knees beside him, her laugh resembling his. Dotunu smiled and walked over to them. Şiwoolu turned to Oriade.

"The Portuguese, where do they hail from?" Şiwoolu asked again.

Oriade blinked. "Oh, they are from beyond the oceans." He watched Dotunu as the sand trickled through her fingers. Her shoulders shook from laughing at Şomide, who was clearly excited by the novel experience.

Şiwoolu slapped his thigh to distract him. "If I were not so forgiving, I would have you beheaded, Oriade."

Oriade turned his full attention to Şiwoolu. His eyes danced. "I apologise, Your Highness. I am sure you get this reaction all the time; your wife is beautiful. I apologise."

He paused as a noise floated towards them. It sounded like nothing Şiwoolu had ever heard.

"Your Highness," Olatunde whispered. He was frowning again. Şiwoolu hadn't seen him frown this many times in the entire time they had known each other.

"It's coming from the ship," Oriade said. "Would you like to go aboard?"

"Did you hear that too?" Dotunu asked, walking back. Behind her, Ireti pulled a disgruntled Şomide along.

"I am familiar with the people on board. They may allow you to see."

Now that they were beyond the shadow of the first ship, they had a better view of the five sails on this mighty vessel. The hulky shapes of men moved back and forth on the platform. They were moving together, dancing.

Oriade cupped his left ear towards the water. "That sound is heavenly!" He pointed. "More men are coming. Maybe we can ask them where on the ship the music is coming from." He began walking to the water's edge.

He waved to four men approaching a canoe. Their skin was darker than that of the white horseman from the day before, as if they had been in the sun for too long. The one sitting in front was twice the size of the others, and from the way he spoke to the others and their bowed heads, it was clear that he was the leader. He jumped out before the canoe reached the shore, and pulling off the cloth tied to his head, he dabbed his face with it. His sparse dark hair was plastered to his scalp. The others disembarked and walked towards them. Oriade said something to the leader and held out his hand. Dotunu gasped.

"Why didn't he tell us he could speak the white man's tongue before now?" Olatunde asked.

The man took the hand Oriade offered.

"Ask him if we can go into the ship," Dotunu said. The leader nodded, and as he spoke a glittering gold tooth appeared. His voice was deep and raspy, as though he had been shouting. He studied Şiwoolu for several seconds, then his eyes moved to Dotunu and Ireti. He said something to Oriade.

"What does he say, Olatunde?" Şiwoolu asked.

"He says yes."

Dotunu clapped her hands. She swivelled to Şiwoolu, lips spread into a smile. "Can we go, my husband? Can we?" she asked.

Oriade began to speak.

"Not so fast, Oriade. Ask him to tell us more and whether it is even worth going on board," Şiwoolu said.

As Oriade began to translate, the leader's eyes returned to Şiwoolu, growing wider as they took in the staff in Olatunde's hand. When Oriade finished, he spoke and pointed to the ship.

"Your Highness, he said it is a musical instrument with strings. It's being played for the workers on board. He can take you on board to see it," Oriade said.

The leader waded back into the water and climbed into the canoe. He hit the side and smiled wide, inviting them with his shiny tooth. Dotunu fidgeted beside Şiwoolu, unable to contain the anticipation rising within her.

Şiwoolu leaned closer to her. "I'll send Olatunde with two guards and they will report back."

Dotunu shook her head. "That will take too long. You know we leave today."

Şiwoolu paused, knowing this was the only way he

could bring peace between the two of them. He turned to Olatunde. "The queen cannot get on that in her condition."

Suddenly, Ireti gasped and pointed at the moving ship.

Dotunu went to her. "Is it really moving, olowo ori mi? Is that ship really moving?"

It was slow, but it was heading towards them.

Oriade smiled. "They are coming to shore." He ran into the waters and waved. "Over here!"

The ship inched closer, and they could feel the eyes of the occupants on them. A wooden plank appeared over the ship's side, guided by the long ropes tied around it.

"Move back!" Oriade shouted, running to Dotunu and Ireti. He stepped in front of them as the plank hit the water, drenching him from head to toe. Heads appeared over the side of the ship.

"Your Highness," Olatunde called.

Şiwoolu turned to him. He pulled him aside and they spoke in hushed tones.

"It looks like a merchant ship, but I have to be sure, Your Highness."

Şiwoolu nodded. "That is why I hired you. Go and report back."

"I will see what is there and will signal from the top after I have had a look around and confirmed the instrument we hear is there." Olatunde handed the staff to Şosan, his second-in-command, and walked up the plank. The leader with the gold tooth ordered one of his men to follow Olatunde. The others could hear their footsteps overhead and as they descended to the lower level.

The musician played louder, even to Siwoolu's ears, it sounded as though the player was fighting with the instrument. He chuckled and waited for what seemed like a long time.

"Your Highness, it is just below the main level," Olatunde said, suddenly appearing above them. "It should take but a few minutes." Ireti yelled and waved at him, relief washing over her face.

Oriade looked at Ireti. "Your slave is quite dramatic, is she not?"

"She is not my slave. Why would you think that?" Dotunu asked coldly.

Oriade looked confused as he pulled the cloth from around his neck again to fan himself.

Olatunde's head disappeared again.

The leader with the gold tooth looked at Şiwoolu and spoke. Oriade looked at Şiwoolu.

"He says they moved the ship closer so that you and Olori can go aboard to enjoy the music and see the instrument. Your bodyguard is waiting for you."

Şiwoolu studied the man. His eyes did not waver. Dotunu inched closer to him, placed her hand lightly, flirtingly, on his back, and waited. He bent his head towards her. Her scent filled his nostrils, and he sighed.

"We can't be long, as we must start our journey home today," he said.

"All the more reason why you should take this opportunity to see this instrument, so that you can have some more stories to tell when you return home," Oriade said, his right hand raised towards the ship.

Şiwoolu held out his hand for Dotunu, who grasped

it without hesitation. "Only for a little while, Dotunu, then we must leave," he said.

"Yes, of course," she responded happily.

He knew he had been forgiven when he looked into her twinkling eyes. She pulled Ireti to her side.

"Fall in line!" Ṣosan ordered the guards. They stepped forward in twos, all fourteen of them. Ṣosan stood behind Ṣiwoolu and Dotunu.

"Your Highness, what of your friend? He was to meet us here," Ṣosan asked.

"That is true!" Ṣiwoolu exclaimed.

Oriade raised his hand. "I can wait here for him. What is his name?"

"Sunmonu."

Ṣosan signalled to the leader-turned-guide to go ahead of the guards. The man smiled and stepped onto the plank. The guards followed, but Ireti hesitated.

"It is fine. We are behind you," Dotunu said reassuringly. Ireti nodded, swinging Ṣomide onto her back and tying the wrapper around him firmly. Taking the hand the guard ahead offered, she walked slowly up the plank. Ṣiwoolu held Dotunu by the elbow and followed.

"I will be waiting here when you return," Oriade shouted behind them.

Ṣosan frowned. "You are not coming?"

"Oh no. They will not allow a commoner like me on board. Trust me, I have tried."

"All right. We will see you when we return," Ṣiwoolu said, looking behind him, but Oriade was already walking away.

It was a short walk up the plank, and in no time they had boarded the ship. There were about a dozen men standing on the deck or leaning on railings; they were the same ones who had been staring down at the entourage when they were on land. They were all dressed in similar attires: billowing shirts with dark, long kembe-like trousers that were much slimmer and longer, tapering off at their ankles. Many had small red or white pieces of cloth tied around their necks or heads. They made way for the guide, who pointed a finger downward.

"It's down there?" Dotunu asked. "Why did the music stop?" They had not noticed it during their journey up the plank, but now the absence of sound was deafening.

"And where is Olatunde? Olatunde!" Şiwoolu turned to the leader. He smiled and pointed his finger downward. He stomped on the floor and the music started again. It started slower this time, as though someone were teasing the strings. Some of the notes were prolonged, others a quick release. Şiwoolu's soul begged for each new sound. His feet moved of their own volition in response to the music. "Shall we?"

Şosan turned to the guards. "I will go ahead. Stay behind me, Kabiyesi."

"We don't need all the guards with us. At least we know Olatunde is there," Şiwoolu said. "Just take three."

Şosan walked behind the guide to a stairway, the staff thumping the floor beneath. One guard followed him down the winding descent while two walked the royal family. Şomide squirmed and opened his eyes. Ireti stopped, pulled him out of the wrapper, and held him on her hip.

"Ireti, don't let him jump out of your arms, and please, don't trip. These ... what do you call them, olowo ori mi?" Dotunu asked.

"Stairs," Șiwoolu said.

"Yes, these stairs, they are more than the ones at Sunmonu's house. Wait for us when you get down there," Dotunu said.

The music was louder when they stepped onto the lower floor. An orange light filtered in through a crack in a door at the end of the hallway. The three guards circled the group and waited for Șosan's command. The leader-turned-guide stopped in front of the door, turned and beckoned to Șiwoolu to come forward. The guards pressed closer around the royal couple and their wards.

"I go first," Șosan said, thumping the staff on the floor and pointing to it. The man smiled and walked in. The music teased and pulled at them until they stood in front of the wooden door. Ireti made a noise and pulled at Dotunu's hand. The man pushed the door open and stepped in as the orange light filled the doorway.

"It's all right, Ireti," Dotunu said in a soothing voice as her hands fell on Ireti's heaving shoulders. "See ... light." The music drew them in, Șosan strode through the door and they followed.

The source of the sound was immediately obvious: A musician, small in stature, cradled an object in his slim, pale arms. The golden-brown wooden instrument was unlike anything Șiwoolu had ever seen. The musician's fingers pulled on the strings, which ran from the handle to the rounded bottom pressed against his chest; there were at least ten of them, each held by a dark peg. The orange light in the glass on top of a wooden box bounced off the polished instrument. The musician's eyes were closed as he played. In proximity, Şiwoolu could see that this was a mere boy, close in age to Ireti.

Dotunu took a step and tripped over a plank, dislodged from the wood flooring. She gripped Şiwoolu's arm as she fell against him and cried out. The music stopped and the musician's eyes flew open. Orange flecks lit up familiar eyes as they fell on Dotunu. They were the same grey colour as the black man's on the horse. His clothing was cleaner than that of the others on board, his shoes, laced with ropes, were as polished as the object in his hands.

The guide moved close to the boy and spoke. The boy stood and shifted his eyes to look at Şiwoolu. He was a few inches shorter than Dotunu. He bent to his waist and looked up.

"Ẹ ka bọ."

The entourage gasped. His Yoruba was tinged with an accent, but they understood. He smiled and straightened his slight frame. His eyes moved to Ireti, who was trying to keep Şomide from jumping out of her arms. He touched the baby's fingers and Ireti pushed his hand away. Şomide giggled and bounced in her arms.

"You understand?" Dotunu asked hesitantly.

He nodded. "A little," he said again in Yoruba.

Şiwoolu stepped forward. "How?"

The boy swallowed and said nothing. Then he spoke in the white man's tongue.

"My mother was Yoruba."

The ship rocked. Ireti clung to Dotunu. Şosan and the other guards reached under their buba. Their guide held up his hands, but his gold tooth glistened as he smiled, as though unable to hold back a secret any longer.

"What is happening?" Şiwoolu, and then it dawned on him. He turned to Şosan. "Where is Olatunde? Was he not supposed to be down here waiting for us?"

Şosan pulled out a dagger and demanded to know from the man. He shrugged. The boy cowered behind him. His eyes fell on the rise of Dotunu's stomach under her wrapper and he started to scream the same word repeatedly.

Şiwoolu pulled Dotunu into his arms. "What is he saying?" he asked.

Şosan's eyes flashed and darted around the room. He looked at Şiwoolu as his arms tightened around Dotunu. "*Run!*" he yelled.

The guards pulled out their daggers and circled the royal family. Ireti screamed and clung to Dotunu, with Şomide squashed between them and all three of them encircled in Şiwoolu's arms.

"Give him to me!" Şiwoolu tried to pull the crying Şomide from Ireti's grip, but she wouldn't let go. She screamed and held on.

"It is I, Ireti! Let him go!" Şiwoolu shouted as he pried her hands off Şomide's body.

Şosan pointed the dagger at the pale boy. "We must go, Kabiyesi, now," he whispered as he motioned the group backward towards the door. The guide laughed hysterically. The boy stepped backward and fell to the floor. He pulled his knees into his chest and began to cry. The guide barked at the boy; his eyes fixed on them.

"Go!" Şosan ordered. The guards ran out and they followed.

"Down that way!" Şosan shouted behind them. The guide's deep laughter followed them down the corridor and then the door slammed shut, plunging them into darkness. The ship rocked again and Ireti screamed louder.

"Shh! Ireti, we must be calm," Dotunu said, with more composure than Şiwoolu could boast of. The guards called to one another in hushed voices. Tiptoeing slowly behind them, Şosan whispered to Şiwoolu to stay low as they moved quickly towards the stairs. The guards stopped when they reached the foot of the steps and looked up to see a shadow waiting for them at the top.

"Olatunde!" Şosan shouted. The guide's laughter was closer as he barrelled down the hallway towards them.

"Run!" The boy's choked scream reached them down the hall as the door was wrenched open again.

"Olowo ori mi?" Dotunu's voice shook as she stared up at Şiwoolu.

"I will die before anything happens to you," Şiwoolu spat out.

Şosan placed his foot on the first step and shouted for Olatunde again. The shadow came down the stairs, his eyes were the same as the boy's. Ireti screamed like she had seen a ghost, her finger pointed at the body he held by the neck beside him. She slumped against Dotunu and fell to the floor. Şosan recognised the shadow that stepped into their view. He was the black horseman with the strange eyes from the day before – Sigmund. He dragged a lifeless body by the neckline of his buba. It was Olatunde. Blood flowed from his slashed neck and his eyes stared back, defiant.

"No!" Şosan screamed as he charged at him, but the latter was faster. He sidestepped Şosan and lashed out with a dagger. Blood flowed from Şosan's chest as he turned to Şiwoolu.

"Run, my king! Run!" Şosan said with all the strength he could muster. A gurgling sound followed as blood spurted from his mouth. He became limp and fell back against an unmoving Ireti. Dotunu screamed as Şiwoolu pulled her away from the guards who ran towards Sigmund. He held Şomide tightly, sidestepped the guards engaged in battle with the strange-eyed man and ran up the steps with Dotunu and their child.

Silence met Şiwoolu as his foot hit the top of the stairs. The nozzle of a gun barrel was pressed against his temple. Saliva spattered against his face as a voice spoke the foreign tongue again. It was the white rider they had seen on their first attempt to visit the Marina the day before. His hat was gone, and his sparse, curly hair grazed his shoulders as he turned to look at the men on deck. They were many, double the number the group had passed on their way down into the ship, surrounding the royal family with swords and guns. At their feet lay Şiwoolu's dead guards. The white man stepped back, the pressure of the barrel on Şiwoolu's temple decreasing. He snapped at his men as he lowered his gun. A hand grabbed Şiwoolu, and he held on tighter to Dotunu and Şomide amid their screams. It burnt a hole in his heart.

"What is happening, Şiwoolu?" Dotunu screamed as big hands tore her and Şomide from him. Şomide was bundled away, and all they could hear were his screams down the hallway.

"Şomide! Dotunu!" Şiwoolu shouted, wincing as his hands were grabbed from behind. Laughter rang out amongst the men surrounding them. One pointed towards land and laughed harder. Şiwoolu could only see a speck of what used to be the harbour. The ship rocked once more.

"Şiwoolu, what is happening?" Dotunu screamed again. She could feel her body shaking of its own volition. She tried to stop it, but it was out of her control. The ship began to vibrate, gently at first. The vibrations increased, shaking every object on board. The men grabbed the railings and held on. Dotunu heard herself screaming but all she could see and feel was darkness. Even Şiwoolu's voice calling out her name could not reach her for what seemed like an eternity.

"Dotunu, stop! You will kill yourself!"

Şiwoolu's voice finally cut through the chaos. Dotunu dropped to the floor, blood trickling down her nose. She stopped shaking and so did the ship.

The white man grabbed the coral beads around Dotunu's neck and slapped her across the face. The beads broke and scattered across the deck.

"No!" Şiwoolu lunged at the white man with his fists, breaking free of his captor, but a blow to the back of his head threw him to the floor. The last thing he heard was the guide's crazed laughter and his last thought was that the curse had finally manifested.

Chapter Five

Dark Places
Unknown Waters
Circa 1836

"*This is not what you promised me, my fathers!* This is not what the oracle foretold would be my end! Why? What did I do to deserve this?"

The anguished voice woke Şiwoolu. His head throbbed as he opened his eyes. It was pitch black. He gasped for air and wished he had not. The stench of vomit, mingled with urine and faeces, was suffocating. Sweat dripped from his pores. He sat up suddenly and hit his head on a hard surface above him. The force sent him crashing onto his back. He tried to lift his hands but metal cuffs, heavy and cold, pulled them back down onto his bare stomach by means of a chain. Then he snapped his head sideways and smelt it – the smell of decay. The figure beside him was still and human. He stared into what he could barely pick out as an emaciated face. He pulled on his wrists again and gasped when his neck was pulled down into his chest. He moved his feet; they were also bound by chains.

The smell reminded him of somewhere. "What is this place?" He whispered and closed his eyes. How could he have forgotten even for a second? "Dotunu! Do—!" He struggled again to rise.

"You must lie still; else you'll end up hurting yourself." The voice was only a few feet away from Şiwoolu. The man's accent was a soothing and familiar one that reminded Şiwoolu of home.

"What is this?" Şiwoolu screamed, pulling at his wrists yet again. His neck jerked forward, and he hit his head on the hard surface again.

"We have been asking ourselves the same question," the voice said, the deep baritone similar to Olatunde's. Şiwoolu's head reeled from the shock of what he suddenly remembered. A scream tore from his throat.

"Olatunde! They killed him! Get me out of these chains! Get me out!"

"Shh! They will come for you if you are not quiet."

Light flooded the darkness. Manic screams filled the enclosed space as bodies thrashed about on wooden shelves and limbs pulled on chains. As men's cries rent the air, the sound of heavy footsteps approached. Angry foreign voices moved towards the shelf Şiwoolu lay on and rough hands grabbed his neck and squeezed until he was gasping for breath. The attack stopped as suddenly as it has started, and he felt the release on his neck.

"Get away from me. Do you know who I am? I will have you killed." He shouted in a hoarse voice filled with disbelief and rage. Another blow hit his face and took the wind out of him. His tormentor repeated the blows until blood flowed from the side of his mouth. Şiwoolu managed to mutter: "Let me go ... my wife ... my son." The words choked him as he imagined what could be happening to them.

He turned his head sideways as half of a face appeared. The wooden shelf above him restricted his full view. The man bent closer until Şiwoolu could see the man's face. It was Sigmund. His shoulders shook as he laughed and he stared hard at Şiwoolu for a moment. Then he snapped his fingers and a small frame stepped forward, shivering. It was the boy who had played the musical instrument. He whimpered when the man's hand landed on his head, he commanded the child to do something in a loud voice. The boy nodded and looked at Şiwoolu, his face drenched with tears. Şiwoolu wondered why he had not noticed his eyes before – they were the same as the man's.

"He says to be ... behave or he will kill your family," the boy said in Yoruba.

Bodies shifted on hard wood around Şiwoolu, limbs pulled on their chains and rubbed against each other in protest.

"Traitor!" A male voice screamed from somewhere in the room, and soon more voices joined. The bodies thrashed around, beating the wood beneath them. Şiwoolu looked around, as far as his neck could stretch, over the still body to his left, and then to his right where he lay at the edge of the shelf. He screamed at what lay before him in the illuminated room – naked bodies stacked one on top of the other in shelves two feet above each other. Şiwoolu turned back to the boy.

"Why have I been shackled like a slave?"

The child looked down at the floor, then at the strange-eyed man who said something to him.

"Because you are one now. We all are," the boy whispered.

Sigmund hit the boy across his face and knocked him down to the floor. He turned his raised hand to Şiwoolu.

"No!"

The pale-faced man on the horse at Marina, the same one who had attacked him and Dotunu on the stairs, walked in and Sigmund dropped his hand. The newcomer stared down at Şiwoolu, his dark brooding eyes assessing his face. He nodded at Şiwoolu, said something to the strange-eyed man and left the room. The strange-eyed man snapped an order at the boy, who got up immediately and departed with him. The door closed behind them, followed by the sound of something heavy placed across it. Darkness curled its tentacles around the captive men once more.

"My life is over!" A voice in the sea of bodies cried.

"Our lives ended the day that idiot invited us to his house. That clown with the cloth tied around his neck, that man from Ijẹbu Rẹmo. Traitor! Stealing his own people for wealth and using that oversized object on wheels to transport unconscious bodies." A bitter chuckle sounded a few feet away. It was the voice that had woken Şiwoolu. A body stirred to the far left and raised its head as far as the shelf above would allow. He was so close, Şiwoolu could have reached out to touch him if his hands weren't bound.

"A well-orchestrated capture by our own people to line their pockets. Did you not notice him standing at the path leading to the harbour?" Another voice, shaking with indignation, asked.

Şiwoolu's chest tightened. "You mean Oriade? He

was part of this?" His head reeled at the thought of being watched and plotted against. Deep, bitter laughter rose from the shelves of bodies. He pulled at his chains. "Explain yourself!"

The still body beside him shifted, and a dark figure leaned over it as far as the metal around his neck would allow.

"Yes, the very same Oriade, Your Highness." It was the familiar voice that reminded him of home.

"Your Highness? Are you royalty?" The voice that had woken him asked. "How did that man lure you like he did most of us? He and that man with eyes like those of a cat!" The faceless man screamed from his shelf. Then came the sound of chains beating against one another, and shouts for freedom booming in the small space. Şiwoolu twisted his body towards the dark figure still leaning over. He winced when the metal collar bit into his neck.

"It is best you lay still, Your Highness. They have chained three of us together."

Şiwoolu looked at the body between them.

"Is he...?"

"Yes. He's been dead for a day. They should have seen that when they came in, but it seems they were only interested in you, Your Highness," the man whispered.

Şiwoolu could make out the man's sunken cheeks as he grew accustomed to the dark.

"You are from my kingdom. How else would you know I am a king?"

The figure sighed, its bony shoulders trembled.

"You choose not to talk?" Şiwoolu prodded, incensed

at the audacity of the faceless man.

"What more is there to say?" the man shouted.

"Be quiet! They will return to beat us again," another yelled.

"At least then we have a chance to kill them!" the first man screamed. Another agreed by banging his chains on the wood, making a sound that spurred a chorus of chains beating the hard surfaces. The door flew open seconds later, men charged into the room and marched straight to where the clamouring man lay. They grabbed three pairs of feet – his and his shackled companions' – and pulled them up.

"No! Don't let them take me!" The man screamed as his knees buckled under him. His shaved head was bowed from the weight of the metal collar linked to heavy chains and riddled with ringworms. Urine flowed between his legs to the floor, causing the captors to laugh before they dragged him away with his shackled companions. The door banged shut again and they listened to the cries of the men until there was silence. The ship rocked back and forth. Then the sound of a whip cut the silence, followed by the men's screams.

Şiwoolu's stomach turned at the smell of fresh vomit. He grunted as bile rose to his throat.

"Steady, steady," the man with the voice from home cautioned. Şiwoolu took a deep breath and closed his eyes as the screams receded and there was quiet. He shifted and his head touched the still body beside him. It was cold.

"Your Highness, are you still with us?" the man asked.

"Yes. What is your name, and where in my kingdom do you hail from?"

"Demilade, Your Highness. I come from Itesi."

"How did you come to Èkó and fall into Oriade's hands?" Şiwoolu asked.

Demilade's body shook in spasms. "May his life be worth nothing! May his whole family miss the road and never find their way back!"

"Aşẹ!" The shackled men agreed.

"Oriade wooed me and my wife, Labakẹ, from our farm in Itesi to Èkó. He promised to introduce us to exporters to sell our yams, but when we arrived, nothing in his house smelled like food. That is when the man with the eyes like a cat appeared in the night."

Cries broke out as each man relived his ordeal at the hands of the man who had deceived and captured them.

"They put us in these!" Demilade's chains rattled as he raised his hands. "Like animals! My wife, my dear wife's clothes were torn to shreds, just so they could see how attractive she was, even though she is heavily pregnant, and Oriade stood there and bargained!"

Şiwoolu closed his eyes. "Dotunu," he whispered. The vision of the white man striking Dotunu, her coral beads spilling to the floor, filled his head.

"He will rot in hell forever, that traitor," someone whispered.

"Dotunu? Your wife?" Demilade asked.

"Yes, where could they have taken her? And my son?"

Demilade sighed. "They are above us, also hidden away in shelves. I hear the women and children crying and screaming when our own noise does not overpower theirs. Those men, they go in and have their way with them!"

The ship rocked. Şiwoolu rolled to the side of the dead man.

"We are going to die on this water!" A panicked voice screamed over the fearful cries of the others. The ship rocked repeatedly, the men's fears eventually silencing them so that for a while all they could hear were the faint footsteps running back and forth on the platform above them. Another lurch of the ship and the men rolled off the shelves to the floor. Chained bodies lay piled on top of each other, helpless to get up. Şiwoolu groaned as he tried to pull himself from under the dead man. The ship rocked again and steadied.

"They will soon return," Demilade whispered beside him as they lay among the naked and soiled bodies. The sound of footsteps near the door reached them as he finished speaking.

"How did you know?"

Demilade's chuckle was short and bitter. "We are their prized possessions. Nothing must happen to us."

Light flooded the room once more as the captors walked in, pulled the men up, and shoved them back into the narrow shelves. When hands found Şiwoolu and the two others shackled to him, they paused. More pale-faced men surrounded them. They spat out words, pointing towards the door and back at the three of them.

A big man stepped forward and the light fell on his face. It was their former guide. He pulled out a ring of keys tied around his waist and unlocked the shackles binding the hands and feet of the dead man, Şiwoolu, and Demilade. His hands, wrapped around the dead man's neck, inadvertently pulled the other shackled men too. He freed their necks from the metal collars and the dead man was taken out. A man pulled Şiwoolu to his feet, and another, Demilade. Each held a large wooden bowl and began to scrub the men's faces down to their necks. Şiwoolu opened his mouth, thankful for the droplets of water that found their way there. The water tasted like it smelt – dirty – but he was thirsty, and the retching had sapped all the energy from him.

The sponge moved down his chest, armpits, and lower torso. He was ordered to open his legs and his genitals were scrubbed as vigorously as other parts of his body. The man washing him pointed at them and laughed, and the other paused from washing Demilade to laugh too. This irked the gold-toothed man, and he barked at them to stop. The room fell silent. They finished scrubbing and then shackled Şiwoolu and Demilade together again. A long chain hung between them. Şiwoolu's heart hammered against his chest when he realised that they were about to be shoved back into the shelf again. He shook his head in resistance, but it was met with laughter. Hands pushed him forward towards the empty shelf ahead, in the centre of a row of six. Şiwoolu decided he would fight and dug in his heels to prevent being pushed further, which made Demilade bump into his back.

"Not now," Demilade murmured. "The time will come."

The gold-toothed man shouted at him and pointed to the floor. There was a wooden box as high as his knees. Şiwoolu stepped on it and crawled onto the dark, narrow shelf. Behind him, Demilade kept whispering, "Not now."

Satisfied that there would be no trouble, the men left moments later. Şiwoolu turned his head gently to look at Demilade. He knew now not to hurt his chained companion.

"Your Highness," Demilade whispered.

Şiwoolu reached out and touched what he hoped was the face he had glimpsed when they were being scrubbed down. What he touched was hairy. He imagined it was the overgrown beard he had seen. His hands travelled up, getting wet, until they touched the man's eyelids. Şiwoolu stopped when his fingers became entangled in the hair on Demilade's head. Only mad people, unable to care for themselves, allowed hair to grow in this wild manner.

"How long have you been chained here?" he asked, pulling his fingers out of the overgrowth.

"Twenty days."

"You're that sure?"

"Every two days, these bastards come to wash us down for fear that we might get sick and die. They have done so ten times now."

The ship rocked and the men groaned.

"They have stayed close to the harbour for that long?"

Demilade sighed heavily. "Every day they stay at the harbour and capture more people."

They were both quiet.

"And before then? You said Oriade took you to a house?"

"Yes, just for a little while, my wife and me. He got

me drunk and beat my wife unconscious. We woke up at night, bound and gagged in a canoe and on the way to this ship, just as the others described. Then they took my wife from me, and before my very eyes stripped her naked." His voice broke and he took a deep breath.

"Where do they take us?"

"The new world. I've heard the traitors among them, our own people within their ranks, talking. You can hear a lot, rammed up in these shelves between the decks – just like we heard the boy play the instrument, and the Olori scream, when they took you."

Şiwoolu pulled his wrists.

"You were the last cargo they were expecting. I heard them talking. We would have left yesterday, they said, but you did not come as they had expected."

Şiwoolu gasped for air.

"Your Highness? Your Highness!" Demilade's voice was sounding further away with every second as the pain and anguish Şiwoolu felt swallowed him whole and he cried out. "King Şiwoolu, we must not faint. The minute I saw you, I knew that the gods had not forgotten me. Are you not the young king that saved Abeokuta from the wave of disasters after your father was murdered? The true king of the Egba? We must not grow faint, Your Highness. We must wait for the opportune time."

Şiwoolu stared into Demilade's hopeful eyes and was reminded again of what he had endured two harvest seasons ago. It had just been three moons after his wedding to Dotunu when the disappearances started again. It started in a trickle – two girls fetching water from the stream

– and then in waves – a family on their farm whisked away, with only their tools proof that they had been there; maidens on their way from a dance; an entourage of traders passing through the kingdom. Fear gripped the people and they needed to blame someone. That person was their newly crowned king.

They were in the inner chambers when they heard the mob's screams as they bombarded the palace. "Dethrone him!"

Dotunu raised her head from his bare chest. "We must go and find out what is happening."

Şiwoolu shook his head. She sat up, pulling her wrapper over her breasts.

"You stay here. I will go." He rose from the mat and flung his agbada over his head. Dotunu sucked on her lower lip but said nothing. She picked up his crown from the bench and waited for him to turn around. His eyes narrowed when he saw her stony expression.

"These are the affairs of the kingdom, dear one. I will see to it." He caressed the hands that held his crown. Her face softened and she placed the crown on his head.

"You must assure them that there will be an end to this," Dotunu spoke softly.

He paused at the doorway and looked at her. "I will. Just leave it to me." He was sure that his mother, Wuraola, Şodękę and the ruling council, including Dotunu's father, Elemere Keşi would be there to support him. At the other end of the door, a tall shadow stood at attention. It was his new bodyguard, Olatunde, whom he had met in Èkó before his marriage to Dotunu. It was the one trip he had to take, even if it was him pretending for a moment that he was a parakoyi. He looked squarely at him.

"Olatunde, is the council present?"

"Yes, all but one."

Olatunde walked a few steps ahead of him, beating the royal staff. Dotunu turned away and bit her lower lip.

After the last villagers left hours later, Ireti ran out of the inner chambers, distraught. Wuraola was able to get it out of her – Dotunu had been taken. The ologun were called to arms and instructed to speak nothing of it but bring the queen back safely. If anyone got wind that the king could not keep even his new wife safe, the kingdom would be lost. The hours dragged into days, and as each one passed, Şiwoolu's heart sank into despair.

Unknown to Şiwoolu, Dotunu was not far away. She had tracked the many footprints all over the kingdom. On the seventh day, humming her song, she followed the tell-tale footprints from the stream she visited every new moon, the same one where she had met Şiwoolu. The prints stopped when they reached the path that divided into two – one leading to the forest, the other to Iporo Ake. She closed her eyes and stilled her body and mind, then turned towards the forest and began to walk with her eyes closed, led by an unseen entity.

Her feet hit an object and she stopped.

"Open your eyes," the voice in her head said.

She stood inches from a decrepit hut adorned with charms and talismans. She was almost afraid, when she realised she was at the hut of Makinde, the recluse and sorcerer everyone avoided.

She stepped over a hoe and entered the hut, dodging more totems and charms. In the corner, the bleeding head of a goat dangled from the roof. The small enclosure oozed of death, but there was no one there. As she exited, Makinde appeared, dragging a rope behind him. He could not see her in the dark, but her eyes glinted like a cat's. His back was half turned as he spoke in hushed tones to the five children gagged and bound at their hands and feet. Dotunu picked up the hoe and her feet lifted off the ground and stayed in the air, catching Makinde by surprise. The hoe fell on his back, cutting deep into his flesh. He howled in agony and fell to the ground unconscious. Dotunu turned to the children who were sobbing and shaken by what they had experienced.

"It is all right, little ones," she said calmly, peering into their faces. "I can tell you're not from these parts. That is a good thing, for you did not see any of this tonight. The smallest of the five, a little girl no older than four harvest seasons pointed her middle finger at Dotunu's nose. She touched it and felt the blood between her fingers and cleaned it away with the back of her hand.

"Don't you worry about that. I am fine. It is just something that happens sometimes. Come, let me get you on your way to the nearest village and then I shall return for this fool."

When she returned less than an hour later, Makinde was waking. She pulled him by his feet with little effort, like he weighed a feather, in the direction of the stream.

"Tonight, you will confess who you are working with, Makinde. I will drown you if you don't." She was on her way to killing him when he refused to talk, his face submerged in the depths of the stream when she heard the war chants of the Ologun.

"You must go," the voice in her head said.

"Yes, Baami," she whispered, pulling Makinde to the soil and pressing down on his stomach. He groaned and his head slumped sideways.

"If you ever tell anyone who I am or what I did, you will ooze out like a rotten carcass." As the chanting got closer, Dotunu ran down the path towards the palace, the water trailing behind her.

At the palace, the mob had tripled from the day before. They stormed the palace walls calling for Şiwoolu's head, unaware of the personal sorrow he bore.

Wuraola walked into the royal chambers, shaking her head. "Hmm! How easily people are swayed by the temporal things of life," she proclaimed.

"Dethrone him!" they screamed again.

Light glowed in the hallway leading to the chambers. Şiwoolu rose from the bench in the middle of the room.

"Where are you going?" Wuraola demanded.

"To face them, of course. Or do you want them to burn down the palace with us in it?"

Şiwoolu's mother ran to the doorway to block his exit, hands on her waist.

"You will not relinquish your throne!" She turned her head, her threaded hair like spikes, casting a shadow on the wall.

Şiwoolu spluttered a weak laugh. "Maami, I am the king who can't even save his Olori from the clutches of the enemy. Dotunu was kidnapped from right under my nose. I can't blame the people for demanding the throne."

"She was not taken!"

"You keep saying that, but where is she then if she was not taken? Do you know more than you say?" Şiwoolu asked, grabbing his mother's arms. Her eyes shimmered with tears.

"I just know," she whispered.

A shadow stood in the doorway. "Your Highness! You must come quickly!" Olatunde shouted.

"I know. The villagers are calling for my head."

Olatunde shook his head. "Not anymore. The ologun have arrived too. They are bringing a body with them."

Şiwoolu's head snapped to his mother. "It cannot be Dotunu, it cannot be!" she shouted. He took a deep breath as Olatunde handed him his irukere – a white horsetail bound at the handle by whitewashed leather – and followed him with Wuraola in tow.

The palace court was full. Five of the six members of the ogboni ruling council, men of his father's age who had selected his father and then him as king, fell to the ground when they saw Şiwoolu. A few feet from his throne lay a long figure. He released the breath he had been holding when it moved.

"Kabiyesi o!" the crowd prostrated.

Şiwoolu was transfixed – it was not the reception he had expected. A few seconds ago, they had been screaming for his head. As they rose, Şodękę, his late father's good friend and one of the leaders who had liberated them from the Oyo empire, walked towards him, a spring in his steps.

"Makinde, the sorcerer, has been captured! Look!" He pointed to the figure on the ground writhing in pain, his clothing soaked. The dark face was skinny, a stark contrast to the bloated body. He held out his arm.

"Mercy, Your Highness!" It was the same voice that had challenged Şiwoolu just days before, mocking him as he deliberated with the council on what to do following the continued disappearances of the villagers.

"Hmm!" A murmur swept through the crowd as they covered their noses with their hands. The smell did not take long to reach Şiwoolu. It was the odour of rotting flesh, and it came from Makinde. His rotund stomach grew before their eyes. People screamed and jostled one another.

"Silence!" Şodękę's voice cracked like a whip as he skirted the figure on the ground. The crowd calmed down enough to hear the harsh, loud breathing of the man before them.

"Confess what you have done, Makinde!" Şodękę shouted close to his ear. The charms on his buba swung back and forth, skimming Makinde's face. A gurgling sound rose from Makinde's stomach. The crowd screamed again. Fascinated, they drew closer. The ologun stationed around the body pushed them back. Şodękę crouched by Makinde's head.

"Confess!" he screamed in his ear.

Makinde raised his hands. "I ... I will."

His stomach made the gurgling sound again. He

grimaced. Clutching the hill that was his stomach, he raised his buttocks to let gas out.

"Hmm!" The crowd murmured again as the smell circulated, clinging to their clothing and wafting through the air.

Şiwoolu covered his face with his agbada.

"We do not have all night, Makinde!" Şodękę growled.

Makinde turned his body towards Şiwoolu, his eyes beseeching him to show mercy. Şiwoolu grabbed the arm of the throne and sat down.

"Speak!" he shouted.

"Your Highness, they came for them," Makinde said through chattering teeth. His body shook as though it was harmattan.

"Who?" the mob screamed.

"They gave me goods in exchange for guiding them through the forest to the villages."

"Haa!" The mob shouted.

Şiwoolu held up his staff, silencing them. "Ask him where *they* took our people."

"The king wants to know where our people were taken," Şodękę said.

Makinde shook his head slowly.

Şiwoolu leaned forward and asked the only question to which he truly needed an answer.

"Where is the Olori?"

The crowd shouted the same question, shaking the palace walls. Makinde twisted on the floor, screaming as if spirits were beating him.

The guards held him down, adding their voices to the

demands for the Olori and the others who had been kidnapped.

Wuraola stepped out of the shadows behind the throne and the mob stopped screaming.

"Please, let him speak. We must find out before... before—"

White foam poured from Makinde's mouth as his body shook uncontrollably. The crowd screamed.

"*They* are taking him before he speaks! He must tell us where Olori is!" Wuraola shouted. "He must confess all!" She ran to Makinde's trembling body as he took a deep breath and went limp. Şiwoolu stood up.

"Is he dead?" he asked.

Wuraola bent her head to his chest and listened. She looked up, eyes blazing, and said, "Everybody, out! Out!"

After the guards had driven out all but the ogboni council and Şodękę, Şiwoolu's legs buckled under him.

"Your Highness!" Olatunde grabbed him from behind and pulled him back onto the throne.

Şiwoolu stretched out his hand to the still body. "He cannot die! He must tell us where to find Dotunu!" he bellowed.

"Take the king to his chambers!" Şodękę shouted.

Wuraola was chanting words over the still body as Olatunde carried Şiwoolu down the dark hallway. He knew that not even his mother's chants would bring a dead man back to life. He resolved in his heart to take the next step. It would take only a few minutes to put together the potion. He had been preparing for this for the past seven days, since Ireti had run in screaming and crying. It had taken some time, but between him, his mother, and Olatunde, they were able to determine what she said, that she could not find Dotunu. They had combed the whole kingdom but could not locate her. What else was there to live for? He closed his eyes and let the tears roll down his face.

Olatunde entered the chambers and gasped at what he saw. "Your Highness! Look!"

Şiwoolu opened his eyes and the darkness gave way to the figure by the window looking at him. Olatunde placed him on the ground and steadied him as he stood. She was wet, her wrapper plastered to her skin.

"Dotunu?" Şiwoolu reached out to touch her cold face. Blood dripped from her nose. He wiped it off, but she stopped him by placing her hand over his.

"I'm sorry," she whispered.

Olatunde retreated.

"Where have you been?"

Dotunu took a deep breath. "I was with my father."

"Your father?"

The tall, dark image of Elemere Keşi flashed before Şiwoolu's eyes. He was the missing member of the ogboni council waiting outside. Dotunu nodded, water dripping from her hair onto Şiwoolu's face and clothing. He felt the water forming around his feet before his eyes slid down to the puddle that had travelled beyond them towards the doorway. Looking up, he asked, "Why are you wet? It's not raining outside."

Dotunu stared at him, her face resolute.

"I thought you were dead ... gone," his voice trembled.

"I'm sorry," she said numbly. She did not sound

remorseful, rather cold, keeping the same composure she had shown when she told him that they should do something about the disappearances.

"Makinde has been caught," Şiwoolu said.

"Good. Did he confess?" she asked without batting an eye.

"Partly. He and some other people were responsible, but he died before he could name the others."

Dotunu nodded. Her eyes whispered things unsaid. "As he should. He deserved it."

Şiwoolu took a step closer and stopped. Her eyes blazed with anger. She turned and walked to the corner.

"I must change out of this wet wrapper."

"Dotunu."

She rummaged through the pile of folded wrappers in the corner. Şiwoolu walked over to her and held her waist.

"Dotunu."

She straightened and turned around.

"Where did you go with your father?"

Her brown eyes glinted in the dark. "We were about the affairs of the kingdom," she said softly.

She turned around and began humming the tune that had drawn Şiwoolu to her the first time they met in the forest.

Chapter Six

War of the Gods
Unknown Waters
Circa 1836

For seven days the gods unleashed their wrath upon the ship. Olokun, goddess of the bottom of the ocean, lashed out in fury as the vessel battled the ferocious turbulence, powerless to stop the assault. It heeled to the left and right until no one on board could keep food down. Şango, god of iron and thunder, raged from above, awakening his sister-wife, Oya, goddess of the wind and lightning. She reached down and struck two men to death on deck, sending the others scampering into the lower level. Their leader's menacing screams had them running back up again. Below, the chained men, toppled by the ship's upheaval, lay in heaps on the floor.

When the storm subsided briefly, their captors came down to feed and clean the prisoners. They made no effort to mask the relief on their faces as they pulled and tugged the men until they were in sitting positions, their knees pressed close to their faces. They placed crusts of bread on wooden plates by their bound feet and waited for them to finish sharing the crumbs, one plate amongst ten or more.

Şiwoolu refused to eat. He pleaded with the gods silently during the day, and at night, he cried out in his sleep for them not to tarry any longer. It would be better if he died with his family than lived in this hell another day. Demilade, his mouth pressed to Şiwoolu's ear, begged him to eat.

"Remember what the gods did when the disappearances started again after your coronation? Did they not fight your battles? Do not lose heart, Your Highness. Remember!"

The others began to ask questions:
"What did the gods do?"
"Is he really a king?"
"Of what kingdom?"
"Will his people raise an army to save him?"
"Can he lead us in the revolt?"

Şiwoolu looked around the room, lips chapped and throat parched. He could feel their hope rising and wished he could tell them not to waste it on him, but he could not summon the energy. Above them, the sound of boots, followed by the muffled screams of females reached them, as the women were pulled off their shelves and dragged out of the room. The door banged shut after them and the men's grunts and the female's screams could be heard below. This happened daily until the day the storm returned, battering the ship ferociously. Şiwoolu prayed once more for death.

The storm subsided on the eighth day. An uneasy calm fell upon the ship. The men heard boots marching one level above their room, where the females were kept. Chained feet trudged above them and for half the day, agonised voices filled their ears.

"What is happening?" Şiwoolu whispered.

"It's the women. They must be..." Demilade choked and became quiet.

"No, this is something else."

The women walked back, crying and calling out the names of their loved ones. Şiwoolu rolled his hands into fists, heartbeat hammering against his chest.

Then boots marched down towards the men's room and the door was flung open once more. The pale-faced men shouted as they were dragged off the shelves and brought up to the deck for the first time.

Şiwoolu's head felt like a drum after a night of repeated beating as he emerged into the sunlight. His eyes stung as he opened them. The reddish sun was merciless as it blazed upon his nakedness. He gulped the air and almost choked when he saw the vast, endless blue water. He looked around with eagerness for a sign from the gods, but all that was before and behind him were the bowed heads and hunched shoulders of the men who had been faceless until now. He imagined the high-strung voice that called for revolt belonged to the man with three vertical tribal marks on his cheeks. Behind him, two voices whispered in a foreign tongue – likely the ones who beseeched Mawu-Lisa, the sun and moon gods of the Dahomey people to intervene as they lay entangled during the storm. Their reddened eyes widened in recognition, as they caught his above the bowed heads, and they nodded. Şiwoolu, thankful for a sign, muttered praises to the gods. These ones were as ready as he was to attack. The chains clanged against each other as he shook his fists. Demilade turned his head to look at him and whispered, "Not now, Your Highness."

"When? What are we waiting for?" Şiwoolu asked as he intensified beating his wrist chains together. Other chains joined his. He looked back again to see more heads raised and eyes waiting for his sign.

Black boots stomped towards him. Şiwoolu looked down at the guide who had brought them on board, holding a whip in his hand. He shouted an order to the first shackled man, one with grey hair and shaking knees, and pointed to the dark man with the strange eyes a few feet from him. In his hand was a red-hot, sizzling object. His devilish grin ignited the fury within Şiwoolu.

Two pale-faced men approached the shackled man, they pushed him to his knees and pressed the fiery object to the upper right side of his back without hesitation. His heart-wrenching scream raised the hairs on Şiwoolu's neck. The others began to struggle against their metal restraints, and the lashes fell on them like rain.

"How dare you?" Şiwoolu screamed as skin tore from his back. More lashes fell, pushing him down to his knees. He gritted his teeth, stopping the screams but not the tears. Had Dotunu suffered this way too? The boots multiplied and surrounded him. One of the captors unlocked his chains, freeing him from Demilade. Several men jeered, spat, and cursed at him, and when that did not satiate their thirst for blood, they began to kick his head and upper torso with their boots.

Şiwoolu pulled himself up slowly and charged at the strange-eyed man with a murderous scream. A blow struck him on the head and sent him crashing to the floor. The slavers laughed even harder, some holding their chests, others banging their hands against the side of the ship. Şiwoolu watched through blood-tipped lashes as the strange-eyed man said something to the men, his eyes never leaving Şiwoolu. Swinging the handle of the fiery object in his hand, he walked towards Şiwoolu. It emitted a reddish glow that Şiwoolu had seen many times in a blacksmith's stall. The men formed a tight circle around Şiwoolu and his tormentor. His grin was the last thing Şiwoolu saw as the iron fell on his back.

The blood-curdling scream that woke Şiwoolu was one he was familiar with. Feet scuffled past him as he lay sprawled on the deck. The female screamed again and paused by his side. A rough push sent her tripping forward. The men whistled as she walked alone, the chains around her ankles limiting her to a few paces at a time. Şiwoolu winced as pain spread across his back. He lifted his head and saw two bodies a few feet from him. He recognised the two foreigners who had been willing to stand with him against their slaveholders. One groaned and touched his back. A large, dark, circular scar was forming on his right shoulder blade. Şiwoolu moaned as his upper shoulder stung from the searing pain he had blacked out from. The pale-faced men glanced at him and turned away, engrossed in the figure before them. Şiwoolu's eyes travelled from her feet up to her legs and thighs, which were covered with welts. Pieces of skin dangled on her back. Neither her hunched shoulders nor small hands could hide the budding breasts she attempted to cover. The men pulled her hands off as she passed between them. A calloused hand slapped her buttocks. Şiwoolu groaned when his eyes fell on her lowered face. He summoned all the strength within him and called out.

"Ireti!"

She whimpered like a cornered animal and looked around.

"I'm here, Ireti," Şiwoolu whispered.

She screamed and ran towards him. A hand hit her across the face and sent her to the floor. The men pointed at her and laughed, but their glee was cut short by a boom that shattered the side of the ship, sending fragments of wood into the air. Bodies hit the deck as smoke engulfed them. The men began to run, shouting orders and pointing towards the darkened horizon. Şiwoolu blinked to get the blood out of his eyes. The ship was thrown into pandemonium as more men ran across the deck towards a long, cast-iron cylindrical object aimed at something Şiwoolu could not see. He could taste their fear. The pale-faced leader barked orders at the men as he got closer to Şiwoolu and then paused by his head. The strange-eyed man was not beside him. The ship rocked violently, with water rushing onto the deck this time. It drenched Şiwoolu's naked body and filled his ears until all he heard were muffled shouts. The pale-faced leader straightened up to steady himself and gasped on seeing what had caught them by surprise.

Something bigger was upon them. Its shadow closed in and the men ran. Those who had brazenly hit and kicked

Şiwoolu fled into the crevices of the ship. The pale-faced leader yelled at them as they ran past him. Then he pulled something from his pocket and pointed it at one of the men running past; the man immediately halted to listen to what his leader was saying. He then nodded, grabbed Şiwoolu's feet, and began to drag him in the direction of the stairs. Şiwoolu turned his head in search of Ireti.

"Ireti! Ireti!" he shouted, looking around to catch a glimpse of her amid the confusion. But he could not see her, he could only hear her maniacal cries for help as his head hit the steps.

PART II: DOTUNU

Serra Lyoa
1836–1841

We yu go na kontri, if yu mit pipul den de dans wit wan fut, yusef fi dans wit wan fut. But if yu dans wit tu fut, den go kut di oda wan unda yu.

When you go to a country where the people dance on one foot, you should dance on one foot as well. If you dance on two feet, they'll cut one of them from under you.

– Sierra Leonean saying

Chapter Seven

A Reckoning
Circa 1836

When all that separated Dotunu from death was the shaky hand that held her by the ankles over a bonfire six moons after her birth, she had been told that her eyes held no fear. When she came of age and her father told her of the sickness that ravaged her mother's brain – a sickness that visited and eventually stayed with the women in her mother's lineage, the same sickness that made her mother dangle her only child over the bonfire – even then, she felt no fear. But now, naked, chained, and pressed in on all sides by strangers in the dark bowels of this moving house, Dotunu feared the madness had finally found her. Even though she had been fortified from the moment she could walk – the sacrifices and pilgrimages, the midnight baths – nothing had been powerful enough to protect her; otherwise, why would she be here? Why would she find herself in this nightmare, interlocked with others, fused by tears and bodily fluids? These questions filled her mind, and slowly, fragments of what had transpired began to return.

The last thing she remembered was the white man grabbing the coral beads around her neck and hitting her.

She turned her head, which lay on her knees, and sucked in her breath as she took in the number of women in the room. They were a multitude, all seated with knees pressed against their faces, sweaty shoulders digging into the next. She screamed for Şiwoolu, Ireti, and Şomide, but how could they hear her when the others' screams overpowered hers? When they paused to catch their breath, they heard females screaming through the wall separating them, crammed like they were, into shelves of the ship.

The women seemed to have been forgotten for days, while on the other side of the wall they could hear female voices screaming and begging as their captors closed in on their prey. Soon, the men's groans, grunts, and bodies thrusting against the thin wooden walls overshadowed the women's agonising screams. Dotunu prayed that their captors would not appear in her room, though her heart sank, knowing that if Ireti was not with her, she was being violated in the other room. When the storm came, Dotunu thanked the gods for their protection.

The men brought them up to the deck days later, when the sun was up. Dotunu scanned the rows of women behind her; they covered the expanse of the ship. Her eyes were blank, seeing but not absorbing the enormity of what was happening. One of the men standing in front of them singled out Dotunu. His eyes burnt holes into her breasts, the swell of her belly, and the dark, soft mound between her legs. He pointed at Dotunu and whistled, and she turned her head to look. It was Sigmund. His tongue slithered out between his thick, darkened lips as he leaned against the side of the ship. But the pale-faced man with the gold tooth came forward instead, in his hand a ring of keys. He grabbed her wrists and turned the key in the lock, leaving her hands to fall to her sides, then pushed her towards the other ten unshackled women in varying stages of pregnancy, who were wailing and covering their breasts and pubic areas with their hands. Then a piercing scream tore through the air, a sound that Dotunu recognised too well.

"Ireti!" Dotunu shouted as she jerked her head from side to side to locate the girl among the many heads. Ireti screamed louder as the sound of a whip fell on bare skin. Moments later, a body fell with a heavy thud on the floor, and Ireti's screams grew in intensity. Dotunu winced.

"Ireti," she whispered, crying silently as the white man shouted and pointed at the pregnant women huddled together. He swung the whip in his other hand on the floor, and she trembled. The sight of it nailed her feet to the floor. Sigmund walked up to her, his hands behind his back. He towered over her small frame. His shaven head glistened from the sun's rays. He looked down at her and softly and slowly said something she did not understand. This drew loud guffaws and whistles from the other men watching the spectacle. When he moved away towards the other pregnant women, his eagle eyes hovered over each one and settled on the one who looked like she could deliver her baby any day. He squatted before her, using a finger to poke her belly and make the baby stir several times within her. Grabbing her hand, he rose and headed for the stairs below as the woman cried. Dotunu watched with trepidation as the woman snatched her hand away inches from the stairs and ran towards the ship's railings, screaming: "Ọkọ mi, Ololufẹ mi, odabọ na o!" She bid her lover goodbye before hauling herself overboard. Dotunu's screams, like nails clawing on stony ground, blended with the others. The men, initially transfixed by the woman's boldness, ran towards the railings with raised weapons, but to no avail.

"So she was one of us," the woman in front of Dotunu said. Her scalp, visible between patches of short greying hair, shimmered with sweat. It ran down her temples and sat in little balls over her top lip, but her eyes remained as clear as the sky above them, untouched by what they had just witnessed. Dotunu covered her mouth but could not hold the sickness back.

"Let it go."

Dotunu felt a hand on her back as she lowered her head, releasing the fear that had clung to her since her nightmare began. It was lumpy, this fear, spattered on the wooden floor – the food the men had given them in the bowels of the slave vessel consisted of rotten, tasteless vegetables.

The tremor of the men's boots as they marched towards the women shook the floor. They advanced, waving their pointed weapons in the direction of the stairs.

"Stand up, child!" The older woman whispered with urgency to Dotunu. She patted the floor, unaware that she had slid to her knees. "We must go below. Come," the woman whispered again before she turned around to face the back of the woman in front of her. As the bodies moved slowly towards the stairs, weary with fatigue and despair, Dotunu stole a glance at the spot from which the pregnant woman had thrown herself into the ocean. Her eyes must have settled on the spot for too long, for the man with the strange eyes suddenly grabbed her by the elbow and said in Yoruba with a foreign accent, "You dare not!"

His eyes lit up as they fell on the gold chain around her neck. But when he reached out to grab it, he found no clasp. Dotunu thanked her father silently that he had requested that the goldsmith melt the chain into an infinite circle around her neck. Frustrated, the man pushed her towards the stairs, and Dotunu gasped as she bumped into the woman ahead of her.

"Just follow, child. If you plan to find your children again, don't look at him," the woman murmured, still staring ahead, but Dotunu looked behind her once more and saw him watching. She caught his eyes as he licked his lips in a manner that made it clear what he wanted to do to her. Dotunu turned away, praying he would not come after her.

They remained in the bowels of the ship for two days. Days listening to men weep as the lashes fell on their backs, days searching for Ireti and Şomide in the dark, clawing through chained bodies, whispering their names while she pressed her face into strangers. Her hands became eyes as she touched the contours of their faces. On the eighth day after the storms had come, Dotunu heard Ireti's screams again. Sounds of a body being dragged down the wooden floor, the *thump thump* of boots, and the blood-curdling screams of her ward woke her up. The men's laughter followed. They were taunting her. The sound of shuffling feet followed the thumping of boots.

"Ireti! Ireti!" Şiwoolu's hoarse voice carried down into the room as a body was dragged above them.

Dotunu sat up and pushed against the bodies, trying to move towards the barred wooden door. She heard whiplashes falling on flesh, then a gasp and a whimper. Tears welled up in her eyes and flowed freely when she realised it was her love. He was up there with Ireti. The knowledge comforted her but also plunged her into more pain.

"Let me go, I beg you!" Dotunu screamed in the dark.

"Hush, child! They will come for you."

It was the older woman a few feet away in her crouched position. They had been separated as they were shoved into orderly rows to fit into the space.

"Mama, they have my family up there," Dotunu whispered. "My family is up there!"

"You must be quiet, child, or else there will be no you and no family."

Dotunu pressed her hands over her stomach to calm the baby that kicked inside her. Suddenly, the ship lurched to the side, throwing Dotunu onto the body to her left. The ship shook, something had hit it. She heard the voices of the men who had laughed and taunted them tremble in fright as they screamed orders and ran helter-skelter on the deck. *Boom!* The ship rocked back and forth repeatedly, and the women held onto one another.

"One who is more powerful has arrived!" It was the older woman again.

"Who?" Dotunu shouted above the noise of screams from their captors and the captives on deck.

"Yes, who?" asked another woman in the darkness.

"Their enemies, our allies," She whispered. "You will see.

The sound of more boots hit the deck above them, followed by the loud sounds of weapons clashing against each other. Bodies fell like torrents of rain. Huddled together in the darkness, the women waited as a fight ensued. Dotunu called on the gods to keep her family safe.

The door swung open long after the harsh clash of metal against metal had been reduced to the quieter sounds of kicks and punches. Black smoke rushed into the room, and Dotunu blinked several times until the faces of men at the door appeared. They were pale skinned like the women's captors, but their clothing was different: they wore dark outfits decorated with a single row of round metallic buttons from neck to abdomen. Their bottoms, once white, were now brown and spattered with blood. Their legs were covered in black leather contraptions up to their knees and their black protruding hats covered the upper parts of their faces. Twelve of them lined up in a row before the women, their noses covered with their palms to minimise the putrid smell of faeces and other bodily fluids in the room.

A man with a white moustache entered. He was dressed differently: he wore a larger hat, and his dark outfit was decorated with medallions on his shoulders and chest. He had a gold belt around his waist and a sword dangled from his side. The men stood to attention as he walked past with a small white cloth pressed to his nose. He paused and pointed at Dotunu, who shrank into the naked body behind her. Though he spoke in a foreign tongue, his tone was not like that of their captors; it was soft. He beckoned to her to come forward, but Dotunu whimpered and pressed further into the body behind her.

"Come," he said as he held out his hand to her. In his next breath, he said something to the men standing behind him. They walked between the women and began to pull out the pregnant ones who remained unchained. The man gestured once more to Dotunu to rise.

"He is not like the others," the older woman near her whispered.

Dotunu looked up into his eyes; they were blue - the colour of the sky on a clear day. Then she took his outstretched hand and followed him through the mesh of bodies to the door. When the pregnant women were assembled, the men held out pieces of brown clothing to each one. Dotunu's was warm as the man placed it around her. It was only when he dabbed at her face with a white cloth that she knew she was crying.

"Come," he said again.

She followed him and the other pregnant women as they were led up the stairs.

The white men dressed in dark clothing paraded their former captors before them in chains. Sigmund jerked in his chains, spitting out words Dotunu knew were foul just by the way he said them. Of the men who had abused them, only half remained. The other half lay lifeless in a pile at the front of the vessel. Smoke still billowed from holes torched by the explosions, creating a fog that affected Dotunu's visibility.

Dotunu strained her neck to see above the heads as naked, shackled men were led from the bowels of the vessel and walked past the women. Their dark bodies, riddled with whip marks, filed past. Dotunu, like the other women, had not laid eyes on any of them since she had been captured. Her heart beat faster as a tall, broad-shouldered man came closer. His tightly curled hair had grown even in such a short time.

"Şiwoolu!"

The man turned around and Dotunu could see that the shape of his head was where the resemblance ended. He had a blend of diagonal and vertical tribal marks that met at the corners of his mouth; she could not tell its origin. The man nodded in her direction and walked past. Dotunu began to sob when the last set of men stepped out and Şiwoolu was not among them.

"Shh, child! See, they are bringing more women from below, and the children are with them. Maybe your sister and son will be there," the old woman said. Dotunu nodded, wishing her tongue would loosen so she could thank the woman for staying close, but the waning energy she had was reserved for her loved ones.

More women, their heads bowed, came out with children. Dotunu moved closer to raise their chins and look into their faces, but in the blink of an eye they dropped into the nooks of their necks, shackled by invisible chains.

"Ireti! Ireti!" she screamed. Her cries got louder as the line snaked to an end. Then a child squirmed and cried out in the sea of bodies. Dotunu's heart lurched in her chest.

"Ṣomide! My son! Let me have my son!" She screamed and pushed through the lines, guided by his weak cries.

The boy's face was lean and plastered with dirt. He sat in the arms of a pale-faced man, swaddled in the thick brown cloth, and when he saw Dotunu he stretched out his hands towards her.

"Ṣomide! Ṣomide!" Dotunu screamed.

The women made way for her; their faces lit with joy.

"She found her son!" They whispered into each other's ears. The pale-faced man handed Ṣomide to Dotunu, who trembled as she grasped and clung to him. The men passed out more children to women calling and reaching out for them. The man whom Dotunu had come to believe was their leader came forward and raised his hand. He said something and gestured for everyone to be quiet; his voice was soothing. He pointed to the other vessel on the water. It was majestic, with a huge flag made of yards of white cloth floating above it. On board were many more men dressed like the ones with him on the slave vessel, holding their weapons close and pointing them at the sky. Dotunu cringed and pulled Ṣomide close.

The men instructed the prisoners to line up and counted them while one wrote with a slim pen in a large book similar to one Dotunu had found in a room in Sunmonu's house. This, like the other one, had scribbles in columns and rows. Sunmonu had grabbed it from Ṣomide when he was playing with it.

One of the pale-faced men waved to them to follow him down the winding line until they were close to the edge of the vessel. There, a short plank connected their ship with the bigger one. A man on the plank held out his hands for Şomide. Dotunu tightened her arms around him.

"I take him."

He pointed to himself and then to another man dressed like him at the end of the plank on the larger vessel. Dotunu shook her head and tightened her grip. He nodded and shouted to the next woman in line. She came forward holding a girl who looked about four harvest seasons old. He held out his hands for the child. The woman glanced at Dotunu.

"I take her," he said again, stretching his arms out further. She looked at him and back at Dotunu. The man smiled, his hands steady and waiting. The woman sighed and gave him her child. The girl cried while her mother soothed her in a foreign tongue. He climbed up onto the plank. The mother followed. It did not take them long to get across. With the help of the men, three more mothers and their children crossed over to the bigger vessel. Next in line again, Dotunu heaved a heavy sigh and handed Şomide to the man, whose pale face was marked with red pustules. He did not look much older than her nineteen harvest seasons. Dotunu followed close behind as they stepped onto the plank. She held her breath and looked straight ahead as they crossed. When her feet touched the floor of the new vessel, she grabbed Şomide, who was crying for her.

"I'm here," she whispered in his ear as she joined the women cradling their children at the end of the vessel and waiting for everyone to be brought on board. They came in their hundreds, eyes rekindled with hope. Had they been rescued? Who were these kind pale-faced men who gave them clothing? Were they still in their nightmare, soon to be woken up by whips on their backs? They dared to hope.

The men began to join them on the deck. Freed from the shackles, their limbs, necks, and feet moved awkwardly, and for a few seconds they looked around numbly, unsure of what to do with their unexpected liberation. They came close, those with families, seeking them out with their eyes. Shouts of joy rent the air repeatedly as they found their significant others. When the vessel began to fill up, Dotunu wailed at the absence of Şiwoolu and Ireti.

"Hush, child, or you will make yourself sick!" Dotunu turned around to see the older woman behind her once more.

"I ... I can't find them!"

She shuddered at the prospect of losing Şiwoolu and Ireti forever. The people near her began to spin around her. Calloused hands grabbed her before she fell.

"Captain!" The man who had carried Şomide across caught Dotunu as she collapsed, and Şomide was swiftly taken from her hands by one of the women.

Dotunu woke with her face pressed into the man's clothing. He smelled of dried sweat and the smoke that had engulfed the slave vessel they had just been rescued from. His boots thudded on the floorboards as he transported Dotunu deep into the ship. She felt her chest tighten in fear of reliving the nightmare and began to scream, hitting his chest and face and kicking her feet feebly against the walls.

"Shh, shh, shh," he said repeatedly as his walk slowed

to a halt outside a door. He knocked with the tip of his boot.

"Well, come in then!" a male voice shouted from within.

"A little help, doctor!" the man shouted above Dotunu's head.

The door opened and a grey-haired, bespectacled man wearing a white coat spattered with blood opened the door. His eyes widened when they fell on the slumped figure in the naval officer's arms.

"Well, what are you standing there for, David? Bring her in!"

He swung the door open and hurried to a wooden table. With one hand he pushed the bottles and metal objects on it to the edge, then patted it.

David placed Dotunu on it. "She fainted. I'll bring her child in a minute, doctor, or she'll get agitated again." His voice was squeaky and his eyes roamed the room.

"Of course, I'll check him too while I'm at it," the doctor said.

David looked at Dotunu and pointed towards the back of the mid-sized room. "The doctor will check on you now, but don't be afraid. We have a few injured here too."

She turned her neck in the direction in which he pointed. It felt like a long time, but finally her eyes focused on the bare feet lining the floor. There were ten of them, pressed in close together, aligned in a straight fashion to the end of the wooden wall at the end of the room. Dotunu's eyes travelled up and down the row of bodies, moaning with pain. One whimpered and then began to scream.

Dotunu gasped. She attempted to sit up. The doctor came closer, and with each step, the stark red splatters on his white coat grew bigger. She screamed and scrambled backward on the table, kicking the medicine bottles to the floor, shattering them to pieces. The sound startled the injured on the floor, and one of them moaned in despair. Dotunu grabbed the ends of the table on which she lay.

"*Ehn?*" she whispered.

It was the same sound that had assailed her ears every night for many moons after her father had brought Ireti back from one of his travels, starved and fearful of anything that moved. The doctor and David pulled her gently into an upright position, and Dotunu's eyes fell on the thrashing body a few feet below. She was in the middle of the row. To her immediate right, was a man with a black eye patch over his left eye. Her eyes darted back to the girl, gasping on noticing the marks on the ebony skin.

"Ireti!" Turning to the doctor, she signed for him to take her to Ireti.

"What? You know this child? My goodness. All right, you want to go to her?" Dotunu nodded when he pointed at her and then at the bodies below. "We must be careful. First for the broken glass, and secondly, for the injured. I wouldn't want them hitting your belly by accident."

Dotunu pulled on his blood-stained coat and pointed to the bodies again. The man obliged with David's help. They placed her on the floor and she moved closer to the girl, brushing aside the arm of the man with the eye patch. Black crusts of flesh and blood covered his cheeks. His other eye watched her. He whispered something and repeated it. Dotunu shook her head.

"I don't understand you," she said, and turned around to Ireti. Ireti's bloodshot eyes found Dotunu's gaze and she stopped screaming. Dotunu grabbed the girl's hand and Ireti squeezed weakly. Dotunu leaned in and pulled her head into her bosom, her body shook as she cried.

"Yes, it is I, my sister. It is I." Dotunu sobbed into her neck, and Ireti flung her arms around her and cried too.

"Dotu-nu?"

It was faint. The raspy voice called to her again. She looked up, her eyes scanned the bodies on the floor, to the left of Ireti where four bodies lay lifeless, and then to the right, first at the man with the eye patch and past him to the four bodies to his left. Her eyes were drawn to the body at the end, next to the wall. He was naked like the others, but it was too dark to see his face from where she was. She placed Ireti gently on the floor amid her soft cry of protest.

"I will return," Dotunu whispered. She looked up at David and the doctor with the bloodied clothing and pointed to the figure at the end, whose heels were now hitting the floor. They took her hands, lifted her up and led her to the body. When they set her down, she moved forward until she was close to his face. It was battered. Blood flowed from everywhere – his chest, arms and thighs were slashed. He opened his mouth.

"Do-tu-nu?"

The scream came from a hidden place, one she did not know existed. They had butchered him. His face was disfigured: one eyelid swollen and shut tight, the other a mere slit. His jaws looked as though he had two drinking gourds in his cheeks. He winced as he lifted his chin to look at her.

"Is it you?" he asked through the small hole his mouth managed to form.

Dotunu cupped his face. "It is I, Şiwoolu! It is I!" she screamed, placing her head on his scarred chest. The touch on her back was so light she thought she had imagined it until he squeezed. The cloth David had placed around her fell, discarded on the floor, as they held each other tight.

Chapter Eight

Serra Lyoa
Freetown
Circa 1836

Şiwoolu and Ireti slowly regained their strength over the next few days. For Şiwoolu, the progress was evident when the tears that fell when he moved subsided to whimpers and he was able to swallow food. Ireti's was in her firmer grip when she held onto Dotunu's hand. It was hard for Dotunu to hold back tears when she looked at her husband's face, which had once been lean and handsome but was now battered to a pulp. He could only whisper, and when he did, it was difficult to decipher. She resorted to making signs as she typically did with Ireti to communicate with him.

"Şiwoolu," she whispered close to his face, hoping to see a flicker of life in his eyes. They were as blank as the night she had encountered him in the forest as he stole away from the village after his father's burial. It had been another full moon, and she had gone to the forest to pay customary homage to Aroni, god of the forest. She had danced more exuberantly than in the past, grateful that the herbs from the forest, the ones Aroni had led her to find, had kept the madness at bay. As she sang, her voice filled the silence in the forest, and she felt completely alone with nature, until she heard the footsteps creeping forward like a child's first tentative steps.

They often argued about who saw who first. Şiwoolu said the beads on her ankles had placed a spell on him and he could not resist the pull to the stream where she danced, oblivious to the world. Dotunu remembered the head peeking from behind the tree trunk. That seemed like a hundred moons ago now as she lovingly cleaned the fresh wound on his back. His skin was burnt and had darkened into a round scar similar to the ones on the backs of the two men to his right, thrashing about on the floor, screaming for Mawu-Lisa and other deities familiar to her. Her father, in his quest to prevent her mother's madness from passing on to her, had travelled far and wide, deep into the kingdom of the Dahomey, and had learned the names of their male and female deities. He was taught by their priests to pray and offer sacrifices to protect his daughter day and night, and had in turn taught her to do the same.

She had once asked her father: "Baami, why do we pray to so many of them?" To which he had answered: "Who are we to favour one over another? Who knows which holds a possible cure for this madness lurking in the shadows?"

On the ship, the doctor ran back and forth among the injured, his forehead creased with worry as he administered ointments and medicines from glass bottles. Like them, he hardly ate the food the pale-faced men – dressed in what Dotunu discovered were war clothes – brought them two times a day. They had ranks too, just like the ologun, the warriors of Ẹgba kingdom. On the third day, David brought food and medical supplies and assisted the healer. Moments after he arrived, there was a rap on the door. It was the leader who had singled Dotunu out when they were rescued. Her thick infinity gold chain had not been lost on him, especially noting that none of the other women had any jewellery on. David sprang up from where he was cleaning the wound of one of the men. He stood erect with his hands rigid by his sides.

The leader spoke to the doctor, who turned to point at Dotunu who was holding a sleeping Şomide in her arms. Her back was against the wall and her shoulders slumped. She sat up when the leader walked towards her. He paused a few feet away and smiled. His white moustache moved when he spoke.

"We arrive soon, ma'am. I am sure you would be happy to know that if you understood." He pointed to the door and then stretched out his hand to her. Dotunu looked at the doctor, his round spectacles inched higher on his nose as he smiled and nodded his head.

"Come. Let me show you the Lion Mountains, your new home," the leader said.

She did not understand, but she was drawn by his friendliness. She laid Şomide down and followed him to the upper level. David followed. Some of the rescued in their path made way for them to walk through. When they reached the front of the vessel, the leader pointed through the mist. She felt the droplets of water on her face but could not see through the heavy fog. Then he said something to David, who moved closer to her and also pointed into the mist.

"Serra Lyoa, my queen," he said, as his eyes dropped to the gold chain around her neck. His pink-dotted face broke into a smile. He turned to look towards the mist again, and this time she followed his eyes more keenly. The sight before her made her gasp – mountains sat like lions lying in wait. Lightning flashed above and the mist turned into showers – pellets falling on Dotunu's face as she looked up at the grey sky. She gripped the railing of the vessel, her eyes welling with tears. Then she sank to the floor, screaming for her father and deceased mother, "Baami! Maami". If the gods could not be at peace with what had happened, Dotunu knew her mother could not be either. David knelt beside her.

"Captain?" He shouted above Dotunu's head with a worried look.

"Let her," the leader said.

He stood again beside the captain, and they both looked forward at the new land while Dotunu's anguished cries filled their ears and left her empty.

As the vessel moved closer to land, Dotunu, weakened by her cries, watched from behind wooden crates near the captain. He had pushed the hat away from his forehead and was barking orders at his men, who ran back and forth across the deck and pulled at the ropes above their heads. When the vessel finally stopped, the men pushed a plank from the ship across the waters and onto the white sand of the beach. The soldiers lined up in rows before their leader, with chests out and arms held stiffly at their sides.

David stood in front, his eyes intermittently wandering to Dotunu's hiding place.

The soldiers saluted him and then shouted orders to the freed people to come forward. Dotunu stood up to see what was happening – a soldier sat behind a table with a slim pointed object, an open bottle with dark liquid, and a large book. Another soldier stood beside him and motioned to the first row of women holding their children to come forward. As they came, the one standing called out something, and the one seated dipped the end of the object into the bottle and scribbled in the book.

Another soldier stood where the plank was lowered down to the land. He called and waved to the first woman with her child clasped to her chest. Her eyes roamed the perimeter of the ship. He called to her again. She took a tentative step forward. He walked towards her and took her by the elbow to help her up so she could walk down the plank. Suddenly, another voice shouted from below, and clapping erupted when her feet touched land. The action was repeated until all the mothers and children were below and only Dotunu remained. The captain turned and held out his hand.

"Come along, ma'am. Let us get you and your family to land."

She took it and walked with him towards the stairs. As they passed the rest of the women waiting to walk down the plank, she looked up into the ashen faces. One raised her hand; it was the older woman who had been with her in captivity. The woman was crying.

"We have been rescued, dear child!" she shouted.

Dotunu nodded and waved at her, overcome with tears that blinded her vision and made her feet buckle beneath her.

"Careful," David said as he appeared beside her. He said something to the captain and led her below to where the doctor was lifting the wounded onto long planks with the help of four soldiers and two plain-clothed, dark-skinned men. The two nodded at Dotunu in greeting. Şomide stirred on the bedding and opened his eyes. Upon seeing his mother, he cried out for her. Dotunu picked him up and waited for Şiwoolu and Ireti to be moved onto the planks. She followed behind as the men took Şiwoolu up the stairs. Behind them, Ireti moaned on a plank carried by two soldiers.

"This way! This way!" David cried out above the noise of the crowd as they walked down the plank onto the shore. Dotunu's toes curled into the white sand as she breathed in the fresh air. She turned to look back at the emptying ship that had brought them ashore and then looked away. The lines of the rescued had dwindled to the ones who had no strength left and were being assisted by the soldiers who worked deftly to get them to the wooden structures at least thirty feet up the beach. Following closely behind them were more soldiers carrying sacks of items filled to the brim. One of them tripped over a stone and the items – jewellery, beads, and expensive-looking embroidered clothing – scattered across the white sand. He bent down immediately and began to scoop them back into the sack, then placed it back on his shoulder and ran to catch up with his mates.

Two men stood waiting on the shore, different as night and day. The first was older and pale-faced, like the soldiers, with curly black hair growing down to his temples. A round white collar wound around his neck and a long-sleeved outfit flowed down to his shoes. Beside him was a young, dark-skinned man dressed in a black, three-piece, buttoned ensemble with a round-necked white shirt. His face was long and lean with deep-set warm eyes, and his head was covered in coarse black hair. He nodded to Dotunu as she walked towards them.

"Ẹ pẹlẹ. Ẹ ku idanwo na."

She gasped at his acknowledgement – in fluent Yoruba – of the ordeal she had endured.

David spoke and pointed to a bench ahead. He took Ṣomide from her despite his cries, and the two men helped Dotunu to the bench. When she was seated, she looked up into the young man's face as he stood hovering.

"Ẹ pẹlẹ," he said again, bowing his head.

"Ẹ ṣe," Dotunu thanked him.

He smiled at her. "Are you from Abeokuta?" he asked, straightening to his full height. Ṣomide wiggled in David's hands and cried for Dotunu, who leaned forward to take him.

"Yes. I am Dotunu. How did you know where I am from?"

He touched his plain cheek with one finger. "Your tribal marks. I myself was born in Osogun, not too far from Abeokuta." He gazed at Dotunu while David and the other pale-faced man spoke.

"They tell me your husband and sister are also on

board. You are fortunate," he said.

Dotunu nodded, her eyes drawn to the object swinging lightly on a long chain lying on his chest. He smiled when he realised what she was staring at.

"I am Samuel Ajayi Crowther," he said, holding out a large hand.

"Ajayi," she said softly. She glanced at the hand and then at David.

He stepped forward and took her hand. His palm was warm. He squeezed hers softly and then released her hand as David began to speak to him. When David finished, Ajayi turned to Dotunu with brows raised.

"David says that it has been a pleasure meeting you ... Olori?"

His eyes widened when she nodded.

"He must go back and bring your husband up to the registration quarters, he says."

"Oṣe, David," Dotunu said, turning to him. Ajayi said a word to him that made him turn bright pink and nod. Then he ran back towards the looming vessel, holding down his hat against the strong wind.

"You have stolen a heart so soon, Olori," Ajayi chuckled. He turned to the older man. "Let me introduce you to Minister Daniel Coker."

The pale-faced man with the curly black hair bent slightly at the waist, his eyes were the colour of the waters Dotunu had crossed. He spoke in a soft voice.

"Olori, on behalf of the people of Serra Lyoa, we are sorry for what you have gone through at the hands of these savages. We welcome you to this safe haven," Ajayi translated. The minister held out his hand, his eyes filling with tears as Dotunu laid her hand in his.

"I apologise," he said, blowing his nose with a handkerchief. He stuffed the cloth back into the slit in his layered outfit and smiled. His accent was unlike that of the captain and soldiers on board the vessel; his words drawled in an almost rhythmic tone. Ajayi translated what he said: "I am always emotional when I meet freed slaves, given that I also was one."

"Slave?" Dotunu asked.

The man before her was as pale faced as the others she had encountered, many of them evil men whose white skin camouflaged their dark hearts. How could it be? She only realised she had been thinking aloud when Ajayi answered.

"Not all are so, Olori. Minister Daniel may look white, but he is only half white. His mother was white, his father black. He was born across the waters in a place called Maryland, a place where the black man is unfortunately a slave. He came here to be free."

Dotunu gazed at the minister, who had turned his attention to Şomide. Laughing with glee, he picked him out of her arms. The child, without resistance, pulled at the hairs on his temple, intrigued by them.

"Is that your husband on the stretcher?" Ajayi asked.

Dotunu turned towards the two dark-skinned men carrying Şiwoolu. Close behind was Ireti.

"Yes, that is my husband, Alake of Ẹgba Kingdom, Oşiwoolu, son of Alade Okikilu. Did you not know of him in Abeokuta?"

A shadow crossed over Ajayi's face as he shook his head.

"No, I have yet to visit Abeokuta, though I hope to someday. Come, let us get you registered under the Coker quarters with Miss Abigail, Minister Daniel's wife."

Dotunu did not know these men, but for the first time since she had been lured onto the slave ship her heart did not beat so fast that it hurt her chest. Having her family with her was all that mattered. Ajayi's soothing voice followed her as they walked towards the wooden structures.

Minister Daniel's wife was as pale as the men on the vessels, even her hair, peeking from under a frilled hat, was as fair as the sand beneath Dotunu's feet. She was standing behind a table with three women when Ajayi, Minister Daniel, and Dotunu arrived. A few items of clothing were folded into a neat pile on one side of the table, and Dotunu could see that footprints decorated the wooden floor. Minister Daniel led them to his wife.

"Abigail, I'd like you to meet Dotunu and her son. Dotunu, this is my wife, Abigail." Ajayi interpreted as the woman came around the table with arms outstretched, the hem of her dress sweeping the ground with a swish. It was the colour of lush grass, the same colour as her eyes.

When Abigail lowered her head to enfold Dotunu in her arms, she exclaimed, "Dear God, you are so small to be carrying such a big baby! How far along are you?" She spoke with the same drawl as her husband. "Come with me. Let me introduce you to these wonderful women who have been the pillars of our communities."

Abigail took Dotunu's arm and guided her to the three women. The first one to their left was dark-skinned like Dotunu, plump with small eyes that lit up when she smiled. She grabbed Dotunu's hand and shook it as she spoke.

"Mighty glad to make your acquaintance, miss. I am Daisy. Welcome to Serra Lyoa." She tapped on a book on the table. "If you don't mind, I just want to record your family's names in the register. You'll be listed with a Coker last name since you will be living in the Coker Quarters with Minister Daniel here. Isn't that just wonderful?"

Ajayi interpreted slowly while Daisy nodded and smiled. When he was done, Dotunu asked him what Daisy meant when she said they would be listed under the Coker name.

"We have several missionaries here who are responsible for settling returnees into the communities, which are organised in quarters," Ajayi explained. "To ensure that everyone is accounted for, returnees must record their last names as the name of the missionary who heads their quarters and is responsible for them. In this case your name will be Coker, since you will be under Minister Coker's care in Hastings."

"This man?" Dotunu asked, pointing at Daniel. He smiled at her and nodded.

Ajayi laughed when Dotunu gasped. "Yes, Minister Daniel understands a bit of Yoruba."

Daisy asked a question and Ajayi said, "Please give us all of your family members' names."

After Daisy had recorded all the names in the book, Ajayi smiled and nodded at the tall dark woman with a long angular face and pointed nose, standing quietly next to Daisy. White frills lined the cuffs of her long sleeves and peeked from the bottom of her dress. She came around the table too.

"Meet Susanna, formerly called Hassana, my wife," Ajayi said proudly.

Dotunu took the hand she offered.

"Much obliged to meet you, miss," Susanna said gently. "I am sorry for the hardship you have had to go through. No one should have to endure that." Her eyes filled with tears as she bent down to place her arms around Dotunu.

"Come, Oṣuntade," Ajayi said.

The last woman stared back at Dotunu, unsmiling. She was tall and lean. The black head tie around her head pulled back her long face. Only her grey eyebrows proved that she was older than the others. The pattern of the wrapper across her chest reminded Dotunu of one she had at home. She walked towards Dotunu, her bare feet soundless on the floorboards. Two round earrings dangled from each ear, and beaded necklaces rested on her prominent collarbones. Her long neck stretched as she appraised Dotunu from head to toe.

"Good afternoon," Dotunu greeted when she refrained from speaking.

"Much obliged to meet you." Oṣuntade's voice was deep and her accent was foreign, different from those of the others. Bangles jingled as she held out her hand, and her scent – a mixture of incense and shea butter – filled Dotunu's nostrils.

"Oṣuntade, that is a Yoruba name," Dotunu said as the woman released her grasp.

Ajayi came closer. "Yes, Oṣuntade came from Jamaica. It is the name she chose for herself when she arrived. She's one of the first Jamaican Maroons to arrive here," he said.

Oṣuntade nodded and said a few sentences to Ajayi. He looked surprised for a moment but resumed translating.

"She says she has divested herself of anything foreign and embraced all things she believes are her true heritage – Yoruba. Her grandfather was taken from Ilesha. She understands a little of our language and continues to learn."

Oṣuntade's eyes shone, a smile appeared fleetingly. She held out her hands for Ṣomide, who had suddenly grown sleepy in Minister Daniel's hands. He went to her without a fuss. These were good people, even Ṣomide could feel it, Dotunu thought.

Abigail said something that started a new conversation between her husband and Ajayi. It was hard to tell that Minister Daniel had black blood flowing in his veins, Dotunu mused, he could pass as one of the pale-faced men. He gazed at his wife as she spoke, caressing her lower back. Then Ajayi bent to speak to Dotunu again.

"The final batch of returnees have started to walk to the cotton tree, where they will be taken in groups to their temporary quarters," he explained. "It is not advisable that you walk in your condition. We have arranged for the cart that took the other pregnant women to return for you. Your husband and sister will of course be carried ahead of us with the others."

He led Dotunu to the doorway and pointed at the four planks carried above the heads of the crowd in the distance.

"Where are you taking them? I must go where they go!" Dotunu screamed in sudden panic, grabbing Şomide from Oşuntade and running after Şiwoolu and Ireti.

"You will hurt yourself, Olori, please stop!" Ajayi shouted after her.

A sharp pain cut through Dotunu's lower abdomen, and she screamed and fell to the ground with Şomide, who burst into tears. Oşuntade was the first to reach her.

"Is she all right?" Ajayi shouted as Oşuntade knelt beside her. Dotunu felt warm hands under the thick blanket, and then the dampness. She looked down as Oşuntade's hands appeared, wet with amniotic fluid.

"Baby is coming!" Oşuntade shouted to the others.

"Get Doctor Crawley from the ship now!" Minister Daniel shouted as another wave of pain hit Dotunu.

Chapter Nine

Bringing Forth
Freetown
Circa 1836

*A**fter Oṣuntade pulled the baby* from between Dotunu's thighs, he was cleaned and wrapped snugly in a soft blanket. Oṣuntade could not stop smiling as she prepared the room in which Dotunu would stay, bringing in supplies for the time she and the baby would spend there. Dotunu was placed on a soft bed to make her comfortable. She was sleepy but unable to tear her eyes from the little face in the crook of her arm. Then she heard movement in the next room.

"Come in. She's awake," Oṣuntade said softly as the door to the room opened.

Dotunu turned her head and the baby stirred. Two men came in carrying a body on a plank and placed it on the floor. A gold ring shone as a hand dangled off the side.

"Ṣiwoolu?" Dotunu whispered and attempted to sit up. Oṣuntade walked around and lifted her from behind until her back was against the wall. The baby stirred once more in Dotunu's arms.

"Is that Ṣiwoolu? Where is he?"

A shadow walked past the doorway and Dotunu began to wonder if this was real or a lucid dream.

"I will bring the light. You men, please lay the king by his wife and then you may leave until I call you," Oṣuntade said.

She left the room, returning seconds later with a lantern. The men lifted Şiwoolu onto the bed beside Dotunu, who could barely contain herself.

"I know you're happy to see your husband, but watch the baby!" Oṣuntade scolded as she took the little bundle.

Dotunu cupped Şiwoolu's bandaged face. He touched hers and whispered something. She leaned close and their noses touched as he repeated it.

"Yes, it is just as I said. A son, you have another son," she whispered.

A ghost of a smile appeared. He blinked back tears from the eye that was not bandaged and whispered something again. Dotunu's chest heaved and her shoulders trembled. She shook her head.

"No, my husband. It is not your fault. It was I who wanted to see what was on board the vessel. It was I."

She laid her hand on his chest. "We will go back home," she promised.

Oṣuntade stepped forward. "Let him see his son. Let him have a reason to live," she said. She placed the baby in Dotunu's arms and returned into the shadows once more.

Şiwoolu gasped as Dotunu handed him the little one. His eyes were bright as day as he looked up at his father. Tears fell on Şiwoolu's cheek as Dotunu wiped his face and held him close.

"His oriki, my husband. Chant it over him, here, now."

Şiwoolu looked down at his son, his tongue locked in

sorrow and regret. How could he speak forth his family's oriki in this land that was not his or his ancestors'?

"We had two names selected for him. Do you remember?" Dotunu asked as he stared at his son. He nodded.

"Then let us speak the oriki into his life together."

Şiwoolu looked into his wife's eyes. They were as fiery as the night she had reappeared, when the mob besieged the palace with the bloated body of Makinde, the recluse. Dotunu began to recite the oral poetry handed down from Şiwoolu's forefathers.

> *Oşolu Ajanaku,*
> *Omo Iporo moko*
> *Iyi ko eniyan loran*
> *To ko ni lejo awijare*
> *Omo mule omo Oleyo*
> *Omo esuru o beni lorun*
> *Kole so omo tantan*
> *Omo taken ren Oo sani po*
> *Ajanaku ile Iporo*
> *Eerin mumi pokan*
> *Omo abori isu tombolo*
> *Obi idi isu barakata lebe*
> *Eni ba nwaja Iporo*
> *Ko saso sorule re ko wa wohun Iporo le se*
> *Omo eni ni yeni*
> *Omo aini ko ye yan*
> *Iporo lakesa meguoye*
> *Iporo kobi kete, Şodękę fi gbogbo re bagogo*
> *Dede won wa ri sangan*

Omo Eledie ogogo maga
Tonyin bi awo kegbe

Oṣolu Ajanaku
Warrior of Iporo
A child of small beginning becomes
The foundation of something bigger
Whoever is looking for trouble with Iporo
Should dare to hang his clothes on the roof of a native of
Iporo and see what will happen
A child who honours one
A child without doesn't honour one
Iporo, son of Ake, surrounded by royalty
Iporo does not give birth to small people,
Only those of stature
Iporo gives birth to children that are well-built and handsome
A child who owns fowls that procreate
And lay eggs like guinea fowls.

Everyone in the room and the next broke into applause, Oṣuntade stepped forward with tears in her eyes.

"K'abọ, Oṣolu ọmọ Oṣiwoolu. K'abọ!" she said, welcoming baby Oṣolu into the world. Dotunu finally felt welcomed too.

Moonlight streamed through the open window; a light breeze danced its way in and lingered. Dotunu rolled onto her side. Below, a figure curled like a cat sat in the corner of the room. A small cry came from the direction of the figure. Dotunu sat up as the figure uncurled and its eyes glimmered in the dark.

"You are finally awake, Olori. Your son has been waiting for you to join us."

Dotunu looked around. "Where is Şiwoolu, or was I dreaming that he was here?"

Oşuntade chuckled and rose with the small bundle in her hands. "It was no dream. Your husband had to go back to the Royal Hospital. They have better facilities there, and you will join him soon."

Oşolu's little foot dropped out of the blanket in which he was swaddled. He jerked as Oşuntade drew him closer. Dotunu smiled. His movements mirrored the ones he had made in her womb. She took him and cradled him in her arms.

"He is special, born into the land of the free. He is set for great and mighty things," Oşuntade said.

Dotunu looked up at the woman Ajayi claimed did not speak much Yoruba. Her accent was foreign, but she spoke fluently. Her eyes shone with something other than tears.

"Come with me."

"Will you take me to see my husband?"

"Arrangements have been made for you to see him again in a few days, after you're healed and he is stronger. Tonight, I take you to a place where your ancestors can hear you clearly. Let them welcome you to this land. Let them take your son's essence and welcome him too." She glided to the corner and returned with something dripping in her hands.

"What...?"

Oşuntade held an object placed in a cloth, and Dotunu could see that the dripping substance was blood. The older woman tied the ends of the cloth and tucked it into the front of her wrapper. Dotunu did not hesitate when Oşuntade took the baby and helped her to the door. The long dress in which they had dressed her swept the floor. The sheer overlay around her waist lifted as the door opened and the breeze whispered in her ears. Dotunu followed the woman like one in a trance, down the moonlit dusty road lined with wooden structures, up one hill and down another. Once in a while, a window would open and a head would appear from one of the houses. She would hear: "It's Oşuntade," followed by the clatter of the window shutting.

Oşuntade's pace slowed as they approached a magnificent tree. She whispered words as she knelt with the baby under its branches.

"Come closer, Olori," she said, holding out her hand. Dotunu took it and knelt beside her. Oşuntade placed the baby in Dotunu's arms and began to dig the earth with her hands.

"What are you doing?" Dotunu whispered.

Oşuntade stopped and pulled the long, dripping object from the folds of her wrapper. "We must bury the umbilical cord that held you and your son together under this cotton tree. Once we do, your son will always have a home to come back to. Serra Lyoa, land of the free, will always be his home."

The wind blew, whispering into Dotunu's ears. She looked at Oşuntade, whose eyes were twinkling as she imparted knowledge that reminded Dotunu of her father's wisdom. She nodded, and Oṣuntade arose and took the baby.

"He will be safe here," she said, placing him on the ground a few feet away. "We must dig."

Dotunu's hands joined Oṣuntade's in the soil. It was warm and soft. They worked silently until the hole was deep enough for the umbilical cord to be undisturbed. Oṣuntade then handed it to Dotunu, who placed it in.

"Speak to your ancestors, Olori! Their ears are bent. Speak!" Oṣuntade said, as she turned to carry Oṣolu.

Dotunu looked up into the tree as tears cascaded down her face. "My fathers, my mothers! Do not forget us in this land! We are not free, not truly, until we return home. Do not forget us, my ancestors!"

She covered the umbilical cord with earth and her tears watered the soil until Oṣuntade pulled her up with Oṣolu in the crook of her arm.

Chapter Ten

Relearning
Hastings
Circa 1836

It had been three moons since they arrived at Hastings, the permanent settlement they were taken to after Dotunu gave birth to Oşolu. Şiwoolu, Ireti, and Dotunu had all spent a few weeks recuperating at the Royal Hospital in Freetown, a typical rotation for all freed slaves, before they were moved to their new settlement.

Hastings was a burgeoning community of freed slaves from regions Dotunu did not know existed – England, America, Bahia, Jamaica, Cuba. Other Yoruba were there, too. She could single them out by the marks on their faces. She would greet them in Yoruba, but they would reply in English. Their stiff nods stopped her feet from rushing forward to hug them like long-lost relatives. Their eyes were lifeless when she smiled at them. She would stare at the brandings on the backs of the men as they pushed carts filled with plywood to the construction sites. "Good morning", "Good day", "Good evening" was all they would say in acknowledgement.

One day, Dotunu asked Oşuntade why her fellow Yoruba behaved as though they did not come from the same place and speak the same tongue. Oşuntade glanced at her as she stirred pottage in a cast-iron pot. They were in the communal kitchen with the thatched roof built a few feet from the house Dotunu and her family shared with their landlord, Douglas.

"Many were taken when they were much younger. You remind them of what they could have been," Oşuntade said.

"How so?"

The woman sighed and stopped to look at her, her slender arms stuck out at her sides as she placed her hands on her hips. "You carry yourself like one who was never enslaved. You are one of the fortunate ones. No memories to keep you up at night, no nightmares wrapping their hands around your neck and choking you, waking you in the early hours of the morning." Her voice trailed off as she picked up the ladle and began to stir the pottage again.

"Is that why you and others choose to live up in the mountains? So you will not be reminded?" Dotunu asked.

Oşuntade chuckled. "Dear child, have you looked around this place you call Hastings? Women in frocks and frills, grown men in tights? Do they miss the land of their enslavement so much that they choose to mimic the clothing, the food, even the houses of the places they escaped? I choose to live in the mountains with people who keep to the ways of the ancestors."

Oşuntade's grey brows curved downward as she looked into the pot. The pottage bubbled and splattered on the ground close to Dotunu's feet. Oşuntade stretched out a spoonful of pottage to Dotunu who was sitting on a bench. She leaned forward and took a bit of it with her fingers, licking it before it fell to the ground.

"You have outdone yourself this time, Oşuntade," Dotunu praised. "Where did you get the crayfish? Did you go to the islands again?"

Oşuntade smiled.

"Which one of them?" Dotunu asked.

Oşuntade's smile widened.

"I know the one! Bense!" Dotunu answered herself. Not a week went by without Oşuntade visiting the island.

"It is Bunce, my child!" Oşuntade said with an exaggerated tilt of her head and flutter of her eyelashes. Dotunu giggled.

"Stop that! It's not nice to make fun of Minister David and Miss Abigail!"

The door of the three-bedroom plank house next to Dotunu's flew open, and a man about Şiwoolu's age and height with curly jet-black hair tied at the nape of his neck stepped out. He wore a high-necked, white ruffle shirt under a waistcoat that stretched tautly over his broad chest and matched his deep red trousers, which were tucked into high boots. A black bowler hat dangled from his fingers as he walked towards them. He made his way around the low wall that encompassed the communal kitchen and broke into a grin when his eyes fell on Oşolu sitting in Dotunu's lap.

"Where to this afternoon, Waltz?" Oşuntade asked, her eyes back on the meal that would have neighbours queuing in a few minutes.

"I have to perform at Durand's wedding in two days. They are afraid I'll be late if I start my trip tomorrow, so off I go to help them with preparations." He paused and added,

"I'll be making a stop in Maroon Town. Any message for your kin?"

Oṣuntade frowned and shook her head. Oṣolu bobbed his head and suckled loudly on Dotunu's breast in sleep. Waltz looked down at him and chuckled.

"That child is as selfish as they come. Will he not let you rest even when he sleeps?"

"He knows what's his and claims it," Oṣuntade said.

"I can't blame him then," Waltz replied softly.

Dotunu looked up and caught her breath. His eyes were on her. She looked down again and placed Oṣolu's hand over her breast. Waltz cleared his throat and turned to Oṣuntade.

"Any other requests, Oṣuntade?"

"Bring back some oxtail. I can make a mean sauce for everyone with that."

He bent at the waist. "At your service. See you in a few days." Turning to Dotunu, he nodded in acknowledgment and placed his hat on his head.

"Travel mercies, Waltz," Dotunu said, unable to raise her head to look back at him.

He clicked his heels and walked away, whistling as he travelled down the road and eliciting giggles from the children playing outside the houses. Dotunu watched him as far as she could until he disappeared down the hill.

"You say you knew Waltz from when he first arrived in Hastings? He speaks Yoruba quite well."

"I already told you his grandmother was Yoruba," Oṣuntade replied. "She taught him from childhood. It was his grandfather who was Portuguese. He was a slave trader. You know it was the Portuguese who found Serra Lyoa and named it the Lion Mountains? Well, they were also the Europeans who first trade in humans. Waltz's grandfather fell in love with his grandmother, one of the slaves they were holding to transport overseas." Oṣuntade paused and stared at Dotunu. "I have told you this many times already, have I not?"

"It may be that you have and that I have forgotten," Dotunu said.

"Well, I could have sworn I did." She stirred the pottage again. "Waltz's grandfather could not bear his grandmother being sold off, especially when he found out she was pregnant with his child. So he took her away to an island and made a home with her there. Soon he was called away to sea again, never to return. The rumour was that he was killed during a fight with the English navy."

"Hmm," Dotunu murmured, imagining what life must have been like for Waltz and his family.

Oṣuntade grunted and glanced at her. "Pay him no mind."

"What?"

"Waltz. Pay him no mind, you hear me?"

Dotunu looked down at her child, unable to answer her.

"You hear me?" Oṣuntade's voice rose.

Dotunu took a deep breath and looked into the woman's knowing eyes. "I hear you."

"Good. Now go in there and get some herbal tea ready for Ajayi, he will soon be here. Use the fresh leaves I brought from my last visit to the mountains. I thought he would be too busy to see your husband every day. Most returnees only get to spend a few days with him when they arrive."

Dotunu pulled her nipple from Oşolu's lips. He had finally fallen into a deep sleep.

"You saw how delirious Şiwoolu was when we first arrived. The only time he had any form of peace was when Ajayi sat with him and said those incantations. It still brings him some calm. I will do anything to make him well again," she said.

Oşuntade grunted again as she set the ladle over the pot. "Just because Minister Daniel and Ajayi have offered a helping hand doesn't mean Şiwoolu must embrace their beliefs."

Dotunu looked towards the house. At this time, the sun high in the sky, Şiwoolu would be sitting by the window in their room, holding the black book Minister Daniel had given him. Ajayi would arrive to read with him soon. Those were the few hours in the day that the Şiwoolu she knew would awaken. The two men would talk for hours about the creation of the world by God. Ajayi's story of God forging the earth in seven days and creating only one man and woman – Adam and Eve – was different from the one Baami had told her when she was a child.

Back then, he had said, there was no earth, just the sky. Olorun was the most powerful being, and he lived with the orishas – the smaller gods – around a baobab tree. They had everything they needed, and he gave them free rein to explore the sky. They were happy and content, apart from one god named Obatala. One day, Obatala stared down from the sky and saw a vast expanse of water. He asked Olorun if he could go down and make beings from the water below; he said it would enable him and the other orishas to use the powers they possessed. Olorun agreed, and so Obatala approached Orunmila, the first son of Olorun, who had the gift of prophecy and could tell him what he needed to prepare for his journey. Orunmila laid out a tray and sprinkled powder from the baobab roots over it. He threw sixteen palm kernels on the powder and studied where they fell. He did this eight times. He then told Obatala he would need a gold chain, a snail's shell with sand, palm nuts, seedlings of maize, rice, grass, trees, and a sacred egg. Obatala asked for gold from his fellow orishas. They gave him all their jewellery, which he melted into a long chain with a hook, and presented him with a sacred egg that carried all of their dominant characteristics. Obatala gathered sand and poured it into an empty snail shell with a little baobab powder. He wrapped the sacred egg in a cloth and tied it close to his chest to keep it warm. The final items – palm nuts, maize, and other seedlings – were soon in his possession, and he was ready for his journey.

Obatala hooked the chain to a corner of the sky and began his descent. When he reached the end of the chain seven days later, he looked down into the water beneath, unsure of what to do. Orunmila called to him to pour the sand in the snail's shell in the water below, and when he did, the sand turned into a vast expanse of land. Still uncertain, the god continued to dangle from the chain. His heart beat so hard that it cracked the egg bearing the spirits of the orishas tied to his chest. A bird flew out of the cracked egg, and with it the spirits of the orishas. The spirits blew across the sand, making hills, lowlands, and dunes in their wake. Obatala let go of the chain and fell onto the land. He called the place *Ifẹ* – the place that divides the waters. As he walked, he scattered the seedlings from his bag. They sprouted into greenery – trees, shrubs, and grass – behind him.

Obatala grew thirsty and stopped to drink from a small pond. He saw his reflection in the water and was pleased, so he began to mould clay from the edge of the pond into his image. Soon he had made many bodies.

The hard work made him thirstier. He found a palm tree that had just sprouted and drank its fermented water. Obatala drank so much that he became intoxicated; when he returned to his task of making bodies, he became careless. He made some bodies without limbs, others without eyes. When he realised what he had done, he vowed never to drink again.

When Olorun did not hear from Obatala, he decided to send a chameleon down the chain. The creature returned with news of Obatala making bodies without life. Olorun gathered gasses from the spaces beyond the sky and shaped them into a fireball, sending it down to Ife. The fireball dried out lands that were still wet and baked the bodies Obatala had made in an instant. Olorun looked closer and saw that he needed to do one more thing: he blew his breath across Ife and the bodies that Obatala had moulded came to life. These were the first people made on earth.

When Dotunu rendered her tale of the foundation

of the world, Ajayi had counteracted it with the story of Adam and Eve and the tree of life. Dotunu noted the similarities between the two stories. Of course, Ajayi had responded, one was a derivation of the other. Olorun was the Father, Orunmila the Son, and the breath of Olorun the Holy Spirit. Even the traditional religion acknowledged there was only one God. The orishas were not necessary. The solution was right in their faces – Olorun was the one true God, and he was the only one they needed to worship. Dotunu shook her head. He was blaspheming the gods, but it was hard to find fault with him as he smiled and made his point. He was a congenial man who respected them despite their differences of opinion.

During these meetings, Şiwoolu would smile slightly and listen. Once the session was over and Ajayi's steps had died away down the hallway, he would retract into his shell, and not even Şomide's babbling attempts to gain his attention could bring him back. Later, Şomide would wander off to the corner to play with the carved doll Waltz had given him. So, Dotunu waited daily for Ajayi to appear so her husband would come alive for a few hours.

Oşuntade walked towards her with a huge smile and outstretched arms to take Oşolu from her. Only Oşolu could do that to her; she called him her special boy. He was more than eyes could see, she said with a twinkle in her eye. Dotunu wondered why she thought Oşolu, out of all the children she delivered in the Coker Quarters and beyond, was special. Oşuntade's midwifery services were in high demand, extending even to communities in the surrounding islands. The people had heard of her magical hands that delivered babies quickly and with such ease.

"A good afternoon to you, good ladies," Ajayi said in his amiable tone. His black cassock brushed the top of his black shoes as he raised his arm. Oṣuntade greeted him as she bounced Oṣolu in her arms. Dotunu got up and patted down her gown, one of many gifts from Miss Abigail.

"Good afternoon, Ajayi. Şiwoolu has been waiting for you," she said, joining him at the front of the house. His eyes creased at the corners.

"I am happy to see you are not so busy this afternoon. I would like to speak with you and your husband."

He opened the door, and they went down the hallway into the first room on the right. The room opposite theirs belonged to their landlord, Douglas McCarthy, who was barely around. Intent on making a fortune for himself, he broke ground all over Serra Lyoa, building houses for returnees with his small crew of artisans. He was a suave businessman from Gallinas Country, located southeast of Serra Lyoa, but had spent most of his life in Serra Lyoa.

Şiwoolu was sitting on a rocking chair next to the window, staring at the vegetable garden in the backyard, when they entered. He wore an oversized, long-sleeved white shirt that hung on his thin body, and a grey blanket covered his healing legs. He turned his head and smiled, and Dotunu walked over to him and squeezed his shoulder.

"Are you all right? Would you like some of the pottage that Oṣuntade just made?"

He pointed to the table a few feet away. "I have yet to eat the breakfast you made."

Dotunu's heart sank as she looked at the untouched

slices of yam and fried pepper stew in the bowl.

Ajayi pulled a chair from the table and sat opposite him. "You must stop punishing yourself, Şiwoolu. Eat and gain your strength, King."

Şiwoolu sighed and looked at Ajayi. "King? I am king to no one here, Ajayi."

Ajayi patted his knee and settled in his chair. "I come with good news."

"Ehn! Good news?" Dotunu exclaimed.

Ajayi seemed to be relishing the curious looks on their faces. He chuckled and leaned forward; his black Bible balanced on one knee.

"I will be performing my first baptism of new converts in a few days. The baptism is an outward declaration that you have forsaken old beliefs and traditions and are now starting a new life in Christ."

He paused and looked at Dotunu as she stepped away from the rocking chair. Şiwoolu leaned forward, his eyes bright.

"Yes, we have read that part in this book," he said, pointing to the Bible on Ajayi's knee. "John the Baptist baptised Jesus."

Ajayi nodded. "This time it will be me doing the same to you, turning your life to Christ."

His voice followed Dotunu to the corner behind the table that served as their food storage area. Ireti stirred on the floor next to the wall, and Şomide was as still as a mouse beside her. He had tired himself playing with the older children earlier in the day. Dotunu picked up two tin cups and turned around to leave the room.

"Olori, you are most welcome to join us. The angels will rejoice in heaven as another one joins the fold," Ajayi called to her.

Dotunu attempted a smile and excused herself. The door slammed behind her as she ran to meet Oṣuntade and Oṣolu outside. Oṣuntade was sitting on the bench and looked at Dotunu with raised brows when she sat down beside her.

"Back so soon? What do you need those for?" Oṣuntade pointed at the tin cups in her hands.

Dotunu blinked away angry tears and placed the cups at the edge of the bench. "I am so tired! Ajayi keeps coming here, talking to my husband about this white man's religion. What good will that do him or us? What we need to do is find our way home. They must be looking for us everywhere."

Oṣuntade shook her head. "He tried that on me when I first arrived, too. It is not so bad, just nod your head. You know what is here and here." She pointed to her head and chest. "That's all that matters."

Oṣuntade shifted closer to Dotunu until her lips touched her ear and whispered, "Let us go to one of the small islands tomorrow. I want to introduce you to a few like-minded people."

Dotunu's head snapped sideways to search Oṣuntade's eyes. They gave nothing away.

"Bring Ireti with you. She's held herself captive in that house for too long, reliving her nightmares. It is time she set herself free."

Oṣuntade talked in riddles, but Dotunu understood them. She wrapped her arms around the woman and breathed in the incense that clung to her skin.

Chapter Eleven

Home
Hastings
Circa 1836

*D*otunu *pushed thoughts of Şiwoolu from her mind* as she sat beside Ireti in the stationary canoe. Oşuntade swung her long legs in and her scent filled the space. She shifted to the end of the bench and pulled Ireti close to make room for Oşuntade. In front of them, three women sat patiently, waiting for the canoe to fill up. Then two other women who had been lingering onshore pulled up their white gowns, held up the cloth bundles over their heads, and waded into the water. They murmured Oşuntade's name as they sat down on the row behind them. Oşuntade greeted them as Dotunu closed her eyes and swallowed the lump lodged in her throat.

"Is this all of you?" The question came from the figure standing behind them at the stern, holding an oar. Her white head tie matched the colour of her full gown, and thick, round silver earrings dangled from her pierced ears.

"Yes, Esmeralda, this is everyone," Oşuntade answered.

Dotunu looked at the three women seated in front of them; they too were dressed in white like Esmeralda and Oşuntade.

"I'll get you some white wrappers," Oṣuntade said, following her eyes.

Dotunu smiled. "We will be back by tomorrow?" she asked.

"Yes. Don't worry, your children are safe with Miss Abigail and Susanna. So is your husband," Oṣuntade said, eyes twinkling.

The woman sitting in front of Dotunu pushed her oar into the water, moving the canoe forward. As Esmeralda rowed from the back, she broke into a song. Dotunu, bewildered by the vastness of the waters, grasped the edge of the canoe and held her breath. Oṣuntade sensed her fear and turned to rub her back. She too joined in singing the slow, melancholy tune. Dotunu's breath steadied and her ears perked up as some Yoruba words mixed with the white man's tongue floated into her ears. Then Esmeralda began to sing another song, this one centred on Yemoja, goddess of the sea. All the while, Oṣuntade's hands rubbed Dotunu's back steadily. As they moved farther from the shore and towards the setting sun, Dotunu wondered why they had taken the path they had all been warned was filled with thorns and snakes, devoid of footprints.

The full moon was rising when the canoe emptied its passengers onto the island. Drumbeats heralded their arrival as their feet sank into the sand. The beat was one Dotunu had heard before, had even danced to. Three female drummers dressed in white wrappers and head ties stood behind dancers circling a bonfire. Their palms hit the taut skin of the traditional drums with fluid movements, bodies moving in unison with the beats.

Ireti tightened her hold on Dotunu's hand as they drew closer to the dancing figures. Women with white wrappers tied firmly across their chests and white head ties swung their hips back and forth, their hands swaying above their heads. They twirled and jumped into the air, the motion lifting their wrappers and exposing hues of brown skin; they were oblivious to the presence of the new arrivals.

Oṣuntade gestured to Dotunu and Ireti to sit before joining the dance. Their fellow commuters joined the circle. A few minutes later, Esmeralda walked into the centre and sat down. The drumbeats began to slow down and finally stopped. Then Esmeralda welcomed everyone in Yoruba tinged with an accent and invited them to sit with her. The sparks from the bonfire highlighted her high cheekbones. Her long ponytail swung back and forth on her shoulders as she began to sway from side to side. Her words travelled over the woosh of the waves. Dotunu murmured the words under her breath.

> *Mo juba awo Yemoja.*
> *Iwo ni Ayaba Iya*
> *Iwo ni Iya Orisha.*
> *Iwo ni Inu Iye Odidi.*
> *Iwo ni Ifihan Ti Abo Ase.*
> *Iwo ni Inu Aiye.*
> *Iwo ni Orisha Obinrin Okun Nla ati Odo.*
> *Iwo ni Oluwa Awo Ti Abo Ipilese.*

I humble myself before the mystery of Yemoja.
You are the Queen of Mothers.
You are the mother of the Orisha
You are the womb of all Life
You are the feminine manifestation of the Ase
You are the womb of the world
You are the goddess of the oceans and rivers
You are the owner of the mystery of the feminine principle.

The women followed her motions, their words merging with hers. Their movements and the soothing tone of their voices pulled Dotunu. Ireti released Dotunu's hand, her eyes fixed on Esmeralda, and began to sway. One of the women rose to her feet with a white bowl, placed it before Esmeralda, and fell on her knees. Then followed another woman, then a third, each with a white bowl. The women stood and the drums began to beat again as the bodies moved, faster and faster. Ireti's body pushed into Dotunu's. Dotunu watched Ireti swing in her direction again, then followed her lead and joined the rhythmic dance, swaying from side to side.

After the ceremonies were over in the early hours of the morning, Oṣuntade introduced Dotunu to the fifteen women who completed the circle around Esmeralda. She had seen some of them in the quarters, but some, like Esmeralda, were new faces. They came from neighbouring quarters that had existed long before the Hastings community was constructed.

Esmeralda held out her arms to Dotunu when Oṣuntade introduced them.

"My child, welcome!" She kissed Dotunu on both cheeks. Her eyes danced when she pulled away. Then she bent to peer at Ireti beside her, and the young girl fell into her arms, hugging her around the waist, which made Dotunu gasp in surprise.

"Ah! She recognises a kindred spirit, does she not, Dotunu?" Oṣuntade asked with a big grin.

Dotunu met Esmeralda's kind blue eyes when she finally looked up; she had a calm and peaceful look. The woman smiled at her. Oṣuntade whispered in Ireti's ear and Ireti quickly took her hand and followed her to join the women talking near the bonfire that had been put out.

"So you are Olori Dotunu, wife of King Ṣiwoolu." Esmeralda's eyes told Dotunu more than what she had uttered. They radiated with warmth and empathy as she recalled Oṣuntade's story of the brave young queen who had made it across the waters to give birth and how she possessed a fiery spirit, one that they should let into their sisterhood.

Dotunu nodded.

"Welcome to our community, our place of solace and worship." Esmeralda said.

Dotunu thanked her. "What do you call ... *this*?" She paused as she struggled to find the right words to describe her recent experience.

Esmeralda chuckled. "You know what this is, Olori. You come from the motherland, a place we yearn for each day. We were sold to the white men from the womb. You tell me what this is." She waved her hands around.

The laughter from the women floated around them, and Dotunu could single out Ireti's childish tinkle. She spoke the first words that came out.

"This ... this is home ... for now."

Esmeralda smiled. "Yes, this is home. Welcome, dear sister. Welcome to what some call *regla de ochá* and others call *lukumi*. I call it *Santeria*, our little secret in Serra Lyoa."

At dawn, some of the women, their wrappers now hidden beneath gowns, piled into the same canoe that had brought them to the island. Dotunu ran towards it as it left.

"Wait!" She shouted.

Oşuntade pulled her back.

"Why aren't we going? Oşolu will be crying for me by now!" Dotunu said, touching her aching heavy breasts.

"We must wait our turn; the rule is that we go in the order in which we come. We were the last batch to arrive, so we must return the same way. We go in small batches so as not to draw attention."

"Why?"

"We are still a minority in Serra Lyoa," Oşuntade explained. "We don't want to raise any suspicions from people who won't understand. Many converted to the white man's religion a long time ago. Many were born into it. It is hard, almost impossible, to change a mind that has been bent to submission from birth. Come, let us while away some time until the canoe returns." She took Dotunu's hand and called to Ireti. The young girl threw her arms around Dotunu and giggled when she held her close.

"My sweet girl," Dotunu whispered, tears in her eyes.

Oṣuntade told two of the other women they had come with not to leave them and then turned to Dotunu and Ireti, telling them to follow close and watch for the huge spiders that inhabited the island. Dotunu and Ireti walked behind Oṣuntade through bushes and up a hill. Ireti cringed when an animal yelled from a tree above them.

"They are wild monkeys, but they won't harm us," Oṣuntade said.

Dotunu glanced up at the trees. They were as big as the one under which she and Oṣuntade had buried the umbilical cord. As they got closer, she realised they were the same type. The roots of one of the trees had grown out of the ground and wound their way around its trunk. Oṣuntade paused at its base.

"Mo juba rẹ o," she whispered. Dotunu stepped closer to see what she was looking at: a bowl filled with oil, a folded red cloth, and a jug on the ground.

Oṣuntade pointed into the dense forest. "I want to show you what this place was before they made it a place of refuge. Do not scream or shout. I just need you to see what the white man wants to cover up, wants to make us forget – but we must not."

She took Dotunu's hand and pulled her along, and Dotunu in turn pulled Ireti. They followed Oṣuntade blindly, for the sun was still not fully up. Oṣuntade climbed the small hills like she had been there numerous times before. They brushed spider webs off their faces and jumped at the deep guttural sounds above them.

"It's just wild monkeys," Oṣuntade reiterated. "They won't attack if we don't disturb them."

Dark shadows whispered behind the leaves, and Dotunu thought she saw a face as they passed a tree.

Oṣuntade paused under a cemented arch entrance a few feet away.

"Look." She pointed to her left and right. Moss and grass had grown over a wall towering above them. "This is the entrance to the slave castle, child. This was the last place some of our people passed through before they were transported to hell. Follow me."

They entered what was once a large courtyard, wide enough to fit two hundred people or more. On the side of the wall was a curved podium.

"This is where they used to trade slaves for weapons and whatever else pleased them." Oṣuntade's voice shook. She beckoned to Dotunu who reached out for Ireti's hand but clutched air instead.

"Ireti!" she screamed.

"She is right there!" Oṣuntade said with a hint of amusement in her voice.

Ireti was a few feet behind Dotunu, examining a huge cotton tree and running her hands up and down its trunk. Dotunu ran to her.

"What is that, Ireti?" Dotunu asked, pushing her hands away to see what was etched into the tree. They were letters: deep curved lines dug into the bark, a message for whoever cared to pause. Dotunu wished she could read and understand them.

Oṣuntade walked back and gazed at the tree. "That was written by the slaves. There, it looks like their names. The native people told me that was a way they left part of themselves here before they were taken."

"Which native people?" Dotunu asked.

Oṣuntade chuckled. "You think this place was uninhabited before we came? There are local tribes here, the Temne, Mende, Loko, so many with their own customs. You have a lot to learn, child."

Dotunu took Ireti's hand and followed Oṣuntade again, through the overgrown grass wet with the morning dew. Oṣuntade stopped in front of two openings in the wall before them. Her chest rose and fell. Dotunu pulled Ireti behind her as she rushed to the woman. Oṣuntade's face writhed in pain. She touched her chest and whispered, "Look."

Dotunu eyed the view holding Oṣuntade's attention. "I see two doorways."

Oṣuntade shook her head. She walked past a crumbling staircase and through the arched doorway on the left. "Not just two doorways, child. This is where they separated the men and women, when they took them out of the dungeons below, shackled. They did that."

Her voice was hard as steel. She grabbed Dotunu's hand and walked back through the first arched opening and up the flight of stairs. Rusted canons positioned in the spaces between the high walls overlooking the waters came into sight.

Oṣuntade stopped beside the one closest to her and said, "See. See their weapons of destruction. Placed high up here, they could see anyone coming in and attack."

"This was used to kill?" Dotunu asked. She kicked the object with her foot.

"Yes. This shot at any ship that dared to come close and would destroy it instantly."

Dotunu nodded. How could she have so quickly forgotten the fire that had engulfed the slave ship?

Oṣuntade raised her arms and turned around. "Welcome to Bunce Island."

Dotunu gasped. It was not what she had expected. "Bunce Island," she whispered.

One of the women called out to them from below. It was faint but they could still piece together what she said. Oṣuntade looked surprised.

"The canoe's here? That was fast! Let's go."

They descended the hill by the same route which they had come.

The two women on the beach were speaking with a man. His bare back was turned to Oṣuntade, Dotunu, and Ireti as they skipped over the sand. Faint scars covered his light brown skin. His trousers were hitched up around his thighs, and his curly, jet-black hair fell around his shoulders in ringlets. He turned around when he heard them approach. His eyes locked with Dotunu's.

"Waltz, what are you doing here?"

He blinked and looked at Oṣuntade. "A canoe of six women capsized not far from here. It hit a rock that cut a hole in its side. Good thing I was passing by. They said there were a few of you still here."

"Where are they now?" one of the women asked.

"I took them back to Sablama."

"To the wedding?" Oṣuntade asked, frowning.

Waltz's chest muscles rippled when he shrugged. Dotunu looked away.

"I had to. The wedding is in an hour." He paused. "What are you doing all the way out here?" he asked Oṣuntade, though his eyes had travelled back to Dotunu's small frame.

"Take us to Sablama as well, please," Oṣuntade said, telling the rest of the women to get into the canoe. Then she winked at Dotunu before lifting Ireti into her arms and wading into the water. Dotunu pulled her gown up around her knees.

"She won't tell me what you're doing here. Will you?" Waltz's eyes were slits that trapped Dotunu.

"Nothing. She was just showing me the island."

He chuckled. "This early in the morning? You slept here, surely."

"How would you know that?" Dotunu asked.

He smiled and tilted his head to the side, stretching his hand towards her. "May I?" His fingers ran between her cornrows, sweeping sand granules off her face and neck. Dotunu closed her eyes and waited for the rain of sand to stop.

"Dotunu! Waltz! Let's go!" Oṣuntade shouted.

Dotunu jerked and opened her eyes. He was grinning as she turned to run towards the canoe.

"Wait," he said softly, clasping her wrist. "Allow me." He bent down and swept her up into his arms. Ignoring her pleas to put her down, he carried her to the waiting canoes amid Ireti's delighted laughter. She clasped her arms around his neck and buried her face in it. His heart beat rapidly against her chest, in rhythm with hers.

On the way to Sablama, Dotunu received a quick history of the islands from Waltz as he rowed behind her. His hand would press gently against the small of her back, calling her attention to the little islands they passed by.

"That's Pepel. If you need strong, hardworking people, come here. Beyond Sablama is Bat Island, just as the name implies. If you have a taste for bat meat, I can always come and get some for you."

Dotunu shook her head and told him bats were a bad omen. "I will not be stepping foot there, nor eating its meat."

He laughed, a low rumble in his chest. Dotunu glanced back to see him staring at her. She did not look back for the rest of the journey.

Sablama was crowded with people disembarking from canoes at the harbour. Many carried baskets of produce in their hands or pressed close to their bodies, making it hard for Dotunu and the others to pass through.

"Waltz! Durand has been looking for you!" A plump woman dressed in a billowing navy-blue gown shouted, arms akimbo.

Waltz bent and kissed her cheek. "Você é linda!" he shouted.

The woman's fair face turned pink at the compliment. She clucked her tongue and patted down her gown. A smile played on her lips as Waltz circled her, his voice rising as he praised her looks. Onlookers smiled and clapped at the exaggerated show.

"Waltz! Waltz! Waltz!" They chanted. Waltz took a step forward. His hips twisted with the fluidity of one born to dance. His feet moved quickly across the sand as he circled the beaming woman. Then he took her hand and twirled her around. The crowd cheered and drew closer.

As Dotunu moved forward to see the spectacle, Oşuntade grabbed her arm. "No. We must go now before the crowd comes. Waltz can take care of himself. The sooner we find someone to take us back to Hastings, the better."

The celebration had started when they stepped into the open space filled with people dressed in the brightest colours Dotunu had ever seen. The fusion of the drums with stamping feet shook the ground. It made Ireti giggle and run into the crowd of dancers.

"Ireti!" Dotunu ran after her.

The girl disappeared between the folds of two gowns, and Dotunu apologised as she pushed through the two women wearing them. Ireti twirled around, her hands pulling at an invisible string in the air. Dotunu called to her again, but she was gone by the time she got to the man she had just stepped on. She apologised on Ireti's behalf and asked him the direction in which she had gone.

"She went that way, towards the newlyweds," he said, pointing at the couple in white and purple attire. The woman's head tie was intricately folded in pleats to form a peacock fan style. Her long gown fell around her hips and swept the floor as she twirled, its cut and deep neckline accentuating her bosom and small waist. The man's hand held hers above her head. He smiled adoringly at her, oblivious to Ireti standing a few feet from them, grinning.

Dotunu waved at Ireti to come to her, but the girl glanced at her, giggled, then stepped closer to the couple as Dotunu reached out to grab her. A heavy set man dancing close by accidentally elbowed Dotunu in the ribs. She clutched her side and fell headlong into the sea of legs. The drums drowned out her screams. She shuddered as darkness engulfed her.

She was back in the lower deck of the ship again. Hands appeared in the dark and grabbed her. She broke out in a sweat and screamed, "Let me go! I don't belong here!", beating back the hands that wanted to take her. The face of the dark man with the strange eyes appeared and she jumped back. The buttons on the back of her dress tore off as she scrambled back to her feet and stepped on its hem, revealing her bare back. She stumbled again.

"Wake her up! She's hallucinating!" Oşuntade's voice came to her through a long, dark tunnel.

Ireti called to Dotunu. "Do-Do."

Dotunu followed their voices, through the huddled naked bodies in the lower deck, up the stairs, over bodies cut down by swords. Olatunde's head rolled past her, followed closely by those of the bodyguards. More heads followed suit along the deck as the ship capsized. She screamed as she felt bodies rolling over her and toppling into the waves.

Water drenched her face and she jerked awake. She spluttered and coughed it up.

"She's awake!"

A multitude of faces stared down at her.

"Olori," Oşuntade whispered. She brushed the water from Dotunu's face. "You scared us."

Ireti's lashes were wet. She pushed through the people and pressed her head into Dotunu's chest.

"No, Ireti. She's too weak," Oşuntade said, pulling her back. "Someone, please help me carry her. Watch her dress! It's ripped at the back."

The crowd surged forward.

"What happened?" Waltz's voice thundered as he pushed the crowd back, spitting out words in Portuguese when they resisted. He fell to his knees beside Dotunu and gazed at her. "Dotunu! Dotunu!"

She blinked as his face became clearer.

"Be careful, Waltz," Oşuntade cautioned as he picked her up, shouting at people to clear the way. Oşuntade spoke into her ear as they pushed through.

"You're safe here, Dotunu. Nothing bad will happen to you here. We're taking you indoors to lie down. You are safe ... you are safe here."

"I'm safe," Dotunu murmured as her eyes closed again.

When she awoke in a large bed, Oşuntade and Ireti were hovering over her. The room was larger than the one in which they lived at Hastings. The bed, made of beautiful black oak, took up half the room. A light breeze floated in through the window next to the closed door on her left. She turned her head and looked into Ireti's eyes. The child threw her arms around Dotunu, overjoyed. Oṣuntade leaned into the bed and patted Dotunu's cheek.

"Mo juba rẹ o." She raised her hands in the air and thanked the gods, then looked at Dotunu. "You have rejoined the land of the living, Dotunu. You slept for three hours at least."

Oṣuntade gently pulled Ireti away and helped Dotunu sit up for a drink of water.

"We must leave soon dear child. Let me help you change out of that ripped dress."

Dotunu shook her head.

"No? You'll do it? When you're finished, join us. We will be down the corridor outside the door."

They exited through another door on the right, and their footsteps echoed down the hallway. When all Dotunu could hear was the rush of waves through the open window, she swung her feet off the bed, buried her head in her lap, and cried. The nightmares had returned. She thought she had conquered them after three moons of wrestling with them, but today, seeing the crowd of strangers, feeling their bodies pressing into hers, she had been pulled back into the bowels of the slave ship.

Dotunu wiped her face and took a deep breath. She had to leave. She undid the remaining buttons on her gown, her hands feeling through the rips to her bare back. She pulled it off and picked up the dress at the foot of the bed. It was a pale pink. It fitted perfectly except at the bottom, which was too long. She searched for her sandals on the floor. They were gone, though she remembered still having them on when she fell.

Dotunu turned the knob of the left-hand door and stepped into the wet sand and cool breeze. The backyard led straight to the bank of a river, which was still and quiet. She walked past the trees growing along the bank with arched branches that provided shade on the path. She came across three houses, but no one else was in sight. Eventually she stopped at the water's edge.

"Were you leaving?"

Dotunu turned to see Waltz holding her sandals in his hand. His long blue shirt with frills on the sleeves and neck was unbuttoned to his waist, black trousers fit his lower torso like a second skin, and his hair was pulled back with a black string. He smiled and walked up to her.

"Here, you cut a strap when you fell. I had it repaired."

Dotunu took them and thanked him. "I, I wasn't leaving. It just looked so peaceful out here."

"I know. I used to come out here too when I was growing up."

He smiled when she looked at him in surprise. "That's my room you were taken to. Hope you slept well."

"Your room?"

He nodded. "I grew up in Sablama."

"Why would you leave all this?""

Green embers around Waltz's light brown pupils sparked when he smiled. Dotunu had not noticed them before.

"I needed to make a living. Sablama became too small after a while."

"So you went to Freetown and Hastings."

Waltz made swirls in the sand with his big toe. "Not just Freetown. I visit many other islands in Serra Lyoa."

"You make a living from dancing?"

Waltz smiled. "Yes, dancing and carpentry. I help build new houses for returnees."

"Oh, with Douglas?" Dotunu asked.

He nodded.

"So you leave your family here while you travel?"

Waltz picked up a shell and threw it into the water. "It was me and my mother for a long time, 'til she died last year."

"I'm sorry," Dotunu said, looking at him.

"She lived a good life. Every single year of her life, she was free. That's all my grandmother ever wanted for both of us."

His eyes searched hers. Dotunu looked away when Oṣuntade's warning sounded in her ears.

"We should go back. Oṣuntade will be looking for me."

He shook his head. "She isn't. She's been called to perform the libation ceremony. It will take half an hour with the prayers."

"I must go to Ireti, I—"

"She is perfectly fine with Oṣuntade."

Dotunu fiddled with the straps on her sandals, bereft of any more excuses. Waltz's chest rose and fell several times before he spoke.

"Are you feeling better?" he asked, turning to her with his hands behind him. A wisp of hair swept across his face.

Dotunu cleared her throat. "Yes, thank you."

"If you don't mind me asking, what happened?"

Dotunu bit her lower lip, embarrassed by the spectacle she must have made of herself.

"I'm sorry, I shouldn't have asked—"

"No," she whispered. "It's just something that I thought had stopped."

He raised his brows. "Something that stopped? So it started again today?"

She nodded.

"Was it the crowd?"

She nodded again.

"My grandmother used to have similar episodes," Waltz said gently.

"What is the malady called?" Dotunu asked.

"Panic attacks," he answered, turning to the water that now lapped at their feet.

"How did they stop? I have tried everything to keep the nightmares at bay, even gone without sleeping at night."

Waltz's dimple appeared as he smiled at her. "I know. It was right after you had Oṣolu. I could hear you rocking in that chair at all hours of the night."

Dotunu stepped away from him as he paused.

"Don't go," he said softly, his eyes on the water.

"I must, Waltz."

He turned to her. "Call me Amadeus. My family calls me Amadeus."

"Amadeus?"

"It means 'love of God' in Portuguese."

"Amadeus," she whispered.

He smiled. "I like the way you say it, Yoruba queen." His gaze travelled from her eyes down to her cheeks and lingered on her neck. Uneasy, she played with the gold chain that hung there.

"Dotunu, *cada dia que passa eu me apaixono mais por você*. With every day that passes I fall more in love with you."

He said it so softly, she could almost have mistaken it for the rustling of the leaves. When he repeated it a second time without translating, his voice caught in his throat, and his eyes blazed like the bonfire from the night before. Oṣuntade's warning whispered in Dotunu's ears again. She stepped further away from him.

Waltz's hand encircled her arm.

"What's wrong?"

"I ... I have to go to my family."

Her heart beat so fast against her chest.

"I know."

He dropped his hand and began to walk back towards the house. Dotunu gasped at the sharp pain in her breast; a damp spot had formed there, enlarging with every drop of milk that escaped from her nipple.

Dotunu was glad when Waltz did not return with them to Hastings. He still had to perform two more dances with the band. She heard him arguing with the couple, wanting to leave, but they refused, reminding him that he had already been paid. He was the one the guests had come to see.

The two women and Ireti were fortunate to find a family of four going to Hastings Harbour that afternoon. With a quick farewell to Durand and Thandie, the newlyweds, Dotunu ran ahead of Oşuntade and Ireti towards Sablama's shore and canoes, resolute in fleeing from what she feared would destroy her. When the canoe floated into Hastings Harbour, Dotunu jumped out and called to Oşuntade to bring Ireti to the house. She ran all the way, murmuring her children's names with every step she took.

The Cokers' residence was a two-level plank house. The orange light reflected through the curtains guided Dotunu up the small steps to the door. She patted down her dress, knocked, and waited for the door to open, glad that the wetness on her chest had dried on the canoe ride. Susanna opened the door with Oşolu in her arms. Dotunu grabbed him and kissed his face, hands, and feet before Susanna could invite her in. Then she followed and listened carefully as Susanna spoke slowly to her in English.

"We have been waiting all morning to tell you the good news! Did the trip to Big Market take a whole day and more? We thought you would be back this morning!"

Şomide ran to her and pulled on her gown, and she knelt to hug him. Susanna pulled her up, insisting that she come and hear the glad tidings. Dotunu followed her into the parlour, where Minister Daniel and Miss Abigail sat opposite Şiwoolu. Their faces glowed. Şiwoolu's face broke into a smile when he saw Dotunu. He stood up slowly on a walking stick. She took a step towards him when he held out his other hand.

"Olowo ori mi," she whispered.

"Dotunu, I have joyous news," he said in that deep voice she cherished.

She took his hand. "Are we going home?"

Minister Daniel and Miss Abigail looked at each other and smiled. Şiwoolu shook his head.

"No, but this news is just as good."

Dotunu waited for him to speak. His eyes were clear and focused on her for the first time since they had arrived at Serra Lyoa.

"I've been baptised. I'm now a Christian, and so are our sons."

Dotunu dropped her hand.

"I waited for you," Şiwoolu said. "You said you would be back this morning. It doesn't matter, you can be baptised in a fortnight when they hold the next session." He paused briefly and continued. "My Christian name is John. Şomide is Harold – Harry for short – and guess what Oşolu's is?" He chuckled. "It's James."

Şiwoolu's eyes shone as bright as they had the day they were married. He held out his hand. "Aren't you happy, Dotunu? We have been washed clean from all our sins."

Dotunu wanted to scream, but the look on his face stopped her. The Şiwoolu she knew was reborn, and that was all that mattered. She took his hand and drew close. Crying softly, she laid her head on his shoulder.

Chapter Twelve

New Life
Hastings
Circa 1837

*D*otunu *took small steps down the vegetable path* behind the house, a bucket balanced on her head. After tripping and falling several times on the small hill leading to the backyard in the past, she had learned to take her time, especially at this time of day when the sun was just rising. She always took this opportunity to hang washed clothes while the children still slept.

The back door opened behind her. "I'm leaving for the harbour."

Şiwoolu held a black suitcase in one hand and patted down his black necktie with the other. "How do I look?"

Dotunu placed the bucket on the ground and went to him. She stood on her toes to pat down his hair. He closed his eyes when her fingers brushed his brows. She stepped back to appraise him – he had filled out. His black suit, a gift from Minister Daniel, was a tad short at the sleeves. She chuckled when the tail of his shirt peeked out as he turned around. The trousers were the right size, at least.

"You look handsome, Kabi—" She paused when the smile froze on his lips. "You look handsome, Şiwoolu. Is Douglas here?"

He smiled. "Thank you. Yes, he is."

"When will you be back this time?" She took his hand and linked her fingers through his, and he drew her close and whispered in her ear.

"Tomorrow. I'll be back by nightfall tomorrow." He wrapped his arms around her waist and nuzzled her neck with his nose. She giggled and pushed him away playfully.

"You'll be late," she whispered back.

A tall figure carrying logs of firewood appeared around the side of the next house and descended the small hill.

"Waltz! You're back!" Şiwoolu said, looking up.

Waltz stopped in his tracks and took them in. "Good morning," he said, then dropped the logs on the pile Dotunu stored in their backyard behind the clothesline.

Waltz had grown a full beard since the last time Dotunu had seen him in Sablama. His eyes dropped to Şiwoolu's hand around her waist. She took a step back from Şiwoolu and tightened her wrapper across her chest. Waltz held out his hand to Şiwoolu as he walked closer to them.

"Good morning, John. It's John now, isn't it?" he asked.

Şiwoolu took the hand he offered. They stood head-to-head, smiling.

"Yes! Douglas did mention you would be back sometime this week. You've been gone for a year, haven't you? Congratulations on the new constructions in the interior."

Dotunu looked at Şiwoolu, surprised. Not once had he

mentioned to her that he knew where Waltz was, though his name had come up a few times in their conversations.

"Yes, it's been about that long since I left," Waltz confirmed. "It's gratifying to see returnees having a place to lay their heads after such harrowing experiences. Congratulations to you too on the new job. Douglas mentioned you're now working with the government as an intermediary with the natives opening new trade routes."

Şiwoolu nodded. "I have experience in that area – trading. I was actually an apprentice in my village."

"We need that experience as we build Serra Lyoa," Waltz said. He paused as he turned to Dotunu.

"Good morning, Olori."

"Good morning. You don't have to call me that anymore," she said, looking up into his eyes. "Dotunu is fine."

Şiwoolu placed his arm around her shoulders and smiled. "Mary. That's her Christian name."

Waltz raised his brows and Dotunu looked away. "Mary? You were baptised too?"

It had happened exactly a fortnight after Şiwoolu and the boys were baptised in her absence. All Dotunu had wanted the night she returned from the islands was for Şiwoolu to keep that glow on his face forever, and he still had it.

She lifted her chin and looked into Waltz's eyes. "Yes, I was."

Maybe she had expected time and distance to change them, but his irises were still the same – the colour of clay, or "hazel," as Miss Abigail would say, with green around the edges.

"John!" the voice carried from the front of the house.

"That's Douglas. I must go." Şiwoolu kissed Dotunu on the cheek. "See you tomorrow, dear wife."

He shook Waltz's hand again and disappeared around the house.

"I'm glad he's doing well now," Waltz said.

He stepped back and placed his hands on his waist. His chest, covered with curly hair, shimmered with sweat.

He pointed to the pile of wood. "A lot of trees were cut down in central Freetown to make more room for the new buildings. I knew you would need them for cooking now that Oşuntade is away."

Oşuntade had been away for close to three months, visiting the tribal communities and learning their ways. Dotunu had taken over her cooking duties for the community.

"How did you know I was in charge of the cooking?"

Waltz chuckled and looked at the ground. "Word gets around." He paused and looked up. "How have you been?"

"I've been well."

"Your sons? The baby must be walking now."

Dotunu smiled. "He is everywhere! You should see him trying to climb through the window."

With soft chuckles and whispers to avoid waking the children, Dotunu described the day she had gone to get something in the backyard, only to return to the room to find Oşolu stuck in the open window, one pudgy leg dangling from the inside and the other outside.

Waltz's deep laughter cut her off midsentence. He threw his head back, shoulders shaking as the tears trickled from the corners of his eyes.

"I knew that boy was a mischievous one the moment I laid eyes on him," he said, wiping his eyes.

Dotunu laughed. "No, he's just inquisitive. I could tell from when he was in my belly. He would kick and tumble every chance he got." She paused when Waltz's eyes sought and held hers.

"You look well. I'm glad John's doing well too," he repeated.

Dotunu nodded.

He pointed at the pile of wood. "Is that where you want the wood? I can move it to the cooking area in front of the house."

"Oh no, this is fine. I still have a lot out there. Thank you."

Oşolu's cry startled them.

"Ah, he must have heard us talking about him," Waltz said.

Dotunu smiled. "I must go. He will soon be beating on the door if he doesn't see me." She picked up the bucket of laundry and hurried into the house. Oşolu was sitting up in his new bed, rubbing his eyes, when she entered. She placed the bucket in the corner, picked him up, and rocked him in her arms. She could hear Waltz's whistling, its wistful tune floating into the room. Dotunu sighed, then leaned against the wall and closed her eyes.

The morning went by fast. Between getting the children washed and dressing them, Dotunu barely had enough time to walk Ireti down to Miss Abigail's, where she had just started attending lessons every morning. Two months ago, Miss Abigail had called Dotunu aside one evening after she visited. She said she had been watching Ireti for several months and thought she could be taught to communicate using sign language, developed by the white man to talk to the deaf and dumb. Miss Abigail said she could teach them both so they could communicate at home. Dotunu had protested. Ireti and her had done well so far with their nonverbal signs, but she could already see the change in Ireti since Miss Abigail started instructing her.

By the time she finished dressing Şomide, swaddled Oṣolu and tied him to her back with her ọja, Ireti was waiting at the door. She skipped ahead of the three to Miss Abigail's house. Dotunu ran as fast as she could after her.

When Dotunu arrived, Ireti's slight figure had gone indoors and a man was on the porch with a child in his arms talking with Miss Abigail.

"Don't you worry about Magdalene, I will take good care of her until you come back from work. I am so sorry to hear about her mother. I hope she shows up soon."

The man nodded and glanced back at Dotunu. It was Godwin, "the silent one", as the community nicknamed him. He was a black loyalist who had escaped into British lines during the American revolution. Like the three thousand who made it, he emigrated from America to Nova Scotia and then to Serra Lyoa. He was blessed with a youthful comportment that made it almost impossible to tell his age, but it was whispered about that his black hair looked too unnatural to be his. The middle was already balding, so the gossip was that he was possibly in his fifties. His much younger wife also added spice to the gossip. She had delivered a baby girl, Magdalene, a few months before Dotunu had Oṣolu, but this was the first time Dotunu had been near her.

Godwin nodded at Dotunu and touched his sleeping child's cheek before leaving.

"Is everything all right?"

Miss Abigail sighed and looked down at the child. She was beautiful, just like her mother.

"Her mother's gone missing again. Rumour has it that she's run off with a British sailor. It's been a week now and Godwin can no longer stay at home waiting. He's gone back to the harbour to work."

Ṣomide ran to her and buried his face in her lap, and Ireti curtsied, her fingers moving quickly as she spoke to her before sitting at the table.

"Hello Ireti, I hope you had a good night," Miss Abigail signed to her pupil. "And good morning to you too, Harry," she said, kissing Ṣomide's lowered head. She asked Dotunu if he could stay with her for a few hours as he had the day before; he was already grasping the alphabets. Soon he would be ready to start attending the school Susanna taught in a one-room building, with students ranging from three to seventeen years old. The first pupil, Tika, had just graduated, and Susanna was so proud. She spoke about the girl and school every opportunity she got. Susanna was advocating for a girls' secondary school in Freetown with the missionaries, now that her oldest pupil had graduated.

"Yes, Miss Abigail, Ṣomide can stay. That will leave

me with this little one, who is a handful as can you see," Dotunu said, turning her head to Oṣolu, who was tied to her back. He pulled her hair with a grin on his face.

Miss Abigail laughed and waved at him. "See you in the evening, then."

"Yes, see you then," Dotunu said, walking down the steps. Her day had just begun.

Dotunu returned home to make a quick breakfast for the older settlers. They were few: Pa Roland, Sister Cassie, and Sister Nettie. They lived next to each other, and most days sat on the balcony of Sister Nettie's house. They would begin saying a prayer for Dotunu as she climbed the steps. Their laughter warmed her heart, reminding her of the old people she had left in Iporo Ake long before she became queen. That seemed like another lifetime.

The three settlers were there as usual today. Pa Roland waved as she ascended. "Mary, always punctual. God bless you, child!"

"Good morning, Pa. How are you today?"

"Wonderful, now that you're here," he said.

Sister Cassie clucked her tongue.

"You are a shameless man. She's a married woman, you know," Sister Nettie said, her eyes laughing.

"I don't care. Look at her, such a beautiful young woman. Here, give me my kiss."

He closed his eyes and tapped his cheek with one finger. Dotunu laughed and set the tray of food on the table.

"Well? An old man can't wait forever, now," Pa Roland said, tapping his cheek again.

Dotunu giggled and went around to his chair. Leaning close, she planted a kiss on his cheek.

"Ah, wonderful. That will last for just today. I will need another tomorrow," he said, opening his eyes.

They laughed, knowing he would say the same thing the next day.

Dotunu looked down at their wrinkled faces. The forks shook in their weathered hands as they cut into the eggs on their plates – the same hands that had worked the cotton fields of Savannah, Georgia. Sister Cassie looked up from her plate.

"Tonight is story night, Mary. Will you tell us more folktales? The last one about the tortoise was so interesting! It reminded me of the stories my grandpapa told me a long time ago."

"I almost forgot!" Dotunu exclaimed. "Yes, I will think of one or two more to tell." She picked up the tray. "Make sure you're under the pawpaw tree across from my house after supper. Don't worry, I will have dinner brought to you long before then."

They thanked Dotunu profusely and promised to be there. As she bounded down the steps, Sister Cassie called her.

"Mary! I must tell you, your English has improved tremendously over the past few months!"

Dotunu offered a rueful smile. "Yes, the Bible studies and readings have helped."

"Children, you remember what I taught you to say the last time? Before I begin a story?"

Dotunu looked down from her stool at the eager faces of the children of Hastings. The twenty-four children, from toddling Oṣolu to sixteen-year-old Tika, yelled a resounding "Yes!"

"We remember too, Mary!" Sister Cassie shouted from her seat behind the children.

Dotunu laughed when the other adults seated with her nodded or murmured in agreement. "Good! So say it after me, then." She smiled at the eager faces as they waited with anticipation.

"Alọ o!" she shouted.

"Alọ!" they shouted back.

"Alọ o!"

"Alọ!"

"Good! You were paying attention!"

Oṣolu toddled towards Dotunu and grabbed the folds of her wrapper with his pudgy hands. "Stay with your sister," she whispered to him. Ireti reached up and placed him in her lap. Her eyes were wide with expectation, just like those of the other children.

Patting down the buba Oṣuntade had made for her, Dotunu began the story of how the spider came to have its unique body.

"A long, long time ago, the spider was very fat. He was also very lazy; he would rather sleep while others tilled and planted their seeds for a harvest or fished in the rivers.

One particular year, he did not work during the planting season, so when harvest time came, he had nothing for his family to eat. The surrounding villages close to the forest in which he lived were having harvest feasts. He knew that if he visited, they would feed him, as was the custom. So he told his two sons to tie ropes around his waist and to set off in opposite directions to the closest villages. He instructed them each to pull on their rope once the feasts began, so he could hurry to whichever one had started. Unfortunately for spider, the two feasts began at the same time, and his sons pulled him in opposite directions, yanking tighter and tighter when their father did not appear. When the feasts ended, they hurried to find him. What they saw was unbelievable, he was disfigured! The pressure from the ropes had transformed his head into a big circle and left him with a tiny waist. That's how the spider came to have his body."

Dotunu paused, looked into each upturned face, and waited for what would come next. Jane, a little girl with tiny plaits and an impish smile, giggled.

"He got a big-big head and a tiny waist!" she shouted.

Thomas, the most mischievous boy Dotunu had ever met, stood up. This week he had come back from school with a gash on his forehead after teasing the school goat with a nasty kick. The white bandage over his eye gave him an eerie look. He got up, stretched out his arms and waddled out of the crowd.

"Look at me, the spider!" he said in a raspy voice.

The children laughed and got up to mimic him. The elders in the back laughed. Pa Johnson's cackle was the loudest.

Oṣolu took two steps, flopped down on his buttocks, and grinned at Dotunu. She picked him up and nuzzled his neck – his dimple appeared and deepened with joy. Sister Nettie called out for him and soon Dotunu joined the waddling, shouting bunch that had formed a circle around the pawpaw tree. Someone began to clap and they all joined in, Dotunu swaying her waist and hips to the rhythm. Her feet threw sand in the air as she danced in the circle to the delight of the onlookers. Oṣolu jumped with excitement on Sister Nettie's lap, the same way he did when he and Dotunu danced alone in the room when Ṣiwoolu was at work and Ireti and Ṣomide were with Miss Abigail. Soon the adults joined in, even Pa Roland with his walking stick and Sister Cassie with her bad eyesight, both hobbled about. Someone found a stick and began beating on a stool. Then Dotunu heard it: beads beating on wood, the sound of ṣẹkẹrẹ. Everyone paused when it grew louder and closer.

"Waltz!" Thomas shouted, and ran towards him.

Waltz raised the ṣẹkẹrẹ above his head to avoid Thomas' flying hands and shook the small gourd with stringed beads. The children ran to him, pulling on his arm and begging to play with the object.

"No, no, I will play it while you dance with Miss Mary," he said.

Waltz held Dotunu's gaze over the children's jumping heads. He shook the ṣẹkẹrẹ again.

"Come on children, dance!" he shouted, but it was Dotunu whom his eyes challenged.

She called to the children. "Come on, children, listen

to the beat. Move your legs, yes, to the left, the right, go up, down."

They followed her steps around the tree. The beads beat harder and faster against the gourd. The music carried Dotunu to the stream in the forest where she had first spoken with Şiwoolu, her ankle beads jingling against her skin. She could smell the earth beneath her feet. Her toes sank into the damp soil as she twirled, pushing clumps of earth high into the moonlit sky. The beat stopped and she paused. The twirling had made her dizzy. She waited for the world to stand still. An outstretched hand appeared.

"Dance, Mary!" Sister Nettie shouted.

The şękęrę began to shake again, more deliberate and slowly this time. Waltz's face emerged inches from hers as he took her hand in his. A cane beat on wood, followed by the shaking of the şękęrę.

"This time, I will teach you a dance," Waltz said in her ear. He stepped back and pulled her close. Dotunu spun into his chest. He looked down into her face and smiled. The crowd began to clap to the beat. Waltz raised their linked hands over her head.

"Spin," he said, dancing around her. "Yes, like that. You're a natural."

Şomide shouted "Mama" as the crowd closed in and formed a circle to watch the impromptu performance. Ireti's laughter rang aloud. Dotunu could imagine the joy on their faces. Right now they were a blur, for all she could sense, wrapped in this cocoon of winding limbs were Waltz's scent and his whispers.

He placed his hand on her waist and drew her close.

The crowd shouted and clapped louder as they swayed to the beat. They moved as one in the circle, their bodies fitting perfectly like missing parts finally reunited, the music cutting them off from everything else.

"Papa!" Oṣolu shouted.

Dotunu's head jerked sideways and she stopped dancing. Ṣiwoolu stood in the middle of the road with a man by his side. Ṣomide and Ireti broke the circle and ran to him. Dotunu withdrew her hands from Waltz's and stepped away from him. The drumbeats and music from the ṣẹkẹrẹ stopped abruptly.

"That was a wonderful dance, Mary, Waltz!" Pa Roland shouted. The other adults murmured agreement. They clapped as Dotunu walked to Ṣiwoolu.

"You're early!"

Ṣiwoolu nodded as he took Ṣomide's hand. "Yes. I had to come back when I met Demilade at the harbour."

He touched the man's shoulder. "This is Demilade; I told you about him. We were on the slave ship, bound together for those unforgettable days."

The man before Dotunu was lanky, with sad droopy eyes filled with resignation. This was not how she had imagined the man who saved her husband from insanity in the slave vessel.

"Olori, I am happy to finally meet you."

"And I you. Ṣiwoolu has talked so much about you. It is indeed a pleasure. Come in! We were just finishing our evening of folktales."

Demilade looked surprised. "That was telling folktales?"

Dotunu laughed. Şiwoolu shook his head, but his lips curled up into a smile.

"My wife can turn anything into fun. I am sure this started out as an evening of stories."

They laughed as Dotunu ushered them, children in tow, into the house. The music resumed as she closed the door on the image of Waltz dancing in the circle.

"Demilade and I met by a stroke of luck," Şiwoolu said from the table, his voice slightly louder than the music and cheers from the crowd that carried in through the open windows.

Dotunu placed two tin cups of water before them and sat down beside Şiwoolu. "How so?"

"Douglas and I had just finished meeting with Minister Daniel at the Methodist Church in central Freetown. We were ready to board the canoe at the harbour when I heard someone call my name – not John, but Şiwoolu. It had to be someone who knew me from…" His voice trailed off.

Dotunu squeezed his arm on the table and smiled across at Demilade. "You're welcome. I have supper ready. It's as though I knew there would be company, I made enough *res en stew*," she said in the new slang she had learned in the quarters, "to feed twice our number."

"You must be able to see into the future," Demilade teased.

"She has many powers she has yet to reveal even to me," Şiwoolu said, chuckling.

Dotunu smiled and got up to serve them. As she

walked past him, Şiwoolu grabbed her hand.

"Thank you."

"There's no need to thank me."

"There is. You must be tired after taking care of the old settlers and telling those folktales," he said. "Let me help you with the food."

She squeezed his hand. "No, please keep our guest company. Everything is already prepared."

Dotunu called Ireti to help carry the plates to the small table they kept in the corner. Şomide and Oşolu were already curled up on their makeshift bed at the far end of the room.

"Douglas said it would be fine for Demilade to stay in his room for a few days while he is away," Şiwoolu said, gathering rice piled high into cassava leaves with his fingers and rolling it deftly into a small ball. He dipped the ball into the stew thick with fish and chicken and gulped it down. Dotunu sat down beside Şiwoolu again.

"That's nice of him." Dotunu looked at Demilade. "Are you just passing through?"

He looked up from his meal, eyes wide with surprise. "Oh no! I am here to stay. I had heard of Hastings some time ago and wanted to visit. Meeting your husband helped me make the decision."

"Where were you staying before?" Dotunu asked.

"Maroon Town."

Dotunu hit the table gently with her hand. "You must know Oşuntade! She just left for a visit there. That's her original residence, Maroon Town."

Demilade frowned.

"You don't know Oṣuntade?" Dotunu queried. "Everyone knows her. Tall, dark, bald, about sixty years old or so, but it's hard to guess and she refuses to tell me."

Demilade's eye lit up. "You mean Janice, the medicine woman?"

Ṣiwoolu and Dotunu looked at each other.

"Janice?" Dotunu asked.

Demilade described Oṣuntade precisely, from her wrapper and head tie to the handmade beads she wore.

"It sounds like Oṣuntade, doesn't it, Ṣiwoolu?" Dotunu glanced at Ṣiwoolu as she picked up an untouched plate. He nodded.

"Janice, erm, Oṣuntade, hasn't visited for many months now. Her husband has all but forgotten she exists," Demilade said.

The plate in Dotunu's hand fell and clattered on the table as her jaw dropped in shock.

"She didn't tell you she was married?" Demilade asked. "Well, that's if you can call it a marriage. Her husband has disowned her, though he refuses to divorce her. She hasn't committed adultery, but he said that since she set foot on this soil, she has turned her back on God and embraced every ritualistic totem dangled in her face. He says that when they were in Jamaica, she was one of the most God-fearing women he knew. Apparently, it was all a sham to get out of there."

Dotunu wanted to defend the woman who had cared for her like the mother she never had, but her tongue was heavy.

"She must be in one of the tribal communities,"

Şiwoolu said, watching the fleeting emotions cross Dotunu's face.

"She must be," Dotunu whispered.

Demilade cleared his throat. "Talking of marriages, the whole of Abeokuta and beyond were so happy when the daughter of one of the chiefs of the Ogboni ruling council and the son of one of our leading warriors wed. You two put a smile on our faces after your father's passing."

Şiwoolu washed his hands in the bowl of water in the centre of the table, beads of sweat forming on his forehead.

"It was a murder," he said in a firm voice as he grabbed the small towel behind the bowl to dry his hands.

"You said?" Demilade asked, looking confused.

"Have you forgotten that it was I who gave my father the poisoned *garri* the night we returned to Iporo Ake? The same night he was selected by the Ogboni ruling council to be the Alake?"

"Everyone knew that the poisoned *garri* was placed in your father's hut by the real murderer. You just happened to be the one—" Dotunu protested.

"We all know that, Kabiyesi!" Demilade added.

"I was the instrument that was used. Don't you think that is ironic?" Şiwoolu said bitterly. "The son being used to kill the father and then becoming king?"

Dotunu sighed. She'd thought the bad days when Şiwoolu would sink into depression were over. His new faith had been a welcome distraction; if his head wasn't buried in the Bible, he would be having a lively discussion with Minister Daniel or Ajayi. But then there were times such as this when he couldn't help himself – seeing Demilade only brought back the memories. As much as he enjoyed the man's company, he couldn't deny the existence of the demons his presence brought – spewing hatred in his heart and threatening to upstage his new-found peace as a Christian.

He glanced at their guest. "Brother Demilade, it has been a long day and I am sure you are tired. Let me go around to Douglas' to see what you may need."

Demilade raised his hand as Dotunu got up. "Olori, if I may take a bit more of your time?"

Demilade eyes burned into Dotunu's with such intensity that she had to look down.

"I must confess the real reason I am here. My visit to this place called Hastings was not by chance." Demilade paused and looked at Şiwoolu, who sat in his chair and waited. Demilade placed his elbows on the table and stretched out his hands. "I heard that many of the women, the pregnant ones, were taken to the Coker and Davies quarters when they landed at the harbour and were transported here, to Hastings. I've searched everywhere for my wife who was with child on the ship. This is my last hope. Have you seen her?"

His eyes begged for confirmation, but Dotunu needed more information.

"There were many of us, it will be hard to tell—"

"She was heavily pregnant. I know you were, too," Demilade said, pointing at the snoring Oşolu, whose knees were propped up under him, lifting up his trouser-clad buttocks.

"Kabiyesi told me all the pregnant women were together." Demilade paused. "Her name was Labakę."

Dotunu inhaled a sharp breath and held it. The face of the pregnant woman on the slave ship screaming for her beloved flashed across her eyes. She still had nightmares of the woman throwing herself overboard. She was the only pregnant woman who had not survived, and none of the others talked of a husband they were still searching for.

"Are you all right, Mary?" Şiwoolu asked.

Dotunu squeezed her eyes tight. Hoping that the tears would not spill, she opened them and looked at Demilade, who looked like he was ready to lap up her words. She turned to Şiwoolu.

"Yes, yes. I must be tired from the dance. I'm sorry, I don't remember a Labakẹ. Sorry." She muttered and began picking up the emptied plates.

Şiwoolu's eyes narrowed into slits as they watched her walk past him; perhaps he suspected the truth. But Dotunu thought Demilade would be better off living with the hope of finding his wife than dying with the knowledge of what happened to her.

"This is a hard thing to keep secret for so long, Mary! How long did you say he would be here?"

Charlotte Davies, Dotunu's neighbour three houses down, was responding to the news of Dotunu's new houseguest. The two women were pushing through the crowd in Big Market in Freetown. Charlotte was at least ten years older than Dotunu, but that didn't stop her from being as congenial and comforting as a sister. She had just moved to Hastings with her five children and husband from Bathurst, where they had been for several years. When they had heard about Susanna's school, Charlotte and her husband, James Labulo Senior, decided to relocate. They had their hearts set on their children attending Fourah Bay College in a few years, and Susanna's school, with its high achievements, offered the best academic foundation for the children.

It was a rowdy market day as usual, and Dotunu needed to buy fish for the evening's supper. She dodged the hard tails of stockfish piled on a hawker's head and then turned to answer Charlotte.

"Demilade is here to stay, Charlotte, didn't you hear me?" she shouted over the noise as she broke out in a sweat. She searched for Ireti's head in the crowd; the girl had been in front of her just a second ago. "Ireti! Where's Ireti?"

"Ireti is right here, Mary!" Charlotte said, grabbing her shoulder. Dotunu threw a grateful look at Charlotte. She was double Dotunu's petite size and stood as tall as Şiwoolu. Anywhere she went, she commanded attention, and Dotunu liked to go to the market with her since she bargained so well with the traders.

Charlotte pointed to Ireti as her head appeared between two woven bags swinging from the women's arms. Dotunu laughed and patted her head. "I didn't see you!"

Ireti signed with her hands.

"You know I still don't understand what the signs mean, Ireti. I'm yet to start lessons with Miss Abigail," Dotunu reminded her.

Charlotte laughed as she dodged a man running in their direction with a basket of yam tubers on his head.

"You and Ireti, I could watch you both for hours! Are you sure you need to learn this sign language? You understood each other before you knew of its existence, so why must you learn it? Besides, you are so busy with the boys and the cooking for the community. Now that I've joined you, I hope things will be easier."

Charlotte steered Dotunu away from the fire that blew out of the blacksmith's workshop and towards the fishmongers' section.

"Look, I think they've brought another shipment of people. They look so lost," Charlotte said, her voice shaking with emotion as her eyes took on a faraway look.

Dotunu and Charlotte stopped to watch the people following Ajayi and Daisy. Each person had a blanket wrapped around the shoulder and covering their nakedness – it was the first item each freed slave received upon stepping foot in Freetown. The rest, in order of priority, would be food, clean clothes, and a place to lay their heads.

"I wonder under which missionary's name they are registered," Dotunu whispered as they filed past. The faces of the group were downcast. Ireti clasped her hands around her waist.

"It's fine, dear girl. These are good people. They're just like us – free," Dotunu said, touching Ireti's plaited hair.

Ajayi waved to them as he walked behind the last batch of returnees. His new round spectacles caught their eyes, and the women stared at them in admiration.

"A good day to you, Sister Mary, Sister Charlotte. How are your families?" Ajayi asked.

"Well, thank you!" Dotunu shouted above the market noise. "Welcome back! You were gone for some time."

"Yes, you know the work of a missionary is never done. I will visit you all soon. Expect me!" He waved again and picked up his pace. They watched as he spoke softly to the new settlers, patting the men's backs, smiling kindly at the women. Charlotte looked as though she would break down in tears.

Suddenly Ireti's bloodcurdling scream – a sound that dragged Dotunu into the belly of the slave ship once more – jolted them out of their thoughts. The girl was pointing in the direction of the fishmongers. Dotunu grabbed Ireti's shoulders and shook her hard, calling her name repeatedly to wake her from the nightmare only she could see. Ireti's body shook in spasms and her teeth chattered with fear.

"She sees someone she knows there. Someone she's afraid of!" Charlotte said, walking towards the spot Ireti pointed at. Dotunu grabbed her gown and begged her to wait.

"I don't know who it is, but this child is terrified. Don't go," Dotunu pleaded.

Charlotte hissed. "In Freetown? Someone wants to frighten my Ireti? No way! Come with me!"

She pulled Ireti behind her and marched towards the fishmongers. Ireti screamed louder as they approached the men and women cutting fish on concrete slabs. They looked up in confusion.

"Who is it?" Charlotte asked, moving closer to them. They were six in all, each scraping the scales off their fish. Ireti kicked and screamed as they drew closer to the first fishmonger. Black hair fell around the face as the fishmonger lifted a large knife and cut the fish in half. Ireti screamed again as the fishmonger lifted his face. Dotunu burst into tears when grey eyes that haunted her long after they had been rescued from the ship met hers. The boy's long hair had deceived them into thinking he was a woman. He dropped the knife and stammered a greeting.

"This boy shouldn't be here!" Dotunu screamed, pointing at him. "He's one of *them*! They stole us from our home. He can't be here!" She pulled up her dress and ran towards him, shrieking.

Chapter Thirteen

Hope Springs
Hastings
Circa 1838

Ireti had nightmares for days. She moaned and thrashed on the bed so much that Dotunu had to move Şomide away from her to the bed she shared with Şiwoolu and Oşolu. The girl would not eat either, which troubled Miss Abigail. A week after seeing Simon, the boy at the Big Market, she pulled Dotunu aside.

"I don't know what to do, Mary. She can't concentrate."

They glanced at Ireti, curled up in a corner of the parlour.

"It's not her fault, Miss Abigail," Dotunu protested. "Why would Minister Daniel and Ajayi allow that boy to come to Freetown, and worst of all bring him here to Hastings? After everything I told them he did, they still allowed him to stay? There are so many settlements. Why here? Must we relive our nightmares every time we set eyes on him?"

Dotunu held back the sobs that had wracked her body every night since Ajayi had broken the news to them that Simon was in Hastings to stay.

Miss Abigail squeezed Dotunu's folded arms. "He is

only a child who was manipulated by evil people. He has nobody, but we have an orphanage here that you know Daisy oversees. It made sense to transfer him here."

"His father was responsible for our bodyguards' deaths. He killed all of them. One was like a brother to John!" Dotunu whispered in Miss Abigail's ear.

Ireti fidgeted in the corner and pulled her legs closer, almost disappearing into the wall. Miss Abigail pulled Dotunu outside and begged her to take a chair. They sat in silence, watching and waving at the neighbours who were walking by.

"I beg of you, Mary," Miss Abigail pleaded. "Ireti looks to you for everything. She will take your lead. I know you stopped attending the midweek service because of Simon. At least come to church this Sunday. Just come, please."

She placed her hands over Dotunu's clenched fists on the table. Her green eyes filled with tears as she whispered words that might have comforted Dotunu had Simon's strange, cold eyes not held her captive still.

Church was full on Sunday. Maybe it was because Ajayi had just returned after months, first in England and then in the interior regions of Serra Lyoa, ministering to the natives and learning their languages. His smiling face always warmed the congregation's hearts. They loved Minister Daniel but considered Ajayi their own. He was the living, breathing testimony of a son of the soil who had overcome every obstacle in his way.

After the welcome and introductions by Minister

Daniel, Ajayi approached the wooden podium with his Bible. Word had been circulating that he was next in line to join the ministry. Many prayed it would not be too soon, since that would require him to leave for England again, like in 1826, when he had attended the Saint Mary's Church and parish school in Islington.

Ajayi's deep-set eyes twinkled behind the round spectacles perched on his nose. "Greetings from the church in England and from our Temne brothers and sisters. It is good to see you after many months."

The congregation responded with a hearty "Good morning." Ajayi looked around, nodding at as many people as his head would allow. Dotunu leaned forward to check on Ireti, who was sitting in the front row to Ajayi's right, watching Miss Abigail's hand movements as she sat on a chair directly opposite Ireti, facing the congregation. She was still sullen, but she was not cowering in a corner.

Ajayi's voice cut into Dotunu's thoughts. "I am happy to see you all. Over the past week, you have all heard of the new returnees who have joined our communities. We also have others who have moved from other settlements."

He paused and looked to his left. Seated in the front row were new faces, some of whom Dotunu had seen at Big Market on that fateful day. Simon sat stiffly with his head lowered between two women. Ajayi nodded in their direction.

"Don't feel sorry for yourselves. Look at me, for instance. What do you want me to say about the hand life dealt me? My village in Osogun was raided when I was thirteen. I witnessed the carnage of my people perpetrated by the Mohammedans. I can still see the explosion of our huts; I can still smell the burning flesh of my people. I can feel the rope thrown around my neck, pulling me away from everything I knew and loved. The worst part was seeing the slaughter of those who could no longer travel and were of no use to our captors. They were cut down like animals. I was sold into slavery six times. Six times!" His voice shook and he paused. Sorrowful moans filled the church, but Ajayi raised his hand and smiled.

"We must look forward, my dear ones," he said with a firm voice. "We must press forward. Where there is life, there is hope." His eyes darted along the pews and found Dotunu's. "Embrace these new brothers and sisters of ours, just as Christ has embraced us all. They need our love and prayers."

Şiwoolu murmured in agreement with the rest of the congregation. Dotunu glanced at him and looked away. A figure behind him caught her eye. It was Waltz. He towered over everyone – except Şiwoolu, in a navy-blue three-piece suit. His beard was neatly trimmed, his hair pulled back into a knot at his neck. A woman who looked a year or two younger than Dotunu sat beside him. She touched his arm. He leaned close to listen as she whispered in his ear, eliciting a smile from him. Dotunu looked away just as he turned his head and Ajayi's voice thundered through the ten rows of the small wooden church, preaching forgiveness and acceptance.

After the service, Dotunu hurried to stand beside Charlotte

and a few other women behind a long table where they served lunch to the congregation. They always broke bread together under the large cotton tree behind the church building; the contributions from each family resulted in a large spread of delicious food. The children stood in line to be served first. Charlotte made conversation as she spooned rice and vegetables onto plates. When Simon stepped up to the table, she smiled at him. He was dressed in a white, long-sleeved, cotton shirt, brown trousers and sandals and his hair was combed behind his ears.

"Well, hello, Simon. How are you settling in?"

The boy kept his head down and didn't say a word.

"Move on over to Miss Mary so she can give you some bread. You need to put some flesh on that scrawny body!" Charlotte commanded.

She handed Dotunu the plate and waved him to the right. Dotunu's hand shook as she reached for the bread roll in the basket and placed it on the side of the plate.

"Thank you," Simon said softly. He walked to the table of newest settlers and sat down.

Charlotte squeezed her shoulder. "Now that wasn't so bad, was it?"

Dotunu shrugged and turned to the next person in line. They worked in silence until all the children were served. Out of the corner of her eye, she saw a lone figure carrying a child and walking away from the building. It was Godwin and his daughter Magdalene. She called him to get a plate of food. He paused and looked like he was about to go on, but something changed his mind and he strolled to the table and thanked her for the food. Charlotte cooed at the little cherub Magdalene had turned into, with her two pigtails and expressive eyes. She clung to her father.

"She's very shy," Godwin said. He thanked them for the food and turned to leave.

"What a strange man," Charlotte whispered.

"He likes to keep to himself. Who wouldn't, after his wife eloped with a sailor and left him to care for his daughter alone?"

"He's still strange, Mary. Admit it." She looked up as their husbands approached. "Here they come!" Oşolu almost jumped out of Şiwoolu's arms when he saw Dotunu. She blew him kisses and quickly filled their plates amid his cries for her to carry him.

"Mama will soon join us," Şiwoolu coaxed when the baby cried louder. He brought Oşolu close to Dotunu and she kissed his ruddy cheeks. His dimples split his face and for the moment he was content. "Was that Godwin?"

"Yes."

"Did I tell you I hired him as my secretary? His English is impeccable, exactly the person I need to help write my letters."

"That's wonderful! At least now he can rest assured that there will be money to take care of Magdalene. Please let him know I am here to help with her anytime."

Şiwoolu nodded and looked sideways. "Let me call Demilade to sit with us, he's at the children's table," He bounced Oşolu in his arms as he walked away.

James, Charlotte's husband, took a step closer. He was a quiet man who listened more than he talked. Their last child, James Junior, who had just turned ten, held on to his father's trousers as he stepped up to the table. His face was wet with tears. He was small for his age, taking after his father, but was a strong and energetic child.

"What's wrong, James Junior, or do you prefer to be called Labulo? You want to be like your namesake over there?" Dotunu teased, nodding at Oşolu, who had resumed crying.

The boy made a face that made Dotunu laugh. His father patted his head.

"He wants to play by the water," Charlotte said, shaking her head. "Here, make sure you finish your food and I'll take you and the other children down to the riverside," she said, handing him his plate of food.

James Junior grinned at his mother and skipped off with his food, ignoring his parents' calls for him to slow down. Dotunu laughed and reached under the table for more bread to refill the basket.

"Mary, hurry up, there's a line forming!" Charlotte said. Dotunu looked up quickly, hitting her head on the edge of the table.

"Are you all right?"

As Dotunu rose to her feet, she saw Waltz standing before her. The dainty hand holding onto his arm belonged to the woman who sat beside him in church. She was a few inches taller than Dotunu. The frills on her pretty pink bonnet fluttered when she turned to look up at him with her hazel eyes, and two dark curly tendrils swung slightly at her temples, framing her freckled face. Like Waltz, she had that light complexion that was the product of the union between dark-skinned natives and slaves and white slavers who had once occupied the land. Dotunu rubbed the lump forming on her head.

"I'm fine, thank you."

Waltz leaned forward, pushed her finger away gently, and felt beneath her hair, which was pulled into a tight bun. His fingers massaged the lump.

"That doesn't feel fine. You should have the doctor examine that, just in case."

Waltz's companion coughed and lifted a hand to her throat. He glanced down at her and dropped his hand, much to Dotunu's relief. She grabbed the half-filled plate Charlotte had handed her while engaging them in conversation.

"I'm Charlotte. Welcome to Hastings." Charlotte leaned over to shake the woman's hand.

"I'm Serita. I'm visiting from Sablama," the woman responded.

Dotunu glanced up at Waltz. He nodded.

"Serita's like my little sister. We grew up together."

Serita's laughter sounded like tinkling bells. She slapped his arm. "Amadeus, I am not like your little sister! How would you know when you don't have one?"

"How long will you be here for?" Charlotte asked.

Serita shrugged. "I'm not sure yet. I've heard so many good things about Hastings, I just might be relocating," she said softly.

Charlotte nudged Dotunu. "Why are you being so rude?" she asked playfully. "Introduce yourself!"

"Oh, I'm Do—I mean, Mary. Here." She pushed the plate of food on the table towards Serita. Waltz picked it up and thanked her. Charlotte handed Dotunu the second plate. She added the bread roll and pushed it towards him. Serita's throaty thank you curled around Waltz's as they walked away together.

Charlotte slid close to Dotunu as they watched the two leave. "Do you know her?"

Dotunu shook her head as she rearranged the bread in the basket.

"I thought maybe she had upset you."

Dotunu shook her head again, watching from the corner of her eye as Waltz and Serita sat at the table with Şiwoolu, James, Demilade, Ajayi, Minister Daniel, and their wives.

"Why would I be upset? I don't know her," she said.

Charlotte studied Dotunu for a few seconds while she moved the plates on the table.

"Hmm. Well, hurry up so we can join them before they finish eating."

The men were discussing the arrival of the new governor of Serra Lyoa, Colonel Doherty, when the women sat down. Şiwoolu mentioned his recent encounter with the governor in town.

"He seems invested in building a cordial relationship with the Temnes and Mendes especially," he said, struggling to prevent Oşolu from playing with the food on his plate.

"I'm glad the government sees the importance of building, or should I say, *rebuilding* a relationship with the natives. We all must realise how crucial their acceptance is in building a successful state," Ajayi said. His eyes danced behind his spectacles as he leaned closer. "That reminds me, I have some news that some of you may find beneficial."

Minister Daniel and Miss Abigail smiled. Waltz crossed his arms on the table across from Dotunu with a knowing grin. She moved closer to the table to listen.

Ajayi chuckled at their increasingly impatient-looking faces. "All right, I will no longer hold you in suspense." He placed his fork on his plate and looked at each person seated at the table.

"Speak, Ajayi!" Charlotte chimed in. They laughed briefly.

"All right. During my recent visit to England, I witnessed a lot of slave ships seized by the British navy rotting away at the ports. An idea came to me that you all might pool your resources to buy these ships and start trading along the coast. You have the land to till and seeds to plant. All that's needed are the ships and viable trade routes and markets beyond Serra Lyoa."

The group was quiet. Dotunu sprang to her feet, heart bursting at the thought that had come to her mind.

"I think that's a wonderful idea! Maybe with this new venture, we will be able to find our way back home!"

Şiwoolu grabbed her elbow, pulled her down and whispered in her ear. His words made her lower her eyes.

"Let her speak, John!" Minister Daniel chided.

"Mary is right. The trade routes may very well lead *many* of us home," Ajayi said, his voice rising at the added possibilities of this new idea.

Şiwoolu rubbed Dotunu's back, his typical way of

apologising. Waltz tapped the table and leaned in, closer to Dotunu.

"I'll invest in this venture."

Dotunu blinked away the tears and looked up. Waltz's eyes sparked as he looked from Şiwoolu to Dotunu.

Minister Daniel, Ajayi, and Miss Abigail clapped. When they were quiet, Charlotte nudged her husband. He cleared his throat.

"We will support this venture too. If there is any opportunity for us to find our way back to Abeokuta, we will take it."

Dotunu wiped the tear sliding down her cheek and waited for Şiwoolu to add his voice to the discussion.

"We will, too," he finally said.

A loud cheer filled the air. Waltz drummed on the table while Charlotte made that peculiar noise with her hand over her mouth that meant she was happy. It made Dotunu laugh every time.

"Ah, finally, a laugh from Olori," Waltz said above the noise. Dotunu looked at him and smiled.

Şiwoolu swung his arm over Dotunu's shoulder and looked pointedly at Waltz. "My wife laughs all the time," he said in a cold tone.

The two men stared at each other, and the others fidgeted in the sudden awkward silence.

"Men of God, please, let's eat!" Ajayi said, picking up his fork again. The group followed his lead.

Charlotte threw quizzical looks in Dotunu's direction long after the topic was changed, but Dotunu avoided everyone's eyes, especially Waltz's.

"What did your husband tell you, Olori?"

The wet washcloth slid from Dotunu's fingers to the ground as she turned around. Waltz, in shirt and trousers, stood barefoot a few feet from her. The clothesline swung back and forth between them with the weight of the clothes Dotunu had just hung. She glanced at the window of the house and remembered that Şiwoolu had left for town at the break of dawn.

"What are you talking about?"

Waltz stepped under the clothesline, picked up the cloth, and handed it to her.

"I'm not a fool," he said softly, looking down at her.

Dotunu grabbed the dirty cloth and dropped it in a bowl. Her heartbeat quickened when Waltz took a step closer. His eyes had followed her throughout the rest of lunch the day before, and Charlotte's questions during their walk home had left her even more uncomfortable. But Şiwoolu's silence had bothered her the most. He had not once mentioned the incident, and it was as though nothing had happened.

"Is he hurting you?"

Dotunu stared at Waltz in amazement. His eyes sparked with anger when he grabbed her arm.

"No," she whispered. "Why would he?"

Waltz ground his jaw. "I know some men are like that."

Dotunu shook her head. Waltz's grip loosened, but he didn't let go.

"Then what's wrong with you? You've changed since the last time I saw you."

"You mean since last year, when you disappeared without a goodbye?" Dotunu challenged him.

Waltz dropped his hand and stared at her. "I thought you wouldn't notice," he finally said.

"Why wouldn't I? You live next door," Dotunu answered, surprised.

"That's not what I mean," he said softly, stepping back. They stared at each other until his eyes broke away from hers.

"I vowed I wouldn't do this if I came back," he said under his breath.

Dotunu gulped but still managed to speak. "Do what?"

He groaned and pushed the words out. "Tell you I love you again."

The words Waltz had spoken that day in Sablama had haunted Dotunu for a year.

"You can't," she whispered.

"Do you think I haven't told myself that?" Waltz asked, looking away.

Dotunu grabbed his wrist so he would look at her.

"I am married!" she said, angrier with herself than with him.

He wrapped his hand around hers. "God help me, I wish every day that you weren't."

"You must stop this nonsense talk! We can never, ever!" she pulled her hand away and broke into tears.

"I'm sorry. Forgive me. I know I've crossed too many boundaries," Waltz whispered.

Dotunu searched his face, and all she saw was his soul laid bare. "You must forget about me, for both our sakes."

His eyes sparkled with tears.

"Find a nice girl ... like Serita." Dotunu's chest tightened as she said the words. Waltz gave a short, dry laugh.

"Yes, ma'am."

She cleaned her face with the backs of her hands while he watched.

"I promise you something, Dotunu," Waltz said, taking her hand again.

"What?"

"I'm going to do everything possible to help you find your way back home, even if it's the last thing I do."

His eyes told her he meant it.

Feet shuffled behind them. They turned around to see Oşuntade standing there with a cloth bundle on her head.

"What has changed since I left?" she asked, frowning at their intertwined fingers. Dotunu screamed with joy and ran to her.

Oşuntade's return to Hastings was met with little fanfare, exactly the way she wanted it. She kept her whereabouts for the past few months a mystery. Minister Daniel invited her to stay permanently, but she declined, stating that she would rather come and go as she had always done. Waltz offered her a room in his house for whenever it got too dark and it was safer to stay the night, and she grudgingly accepted.

The living arrangements in Dotunu and Şiwoolu's house had changed. Douglas moved to the house he had built in town and decided to rent out the large room that had been vacant for so long to Şiwoolu and his own former room to Demilade. With an extra room for him and the family, Şiwoolu carved the large room into two bedrooms and the existing one they made a parlour to receive guests.

Life had taken on a form of normalcy. Şiwoolu now had a full-time position in the government, with an office in Freetown. He was instrumental in helping the group locate the first slave ship offered for sale. Within a few weeks, everyone at the table that Sunday had gathered funds to pay for the ship. The first meeting on how to bring the ship to the harbour was held in Dotunu and Şiwoolu's house. James, an investor who already farmed hectares of land, advised that cocoa would be a viable export to start with. They could go as far as the Gold Coast to trade.

"What do we do for labour?" Şiwoolu asked, looking up from the map on the table during one of the meetings.

"There are a lot of young, able-bodied men who are looking for work here in Hastings as well as in town. We can recruit," Waltz said.

Şiwoolu nodded but said nothing. The men had at least been cordial to one another since the incident at Sunday lunch six weeks ago.

"We will have to buy more trees to plant," James said.

"And more land," Şiwoolu added.

Dotunu took a deep breath. It was a humble start, but they would plant the seeds and watch them yield fruits.

"Here, give him to me. He's getting too big for you," Şiwoolu said as he lifted Oşolu from Dotunu's arms.

She smiled as Oşolu protested but grew quiet when he realised his father was lifting him onto his shoulders. Şomide looked up, his hand tightening around his mother's, and whined for his father to carry him too.

Şiwoolu laughed. "When you are ready to release your mother from that hold of yours, then I'll know you're ready to go up there." He pointed to a ship close to the docks. "Look, over there," he shouted, manoeuvring Dotunu with a hand on her back through the shouting crew of labourers running back and forth to the lone large ship.

Dotunu stared at it. The paint was peeling off the sides, and it was impossible to make out the vessel's name, but it looked sturdy. Its sails were down as the labourers were busy working on the deck, talking and laughing. One man was overhead with a rope tied around his waist, banging away with a hammer.

Şiwoolu turned to look down at Dotunu. "Do you want to go on board? Every one of the investors has been on the ship except us."

Dotunu took a deep breath and looked up at him. "Not with the children. There may be nails on the deck, and I don't want them stepping on anything."

Şiwoolu nodded. "All right. Well, since we have all of this lovely Saturday in town to do what we please, why don't we go to lunch? I will take you to the place where I sometimes eat with the governor."

Dotunu smiled with relief. It was harder than she had thought to try to get on a ship after their ordeal. An object dropped onto the deck with a loud bang. The labourers called to one another, but only one name echoed in Dotunu's head.

"Simon!"

Dotunu's hand tightened around Şomide's. "Simon? Which Simon?" she whispered as her eyes travelled the length and breadth of the ship's deck.

A curly head, followed by a hand, appeared on the side of the ship. The figure straightened up and Dotunu put her hand to her chest and gasped.

"Dotunu, please..." Şiwoolu whispered.

"No! No, Şiwoolu! Why is he here? On our ship?" Tears filled her eyes.

Şiwoolu swung Oşolu off his shoulder and placed him on the ground between them. His eyes pleaded as he began to speak.

"He needed a job. Ajayi came to me and asked me to take him on. What he said that day in church almost three months ago spoke to me. Besides, he has nautical experience. He's lived on ships for years. We – Waltz, James, Minister Daniel, even Oşuntade and Charlotte – agreed—"

"How long has he been working here?" Dotunu asked incredulously.

"He only started about a month ago."

"But you didn't ask me! Why? Why, Şiwoolu?"

"I beg of you, don't do this," Şiwoolu whispered. "Look, he's finally coming out of his shell. Look at him."

Dotunu lifted her head with difficulty and looked at

Simon. He was shouting back at the men.

"I'm fine! It fell beside me, not on my head, thank God!" His voice was no longer the shy one that had thanked her at the Sunday lunch months ago. It was now the deep, robust voice of a young man coming into his own.

Simon picked up the hammer on the floor beside him and waved it at his colleagues. The others hailed him while Dotunu bristled with anger, wishing that it had not missed.

Dotunu could feel the strange grey eyes on her every time she passed the orphanage, the largest house on the fringes of the Hastings community. She was most uncomfortable when Simon stopped at the communal kitchen on an errand from Daisy, asking for extra logs of wood. She never said a word to him, only nodded to the pile in the corner and continued cooking.

On the fifth anniversary of the church foundation in Hastings, three weeks after Dotunu had discovered that Simon was working on the ship, the community was agog with activity. Plans for a feast, complete with street parties to end in the late hours of the night, had been forming for weeks. The church service had been replete with hymns from the choir – dressed in new robes sent by their sister church in England. Portly Mr. Durand, the choirmaster, made the congregation chuckle: his maroon-coloured robe was too long for his short frame. His stomach protruded like a six-month pregnancy, and when he swung his arms to lead the choir, they disappeared into the billowing sleeves.

After a fire-cracking sermon, Minister Daniel called for donations to renovate the church and everyone reached into their pockets and purses and gave. At the end of the service one of the deacons ran up to Minister Daniel at the podium with the offering bag. On any other Sunday it jingled with coins, but today there was no clanking metal because the bag was padded with pound notes that peeked out of it. He whispered excitedly to Minister Daniel, who in turn looked up with a huge smile on his face.

"The Lord be praised! This is the most money raised to date by this church! Thank you for your donations!"

The congregation broke out in a dance that soon spilled outside, where the food was about to be served.

Like the other women, Dotunu ran back and forth between the storage room where the food was kept – next to the vestry – and the back of the church, to serve food. When Charlotte shouted from the table next to hers that they had run out of bread once more, Dotunu pulled up her gown and headed to the storage room for the last basket. She stopped in her tracks when she saw Simon coming out of the vestry with a bench. He began to smile at her, but Dotunu stepped back and looked away until he walked past. She waited until his footsteps faded and her heart resumed its normal beat before she continued her walk. She spent the rest of the day watching Simon talking and smiling with church members who had grown to love the curly-haired young man.

The next morning, Charlotte appeared at Dotunu's door, out of breath.

"What is it?" Dotunu asked, pulling her in.

"There's been a theft at the church!"

"The church?" Dotunu asked, baffled.

"All that money that was raised, gone! Gone!" Charlotte shouted.

Şiwoolu appeared behind Dotunu, his briefcase in his hand. "Good morning, Sister Charlotte."

Charlotte smiled at him. "Good morning, Brother John. On your way to work?"

"Yes. How did you hear about this theft?" Şiwoolu asked.

"A neighbour. He heard Minister Daniel mention this morning that he could not find the bag with the money."

"I see," Şiwoolu said, turning to Dotunu. "I will be back at the usual time." He kissed her cheek and walked out, nodding to Charlotte as he left. "Have a good day."

Dotunu turned to Charlotte as the truth dawned on her. "I saw him," she whispered.

Charlotte frowned. "Saw who?"

Dotunu pulled her further into the house and shut the door. "Simon. I saw him coming out of the vestry yesterday."

Charlotte's eyes grew bigger as Dotunu gave her a detailed description of what had happened. Dotunu knew it would not take long for the news to get out, and her heart leapt for joy for the first time in months.

By the time Şiwoolu arrived home that evening, Minister Daniel had summoned the church deacons and Dotunu to the church. She told them exactly what had happened and returned home to face Şiwoolu.

"But did you see him with the offering bag of money?"

he asked, looking down at the papers he was pretending to read at the table.

Dotunu sighed and kept stirring the bowl of corn meal in her hands. "I only told them what I saw."

He shook his head. "You have crucified this boy."

"I only told the truth."

Şiwoolu grunted.

Dotunu placed the bowl gently on the table and got up. "I never said I saw him with the offering bag, nor did I say he stole the money. The deacons will make their decision on their own."

"We all know what that will be."

Simon did not attend the midweek service. Minister Daniel looked downcast as he gave the sermon but did not mention the incident.

"Won't he talk about what happened?" Charlotte whispered beside Dotunu as he gave the benediction.

At the end of the service, the congregation poured out of the building, many pausing to shake hands with Minister Daniel. When Şiwoolu and Dotunu approached, he reached out to shake their hands as well.

"Have you heard from Simon?" he asked Şiwoolu.

"Simon has decided to live on the ship until it's fully renovated. He doesn't feel welcome here with everything going on," Şiwoolu said, looking sideways at Dotunu.

Minister Daniel sighed. Dotunu tried to stop the boiling emotions within her from surfacing.

"I understand. No one is pointing fingers at him, but yes, I understand," Minister Daniel responded.

Dotunu looked away, content that she had not had to lift a hand for this to happen.

The mood in church the next Sunday was subdued. Dotunu, like the others, noticed that the new returnees who had joined at the same time as Simon were also absent.

After the service, Dotunu was busy serving outside when someone shouted from the vestry.

"What is it now?" Charlotte asked.

It was Mr. Durand, the choirmaster, waving the offering bag and screaming, "I found it! I found the money! It was underneath the old choir robes!"

Oşuntade threw Oşolu up in the air again. He giggled with glee and splayed out his chubby arms. Şomide laughed and pulled at Oşuntade's wrapper for a turn when she caught the baby.

"You're a big boy now, Şomide. Look how you've grown!" Oşuntade flopped down on the bench with Oşolu on her lap in the communal kitchen and turned to Dotunu. "Children will be children! Can you believe it took Şomide a few minutes to remember me? Forget Oşolu! He did not know who I was anymore!" she exclaimed.

"A lesson to you for leaving unannounced as you did. Where did you go for four months?"

Dotunu had been waiting to ask this since Oşuntade had returned a month before, but she had left town again a few days later, leaving a message that she was going to Maroon Town.

Oşuntade smiled. "Learning and growing, dear one, learning and growing." She moved closer with Oşolu in her lap. "Did you know that this British Squadron, or whatever they call themselves, have been deceiving us all along?"

Dotunu frowned and leaned in. "Have they not been saving slaves for many years? What have you found out?" Dotunu asked.

Oṣuntade rolled her eyes and continued. "They have been receiving payment for every slave that's freed! This is a lucrative business for them!" She spat on the ground. "You told me how you saw the British soldiers carrying jewellery and clothing belonging to the returnees from the slave ship onto their own ship and never once locating the owners to return the items. Even your husband's crown and staff are yet to be found."

"That is true. But we did find the scalloped ring," Dotunu muttered.

"That was sheer luck. It fell on the street and only the honesty of a pedestrian made that possible. Besides, you said he hates the ring and never wears it, so that doesn't count."

Dotunu touched her arm. "All right, so what? What if they take our things away? What if they make money off us? At least they saved us. What can we possibly do?"

"Yes! That's the question I expected from you." Oṣuntade paused when Oṣolu pulled on her beads, and then smiled. "Where is the money going? That is the first question that must be put to them. We also must demand that the money they have received to date be shared with all freed slaves."

Dotunu gazed at this warrior who reminded her of her mother-in-law, Wuraola. Oṣuntade pulled Ṣomide onto her lap beside Oṣolu and murmured a prayer over the two of them.

"Oṣuntade, we must tread with care," Dotunu cautioned. Oṣuntade eyed her, but she continued nonetheless. "Let me finish. These people have been kind to us. They still provide food for some of the settlements."

"Must we be indebted forever?" Oṣuntade asked, exasperated.

"Not forever but let us be wise. As Minister Daniel says, 'I am sending you out like sheep among wolves. Therefore, be as shrewd as snakes and as innocent as doves—'"

Oṣuntade cut her off with a wave of her hand. "I was obviously gone for too long. They have indoctrinated you. I thought you were baptised in name only, not in head or heart. I thought you did it only for your husband!"

Dotunu waited patiently for Oṣuntade to spit out all the hate she had for the white man's religion.

"Are you finished, Oṣuntade?"

"I will never be finished until they leave!"

Dotunu shook her head.

"No, don't shake your head, Dotunu. You have become one of them. Look at you!" She glared at Dotunu's flowery pink gown with the pink sash tied at the waist. "Where are all the wrappers I sewed for you? Are they at the bottom of the river?"

Dotunu sighed and closed her eyes.

"Answer me, Olori!" Oṣuntade sneered. "What has made you change so much? Was it the love for your husband? Have you not sold your soul just to get him back?"

"Stop it."

"Why should I stop? Is it because I speak the truth?

Şiwoolu has decided to turn his back on his beliefs and kingdom and I can see that he has been successful in dragging you and these children down this dangerous path."

"No, he hasn't." Dotunu closed her eyes tighter, but Oşuntade's words drummed in her ears.

"You know I speak the truth. He runs after these white men, making money from the backs of freed slaves just like him."

"I said stop it, Oşuntade! Şiwoolu works for the Liberated African Trade Department. Yes, it is under the British government, but it is for the well-being of freed slaves," she said, opening her eyes.

Oşuntade snorted. "Suit yourself, Dotunu, but in your heart you know the truth." She bounced Oşolu on one knee when he started to fuss. "Esmeralda tells me you stopped going to Bunce Island the moment I left."

"What did you expect? My excuse to Şiwoolu when we used to go was that we were buying shrimps on the neighbouring island. Once he realised there was a seafood section in Big Market, I had no more reason to go."

Oşuntade offered a short, dry laugh. "Don't insult my intelligence. Do you think I don't know how well you've hidden your powers? How you have killed that gift you were born with? Esmeralda saw it in you, and I recognised it the moment you set foot on this soil."

Dotunu gasped. No one knew but Şiwoolu. No one could know.

Oşuntade stopped the bouncing and changed the subject. "It looks like things are getting serious between those two," she said as Waltz appeared on the street with Serita on his arm. She glanced at Dotunu. "I'm glad his infatuation with you is over, or is it the other way around?"

Dotunu sighed and waved at the couple. They called out greetings as they walked by. "Where are they going?" she asked.

Oṣuntade shook her head. "Ah, it is not over! I told you to pay him no mind from the start. Did I not tell you?"

Dotunu ignored her and stood. "I must go. Ṣomide, come. Ṣiwoolu is expecting me in town to attend an event with the governor. Can you please check on Ireti and these two later?" Dotunu asked.

Oṣuntade nodded. "What about supper?" she asked.

"Charlotte will be here to start it soon. Oh, I meant to tell you: starting next week, we will be stopping the communal feeding, except for the old people. Charlotte and I will alternate cooking for them in our homes."

Oṣuntade's brows shot up.

"I knew you would react that way. So many of us are going into town to work now, and the children are also settled in school. It doesn't make sense to make all this food when no one is here to eat it."

"This place is evolving into something I no longer recognise." Oṣuntade's shoulders slumped.

"Is everything all right?" Dotunu sat down and touched Oṣuntade's shoulder gently.

She sighed and shook her head. "No, Dotunu. Nothing is all right."

Dotunu held her breath.

"Sherman is dead."

"Sherman? Who is that?"

"My husband. I had this nagging feeling to visit Maroon Town. I hadn't been there in close to a year. I ... I—" Oşuntade gulped as a tear fell down her ebony cheek. "He was already rotting in the room when I got there. He had been dead for at least a week."

"Dead!" Dotunu's cry startled the boys.

Oşuntade stared into space. "Sherman is gone."

Dotunu wrapped her arms around her. This time, it was Oşuntade who cried on Dotunu's shoulder.

"What a lovely dress you have on, Mary!"

Dotunu paused before the flushed woman fanning herself with a purple feather fan that matched her bonnet and cotton dress. Sweat was dripping down her face, though it was just half past nine in the morning and a breeze was blowing onto the dock where the crowd of guests mingled.

"Why thank you, Mrs. Whitford. How do you do?"

Mrs. Whitford beamed at the petite creature before her in a baby blue taffeta dress with mancherons – silver ornaments trimmed on the upper part of the long sleeves – and a matching bonnet, which drew admiring glances from other guests. "Is that not a round dress you're wearing? How did you get it so quickly? I placed an order months ago from the material shop!"

Dotunu's ebony skin glowed, her lips glimmered from the shea butter she had earlier smeared on them as she tried to speak, but the woman everyone in Freetown referred to as "running tap" interrupted again.

"Oh, forgive me for prying! Congratulations on the launch of your husband's new ship. We've all been waiting for this day for almost three months now. I guess we will learn the vessel's name this morning." She held out her gloved hand and Dotunu stepped closer to take it in hers.

"Thank you, yes, we will. How is Mr. Whitford? John tells me he was very helpful in the acquisition of the ship, what with his position in the Liberated African Trade Department." She paused on seeing sweat trickle from under Mrs. Whitford's bonnet and down her jowls. "Would you like to use my—" she twirled the white parasol, another purchase from the material shop, over her head.

Mrs. Whitford giggled. "Don't be silly, dear! It was silly of me to forget mine at home. I'll just get a cold drink! Young man!" She called to the man in a black suit with his back turned. He turned around and Dotunu caught her breath. It was Simon. He was taller than the last time she had seen him at church, almost unrecognizable with a straight back and broad shoulders. His long ponytail was gone, replaced by short tightly curled dark hair. He smiled and came towards them with a tray of glasses.

"Good morning, madams," he said in a deep, clear voice.

Dotunu nodded and followed Mrs. Whitford's lead by picking up a glass of juice.

"Thank you!" Mrs. Whitford lifted the glass to her lips. Dotunu also murmured what she hoped was thanks as Simon bowed his head slightly and walked towards another beckoning hand.

"Ah, that feels good!" Mrs. Whitford said after her first gulp. The glass shook in Dotunu's hand. "Are you all right, my dear?" the older woman asked, touching her arm.

"Excuse me for a moment, I'm sorry," Dotunu said, walking away from the bow of the ship where everyone was congregating.

"Olori?"

Dotunu sighed. Only one person still called her that. "Waltz, good morning," she said, looking up.

Waltz looked immaculately dressed in in a three-piece burgundy suit and crisp white shirt.

"Good morning," Serita said beside him. She was in a round dress too, the colour a soft pink that complemented Waltz's suit. Her pink lips pouted up at Waltz. "I hope we're not late! I told you that late night we kept wasn't a good idea."

Waltz glanced at her and patted her hand, then he looked down at Dotunu.

"Are you all right?"

"Of course, she's all right," Serita said, glancing at the glass in Dotunu's hand and patting his arm in return. "Aren't you, Mary?"

"I ... I just need to see ... to get something. I will be back." Dotunu looked up at Waltz. "Şiwoolu has been waiting for you, he's at the bow with the others. I'll be back shortly." She picked up her dress and hurried away before he could speak. Seeing Simon acting like nothing had happened was too hard for her to bear.

Dotunu hurried up the steps to the wharf, farther

from the docks and the jubilant cries of the guests, the parasol shaking in her hands. She was embarrassed to see Simon again. She knew the day would come when she would have to face him, but today was too soon. She paced the empty street above the docks and lost track of the time. It took two servers and Şiwoolu to bring her back to the guests.

"What happened to you?" he asked, as they made their way through the crowd waiting for them at the bow. The smiling faces of the other investors, and even Oşuntade decked out in her new wrapper and head tie, did little to quell the rising lump of guilt in Dotunu's throat.

Dressed in his white and navy-blue uniform, Governor Lieutenant Colonel Doherty smiled congenially at Dotunu and Şiwoolu when they stood beside him.

"It is my pleasure to launch this ship, once used to wreak havoc on humanity, but now primed and ready to foster trade and commerce," the governor proclaimed proudly. He lifted the champagne bottle in his hand. "I hereby name this ship *The Overcomer*," he shouted as he smashed the bottle against the hull.

The guests cheered and Dotunu clapped her hands while her eyes searched for the curly dark head that now seemed like a figment of her imagination.

Days after Dotunu had laid eyes on Simon at the harbour, she still could not get him out of her mind. She thought of asking Şiwoolu where he lived and how he survived on his own, but when she eventually summoned up the courage to ask, he was making plans for a trip with the governor of the interior to meet with the village chiefs. It was his first trip with the governor, and he was nervous. The night before he left, he talked nonstop about the planned activities, first picking up Şomide, then putting him down and lifting a drowsy Oşolu.

"Şiwoolu, please, that boy has finally tired himself enough to sleep, put him down. We need peace," Dotunu pleaded.

Şiwoolu sat quietly with Oşolu on his lap on the couch and looked up at Dotunu. "What is worrying you? And don't lie to me this time."

Dotunu sighed. "Şomide, go to the bedroom. Ireti is there."

The boy left the room and Dotunu turned to Şiwoolu. "It's Simon."

"What about him?"

"He was a server at the launch."

Şiwoolu raised an eyebrow but said nothing.

"Why didn't you tell me?" Dotunu asked. She pulled her favourite blanket, a reminder of their rescue from the slave ship, from the armchair next to Şiwoolu and wrapped it around her. "Why didn't you tell me he would be serving?" she repeated.

He shook his head. "What does it matter? Didn't you notice that all the servers were employees? Shipmates?"

She shook her head and pulled the blanket tighter around her.

Oşolu stirred in Şiwoolu's arms and he looked down at the child. When he looked up, Dotunu was turning away towards the door.

"Wait." Şiwoolu laid Oşolu on the couch and went to her. His hands caressed her shoulder blades through the blanket. "There is no need to feel guilty about anything."

"But—"

"I know you do. I know you too well."

Dotunu's shoulders slumped.

"No, don't do that," he said softly, lifting her chin so she would look him in the eyes. "He's happy. He found a room in town and has a job with the company. Everything has worked out well. There is no need to feel bad about what happened at church, all right? You told the truth about what you saw, that was all."

She nodded as he pulled her close.

"I'm sorry I won't be here to send off the first trade mission," he said softly in her ear.

"That's fine. I will be there," Dotunu responded.

"You know Simon will be traveling with Waltz and James and the other men. He will of course be there for the send-off."

Dotunu's body stiffened in his embrace, then she relaxed against him. "Thank you for telling me."

He kissed her forehead and tightened his arms around her.

The send-off party for the shipmates was the talk of Hastings, the other settlements, and Freetown. The news that a small group of returnees could form a shipping and trading company and buy a ship had spread like forest fire, and people from the islands and beyond planned to attend. Still, Dotunu was not prepared for the crowd that spilt out of the Freetown restaurant and into the surrounding streets. There were many new faces but also familiar ones, including Esmeralda's and the other women from Bunce Island, their neighbours in Hastings, labourers and shipmates. She smiled and waved at them as Charlotte pulled her along towards the restaurant.

"Watch your step, Mary! That dress cost too much to be ripped before we get to our destination!" Charlotte shouted as she avoided a puddle.

"Slow down, Charlotte," Dotunu yelled back above the sounds of the balo – a xylophone made of wooden bars – and drums coming through the restaurant doorway.

Charlotte stopped and turned to her as she adjusted the black beaded pelerine over her gown.

"Look, my sister, this is the first time I can remember going to a party without my children. I want to milk the enjoyment out of today, so don't waste time."

Dotunu giggled. "You're right! I hope Oşuntade and Daisy can manage with all those children."

"Everyone listens to Oşuntade, don't worry. Come on!"

The hall was filled with round tables and chairs and a dance floor already packed with gyrating guests. James waved to them from a table close to the dance floor. He got up when they approached and pulled out seats for them. "You got here just in time."

Charlotte looked up at him. "Really? What's going on?" she asked, reaching up to straighten his tie.

"Some talk has been circulating that Waltz has some news," James said.

Dotunu looked around the room, determined to find Simon.

"News? What news?" Charlotte looked at Dotunu when she didn't say a word. "Are you looking for someone?"

Dotunu looked at Charlotte and shrugged. "No, I'm just looking at this crowd. We barely know anyone!"

Charlotte laughed. "Of course, everyone, even the ones we don't know, will be here. You know how much people like enjoyment! Come, James, let's dance!"

She sprang to her feet and grabbed her husband's hand. He threw Dotunu a look that made her burst into laughter.

"Don't worry, James, I will save you soon!" she shouted as Charlotte dragged him to the dance floor.

A figure pressed against the table. "What would you like to eat, madam?"

"Ah! You scared me!" Dotunu exclaimed, looking up at the amused man with an oversized tray filled with plates of food.

"Sorry, madam. Mr. Waltz told me to come here and ask before all the food is finished."

"Waltz? Where is he?"

The man pointed to a figure on the dance floor in a dark blue silk shirt, black trousers and shoes twirling a curvy figure in a red dress. Waltz nodded at Dotunu and then turned his full attention to Serita, whose seductive hip sways elicited vocal appreciation from onlookers.

"I see," Dotunu said, looking away. "Just give me whatever is on your tray."

The server placed a bowl of couscous and chicken

stew before her and promised to return with drinks.

As Dotunu lifted the wooden spoon to her mouth, Waltz shouted, "Please, everyone!"

The music stopped.

"I want to thank you for coming. It is an incredibly exciting time for our families and communities. But before I lose track of time, there is something I'd like to announce."

Dotunu dropped the spoon in the bowl.

"As you know, Serita here has been visiting for a while, trying to get to know Freetown and Hastings—"

"And you!" Charlotte shouted and the crowd burst into laughter.

Waltz chuckled while Serita turned a bright red.

"Well, if you say so," he said as his eyes fell on Dotunu for a second and then returned to the crowd.

"I asked Miss Serita here to be my wife earlier today … and she agreed."

The crowd screamed and clapped their hands. They began to surge forward towards the couple to congratulate them.

An elbow brushed Dotunu's shoulder. "Sorry, madam," its owner apologised. A large foot came down hard on hers and she gasped in pain. The music resumed and the crowd continued to push past her. Her heart began to race, and she wasn't sure if it was because of the crowd or the news.

Dotunu got up and started to push her way towards the exit so she could get some fresh air. The walk was like swimming against a current; bodies pushed against

Dotunu's small frame and her hands stretched outward, trying to find an escape. The crowd jostled her in unseen directions, and when she was finally able to look up and breathe, she found herself on an unfamiliar cobbled street. The music sounded farther away than she wished, and the dark street was almost deserted except for the few bodies leaning against the walls of some plank houses.

A cat whistle pierced the air as she walked past a tall, faceless man leaning against a wall. He pushed himself off it and followed her. His pace quickened and so did her heart rate. Dotunu pulled up the folds of her gown and made a left turn on the next street, praying that it was in the direction from which she had come. As he turned the corner, she picked up speed. He laughed and broke into a run behind her. The street curved up and became steeper. She felt his breath on her neck and tears sprang to Dotunu's eyes. He grabbed the back of her dress and she fell.

No!" she screamed as he climbed on top of her.

The man laughed again and spat out a word she did not recognise. His hands fondled the top of her pelerine, looking for an opening. She struggled against his hold, neither of them noticing the shadow that stood over them until the punch fell on the man's head and he slumped and rolled off Dotunu.

She burst into tears as she struggled to sit up. A hand reached out to touch her shoulder.

"You are safe now."

Dotunu looked up at the curly-haired youth and grasped the hand he held out.

"Simon?" she whispered.

"Yes, it's me. You're safe now." He helped her rise on shaky legs.

"Simon," she whispered, grasping his hands tighter.

He looked at her. "Yes, madam?"

"Come back to Hastings…"

The dark street began to spin as Simon spoke, and the last thing she felt was the cobbled street beneath her once more.

Dotunu moaned as she opened her eyes and gasped on seeing the hunched-over figure inches away.

"Dotunu, it's just me," Waltz whispered, leaning closer to the bed.

She felt his hand over hers on the blanket. "What happened?" she murmured.

Another figure ran into the room. "Is she awake?" Charlotte asked breathlessly.

Dotunu groaned as she sat up on the narrow bed, and Waltz withdrew his hand. Charlotte squeezed into the space between Waltz and the bed and peered down at her.

"My dear, we were so worried when Simon ran to get us in the restaurant! You mean a man just attacked you? My God!"

Dotunu looked around the small room with the table near the window, and the memories began to return.

"Simon? Oh God…" Tears welled up in her eyes.

"You're safe now, Mary," Charlotte said, wrapping her arms around Dotunu's shoulders.

Waltz sighed. "Don't worry, your attacker has been taken to the police cell. Simon had to go and write a statement. He'll be back here soon. I'm just glad his room was only a few doors down from where…" He bit his lip and got up from the chair. "Sit down, Charlotte. I'll stand outside until morning."

Charlotte looked at him. "Are you joking? The guests are still at the party, and your fiancée is waiting. I will stay with Mary."

"This part of town is not exactly the safest place for two women to be alone."

Dotunu pulled away from Charlotte and cleaned her wet face. "I'll be fine. Please, go back to Serita."

Waltz dug his hands into his pockets and stared at her without saying a word.

"Waltz?" Charlotte prompted.

He blinked and glanced at Charlotte, then he nodded and walked out of the room.

Charlotte turned to Dotunu, her eyes brimming with questions, but Dotunu avoided them and lowered her head onto the soft pillow.

"Yes, rest for now. Tomorrow we will go home," Charlotte whispered as she leaned over and brushed a thick strand of hair from Dotunu's face. Outside, Waltz paced back and forth.

When Dotunu returned to Hastings the next morning with Simon by her side, the community welcomed him back like a lost son that had just been found. The news of his chivalrous rescue had spread. The women hugged him and rained blessings on him, and the men pushed palm wine gourds into his hands as they made their way to Dotunu's house. Dotunu paused at the foot of the steps, unsure of what Ireti's reaction would be when she saw Simon. The front door swung open and the three of them – Oşolu, Şomide, and Ireti – stood there with Oşuntade behind them. They screamed and ran to her. Through tears and laughter, Dotunu lifted her head up to look sideways at Simon. He was laughing and holding Oşolu in one arm while Ireti hung on the other. They dragged Simon into the house and left Oşuntade and Dotunu in the front yard. Oşuntade smiled and pulled Dotunu into her embrace.

"You are loved, my child. So loved."

Dotunu basked in her motherly warmth and then pulled away to look into her twinkling eyes. "What is so funny?"

Oşuntade shrugged her thin shoulders.

"What?" Dotunu pressed her further.

Oşuntade placed her hands on her waist and looked at Dotunu. "It is not only the news of your rescue that has reached us all, child."

"What do you mean?"

Oşuntade shook her head. "I told you all to pay each other no mind," she said softly.

Dotunu held her breath.

"That boy has gone and broken off his engagement!"

"Waltz?"

Dotunu's head swung towards the next house as though Waltz would materialise.

"Yes, him! What really happened yesterday, Dotunu?"

Dotunu released a breath and shook her head.

"Nothing," she whispered, remembering how the soft sound of Waltz's shoes pacing back and forth on the other side of the door had lulled her into a peaceful sleep. "He only stayed outside the door while I rested. Charlotte was with me."

Oṣuntade's eyes widened. "Child! You mean he stayed with you all night and left that poor girl at the party by herself? No wonder!" She grabbed Dotunu's hand. "No need to stand out here, we can talk about it inside."

Dotunu's heart felt lighter than air as she climbed the steps into a house filled with laughter.

Chapter Fourteen

News from Home
Hastings and Freetown
Add Circa 1841

The export business expanded rapidly over the next four years. The acquisition of a second slave ship was serendipitous; it not only added trade routes and doubled sales, but it also brought 841 freed slaves and news from home to Freetown.

Şiwoolu came home excited one evening and called an emergency meeting with James, Charlotte, Waltz, Demilade, and Oşuntade, the latest investor. She had finally come to accept that to find her way back to where she believed to be her ancestral home, she would have to invest, like the rest of them, in the business that would most likely take her there.

Events were unfolding on the Gallinas River between the British government and the king of Gallinas Country that would affect the export trade. Governor Doherty had received an angry request from King Siaka, of Gallinas Country, to remove the blockade at the Serra Lyoa station set up by the British squadron on the Gallinas River. This was known to be a clandestine route for slave traders in cohorts with King Siaka – one used to bring slaves into the region and hide them in caves until they were ready to be shipped out to the Americas. In the same month, information reached Governor Doherty that a Serra Lyoa woman and her child had been seized and detained by King Siaka's son, Prince Manna, on the pretext that she owed them a debt. The governor sent a message through Captain Denman, the senior naval officer in charge of the ship that monitored the Serra Lyoa station on the Gallinas River, calling for an immediate release of all subjects of the Queen of England in captivity. While he waited for King Siaka's response, Captain Denman laid in wait for slave ships taking advantage of the route.

At the break of dawn on November 19, 1840, Captain Denman's vessel *Wanderer,* entered the river, and the Spaniards in league with King Siaka were spotted moving slaves from the caves into canoes. The British ship forced its way down the river and apprehended the slave traders, who surrendered their victims. This manoeuvre gave the British government leverage to demand that the Serra Lyoa woman, her child, and all the other slaves be released. In addition, they required that the instruments used for captivity – including the chains, shackles, and bar irons – be handed over. The British also confiscated the canoes used to bring the slaves from the slave ships to the shore and back, and their final act was to raze the places where the slaves were kept in Paisley, Jeinbo, Minna, Jekrel, Comassoon, Comabindo, Teiro, and Dombocorro. This took five days. The 841 slaves boarded British ships and were brought to Freetown. They were immediately handed over to the Liberated African Trade Department where Şiwoolu worked. The result was a sudden influx of people and several empty slave ships. All these Şiwoolu reported to the investors that evening.

The group agreed to purchase one of the ships. With Şiwoolu's position and relationship with the staff of the Liberated African Trade Department, they negotiated a good price and purchased the ship they christened *The Voyager*. Waltz and James, the group's frequent travellers, discussed when the next trip would be; they had gotten as far as Cotonou. Each time they returned, they brought back news of another kingdom and of the constant tug of war between the British and French governments over native lands. Oşuntade would shake her head in dismay and comment on the covert style of the white men to infiltrate and control. Dotunu would listen with rapt attention, holding her breath for any news of Abęokuta.

Dotunu and Charlotte took a trip into Freetown a few weeks after the new acquisition. The material shop had just received a shipment of silk, taffeta, and lace from England, and the women wanted to purchase some before the store ran out. This meant Dotunu had to swaddle Daniel, the newest addition to the family, on her back while swimming through the sea of people in town. Daniel had just turned six months old and his brothers were now full-time students at the new school where Susanna was the schoolmistress.

The streets were filled with strangers looking awestruck and lost. "These must be the new freed slaves Şiwoolu was talking about," Dotunu whispered to Charlotte as two men in threadbare shirts brushed past them. She had grown weary of searching faces for anyone who looked remotely familiar every time a new shipment of freed slaves arrived.

"Olori? Is that you?" one of the men said incredulously. His intonation was that of a native of Abeokuta. His facial marks told it and his eyes confirmed it. He fell, crying, to the ground. Dotunu ran to him.

"You know me?" she gasped in disbelief. She had dreamt of this day. She pulled him from the ground. "You're from Abeokuta! What is your name?"

"Yes, Olori, I know you. I am Bodunde."

Dotunu threw her arms around him and burst into tears. She could hear Charlotte shouting at the crowd to move aside for her to pass through.

"Who is this, Mary? What has happened?" she demanded.

This was what Dotunu had been waiting for – a sign that it was time to find their way home. She could not speak. Her heart was full.

Rather than wait until Şiwoolu got home to give him the news, she dragged Bodunde and Charlotte to Şiwoolu's office in central Freetown. It was a white, colonial-style building next to the governor's office, which was even grander. Şiwoolu was reading in his office when Godwin, ushered them in.

Dotunu asked after Magdalene as he closed the door to Şiwoolu's office. She attributed his lack of response to not hearing her and shrugged it off.

Şiwoolu leapt from his chair and walked around the oak table when he saw Charlotte and the man behind Dotunu.

"Kabiyesi!" Bodunde shouted as he dropped to the floor and rolled from side to side. "K'ade pe lori, ki bata pẹ lẹsẹ."

Şiwoolu's gasp sliced the silence. Dotunu took his hand and said, "He's from home."

Şiwoolu searched her eyes and she nodded. He took a deep breath and invited them to sit on the cushioned seats in his office. After calling Godwin to bring some water, he sat beside Dotunu.

"How long were you on the ship?" Şiwoolu asked. Bodunde answered with his head bent in reverence, one knee still on the floor and buttocks grazing the edge of the chair.

"I think it was ten days, Kabiyesi. I was captured while working on my father's farm. It was early. They had been hiding there all night."

Charlotte exclaimed and placed her hands on her head.

"I was sold to a Brazilian man, Joaquim Almeida," Bodunde continued.

Something sparked in Şiwoolu's eyes. "I have heard that name before. Olatunde pointed him out in Èkó, before we were..." He tapped his crossed knee and stared into space while Bodunde waited for his next question. Dotunu leaned forward.

"How about home, Abeokuta? Are they still looking for us?"

Bodunde's mouth fell open.

"What?" Dotunu asked.

"The news did not travel this far?" he asked quietly.

"What news?" Dotunu, Şiwoolu, and Charlotte all asked at once.

"We all thought you had died. Someone came forward

saying he was next in line to be king, someone from the ruling house of Jibodu, Kabiyesi. He swore he had seen you board a merchant ship that sailed away." Bodunde's head dropped in embarrassment. "The people are afraid that if the kingdom is left without a leader, the Oyo Empire will attack again. They are demanding a new king."

Şiwoolu pulled his legs close and leaned in. "Who?" he asked in a strangled voice.

"Your kinsman with the clubbed foot, Sunmonu."

Dotunu slumped in the chair, and neither Charlotte's screams to take the baby from her back nor Şiwoolu calling her by her true name after so many years could pull her out of the dark hole into which she was falling.

The oil lamp was burning on the coffee table when Dotunu woke up. Şiwoolu was sitting in the chair opposite the couch where she lay, staring into nothingness. She called to him twice before he responded. He fell to his knees beside the couch and touched her cheek. His hand was warm.

"You scared me."

Dotunu sat up slowly and looked around. They were alone.

"I asked them to leave. Charlotte took Daniel home. You woke up once, after we splashed water on you. I had to send Charlotte to buy you another dress after that," Şiwoolu said, almost chuckling.

Dotunu looked down. She was no longer in her blue gown. Instead, she wore the ready-made gown that she had seen in the window of the material shop and had wished she could buy. Şiwoolu sat on the floor. The orange light from the lamp flickered behind him. He made a noise, a cross between a sob and a sigh.

"Şiwoolu," she whispered.

He kept his eyes averted, but she grabbed his chin and turned it towards her. His eyes were laden with tears.

"Sunmonu betrayed us," she whispered. "It makes sense. Everything makes sense now."

He stared at her, still in shock from the news.

"We must find our way back, Şiwoolu. We must take back what is ours."

Şiwoolu shook his head. "It can't be Sunmonu," he said.

"Did you not hear what that young man said?" Dotunu demanded.

Her husband chuckled darkly as his hands flicked away the tears that had dropped onto his cheeks.

"Şiwoolu," Dotunu whispered again.

He got up and began to pace the room. She whispered his name again, but he ignored her and kept pacing. Dotunu got up and met him in the centre of the room. Her palms fell on his buttoned waistcoat. She pressed her hand over his racing heart and looked up. His eyes were wide and sad.

"We must find our way back," she said.

He shook his head. "Back to what? To a kingdom that no longer needs me? Look how quickly they have forgotten about me, about us."

Tears stung her eyes. "They are dying each day we don't return – your mother, my father," she whispered.

Şiwoolu shoved his hands in his pockets and walked to the window. Dotunu followed him. She felt more than physical distance between them; she was losing him again. She placed her head on his back and held him around the waist. The moonlight streamed in, casting their shadows on the carpet, as the clock chimed eight times. Şiwoolu sighed as he placed his hand over hers.

"We can't go back. What subject wants a king who has been captured as a slave?"

Dotunu pulled away and walked around to face him. Grabbing his face and pulling him close, she said, "It's not your fault!"

"Do you remember what I told you I had done?"

Claws wrapped around Dotunu's heart when he whispered the same words that had made her sit down, at that fateful church lunch, after her outburst that the business venture might help them find their way back to Abeokuta. The very words Waltz had demanded she tell him.

"The curse."

"That was not your fault! That man was sent to kill you, just as they killed your father! You were defending yourself."

He shook his head. "A king's hands cannot be stained with blood. I lied to the kingmakers that night, the night of my coronation. They asked me..." He paused, still shaken by what he had done and what he had told Dotunu, the night they had told each other everything. "They asked me if I had ever killed a man. I said no. I should never have lied."

"We all do things we regret," Dotunu said softly, her thoughts floating to the night she had returned, drenched from head to toe, just as the mob arrived at the gates of the palace in Ake, demanding the removal of Şiwoolu as king.

"I brought a curse upon Abeokuta because of my lies. I brought a curse upon my family," he said, turning towards the window.

Dotunu pulled him around again. "No, you didn't, Şiwoolu! Did you really believe the nonsense that old recluse, Makinde, accused you of? That you were responsible for the disappearances in the villages because of a curse? Those started long before you became king!"

Şiwoolu sighed. "We have created a new home for ourselves here in Freetown. God knew what He was doing when all this happened. Our boys can get a good education. Harry and James have already started at an excellent school. Eventually they will attend Fourah Bay College, and you know it's the best university on the continent. They would never have had such an opportunity if we were still in Abeokuta."

Dotunu stared at the stranger before her, unable to speak, for fear had stolen her voice. Şiwoolu's hand shook as he held it out and called to her.

"No!" she screamed.

"Mary," he said again.

"Don't call me that! I will never be Mary!"

Dotunu turned around and ran into the wall.

"Mary! Are you all right?" Şiwoolu shouted.

She groaned, grabbing her head with one hand and touching the wall with the other. The building shook and windows rattled.

"Dotunu, no. Not again. Don't hurt yourself."

Blood gushed from her nose, and she felt strength flow from her.

Taking a few deep breaths, she willed herself to stop the shaking. The tremor ceased, and silence weighed heavily between them. Her heart begged silently for him to speak words of hope, but every second that passed proved otherwise. She braced herself and walked towards the double doors.

"Don't go, Dotunu!" Şiwoolu's choked voice called out, but she turned the knob and ran down the dark hallway, past the many double doors and out into the moonlight to the place she knew would receive her.

Esmeralda sat on the sand beside Dotunu and smiled. She hadn't aged a day since they last met.

"Welcome, Olori. It has been too long. Did you enjoy the ceremony last night?"

Dotunu nodded, eyes on the waves rushing onto the shore. She had danced her fears and tears away, and it was exactly what she had needed to calm her turbulent heart. Today she would face Şiwoolu, unpretentious and unafraid to be her true self.

They sat quietly for a few minutes while Esmeralda waved at the women who called out goodbyes as they boarded a waiting canoe.

"Oşuntade had said on her last visit, which has also been a while now—"

"She has been having some joint pains. Age is telling on her," Dotunu said.

Smiling, Esmeralda responded, "Don't let her hear you say that. Oṣuntade believes she will never die."

They laughed and became quiet again. Esmeralda turned and took Dotunu's hand.

"I'm happy you remembered after so long that we meet on the first day of the full moon. You are always welcome here. We are your sisters."

"Thank you. This was the only place I could think to come," Dotunu said, holding back her tears.

Esmeralda sighed and squeezed her hand softly.

"I knew you would come back. I saw it before you arrived. I saw it all."

Dotunu looked closely at the woman she had known for years but not been able to read.

"From the moment you climbed into the canoe years ago, I felt your power, Dotunu. Everything that you are, that you've tried so hard to hide."

"You did? So you must possess the same powers my mother had." Dotunu searched her eyes.

"I have the gift of clairvoyance," Esmeralda said. Her hand went up to touch the streak of grey hair woven into the cornrow in the centre of Dotunu's head. It had sprung overnight. "Tell me about your mother Dotunu."

"She tried to kill me first by fire when she saw my future. The future my father never told me about and tried to fortify me against. I understand it all now. This future that is now my present. She did not want it for me. It drove her mad, so she killed herself. No one talked about her anymore when she did. It is a taboo to kill yourself back home. You no longer exist once you do. So everyone erased her memories from their minds. Even me..." The guilt she had carried all her life weighed heavily on her.

"You must stop blaming yourself for something you had no control over. This was all meant to be. We are only pawns in this game of life," Esmeralda said, looking to the waves. She turned back to Dotunu. Her eyes glazed over as she spoke. "But you can no longer use your gift."

Dotunu held her breath, as the events of the night before came crashing in – her life source flowing out of her as the building trembled and the windows rattled.

"If you attempt it one more time, you will die."

Esmeralda began to hum under her breath, and it eased Dotunu's thumping heart. She pulled Dotunu's hand to her chest and began to sing. The sound of the waves coupled with her soulful voice soothed Dotunu. Her eyes fluttered and shut.

"Dotunu! Dotunu!"

She opened her eyes. A tall man standing in a canoe rowed quickly to shore.

"Who is that?" Esmeralda asked, getting up.

The canoe filled with the worshippers stopped close to the man's canoe. They pointed at Esmeralda and Dotunu. He jumped out and pulled the canoe onto the shore. Dotunu got up when he came closer.

"Waltz?" She whispered.

Esmeralda looked at Dotunu and smiled. "Ah, the one who is always there for you. I will leave with the others. You are in good hands."

She grabbed Dotunu's shoulders and kissed her on both cheeks. Waltz spoke with her as they passed. She nodded and replied before entering the canoe. Dotunu took a few steps towards Waltz and stopped. Water dripped from his clothes as he took the last few steps to her. When they stood a few inches apart, he broke down.

"I've been looking everywhere for you! I thought you were gone." His shoulders shook uncontrollably as he covered his face.

"Waltz," she whispered. The sound of her voice only made him weep louder.

Dotunu took a step closer and pried his fingers from his face. His eyes were red from hours of crying.

"I'm here," she said softly. "I'm here, Amadeus."

He nodded as the tears rolled down his face. He pulled her close and buried his face in her hair as the waves rushed towards them. A strong wind followed, lifting her gown and wrapping them in a cocoon.

Dotunu did not go straight home when Waltz brought her back to Hastings, she stopped at his house first. Drops of water from their clothes trailed down the street and up the steps into the house. Oṣuntade sat in her chair in the parlour, looking pensive with her hands wrapped around her. She sprang to her feet upon seeing Dotunu and ran to her as fast as her legs would allow. She grabbed Dotunu and embraced her. Finally, she raised her head and looked at Waltz.

"Was she where I said she would be?" she asked.

"Yes," Waltz answered.

Oṣuntade pulled Dotunu gently to a chair at the

dining table. She touched her face and shoulders as though Dotunu might be a figment of her imagination and would disappear. Her eyes, like Waltz's, were red.

"What happened, dear child? What happened to you?"

Dotunu felt Waltz's burning gaze on her before she turned her head to look at him. She had told him everything on their trip back, now she told Oşuntade too. Silence was the last thing she expected when she finished. Dotunu squeezed the hand that was still clasped in her lap.

"Did you hear what I said, Oşuntade?"

Oşuntade nodded. "Yes. Şiwoolu's throne may already have been taken from him," she said.

"Şiwoolu refuses to return and take back what is his!" Dotunu shouted, jumping to her feet. Oşuntade pulled her down onto the chair again.

"Sit, child. Don't work yourself up like that. You'll only get sick."

Waltz walked out of the room. They sat quietly as he moved around in the next one, picking up things and dropping them, shifting chairs. They could feel his pent-up emotions through the thin walls. Dotunu glanced up at the wall clock.

"The children are already in school. Charlotte kept Daniel with her overnight," Oşuntade said.

Dotunu smiled. "You could always tell what I was thinking."

Oşuntade patted her shoulder. "So, what are you going to do now?" she asked as Waltz walked back into the room in dry clothes. His hair was pulled back into a ponytail. He came towards Dotunu with a towel in his hand.

"Thank you," she mumbled and took it. Oṣuntade pulled the towel from Dotunu's hands and began to dry her hair. Waltz leaned against the wall and crossed his arms over his chest.

"I'm leaving. I'm going to find my way back to Abeokuta," Dotunu said.

Waltz pushed himself off the wall and made for the door. "I'm going to work," he said to Oṣuntade.

She looked up, surprised. "Which work? I thought construction in town has been stopped for a few days while the new governor takes a tour."

Waltz turned the front doorknob. "I'm going. Please, talk some sense into Dotunu. How is she going to find her way to Abeokuta when James and I have gone on these trading trips for years and have yet to find it? The closest we've been is Cotonou, and that was by chance." He looked at Dotunu, his eyes filled with fury. "Do you want to get lost? Or worse, die?" Turning back to Oṣuntade, he said again in a clipped tone, "Talk some sense into her," and closed the door behind him. They heard him walk briskly down the steps and out of earshot.

Oṣuntade turned to Dotunu. "It seems you have already had this conversation with Waltz."

Dotunu shrugged, reluctant to divulge the details of the heated argument they had had during the canoe trip.

"All right, all right. Let me take you home to rest."

"But I need to get Daniel from Charlotte."

"No, no children. He's safe with Charlotte. You have had a harrowing time, child. I will make you some hot soup and put you to bed." Oṣuntade pulled Dotunu to her feet. "Not here, though! In your own house, child. We don't want tongues wagging. Your husband had to go to work because of the governor's tour, but he stayed up all night waiting for you. He will be home soon. Come along."

Dotunu's heart sank at the thought of Ṣiwoolu going to work rather than searching for her.

Ṣiwoolu devoured every inch of Dotunu's face as she lay on the bed, dead to the world. The night before had been the longest of his life. His mind had run wild with what could have happened to her, and it didn't help that Oṣolu would not stop crying for his mother. He sighed and touched her cheek, willing her eyes to open so he could see that fire that nothing could quench. It was that fire that kept him alive, the one that gave him hope and reminded him that he was still hers. The same fire that he remembered when she reappeared, when everyone in the kingdom feared she had been kidnapped like the others. She had reappeared the day the mob converged on the palace in Ake demanding that he be dethroned.

Ṣiwoolu's thoughts were still in Ake as she opened her eyes in the darkening room. It was dusk, and most families in Hastings were indoors eating supper.

Dotunu sat up on the bed, her back to the wall.

"My love, you are finally awake." Ṣiwoolu pulled her to his chest and inhaled her scent of shea butter and coconut oil. He had forgotten how it made him swoon every time he was near her. Dotunu lay still in his arms and his heart skipped a beat. He looked down into her eyes, and what he saw almost broke his heart. They were lifeless. "Dotunu? Talk to me. Where have you been?"

She looked down at the sheets but remained mute. He dropped his hands and pulled back.

"I beg of you, Dotunu. Talk to me."

Her eyes filled with tears.

"Dotunu! Did someone hurt you?" he grabbed her by the shoulder.

Tears tumbled down her face like a waterfall. He fell to his knees beside the bed to look into her eyes and began to wipe her tears.

"I will kill the person who hurt you, my love. Just tell me."

Dotunu grabbed her chest and sobbed harder. "It's you, Şiwoolu! You hurt me!"

Şiwoolu's hand went still on her face.

"You've hurt me more than anyone in the world, Şiwoolu! You are killing me by telling me not to return home!" she screamed at him.

"I beg of you, Dotunu!" Şiwoolu whispered as tears filled his eyes. "*You* will kill *me* if you leave. I've been running mad all night and day. I can't imagine life without you."

They were silent for minutes. Dotunu looked towards the mini shadows waiting behind the door to be let in. "I have to go to the children. Have they been fed?" she asked, swinging her feet off the bed.

Şiwoolu's hands found her waist. Chanting her name as if his life depended on it, he pulled her close and buried his face in her lap, sobbing uncontrollably. His wide shoulders shook and his hands tightened around her until she could hardly breathe. Dotunu's hands caressed his head and shoulders as they cried together. When they were spent, he raised his head and stared at her as if he were seeing her for the first time.

"I promise you this. When it is safe for us all, we will return with the children. It's all of us or none at all."

Dotunu sat still, torn between her love for him and her longing for home. She cried silently and his arms tightened around her once more. Then she lifted his face towards hers and whispered, "You promise?"

"Yes, I promise, my love. All of us or none at all."

It was Ireti who gave Dotunu another sign that it was time to find their way back to Abeokuta a few days later. She had come home after her day in town working with Miss Abigail as a teacher's assistant for the deaf and mute students at the new missionary school. Her hysterical calls had brought Dotunu running out of her room into the parlour. Ireti pointed down the road, repeating "Miz Abby." Impatient at Dotunu's slow pace, Ireti had grabbed her hand, begging her to hurry. Dotunu had insisted on setting the table for Şiwoolu and the boys when they returned together from town, then followed her with Daniel tied to her back.

Miss Abigail was talking animatedly with Minister

Daniel when Dotunu and Ireti entered their house. Minister Daniel took little Daniel as Dotunu untied the wrapper holding him to her back.

"Ah, little Daniel, how are you today?" Minister Daniel asked as he held his namesake. Dotunu had gone into labour while visiting Minister Daniel and Miss Abigail, and he had extended the same generosity that he had when Oşolu was born. He had taken charge and ensured that Oşuntade and the doctor were there to help Dotunu through a rather quick delivery. Şiwoolu and Dotunu had honoured him by naming their third son after him.

With the two Daniels entertaining one another, Ireti pulled Dotunu to Miss Abigail, whose face was flushed with suppressed excitement. Miss Abigail grabbed Dotunu's shoulder when she was close.

"Dear Mary, you will not believe what Ireti was able to tell me this morning! Come, sit!"

Miss Abigail seated Dotunu on the couch and squeezed in next to her, with Ireti on the other side.

"What is it?" Dotunu asked.

Ireti signed at Miss Abigail, who giggled and said, "Ireti says to carry on! All right!'"

The teacher took Dotunu's hand and began to explain. "You know how I've been adding an extra half-hour to my sessions with Ireti – more like a therapeutic session to share her ordeals of the capture and torture on the slave ship? I thought it would help since I could already see the change, having started it with the new returnees and the older ones who have been having a hard time adjusting to life here."

"Yes, and I thank you for that," Dotunu answered in a heartfelt voice. "Look at her. She is not the same Ireti who set foot here five years ago. She has blossomed into this beautiful, confident young lady."

Miss Abigail's eyes twinkled. "She told me something that I knew would interest you."

She nodded at Ireti, who took that as a cue and began to sign with the mastery that had come with time.

"She's asking if you remember that day in Èkó when you left for a walk with your husband," Miss Abigail said, her eyes on Ireti's hands.

Dotunu nodded.

"Do you remember when you came back, and she was too afraid to go to the back of the house?"

Dotunu's chest felt as though it were falling to the bottom of the ocean. She pulled her hand from Miss Abigail's and grabbed Ireti's.

"Let her talk," Miss Abigail said softly.

Dotunu released Ireti's hands, and the young woman continued to speak with them.

"She saw two men who later imprisoned you on the slave ship – one with grey eyes and a white man with a hat. They were talking to a man whose back was turned to her. They were all standing next to the small house hidden by leaves and branches. It was dark, and she couldn't see his face."

Dotunu gasped. Ireti signed again and Miss Abigail continued.

"Simon confirmed it. He said his father had a contact

in Èkó for the slaves he bought. He said it was a man with a clubbed foot."

"So it *was* Sunmonu," Dotunu whispered. She looked at Ireti. "Simon told you this?"

Ireti nodded and smiled. Dotunu had noticed their closeness of late. They sat together at church, and most times he walked her home from work.

Miss Abigail signed to Ireti and she responded.

"The man worked for someone else, she said ... a woman," Miss Abigail said and continued. "I think it's wonderful how Ireti's able to talk through her experiences with Simon in a safe environment, don't you think? It's all helping to bring back buried memories."

Dotunu scratched her head. "Yes, yes, of course. But did you just say that the man, Sunmonu, worked for a woman? A woman can also participate in this horrible trade? How heartless can she be?"

"Don't fret, Mary. Your knowing that does not help matters."

Miss Abigail's eyes, which had dimmed during Ireti's tale, now lightened with knowledge. "I ... we," she paused and glanced at Minister Daniel playing with Daniel in the background, "we bear good news."

Minister Daniel walked towards them with little Daniel in his hands. "I was hoping Ajayi would be here by now so we could all give you the news together, but I don't think this can wait," he said, as excited as his wife, who waited with bated breath. "The new governor, John Carr, has approved a government expedition to the Niger River."

"Does this mean what I think it means?" Dotunu asked.

Miss Abigail nodded.

"Yes, Mary!" Minister Daniel shouted as he bounced Daniel on his hip. "The Church Missionary Society is part of a larger team that includes the commanders of the three vessels of the expedition, the commissioners who will make treaties with the native chiefs to abolish slave trade, and the African Civilization Society, which will bring with it scientists, to assess the agricultural viability of the areas. As members of the Church Missionary Society, we will be sending missionaries along to explore the possibility of establishing missions on the banks of the Niger."

Dotunu got up. "You can select whom you want on this trip?" she asked.

Minister Daniel smiled. "Yes, dear Mary. Of course, the Very Reverend Schon, who is based in Freetown, will travel with them. Ajayi and some of our teachers will be going as well – but most importantly, we will need interpreters."

Dotunu looked at Miss Abigail's smiling face, any wider and she would have burst a vein. She sprang to her feet and took Dotunu's hands.

"Your dream to return home is no longer a dream. It will be a reality!" she said.

"Şiwoolu will definitely go," Dotunu whispered. "Won't he?" She searched Minister Daniel's face for an answer.

His smile reassured her that Şiwoolu would.

An emergency meeting was called in church that evening. Minister Daniel stood by the podium with a beaming Ajayi to inform the congregation of the expedition that would leave Freetown on July 2 and travel up the Niger River. The room was filled with raised hands before he finished speaking.

Dotunu searched for Şiwoolu in the congregation when she came in briefly. She was helping the other women arrange the food on tables outside, in readiness for the hungry congregation. He was seated in the first row. Mr. Callister, an old parishioner, sat behind a table with a large book, an ink pen, and a small bottle of black ink. He had been tasked with recording the names of the 150 people who would be needed on the expedition. Waltz called the people to order as they began to push forward. He warned that any act of aggression was an automatic disqualifier – that subdued the crowd.

The exercise took several hours. When the line, which had curled around the building to where Charlotte, Dotunu, and a few other ladies stood serving refreshments, dwindled, Dotunu turned to her friend. Charlotte looked back at her with knowing eyes.

"Mary, please don't go," she whispered, pulling Dotunu away from the prying eyes of the churchwomen close by.

"Why not? I've been checking every few minutes to see if Şiwoolu has signed up, but he just sits there!"

"Why don't you have this discussion with him at home? Don't do this here," Charlotte pleaded.

Dotunu's laughter was short and dry. "But we already did! I beg of you, let me go."

Charlotte sighed and released her wrist. Dotunu

marched into the church towards the last ten men waiting to sign up. They turned around when they heard her approach.

"Sister Mary?" Demilade exclaimed from the front of the line.

Şiwoolu, still seated in the front row, looked her way. His brow furrowed, but he kept silent. The congregation was quiet as the men signed up, and finally it was Dotunu's turn. Waltz stood beside Ajayi and Minister Daniel as Dotunu stepped forward to the table, a few feet from Şiwoolu.

"Write my name down, Mary Dotunu Coker," she said.

Mr. Callister glanced sideways at Şiwoolu, his ink pen in mid-air.

"You can't go," Şiwoolu said softly with blank eyes.

Mr. Callister dropped the ink pen on the table and leaned back in his seat. Dotunu grabbed the edge of the table.

"Are you going?" she asked, turning her head to look squarely at Şiwoolu.

He sighed. "We have talked about this."

Dotunu turned to Mr. Callister again and said, "Put down my name."

Minister Daniel stepped up to the table. His smile faded when he looked at Dotunu. "What is the matter?"

Dotunu's nails dug into the edge of the table.

Şiwoolu shook his head. "We've talked about this. We said all of us or none at all," he said softly.

Dotunu looked sideways at him, his elbows on his knees as he leaned forward.

"I will go if you won't," she whispered.

The congregation began to murmur. Minister Daniel touched her elbow.

"Let us discuss this in private, Mary. Look, your boys are here!"

Ṣomide and Oṣolu ran down the aisle and buried their faces in the folds of her gown. Minister Daniel's pleading look coaxed her into taking their hands and walking. As they passed Waltz and Ajayi, the two men began to talk.

"I'll be ready with the artisans we have, Ajayi."

"Good, we need you! I'm happy to know you have signed up."

"I wanted to. I made a promise to someone that I have to keep," Waltz said.

Tears sprang up in Dotunu's eyes as she walked out of the building towards Charlotte.

"Take the boys. I have to take a walk. I have to—" She burst into tears as she pushed the boys into Charlotte's side and ran down the street.

Dotunu laughed at herself as she walked back home. It started out as spurts and then outright high-pitched bursts, like fireballs in the air, slicing the silence. If it were any other night, heads would have been in the windows, searching for the culprit disturbing the quiet. She flung her hands in the air and began to run down the empty streets. She tripped over her sandals and one of the straps tore off, but that did not interrupt her manic laughter. She sat right in the middle of the street and took the sandals off. She attempted to get up, but her legs failed her. She laughed at herself. She was a fool to have believed Şiwoolu. He would never leave. Why would he? He had everything he wanted here in Serra Lyoa – recognition and respect, a dutiful wife, and sons that would carry on his name.

She pulled on the gold band around her neck, and then her hair, willing tears to come. It would be better than this creature on the ground laughing like a maniac, like her mother when she ran mad. This was the laughter she had handed down to her. This was the madness she thought she had escaped. She lay on the ground but did not feel the stones that pressed into her back; worse pain coursed through her heart.

She did not hear the shoes crunching on the ground until they were beside her. Familiar hands grabbed her shoulders and raised her up. She stopped laughing.

"Why are you doing this to yourself, Dotunu?" Waltz whispered. "I promised you I would do everything I can help you find your way back home. That's why I signed up for the expedition." He stared at her but couldn't recognise the shell in his arms. "Where are you, Dotunu? Come back to me," his breath fanned her face. He repeated the words as his tears dropped on her skin. Soon, hers mingled with his and her arms circled his waist. They cried together until they were empty and then he whispered life into her ears.

"I love you, Dotunu, my Yoruba queen. I will go and find your home, but I will come back for you."

Şiwoolu returned to the house hours later. Dotunu listened from the bed as he tucked the children in and made his way into the dark room. He got into the bed and curled up behind her, his hands finding hers in the folds of the blanket.

"Forgive me, my love. We will still return home. It's not the curse, I don't fear that anymore, Dotunu. What I fear is never coming back to you or vice versa. This is the first trip, anything could happen. Let them go and bring back word. Let us raise our boys in peace. When the time is right, we will know, but not right now, my love. I cannot lose you."

She sighed and turned to him. "Promise me, Şiwoo-lu."

He pressed his nose to hers and did. She turned away and felt his arms enfold her from behind. Her eyes closed in sleep, reassured by the first promise made.

The three steamers of the Royal Navy under the command of Captain Trotter – *The Albert*, *The Wilberforce*, and *The Soudan* – departed on July 2 to the cheers of Freetown and its neighbouring towns. Susanna, Miss Abigail, Oşuntade, Charlotte, Ireti, and Dotunu, along with the boys, waved and screamed the names of everyone they could remember on board as the steamers sailed away. It was a bright, beautiful morning with no clouds in sight.

Oşolu demanded to know where Uncle Waltz was. Şomide said with his nose upturned that it was impossible to tell with the ships so big. They could hardly see the faces of those on board.

"No, look! Look at Uncle Waltz!" Dotunu shouted.

Waltz was waving from the last ship to leave the harbour. It was impossible not to see his large, muscular arms over all those heads.

He screamed her name and those of the boys. They giggled and waved back.

"Oh, look! There's my James!" Charlotte shouted.

Demilade's face soon appeared, along with those of many of their neighbours and fellow church members. Ajayi and Minister Daniel appeared at the railing to the cheers of the people bidding them farewell.

"God go with you!" Charlotte cried.

"Olodumare and all the gods go with you!" Oṣuntade shouted.

Dotunu laughed and cried as the ship began to move away and the distance between them increased.

"I'm going there one day, Mama!" Oṣolu called as she picked him up for a better view.

"I know you will, dear boy," Dotunu said and kissed him soundly on his dimpled cheeks.

A large, warm hand encircled Dotunu's waist.

"We all will, my love," Ṣiwoolu whispered in her ear. Dotunu looked up at him and nodded.

It would come to pass, but not the way they had planned.

PART III: JAMES OṢOLU

Serra Lyoa and Èkó
Western Africa
Circa 1853 - 1854

Do not take revenge, my dear friends, but leave room for God's wrath, for it is written: "It is mine to avenge; I will repay," says the Lord.

– Romans 12:19

Chapter Fifteen

Genesis
Freetown
Circa 1853

"Oşolu Ajanaku,
Omo Iporo moko
Iyi ko eniyan loran
To ko ni lejo awijare
Omo mule omo Oleyo
Omo esuru o beni lorun
Kole so omo tantan
Omo taken ren Oo sani po
Ajanaku ile Iporo
Eerin mumi pokan pokan
Omo abori isu tombolo
Obi idi isu barakata lebe
Eni ba nwaja Iporo
Ko saso sorule re ko wa wohun iporo le se
Omo eni ni yeni
Omo aini ko ye yan
Iporo lakesa meguoye
Iporo kobi kete, Şodękę fi gbogbo re bagogo
Dede won wa ri sangan sangan
Omo Eledie ogogo maga
Tonyin bi awo kegbe kegbe"

The walls of Casa do Hernandez merged with faces and limbs. Live music and drunken voices buzzed in the background. Oṣolu grabbed the chair that had evaded his grasp on the first two attempts.

"James Oṣolu Coker! Must you chant those words every time you gulp down a few glasses of whiskey?"

Oṣolu glared at the slumped figure of Stephen, his roommate, across the table.

"Shh!" He pressed a finger to his lips. "Stop mentioning my name! You know how upset my father got when some nosy person reported seeing us here the last time."

Oṣolu dragged the chair across the floor, laughing when the customers in the bar cringed at the sound. He sat down and swung the glass to his lips again, careful this time not to let the drink touch his tongue. Stephen leaned on the table, put the glass down and pointed at him.

"Look, mister, it's best we leave now while we can still walk," he drawled.

"You mean while *you* can still walk. When I said we should pretend to be drunk, I meant that – pretend. Look at you!" Oṣolu spat out in disgust as he watched Stephen's head slump to the table. He shook his head and leaned back in the chair. The bar was not full today. It was Thursday, the best day of the week to leave school and mingle with the residents of Salone, the name Serra Lyoa was fondly called – most people were in churches for the evening services. Abu, the bartender, smiled and then winked at Oṣolu from behind the counter as a woman entered.

"Stephen, Stephen," he whispered, eyes darting to the double doors that opened wide onto the street. "She's back."

A young woman in a red gown entered the bar, her thick black hair was parted in the centre and pulled back. The gaze of the people was drawn to her large, kohl-lined eyes. Her bangles jingled as she twirled between the tables. She sat at the edge of the room, her honey-sweet scent filling the bar.

"Ah, Magdalene is here," Stephen whispered, smiling.

"Shut up! Do you want her to hear you?" Oṣolu whispered back, slapping Stephen's arm across the table.

Stephen chuckled, closing his eyes. "Mr. Loverboy," he whispered, making a pouty mouth and kissing noises. He opened his eyes. "Look, she has a customer already!"

Oṣolu groaned as a burly unkempt man pulled out a seat opposite Magdalene and sat. They spoke for a few seconds and left. Stephen sat up when Oṣolu rose.

"No, James! Don't be so obvious." Alcohol oozed from his breath.

"I'm following her. If you like, come."

Oṣolu rocked on his heels for a few seconds, feeling the effects of the whiskey that had touched his tongue. Magdalene's laughter spurred him to take a step and then another. He followed her scent down a slope into the maze that was Freetown.

The knock on the door got louder as Oṣolu turned on the bed. He opened his eyes and groaned as sunlight blinded him.

"Open this door, James!"

Oṣolu's head began to pound. He pulled the pillow

over his ears and wished the room would swallow him up. The knock got louder.

"You better open the door before your brother knocks it down," Stephen murmured from the bed adjacent to Oṣolu's.

Oṣolu got up and walked to the door. He cracked it wide enough to see Ṣomide push back his glasses and glare at him. His older brother was the youngest lecturer at Fourah Bay College, but he had always behaved like an old man.

Ṣomide pushed the door inward and walked past Oṣolu into the room. "Hmm!" he exclaimed, covering his nose with a white handkerchief and tiptoeing through the clothing strewn on the floor.

"What do you want?" Oṣolu mumbled, holding his head as he sat on the bed. Ṣomide surveyed the compact room with the two mahogany study desks and chairs close to the windows and the two beds bordering the walls.

"So this is why you didn't show up for my class this morning? You continue to disgrace me at this college, carousing all night!" The handkerchief muffled Ṣomide's voice but not the indignation it carried.

Oṣolu fell back on the bed with a sigh and closed his eyes.

"Go ahead, roll your eyes, laugh, but mark my words, you will regret your actions." Ṣomide paused and reached for something on the floor. "What is this doing here?"

Oṣolu opened an eye to see Ṣomide holding up a scalloped object between his fingers. He groaned and waited for the tirade.

"This is mine! Father gave me! You stole it from my room, didn't you?"

"You can have it, Şomide, what does it really matter?" Oşolu said, waving his hand in the air.

Şomide placed their father's ring on his middle finger. "Gladly! If it meant anything to you, it wouldn't be on the floor with all your dirty underwear." He marched towards the door and stopped. "I only came to remind you to show up at supper tonight. Our parents have some news to share."

"Tonight? I have—"

Şomide held up his right hand in the same manner with which he would silence his belligerent students.

"You had better show up, James! Mama hasn't seen you in two months!" He yanked the door open and slammed it behind him. When his footsteps could no longer be heard down the hallway, Stephen rolled over on his bed, a perplexed look on his face.

"Teacher Harry needs to relax a little. What were you even talking about so intensely? Sometimes I wish I understood Yoruba."

Oşolu sighed and turned to the wall.

Oşolu arrived in Hastings as the sun descended. Every visit home left him feeling more like a stranger. He was accosted with new faces on every corner.

"Broda, ow di bodi?"

He looked across the street at the men sitting under the pawpaw tree, where he remembered his mother telling him and other children folk tales. Now, men sat there to play draft, drink, tell jokes, and talk about the government.

"Tell God tenki!" he called out and waved, happy to still recognise a few faces in the group. They all waved back at him.

The emigration of families back to Abeokuta – families that Oşolu had known since birth, that had helped build the community of former slaves from the West Indies and England – had also taken its emotional toll on the families left behind. Many of the friends Oşolu had grown up with had left with their families in an excited frenzy, after the conquest by the British Empire in Èkó two years ago. These signs buoyed up Freetown residents, many of whom were of Yoruba origin and had initially been unsure of relocating.

Oşolu paused before the two-level orange plank house with green shutter windows. It was the same old house that now looked new. His father had bought it from Douglas, and as the family grew, added an upper level. Over the years it had worn many colours, but this burnt orange was the one that suited it best. The burst of colourful flowers from his mother's garden added to the collage: the red hibiscus, yellow allamanda, and black bat-head lily each lent a unique touch to the property.

Oşolu brushed past the flowers and smiled as he remembered the many evenings spent playing hide and seek with his siblings in the garden. Female voices rang out through the open windows as he climbed the steps to the front door. He tucked in his shirt, patted down his blazer and pushed back his shoulders. As he lifted his hand to knock, he heard her voice.

"Come in, Oṣolu. You know the door is never locked!"

Oṣolu pushed open the door and stepped into the parlour. Dotunu was standing with hands on her hips. The light green cotton dress with frills around the collar and balloon sleeves highlighted her still-tiny waist and swept the floorboards. Her thick gold chain glowed when she turned her head, her brown eyes danced as she gazed at her second son.

"Son of mine, where have you been?" Her voice was the same throaty one he could pick out in a crowd since he was a baby.

Oṣolu grinned as she flung out her arms. He took a few steps and buried his face in her hair, which was pulled into a bun on top of her head. Stepping back, he noticed a strand of grey hair – inches from her right temple – that hadn't been there at his last visit.

"Alright, Mama! Can you give the rest of us whatever remains of James to share?" A miniature version of Dotunu skipped across the parlour, as ebony-skinned and petite as her mother. Little Abigael was eleven, a year younger than Daniel and with a larger-than-life personality.

Oṣolu let go of his mother in time for Abigael to jump into his arms. To her delight, he kissed her on both cheeks.

"They let you out of boarding school during the term?" he asked.

Abigael pulled Oṣolu beside her onto the couch and looked across at their mother. "Ask Mama. I have no idea what she told Miss Sass, but it worked."

Oṣolu looked at their mother as she patted down the

front of her dress, a sign of nervousness Oşolu had come to recognise. "Mama, how did you get that strict principal at Annie Walsh Memorial School to let your daughter go? Did you go to Charlotte village to get her yourself?"

Dotunu smiled and turned to Abigael. "Child, must your mouth run nonstop? Look at the time!" she said, glancing at the grandfather clock against the wall. "Anyway, your father will be here shortly to tell you the news, and Daniel should be running down the street any minute."

Oşolu looked at the walls of the room decorated with black-and-white pictures of Şiwoolu with Governor MacDonald and the one picture they had taken as a family in front of the house when Abigael was just a year old. Şomide, dressed in a three-piece navy-blue suit, stood next to Şiwoolu, who was seated beside Dotunu and looked directly at the camera. Oşolu looked cross in a suit identical to his older brother's as he hung on to Dotunu's arm, while Abigael straddled one of her mother's knees and Daniel perched on the other. He chuckled, remembering how angry he had been about sharing his mother with yet another sibling.

The door opened and slammed shut as Daniel appeared, sweating profusely. He was as tall and gangly as Oşolu had been at that age.

"Brother James! Where have you been?" Daniel shouted, running to his brother and hugging him tightly.

Oşolu patted Daniel's head, lost for words at how he had sprouted overnight. The young man was barely two or three inches short of Oşolu's six feet and two inches.

"Where have you been?" Daniel demanded again as he gazed at his brother.

"You know, here, there. How's school?"

Daniel shrugged and lowered himself into the tiny space between Abigael and Oṣolu.

"No! Find your own seat!" Abigael shouted, sliding closer to Oṣolu.

Dotunu and Oṣolu looked at each other and laughed. The two continued to bicker as close siblings did, soon forgetting the reason why they had started arguing. Oṣolu got up and followed Dotunu to the newly renovated kitchen when the argument segued into who should get the bigger room since Ṣomide had moved out of the house.

Dotunu tiptoed to reach for the wooden bowl on top of a cupboard.

"Let me get that," Oṣolu said.

She stepped back and watched him bring it down. "How have you been?" she asked.

Oṣolu placed the bowl on the table already set for supper with china plates.

"I'm well, Mama. How are you?"

Dotunu cupped his chin, and her fingers pulled on his short beard.

"My baby is all grown," she said in a wistful tone.

He chuckled. "Baby? You must be talking about the ones arguing in the other room."

Dotunu smiled and pulled him down onto one of the chairs around the table. "No, you will always be my baby," she said softly. They sat in comfortable silence for a few minutes.

"Are you eating over there at the college?" she asked, patting his chest. Her palm pressed gently and felt his heartbeat for a few seconds.

"Yes. Even if I weren't, your weekly supplies sent through Şomide make sure of that."

Dotunu chuckled. "You need them! I'm sure you don't get enough fruits or protein." She dropped her hand and leaned back in the chair. Oşolu placed an elbow on the table and tilted towards her.

"What is this news you want to tell us?"

Her response was a slight smile. A floorboard creaked in the hallway, and she got up. "That's your father. Come on."

He got up and held out his arm. She tucked her hand through it, and they walked into the parlour.

Şiwoolu was standing with his hands in his pockets, reprimanding Abigael and Daniel.

"Now, Abby, you apologise to your brother. He's older than you—"

"Age doesn't negate stupidity, Papa!" Abigael shouted.

Şiwoolu pulled his right hand out of his pocket and pointed at her. "Abby! That was uncalled for. Now apologise to Daniel! And you, Daniel, next time you call your sister that name, I will wash your mouth with soap. apologise." His voice sounded frail, unlike the booming voice that had sent Şomide and Oşolu scurrying away whenever they got into trouble. Abigael pouted and glanced at Daniel, who responded by sticking his tongue out. Dotunu shook her head.

"Abby! Daniel! Have you no manners anymore?"

Şiwoolu turned around at the sound of her voice. His oval spectacles, balanced on the bridge of his nose, lifted, and a smile appeared when he saw Oşolu. His full head of hair, devoid of greys, was combed into his usual afro, and well-groomed sideburns curved down to his cheeks. He held out a large hand.

"Young man, when did you arrive?" His voice was hoarse, just as it had been the last time Oşolu had visited.

Oşolu grasped his hand and they shook. "Just now," he said, feeling a pat on his back as they hugged.

They walked to the couch and Şiwoolu sat in his armchair, to Oşolu's right. Abigael and Daniel fidgeted and made faces at each other, and their mother pulled their ears.

"Behave yourselves! Now you're going to stand there until I say you can go," she said sternly.

Şiwoolu raised his hand. "Mary, don't excite yourself. You've been cooking all day. Sit." He covered his mouth and coughed for a few seconds. The family murmured to him to take it easy until the cough subsided. When Şiwoolu pulled a handkerchief from his pocket to wipe the resulting tears from his eyes, Oşolu looked from one parent to the other and asked, "So this cough hasn't left? I hope this won't be like the last one that sent you to the hospital, Papa."

Şiwoolu smiled and shook his head. "Far from it, son. I'm doing much better. It will pass."

Dotunu sat beside Oşolu and leaned into his side. He put his arm around her shoulders and squeezed them gently. The gesture instantly produced a bright smile from her.

"It's the job. I've told your father to leave the running

around to his subordinates, especially to those areas less travelled. He came home two months ago with this cold and cough that have refused to abate."

"You should listen to Mama," Oṣolu encouraged. "You're not as young as you once were. You need to take better care of yourself."

Şiwoolu pushed up his spectacles. "I was only one or two years older than you with a wife and child and another on the way when we arrived here, son." His eyes took on a misty, faraway look that lasted for a spell while the others watched in silence. Abigael and Daniel began to whisper to each other, startling him. He looked in Oṣolu's direction, seeming almost embarrassed.

"Papa, is everything all right?" Oṣolu asked.

Şiwoolu cleared his throat and nodded. "Yes, yes of course," he said, crossing his legs, his white socks peeking out from between his trouser cuffs and lace-up shoes.

Abigael and Daniel fidgeted.

"Children, you will remain standing until you do the needful, and maybe I will be kind enough to tell the tale of..." Şiwoolu paused as the two looked at each other, almost bursting at the thought of what they would have to do for their father to tell them stories of their ancestors.

Abigael moved her lips.

"What was that?" Daniel asked, cupping his ears with his hands.

Her lips puckered and eyes flashed. "Sorry!" she shouted.

Daniel grinned and began to dance on the spot, his buttocks pushed out like a dagger stabbing the air in one direction, and his arms in the other. Oşolu faked a cough to hide his smile behind his hand.

"Stop that!" Şiwoolu shouted, and a cough spluttered out suddenly and stopped just as quickly. He pointed at Daniel. "She has apologised. Now it's your turn."

Daniel stopped his dance with mouth agape. "For what, Papa? Abby is so rude. She needs to be punished."

Şiwoolu leaned his head on the back of his chair. "You do not want me to get up, young man," he said slowly.

Daniel looked at Oşolu.

"Trust me, you don't," Oşolu said, remembering the paddles on his buttocks that their father had never held back when he was younger.

Daniel sighed and looked at a smug Abigael. "I'm sorry for calling you a mistake."

"What?" Oşolu's arm slid off Dotunu's shoulders as she sat up.

Şiwoolu looked at her with a frown on his face. "Mary," he murmured.

"Why would you say that about your sister?" Dotunu asked with incredulous eyes.

Daniel shrugged. "She has to be! I mean, three boys and then *her*? Can I go now?"

"No!" Dotunu shouted and stood up.

Şiwoolu caught her wrist as she walked past him. She stopped and looked down at him.

"Don't," he said softly. "We have more important things to talk about."

Dotunu gazed at him for a few seconds – precious seconds the two younger siblings took advantage of to escape. They ran out of the room before Şiwoolu let her go. Oşolu called to them to go straight to the kitchen to wash their hands.

"Thank you, Oşolu. You see, that's what they've been missing since you left for college – an older brother to keep them in check," Şiwoolu said as Dotunu excused herself and followed. They sat listening to the clatter of plates and cups mixed with the voices of Dotunu and the two younger children who had decided to call a truce.

Şiwoolu cleared his throat. "Any news of Magdalene yet? Godwin is worried. He can't concentrate at work."

Oşolu folded his arms across his chest. "None, Papa. She just disappeared from Freetown."

Şiwoolu frowned. "That's strange. This is not such a large place. I've checked the manifests of all the ships leaving the harbour, and there's nothing. She really has disappeared into thin air."

Oşolu bit his lower lip as his father shook his left foot, deep in thought. The front door opened.

"Mama!" Şomide called out.

"We're in the kitchen," Dotunu responded.

Şomide paused as he stepped into the parlour. The two brothers nodded at each other.

"Papa, good evening."

Şiwoolu raised his head and smiled. "Harry, how were your classes today?"

Şomide placed his briefcase on the floor. The ring glittered as he unclasped his fingers from the handle.

"It was fine. How was work?"

"Slow, you know bureaucracy. The new governor is

trying to put his own stamp on everything. This includes bringing to a halt all projects implemented by the last administration."

Ṣomide smiled. "So I hear. We are still waiting for funding from the government to help with the construction of the new library, but that is not your department, is it?"

The two laughed. It was a long-standing joke of Ṣomide's ever since he had declined an offer from the government to work in the Housing Department because of the bureaucracy and politics. He much preferred his position as a lecturer at Fourah Bay College, where he had graduated top of his class two years ago.

"James, glad you made it on time," Ṣomide said in a chilling voice. Oṣolu nodded but said nothing.

"Supper is served!" Dotunu called from the kitchen.

Ṣiwoolu and Oṣolu got up and the three headed towards the kitchen as Abigael ran out with a tray of dishes.

"Hurry up and get that to Granny Oṣuntade and come right back here!" Dotunu shouted.

"Is she going by herself?" Oṣolu asked, trying to quiet the panic in his voice as the door slammed behind her. Everyone sat down and stared at him.

"She's just going next door!" Daniel said and laughed.

With narrowed eyes, Ṣomide observed Oṣolu from across the table. "Yes, she's just going next door. Why are you so skittish, brother?"

Oṣolu placed his hands flat on the table. "I'm not. It's just not right for a young girl to be out at night like this."

"At seven o'clock? Shouldn't Granny Oṣuntade eat? You know very well her arthritis has worsened in the past few months," Dotunu said.

"You would know if you visited," Şomide murmured.

Dotunu smiled and squeezed Oşolu's hand on the table. "Ignore him! I must say, though: how chivalrous you've become, Oşolu!" she exclaimed.

"Chivalry aside, Mama, next time let Daniel take the food or at least go with her."

"He makes a good point," Şiwoolu said softly.

Dotunu and Şomide looked at Şiwoolu and Oşolu, surprised.

"How the tide has turned," Şomide muttered.

Dotunu got up, murmuring an excuse, and left the room. Oşolu's eyes followed her downcast head. He turned to Şiwoolu, whose eyes had not left her either.

"Is everything all right with Mama?"

The front door swung open and shut, ushering in Abigael. She skipped to her seat and sat down with a grin on Şiwoolu's left side.

"So, Papa, tell us again the story of how your father was selected to be king, and about Mama's father."

She grabbed his hand and waited with wide eyes. Şiwoolu smiled down at her. He could never deny her anything.

"All right, daughter. Just one story though, until your mother returns."

"Papa, you mustn't leave out anything this time!" Daniel shouted, wiggling a finger in the air.

Şiwoolu looked shocked. "When have I ever done that?"

The children laughed.

"Papa, you've left out many things in the past, including spying on Mama at the river," Şomide said with his first smile of the evening.

Şiwoolu waved his hand in dismissal. "You believe your mother over me?" he asked with twitching lips.

"She always knew you came to spy on her!" Abigael said, joining the laughter of her siblings.

Oşolu moved his chair forward while Şomide placed his elbow on the table.

"I was barely older than Oşolu here when my father decided to take me to a meeting with the elders to discuss the recent disappearances in the villages." Şiwoolu smiled as he looked at their eager faces and recounted how his father, Alade Okikilu, came to be selected as Alake of Ęgba Kingdom.

Afterwards, he took a gulp of water.

The children had been quiet throughout, eyes wide and entranced as their father replayed the event at Olumo rock.

"Papa! I love hearing this next part every time!" Abigael gushed with her hands under her chin, staring up at Şiwoolu. He smiled at her, a distant look in his eyes.

"Which part?" Daniel asked, kicking her under the table. She kicked him back.

"The part where Papa sees Mama's father seated in the front row with the other members of the ogboni council, silly!"

"Little did he know that that would soon be his father-in-law," Oşolu added.

Şiwoolu looked at him and nodded solemnly. "Such a good man," he said softly.

A shadow fell in the doorway. "Yes, a very good man, and a loving father," Dotunu said as she made her way past Şiwoolu to the other end of the table. Şomide got up and pulled out her seat.

"Mama, what is the matter?" he asked.

Dotunu looked around the table with trembling lips. As she made to speak, the front door opened.

"Good evening, family!" Simon said, holding onto a heavily pregnant Ireti. She signed and waved.

Dotunu was the first to grab her; she kissed and hugged Ireti as if she hadn't seen her in years.

"We weren't sure you would make it! Oh my! I had no idea you were this big!" Dotunu fluttered about, beside herself with joy. She ordered Daniel to get more chairs from the guest room.

Oşolu shook Simon's hand and only had to wait a second for Ireti to pull his neck down and plant two kisses on his cheeks.

When they were all seated, the family plied the couple with questions about their new home in the town of Sherbro, too impatient and excited to wait for answers: "How is Sherbro?" "How is the new house?"

The export business had an office in the port of Sherbro that was managed by Simon. Ireti had joined him there after they were married a year ago.

Abigael picked up the wooden spoon and was immediately stopped by Şiwoolu's tap on her hand.

"Grace first," he said.

They bowed their heads for the short prayer and then dug in. When the last ball of ẹba had been scraped up with Dotunu's famous okra and beef sauce – which the older residents of Hastings still demanded occasionally – the children turned to their parents.

"Well, what's the news Harry and I had to come all the way from Fourah Bay to hear?" Oşolu asked.

The orange light from the oil lamps in the centre of the table flickered as a breeze blew in through the windows. Şiwoolu sat back and looked across the table at Dotunu.

"Yes, that news. Well, do you want me to...?"

Dotunu gulped and nodded her head. Oşolu noticed the tears sparkling in her eyes.

"What is going on?" various voices chorused.

Şiwoolu tapped his fingers on the table and sighed. "Your mother is fine, but we have unsettling news that necessitates immediate action."

Oşolu held his breath when he saw the shimmer in his father's eyes as well.

"As you all know, some twelve years or so ago, the church sent representatives on an expedition to Niger."

Abigael and Daniel frowned. Şiwoolu glanced at them and smiled. "You were too young to remember, Daniel, and you, Abby, were just growing inside your mother, though we didn't know it yet."

Their laughter was a mere sputter, an acknowledgement of their patriarch's attempt to lighten the mood.

"People died on that expedition," Şiwoolu continued, looking at Dotunu, whose face had turned ashen.

"Forty-two white men out of 150, but no casualties from the same number of Africans on board the vessel *Albert*," she added.

"Yes, thank God no Africans died. God spared them. It was the longest five months of our lives, waiting to hear from James Senior, Waltz, and Minister Ajayi," Şiwoolu paused and looked around the table. "Which brings me to the news we have for you." His eyes settled on Dotunu, whose hands had begun to shake on the table. She rolled them into fists before the children could see and hid them in her lap.

"The plan was for us all to return home, but with the perils of the journey, we knew it would not be safe for us to go at that time. You remember what we promised? All of us or…"

"None at all," Oşolu's voice joined in the mantra that they had had recited over the years, especially on the days when they had watched their neighbours and friends pack up and leave, wondering when they too would.

Şiwoolu nodded.

"Yes, but that was only one reason. I know after a few years you all felt that was a flimsy excuse. There was another reason that your mother and I kept from you."

"With Demilade settled in Ota, he was able to monitor from a distance, the lengths Sunmonu—"

Şomide slammed his fist on the table, eyes glaring at an unseen enemy.

"Papa, that man's name does not deserve a mention under this roof! Why bestow any form of dignity on that turncoat and murderer?"

Şiwoolu nodded and continued, "Your grandfather had an informer within the new ruling council. Sunmonu believes he has won him over. He tells him everything. The informer found out that Sunmonu, my bosom friend from childhood, had planted assassins at the Marina in Èkó, and in Badagry should I or any member of my family ever return."

Dotunu's short, ragged breaths filled the room as her fingers travelled to her neck to trace the fine edge of the chain her father had given her.

"What is it, Mama?" Oṣolu asked.

She looked at him, and he fell into the dark pool of pain in her eyes.

"What is it, Mama?" he demanded again. "Why are you not telling us what is really going on?"

The silence in the room seemed to last forever, and then Dotunu whispered something.

"What did you say, Mama?" Oṣolu asked.

"He died," she murmured, looking down at the table.

The rest of them looked from Ṣiwoolu to Dotunu.

"Who? Sunmonu? Good riddance!" Ṣomide bellowed as he crossed his arms over his chest and puffed up like dough.

Dotunu lifted her head and shook it. "No."

"No? Then who?" Oṣolu asked, leaning over to steady her shaking shoulders.

"Elemere Keṣi, your grandfather, the last living member of the ogboni council that selected your grandfather as king and later presided over my coronation – the only one standing in Sunmonu's way of being crowned king – has died," Ṣiwoolu said, looking down the table at Dotunu.

"But..." Oṣolu's voice broke as he sat beside his mother, gathered her into his arms, and rocked her.

"Demilade sent word from Ota," Şiwoolu said.

"Was he sick?" Simon asked.

"He had been sick since we were taken, we knew that, but I think he finally died of a broken heart. He had waited too long for our return," Şiwoolu said, and paused. Şomide placed his hand on his father's shoulder as he regained his composure.

"Sunmonu made life hell for both him and my mother. He ostracised them, decreeing that anyone associating with them would be banished. Even Demilade who initially settled in Abeokuta, had to move to Ota. Thankfully, he made sure foodstuffs were delivered to them. They lived like lepers in the kingdom they had both fought for. That alone can kill anyone."

"How could the people and the council let this happen?" Oşolu asked.

"Sunmonu bought the new members of the council with his blood money. The new head, Sagbua Okukenu, is now pushing to make Sunmonu king, and the people are like dogs lapping water from his hands."

Dotunu sobbed into Oşolu's shoulder.

"Shh, shh," he whispered into her ear.

Şiwoolu leaned his elbows on the table and stared at the white cotton tablecloth as though waiting for a sign. The family sat in silence, the tick tock of the grandfather clock measuring the passage of time. When Şiwoolu raised his head, his eyes blazed with a ferocity that shocked the others.

"Now no one stands in the way of Sunmonu becoming king ... except me."

Dotunu raised her head and squared her shoulders.

"We will return home and I will claim my throne," Şiwoolu said.

Everyone gasped.

"As you all know, a few years ago, Ajayi made a presentation to Her Majesty about the state of affairs in Lagos Colony. The increased slave trade and inability to access Abeokuta resulted in the decision to attack Lagos and dethrone the king there in 1851. I believe his name was—"

"Kosoko," Dotunu said.

"Yes, Kosoko," Şiwoolu said. "Ogun Ahoyaya, 'the boiling battle,' it was called. James Labulo Junior, Charlotte and James' son, fought on the side of the British, and what a tale he told! Kosoko was successfully deposed. A new king has been crowned and has forged a treaty with the British to stop the slave trade. He also has opened the port of Lagos for trade and to allow many of us, taken away as slaves, to return. We have watched for two years to see how things are progressing, and they are progressing well. This is a sign for us to return, and we must, before—" he covered his mouth as his voice shook.

"Before Sunmonu takes the crown," Oşolu said through gritted teeth.

Ireti, eyes wide, signed to Simon. He turned to Şiwoolu.

"You mean to say that we can now return home? Back to Abeokuta?" Simon asked.

Şiwoolu nodded.

She signed again, and Simon's words confirmed what everyone at the table was thinking.

"Won't the assassins be waiting for us?"

Şiwoolu looked at each of his dear ones' faces with a fire they had never seen.

"This informer contacted me. Sunmonu has pulled all his men, including his assassins, back to Abeokuta in readiness for his coronation. Their guards are down. We leave upon my last official trip to Sherbro."

Chapter Sixteen

Sins of the Father
Hastings
Circa 1853

It felt strange to Oşolu to wake up in his old room the next morning and even stranger to see Şomide standing over him. The family had stayed up most of the night, talking about their plans to move back to Abeokuta. Şomide had told everyone how absurd he found the proposition that he resign from his job and relocate to a place he knew nothing about. Oşolu was expected to finish his education at Fourah Bay College in a few months and join the family in Abeokuta.

"Get up, James. We need to talk."

Şomide sat on the edge of the bed. His long legs spread out across the small room comprised of a bed, a study table, a chair, and a wardrobe; it was the same set-up as the college room he had visited few days before. Oşolu sat up and rubbed his eyes, bringing a brooding Şomide into focus.

"What's wrong now?" Oşolu muttered.

Şomide shook his head. "The thing with you is that you never take anything seriously. Did you ever think of what would happen to the shipping business when you all leave for Abeokuta?" he whispered, careful not to wake their parents down the hall.

Oşolu placed his feet on the floor and stretched.

"Don't you have anything to say?" Şomide's big eyes widened in disbelief at his brother's silence.

"We talked about all this last night," Oşolu responded patiently. "Uncle Waltz is going to be managing the business here. Simon and Ireti will be in Sherbro, at least until the baby is old enough to travel, and James Labulo Davies will manage the office in Lagos. His accident during the bombardment was really a blessing in disguise. Now that he is in Lagos full-time, he can coordinate the new farmers he's just employed as well as the transport of goods to the merchant ships at the harbour."

Şomide shook his head. "That all sounds grand, but remember that Uncle Waltz is always traveling."

"He's been in town for the past three months," Oşolu said.

Şomide looked surprised. "Three months? He hasn't visited Hastings all this time."

"Well, he has his place in Freetown. Why come out here when he can be close to the company office and ships?"

Şomide chuckled. "Uncle Waltz, the unrepentant bachelor!"

Oşolu yawned and got up. "You would know if he was in town if you can pull your head out of your engineering textbooks long enough to stop by the Chacha Restaurant. He teaches dance there two nights a week," he said, picking up his towel from the arm of the chair.

"And you would know, wouldn't you? It must be one of the places you frequent," Şomide returned.

Unperturbed by his brother's jabs, Oşolu shrugged,

threw the towel around his neck, and watched as Şomide tapped his feet on the floor. The creases on his head added ten years to his visage.

"Brother, you need not worry about Papa pushing the business onto your shoulders. I'm ready to take it on once I graduate in a few months."

Şomide stood up, facing him. Oşolu was taller by three inches; he had overtaken his older brother when he was ten. Şomide had hated it then and now.

"James to the rescue," Şomide said softly.

Oşolu shrugged and walked to the door. "If you say so. Is that all you woke me up to say?"

Şomide stared at him for a few seconds. "No. I really would like to know where you've been going every evening after classes."

Oşolu placed his hand on the doorknob. "That's really none of your business, brother."

They stared at each other, neither of them willing to back down. A knock on the door caused them to break their standoff; it opened to reveal Dotunu with parted, smiling lips.

"Good, you're both awake! Your father needs to speak with you before he leaves with Simon and Ireti for Sherbro. It's a good thing they came, he'll have company while he travels on official business."

"But, Mama, is that a good idea?" Oşolu asked as they followed her down the hallway.

"What?"

"Papa travelling with this persistent cough?"

"He won't listen to me, Oşolu. You know how he is.

He insists on completing this last task so we can focus on moving as quickly as possible."

Dotunu walked down the hallway with her two sons, outlining the plans for their relocation, oblivious to the storm brewing between the brothers.

Şiwoolu's message was brief, just as Oşolu had expected; his father was a man of few words. He made the two brothers promise to check on their mother, siblings, and Granny Oşuntade while he was away for two weeks. He promised to provide more details about the relocation and the business upon his return.

Şomide pressed him for more information, but his father shook his head with the firmness of one who had dealt with his son's stubbornness for years and told him to be patient.

Oşolu hurried downstairs after the discussion to have breakfast with Granny Oşuntade and the family. Apart from her ailing legs, she did not look a day older than she had ten years ago.

"Maybe it's because I looked old even when I was young and stayed that way," was her usual response when she revealed her age to people who asked and were subsequently surprised.

Oşolu kissed all four women in the house and bid them goodbye. Their mood dampened at the thought of his leaving for weeks again. Dotunu demanded to know what he could be doing on a Saturday; she had expected him to stay at least until after church on Sunday.

"Oh no! I have projects to submit. Lots to do before my final examination," he said, kissing his mother on both cheeks once again. She complained about not seeing him enough as she hurried around the house, filling a bag with a week's supply of provisions. Oşolu showered her with more kisses as he took the bag from her and ran for the front door. Şomide's scowling face was the last thing he saw as he closed it behind him.

Oşolu weaved through the dark, narrow streets of the Quarters, checking every few minutes to see if he was being followed. Mama's warning never to visit this neighbourhood rang in his head as he stepped out of the path of two men, one chasing the other. The houses in these slums were barely bigger than his room in Hastings, yet they were home to half the population of Freetown. The occupants were the undocumented immigrants who had snuck in through the mountains and sea routes off the coast.

Oşolu tried to remember which of the shacks on the slope Magdalene had entered with the burly man, the night he and Stephen had followed her. A child with a big belly, small head, and skinny arms with flies following his shit-smeared buttocks waddled past him.

"Maggie, kam ya!" The demand came from a tall, skinny woman standing with arms akimbo outside a red shack. She was staring at Oşolu.

"Watin?" It was Magdalene's voice; a curtain was pulled back and she stepped out. She gasped on seeing

Oşolu. Devoid of the red rouge, her lips were still pouty with its natural soft pinkness. He had always teased her about it.

Oşolu stepped closer to her. "Magdalene," he said.

She held up her hand. Her gold earrings dangled as she swung her head from side to side. "I told you not to follow me!"

Her voice, soft and low, had not changed since grammar school. The tall, skinny woman started to laugh, throwing her head back in an exaggerated fashion as though she were performing for an audience.

"Loverboy! You kam back?"

Magdalene turned in her direction. "I'll take care of this, Martha."

The woman puckered her lips and blew Oşolu a kiss. "You kin kam back later dis net. Nar ya me dae." She hit the side of her shack next to Magdalene's.

"Come here!" Magdalene grabbed Oşolu's hand and ran down the slope past the shacks. Oşolu did not want her to stop or let go. It had been too long since they had held hands. Finally, she stopped beside a dirty pond filled with debris, panting from the run. Oşolu chuckled.

"Do you need a few more minutes?"

She dropped his hand and glared at him. "Why are you always so stubborn, James? I've told you several times not to follow or look for me again. Do you think I didn't see you at the bar the other day?"

He sighed. "That was Stephen's fault. I told him to act like he was drunk, not to actually get drunk. Why didn't you just come and talk to me?"

"And say what? We've said all that needs to be said." Magdalene crossed her arms over her chest and turned away. Oşolu stared at her thick black hair, which was pulled into a bun on her head. It seemed like a lifetime since his fingers last combed through its wavy texture. She had not allowed him to go any further than that. They were too young, she had maintained, every time he had asked why. Though his fingers itched to swim in the lushness of her hair now, he stilled his hands.

"What do you want me to tell our fathers?" he demanded. "They've been asking again. They know how close we were. I can only keep up this lie for so long."

Magdalene turned around, eyes wide with fear. "You saw my father? Did you tell him where I was?" She grabbed his arm and shouted the same question at him again.

"No! For God's sake, Magdalene, what is going on between you and your father?"

Magdalene turned away and stared into the pond. The edges of her wine-coloured dress dipped into the murky water. A ruckus broke out above them on the slope; it was the two men who had almost run into Oşolu. They whistled and called Magdalene's name.

She looked up and waved at them. "Later, Alfred, Timon! I will see you both later." Her voice had taken on a throaty, seductive note.

The men waved at her and disappeared. When they were alone again, Magdalene turned to Oşolu.

"I will tell you everything, James," she whispered. Her eyes bulged with the weight of the secret she had harboured for so long. "But please, you must promise me something before I tell you."

"What?" His heart hammered against his chest.

She licked her lips.

"What, Magdalene?"

"That you will go back and tell our fathers that you heard that I had been killed in the Quarters."

Oşolu shook his head. "Absolutely not!"

"I'm not finished!" Magdalene cried out.

Oşolu waited as she muttered under her breath. "Finish, then," he said.

"You must also promise me that you will die with the knowledge of what I tell you today." Magdalene looked at Oşolu with such intensity that he gasped. This was a different Magdalene from the one her father used to bring to Hastings – a shy, soft-spoken girl who never asked for anything. As the years went by, he had seen less of her. After grammar school, her father had said she would stay home rather than go on to Fourah Bay College like the rest of their classmates.

Magdalene pulled up her gown as if ready to leave when Oşolu didn't say a word.

"Wait! Let me at least think over the terms of this agreement," he said in a sorry attempt at a joke.

She smiled, but it didn't reach her eyes. "You always found joy in everything, James. I always liked that about you."

"A compliment! Finally!" he chuckled, then sighed. "I promise, Magdalene. What you say here stays between us, forever."

"Alright."

As Magdalene began to unravel the mystery leading to her flight from home two months ago, Oşolu realised for the first time that her eyes had never been happy, even when she smiled.

Making his way back up the slope and out of the Quarters, Oşolu knew he could no longer keep down the pap and akara he had eaten that morning. When he got to Water Street, he stopped to throw up a few steps from the Royal Hospital and Asylum. A man paused and asked if he wanted to go in. He shook his head, too weak to talk. The man called over a girl selling water as he whipped shillings out of his pocket. Oşolu thanked him before splashing the cup of water on his face.

"Go home, young man," the man said, patting him on the back before resuming his walk.

Oşolu's true home was with Magdalene. He felt lost without her and had for a long time. He contemplated what to do; to tell his father would be to betray Magdalene. He leaned against a wall, weighed down by the enormity of what Magdalene had just told him.

"Oşolu?"

Only three people called him Oşolu: his mother, Granny Oşuntade, and Uncle Waltz. The voice was male, and Oşolu knew to whom it belonged.

Waltz strolled up the Portuguese stairs leading from the docks. His once-long hair was now clipped short, the ends curled close to his scalp. His beard, always neatly trimmed, framed his chiselled jawline. He grinned and scaled the last few steps.

"Uncle Waltz," Oşolu said, straightening up to prepare himself for the questions.

"What are you doing here? Did you go to church?" Waltz asked.

Oṣolu chuckled. "It's Saturday, and no, I am not a member of St. George's Cathedral." No one could miss the church with the statue of Tom Peters, the slave from Nova Scotia who had made Salone his home.

Waltz smiled and patted his shoulder. "Young man, what bothers you?"

He always seemed to know when something was wrong. Growing up, he had often taken Ṣomide and Oṣolu out when Ṣiwoolu could not because of his busy work schedule. They had developed a friendship over time.

"Nothing. I, er ... I was just taking a walk," Oṣolu said.

Waltz stared at him. "I see." He smiled and dropped his hand on Oṣolu's shoulder. "I was on my way to have breakfast. Would you care to join me?"

"No, no!" The thought of food made Oṣolu sick. "I just ate. I was actually home overnight, visiting the family."

Waltz's eyes lit up. "You were in Hastings? How is everyone? Your mother, siblings, father?"

"Fine, everyone is fine. I have to be on my way."

Waltz's steady eyes searched Oṣolu's face for a few seconds. "All right, Oṣolu. I know something's going on. You know you can always talk to me about whatever it is."

"Of course. Thank you, Uncle."

Waltz squeezed Oṣolu's shoulder. "Come by Chacha tonight. I will save a table for you and your friend. What's his name again?"

"Stephen."

Waltz laughed. "Yes, Stephen. How could I forget? He was the life of the party last time."

Oşolu smiled, thanked him, and began to walk in the opposite direction.

"Oşolu!" Waltz shouted. Oşolu turned around.

"I'm sorry about your grandfather's passing, but at least something good has come from it," Waltz said.

Oşolu frowned and cocked his head.

"The move to Abeokuta. It's about time," Waltz said.

"How did you know so soon?" Oşolu demanded.

Waltz's eyes lit up when he smiled.

"I really shouldn't have asked, should I?" Oşolu sighed, turning back around.

"See you later?" Waltz asked.

"Maybe!" Oşolu called back.

Oşolu could not stay away from the bar that night even if he had wanted to. He had forgotten to give Magdalene the week's supply of provisions his mother had given him. He usually left it with the server at the bar for Magdalene to pick up, but tonight, after all that he had heard, he felt drawn to see her once more and tell her what was on his mind. He also needed to apologise for his abrupt departure. He was happy to go alone and avoid the ordeal of dragging his drunken friend all the way up the hills of Fourah Bay in the dead of night – Stephen had a study date with a girl he had met in the library.

Oşolu did not have to wait long for Magdalene to enter the bar. She was in her dark blue velvet gown, in the company of Martha and another woman. The third woman was much older and seemed to be in charge. The trinkets on her wrists jingled as she pointed to a table in the centre of the room.

Oṣolu tipped his bowler hat further down his forehead and stared into the frothy glass before him as they filed past. The noise in the smoke-filled room lessened as the men turned to watch the women twirl between the chairs in their large gowns. Oṣolu sighed when Magdalene pulled out a chair and sat with her back to him. Martha's hawk eyes darted to and fro in the darkened room; he had to be careful. The server, Abu, appeared with three glasses for the women and pointed to four men at a table who waved at them. One had a wooden leg. They were sailors in town for a few days; the bar was the best place for most of them to pass the time until their next sail.

Martha and the older woman winked as they raised their glasses to the men, who laughed and clapped each other on the back. Magdalene kept her eyes on the table. The woman reached out and tapped her on the side of the head. She did not look up; her shoulders slumped as Martha and the woman talked loudly and batted their eyelashes in an exaggerated manner. Oṣolu clasped his fingers around his glass, willing his feet to stay put. Magdalene's shoulders began to shake, and he jumped to his feet. Two men walked into the bar and came straight to his table, blocking his passage to the women. They pulled out chairs next to him and sat down. Oṣolu looked across to see the four men standing over the women and he sat down again. The bargaining was quick: soon, the three women followed the four men out. Oṣolu picked up his bag and followed.

It was easy to become invisible in the streets of Freetown when the sun went down; with a port close by, the flow of visitors never ceased. From the eager sailor on his first trip to the Black Continent, to the husband in search of his next erotic fantasy, the night reeked of anticipation. Oşolu plunged into the crowd of pedestrians. Music and laughter escaped from the bars and restaurants, and couples staggered past him down the unlit streets that people whispered about in the daytime.

Oşolu was not surprised when the men led Magdalene and her friends to the low-cost houses rented out to short-term guests. He hid behind a pile of crates and watched them bargain with the older woman. After a few minutes, two of them followed Martha into a green plank house with a vacancy sign hung on the front door. Magdalene followed the man with the wooden leg. The older woman spoke to the last man for several minutes before they walked away towards the Quarters.

Oşolu waited for a few minutes, listening to the moans and creaks emanating from the plank house. It was like this every time he followed Magdalene, but this night had an added element of pain after Magdalene had told him why she had chosen this lifestyle. This night, his heart broke into pieces.

He tiptoed to the side of the house and listened at the first window. Martha and the two men were loud. He moved closer to the second window, hoping it would be Magdalene this time. She was talking quietly to the man.

"You'll do exactly what I paid for!" he shouted.

Oşolu jumped at the sound of a slap. Magdalene gasped as the bed began to creak.

"No! Not like that!" Her voice was muffled. Oşolu tiptoed to the front door and shook the knob. It opened. He ran down the dark hallway to the last room on the left. Magdalene's soft pleas for help were answered with slaps. Oşolu tried the knob to the room and once again, it opened. They were unaware of his entry. The man's trousers were at his ankles, his body pressed behind Magdalene. Her gown was over her head. She grunted in pain as he pushed against her. Oşolu looked about desperately for anything to grab. The only furniture in the room was a chair. He picked it up and broke it over the man's head. He slumped over Magdalene. She froze.

"It's me, James," Oşolu whispered, pushing the thick, hairy body off her. He pulled down her gown and helped her to stand. Magdalene stared at him with tears in her eyes.

"We must go, Magdalene," Oşolu urged.

She shook her head. "I told you not to follow me anymore, James. This," she said, looking down at the still figure on the bed, "is my life now."

Oşolu grabbed her hand and pulled her to the door. "Let's go! We can get away from here, go to Èkó. My family's ship can take us."

Magdalene reached out and touched his cheek. Her finger found his dimple in the dim light of the lamp on the floor, just like it used to years ago when they were still carefree. Oşolu dropped his bag and cupped her face, wishing it was devoid of the kohl eyeliner and red lipstick that made her look older than she was.

"I wish I could," she whispered.

"There's nothing stopping you. Let's go, please."

Something changed in Magdalene's eyes, and she began to nod.

"You're not going anywhere!" the man shouted as he got up. Oşolu pushed Magdalene to the corner and faced him. He swung a sharp object at Oşolu, who dodged and regained his balance. The man yelled and ran towards him. Oşolu jumped over the broken chair, landing a few feet from the window. The man followed, grunting as his trousers, lowered to his ankle and wooden leg, tripped him. He landed on top of the broken chair and spasms shook his body. He gasped and grew limp.

Oşolu looked up at Magdalene in the corner. Her hands shook as she pointed at the body.

"Is he dead? Check him!" she whispered.

Oşolu stepped over the broken pieces of the chair and bent to look. Dark liquid seeped from under the man. Oşolu pulled at him, but something kept holding him down. After several attempts, Oşolu turned him around. He jumped back at the sight. Magdalene sucked in her breath behind him. A leg of the chair was lodged in the man's stomach. His eyes were closed, his body stiff. The only movement was the blood trickling down the corner of his mouth.

"Is he dead?" Magdalene whispered.

"Magdalene?" Martha shouted from the next room. The two men called to their friend.

Oşolu took Magdalene's hand. "We must go."

She shook her head. "No, they'll find us. You go! Go!"

Footsteps hurried out of the next room. Oşolu ran to the window and pushed it open. Magdalene peered down at him.

"I left you the bag of provisions," he whispered. She nodded and closed the window as the door to the room crashed open.

Oşolu ran to the only place he knew no one would come looking. The streets were dark and quiet as he sped down Water Street, down the Portuguese Stairs to the docks. He had played there with Şomide as a child, waiting for the ships to come in. He knew exactly where the *Voyager* would be, right next to the other three ships owned by the company at the end of the docks. It was just as he expected – deserted.

The ship was pitch black, but Oşolu found his way easily down the stairs to the lower level, having spent many years playing there as a child while his parents, Uncle Waltz, and the Davieses talked business. He had mastered every corner of their second home. The smell of palm kernel hit his nose as he turned the doorknob leading to the storage room. His hands felt along the sacks piled against the walls until he found a space big enough to fit into. He pressed his back against the wall and slid to the floor, shivering as a light breeze found its way in through the planks of the ship. The hull rocked and he closed his eyes and sighed.

A floorboard creaked, followed by footsteps.

"James?"

Oşolu sat up when the voice repeated his name. The

figure, which was tall with a muscular build, moved closer until they were inches apart. The eyes that met his sparkled with tears.

"Harry?" Oşolu whispered.

"Brother, what have you done?"

Oşolu hid in the storage room of the *Voyager* for a week. Şomide came back two days after his first visit with news and food.

"A good thing you developed a habit of staying away from home for months. At least your absence won't draw suspicion," Şomide said as Oşolu munched on the bread and fried fish Şomide had taken from the college cafeteria. "We have to talk about what to do. There's nothing out there yet about you being wanted by the police. But that night, when I followed you from school to the bar to *that* place, I remember that other girl running into Magdalene's room and then screaming that she knew it was you. She said something about the provisions you left behind."

Oşolu dropped the slice of bread. "Oh, Martha," he murmured.

"She will go to the police," Şomide whispered. "We must get you out of Freetown."

Oşolu agreed.

Oşolu began to worry when Şomide did not come back for the next three days. A flurry of activity had begun on the ship; workers came with more farm produce, filling up the storage rooms with sacks of palm kernel and cocoa seeds.

It was not long before they entered the room in which he hid, trapping him with more sacks of produce. He could scarcely breathe.

On the fourth day, he heard footsteps enter the room.

"James? James?"

Oşolu tried to push away the blockage in front of him.

"I'm still here!" he called.

"Where?" Footsteps approached.

"Here!" He pushed the sacks again, but they refused to budge. "I'm here!" He shouted at the top of his lungs and pushed with his hands and feet until the sacks moved.

"Shh! Stop the noise, there are still men working on deck!"

The sacks rolled to the ground and Şomide's apprehensive face appeared. Hesitant footsteps approached.

"Who is that?" Oşolu whispered.

Şomide shook his head. "I'm sorry, James. I had to tell them."

The footsteps became louder. They stopped behind Şomide, and two figures appeared.

"Oşolu?" Dotunu whispered. Oşolu looked up. His mother's hand was clasped to her chest as though she were in pain. He scrambled out of his hiding place with arms outstretched. Dotunu fell into his arms, weeping.

"Oşolu, we've been worried sick! The police have plastered your picture all over town," Waltz said, appearing behind her.

"I had to tell them when the police came knocking. As we suspected, Martha told them what happened," Şomide said softly.

"I didn't mean to kill that man," Oṣolu said desperately.

"We know that. You did what had to be done," Waltz said, his eyes fiery in the dark.

Dotunu patted Oṣolu's chest with her hand as she looked up at him. "You must go to Èkó," she said. Looking at Waltz and Ṣomide, she continued, "that will be the best place to hide him. The shipment is almost ready to go to the Marina."

"Yes, you're right," Waltz said. "I will send a telegraph to James Labulo. With his connections there, we can smuggle you from the port to his house in Èkó, and on to Abeokuta to your grandmother, Wuraola."

Dotunu clasped Oṣolu around the waist and hugged him until he gasped for breath.

"Ṣomide told me what happened," she whispered. "I am proud of you, my dear son. So proud." When she raised her head, tears cascaded down her cheeks. "We will soon join you. Olodumare go with you."

Chapter Seventeen

Refuge
Èkó
Circa 1853

The Voyager departed the port of Freetown two days later. Oşolu would never forget Dotunu's face, vacillating between sorrow and pride as she chanted his oriki. When he was younger, he would bury his face in her chest as she rocked him to sleep, chanting those words over him. The day he departed, he held *her* to *his* chest as she chanted them.

"Promise me one thing, Mama," he whispered in her ear.

"Anything, dearest one."

"Promise me you will find Magdalene and get her out of that place."

"Since you have affirmed that her plan is to make enough money to leave Salone, do you think she would be willing to come with us?" Dotunu asked.

Oşolu nodded.

"Then don't worry. The next time we see each other, we will all be together, including Magdalene," Dotunu promised.

Oşolu ground his teeth. "And her father? What happens to that vile man whom everyone holds in such high esteem? Who is going to tell the whole world what he's been doing to his daughter since she could walk?"

Dotunu wiped her face and sniffed. Her eyes flashed with anger. "I will. I should have known something was not right. Every time I asked him to bring her to visit, he did so reluctantly, and then he just stopped." She took a deep breath and raised her chin. "As I live and breathe, he will be brought to justice," she whispered.

Şomide, just inches away, pulled on her arm gently. "If I don't do this, you will never leave, James."

Şomide grabbed Oşolu's shoulders and pulled him in for a hug. "Here," he said as he pulled off the ring on his middle finger. "This is for you. I'm sure Papa would want you to have it."

The scalloped gold ring fell into Oşolu's palm. "I thought you wanted it?" Oşolu asked.

Şomide waved it away as Oşolu continued to protest. Dotunu moved closer and peered down at the ring.

"Oh, this ring! Your father could not stand the sight of it. It reminded him too much of Èkó and that day we were taken. I thought he threw it away years ago," she said.

Şomide looked shame-faced and licked his lips.

Oşolu gasped. "You stole it from Papa?! You told me he gave it to you!"

Şomide raised his finger like the teacher he was and shook his head vehemently. "No, I did not! Like Mama said, Papa couldn't stand the sight of it, so when he threw it in the garbage, I salvaged it."

Oşolu covered his mouth to stop himself from laughing, but Waltz, who was standing close by, could not help the chuckle that escaped him.

"Uncle Waltz," Şomide muttered, visibly embarrassed.

Dotunu smiled at Waltz. His hands were behind his back, his stance attentive to her every need.

"I believe you, Şomide," Waltz said softy, though his lips twitched.

Oşolu pulled Şomide in for another hug and whispered in his ear. "This means you have to come to Abeokuta to get it back."

Şomide patted his back before letting his brother go.

"Say us well to James Junior. He will be expecting you," Waltz said.

"Uncle Waltz." Oşolu stepped across a large sack and held out his hand to Waltz. They shook hands several times.

"Only one person knows you're down here. His name is Lieutenant Savoy, and he's been given clear instructions by James Junior," Waltz said.

"Yes, Uncle Waltz."

Waltz's smile was rueful. "I always knew you would take on more adventures than any of us," he said, glancing at Dotunu. They all chuckled.

"Oşolu, that's a mild way of saying you are always getting into mischief!" Dotunu laughed.

Oşolu gazed at them, grateful for their support.

"Take care of Mama," he said pointedly to Waltz.

"I always have and always will," Waltz said.

Oşolu turned to Dotunu. "Tell Papa—"

"You will tell him whatever it is when you see him in Abeokuta, Oşolu," Dotunu whispered. "We will see you very, very soon."

Oṣolu was in hiding for the length of the journey, which lasted 20 days. Retired Lieutenant Thomas Savoy, a mulatto man from Salone who had fought alongside James Junior on one of the British naval ships during the bombardment of Lagos, came to see him twice a day with a tray of food. They would talk about what was happening in Èkó and around the world as they ate bread and sipped lentil soup.

A few days before the ship arrived in Èkó, Lieutenant Savoy sat on a sack across from Oṣolu, a slim white candle flickering on the floor between them.

"JPL will be happy to see you. Since he's been spending more time in Èkó, he's become homesick."

Oṣolu looked up from drinking his soup. "You mean James Labulo?"

James Labulo was several years older than Oṣolu and a natural leader. He had always led the rest of the neighbourhood children on errands or pranks – whichever took his fancy. Oṣolu remembered the grin that had split his face every time he was caught in some mischief, which was rare. After completing his studies at the Christian Missionary Grammar School in Freetown, he had enlisted as a cadet in the British Navy's West African squadron. He'd trained in seamanship and navigation, progressing from midshipman to lieutenant to captain. James Junior was a household name in Hastings and Salone. Everyone was proud of him for having fought in the war that had ousted King Kosoko, breaking the stranglehold of slave trade in the region. His war injuries had pushed him into retirement at Èkó, much to his parents' relief and delight. They had returned to settle in Ebute Metta years ago among the other Saro – the name given to Yoruba-speaking Christians who came back home from Salone.

Lieutenant Savoy smiled and shook his head. "He doesn't like to be called James Junior anymore, he mentioned something about having his own identity. He prefers JPL – James Pinson Labulo Davies. Pinson is his second name, you know."

"I will try and remember that," Oṣolu nodded.

"We will soon be arriving in Èkó," Lieutenant Savoy added. "I will come for you once the crew has disembarked. It will be dark then."

Lieutenant Savoy shouting orders to the sailors announced their arrival in Èkó. When the ship came to a stop, it took three hours for the crew members to haul barrels and crates out of the storage room next to the one in which Oṣolu hid. Once that room was emptied, one of the sailors rattled the doorknob of Oṣolu's room, calling for someone to open it. From the top of the stairs, Lieutenant Savoy ordered the sailors to leave it until the next day.

Overhead, the port was agog with people shouting in foreign languages and pushing carts of produce and items for sale. The tantalizing aroma of fried food wafted through the wooden boards, reminding Oṣolu that his last meal had been the day before, but he waited patiently for the lieutenant, who returned long after the last sailor had left to find entertainment in town.

"Here," Lieutenant Savoy said, handing Oşolu a buba and şokoto. The last time he had worn a set was probably at the age of thirteen. "It's best you change into these. We want to blend into the crowd here, not stand out."

Oşolu looked down at his European-style long-sleeved white shirt and pants. "They don't dress like this here?" he asked.

"Èkó is a marriage of both the old and the new. But trust me, you will indeed stand out if you wear those clothes. They give off a foreign feel and look, and we still don't know how far the bounty on your head has spread to the other colonies on the coast."

After Oşolu had changed, they took a small boat tied to the side of the *Voyager* to the now empty port. Rolling up the ends of his trousers and tucking his shoes under his arm, Lieutenant Savoy told Oşolu to follow him down the shore towards the light and sound of music in the distance. The music was coming from a storefront; it was the same familiar beat of the Cuban melodies from the Chacha Restaurant Oşolu had often visited at home. Home did not seem so far away after all. Lieutenant Savoy tucked his chin into his chest and walked briskly by the customers laughing over bowls of drinks. Oşolu followed suit. When they had created enough distance between them and the storefront, Lieutenant Savoy looked back.

"There are eyes everywhere. You can't trust anyone, James."

Oşolu nodded and followed him silently down dark streets until they stopped in front of a blue gate and low whitewashed walls decorated with thick columns surrounding a bungalow. Lieutenant Savoy pointed at the orange glow from an open window.

"He's been waiting."

The front door opened, and a man of average height and build stood in the doorway. "Thomas? James?" His voice was deep and welcoming. He opened the door wider and said, "Come in!"

The man shook their hands as they entered. His deep-set eyes smiled at Oşolu, taking him back to the days when they had played under the cotton tree in Hastings after church service.

"My namesake, how are you?" He gave Oşolu a bear hug that belied his stature.

"My parents send their greetings. How are yours?" Oşolu asked, as they followed him a few steps down the dark hallway into a large room lit with glass lamps. A man in a black suit stood beside a long table with an array of dishes.

"They are well. They are bona fide Lagosians now. Serra Lyoa feels like a lifetime ago to them." He nodded to the man in the suit. "My butler, Mr. Baidoo, will attend to us tonight."

Mr. Baidoo's long, slim face was expressionless as he bowed stiffly in his black suit from the waist, one hand behind his back and a white cloth neatly thrown over the arm in front of him.

"Please wash up in the outhouse and come back in for supper. You must be hungry," JPL urged.

The two followed the silent butler down the hallway lined with black and white pictures of JPL with his parents and siblings, another in his navy uniform with Her Majesty Queen Victoria, and one with his colleagues standing in rows in England. Mr. Baidoo led them through a door to the small building in the backyard and waited at the door while they eased themselves into separate compartments. They returned minutes later and sat at the table with JPL at the head. He asked about everyone he could remember during the meal. His favourite was Oṣuntade.

"We used to tell tales about her being a witch, you know," he said.

Oṣolu chuckled. "She knew and encouraged us to keep spreading them," he said.

JPL's shoulders shook with laughter. "She made Hastings very interesting. Will she also be coming? I did not see her name in the telegram Uncle Waltz sent."

"Not now, maybe later. Her health has been a bit poor."

JPL nodded and turned to the lieutenant. "Thank you for your loyalty, Lieutenant. I will never forget this."

"I am always at your service," Lieutenant Savoy said. He nodded at Oṣolu. "Though I don't know the circumstances that brought him here, this young man seems to have a good head on his shoulders."

"All Jameses do!" JPL said, leaning forward to pat Oṣolu's back.

They all laughed, temporarily forgetting the arduous journey to Abeokuta that lay ahead. After supper, Lieutenant Savoy thanked JPL for the meal.

"I leave at the crack of dawn tomorrow, Captain," he said, rising from his seat.

JPL stood and shook his hand. "I will forever be in your debt, old friend."

Oşolu stood up and came forward to hug the man who had saved his life.

"I hope to hear only good things about you, young man," Lieutenant Savoy said, pumping his hand.

"You shall, Lieutenant. Thank you," Oşolu said.

Mr. Baidoo, who had been waiting in the shadows, moved towards the door and the lieutenant followed.

"Sit, James," JPL said as the door closed. "We must discuss next steps." He intertwined his fingers and laid them on the table. "First, you must stop calling yourself James. The Freetown police are looking for a James Coker. You must change your name. What is your Yoruba name?"

Oşolu cleared his throat. "Oşolu. It's Oşolu."

"Good. And you do remember your father's true surname, do you not?" He smiled.

"Of course! Mama never let me forget it. It's Okikilu."

"There we have it, then! Henceforth, you will be called Oşolu Okikilu. Tomorrow we will begin our journey to Abeokuta. Your grandmother is still alive and well. She has not been told yet that you and your parents are coming. She has had her hopes up for so long that we didn't want to disappoint her should things not go as planned."

"I understand," Oşolu nodded.

"But first," JPL said, raising a finger, "I must stop at one of my debtors' stores here in Marina. He's been dodging me for more than a year now, and he has no idea I have fully recovered from my wounds since the bombardment and can check on him. With this new cocoa farming that I am venturing into, I need all the funds I can lay my hands on."

JPL pushed back his chair and got up. "Mr. Baidoo will show you to your room. May God keep us until tomorrow, Oṣolu," he said, holding out his hand.

Oṣolu got up and grasped it. "Thank you, JPL. May God keep us until then."

The next morning, Mr. Baidoo walked silently behind JPL and Oṣolu as they approached the stores lining the busy street in Marina. They stopped in front of the store with the dangling signboard marked M.T. Agents. The wooden double doors were thrown open, and a few feet into the hovel sat a wooden desk to the left side of the room with a chair behind it. JPL frowned and looked around.

"That rascal! How could he have gotten wind that I would be stopping by here today?"

A shadow stirred on the floor behind the chair.

"There's someone there," Oṣolu whispered as he took a step closer. When the shadow began to get up, JPL pulled him back and signalled to Mr. Baidoo, who seemed to have been waiting for this. He felt for something in his pocket and sprang forward with it in his hand.

"Who is that?" The voice shook with age.

"Show yourself!" Mr. Baidoo shouted, pointing a shiny black object at the unseen enemy.

The shadow transformed into a figure, flung back the cloth on its head, and stood up. Mr. Baidoo raised the object in the air as a withered woman's face appeared.

"Stop!" Oşolu shouted. He imagined his grandmother, Wuraola, looked just like this – small and willowy with sparse grey hair and thick grey eyebrows arched over the most knowing eyes he had ever seen.

The woman stepped forward and blinked multiple times when the sun's rays hit her eyes.

"It is fine, Mr. Baidoo, you can step back," JPL said to his butler, who had a crazed look in his eyes. He stood to attention.

The old woman's watery eyes shifted to the two men. "Welcome, my sons. Are you looking for Oriade?"

"Good morning, Mama. Yes, who are you?"

The crone cupped one hand in the palm of the other and shrugged. "I ask myself that most days now," she said softly. "Some days I am Oriade's mother, others I am just someone he fears will tell all his secrets."

JPL frowned and looked around the room. "Is he here? Is this where you sleep?"

She shrugged her thin shoulders under the buba again. "Two days ago, he locked the house and brought me here to stay. All he said was that he had to go and teach someone a lesson."

The old woman stepped forward, tripping over the cloth she had flung away seconds before. Oşolu reached out and grabbed her outstretched arms in time. She gasped and looked up at him as he steadied her.

"Don't I know you?" she asked.

"No, Mama, I don't think so." He pulled the cloth gently from under her feet and folded it. "Here," he said, placing one hand over the clothing and the other under it.

The rays from the sun fell on the scalloped ring Şomide had given him. The old woman touched it and instantly whipped her head up to look at him.

"This ring, from whom did you get it?"

"It was my father's," Oşolu said, watching the changing expressions on her face.

Her eyes widened. "I thought so!" she shouted with the force of someone half her age. "You are the son of the young king, the Alake of Ęgba Kingdom who went missing. You look just like him. I gave him this ring!"

Open-mouthed, JPL asked her, "Mama, are you sure?"

The woman hissed and threw him an angry look. "Do I look crazy? I said I gave Oşiwoolu, son of Alade Okikilu this ring, the day he came to the Marina with his pregnant wife."

Oşolu staggered backward.

"Are you all right, Oşolu?" JPL asked as both he and Mr. Baidoo grabbed his arms.

Oşolu nodded and looked at the old woman, whose eyes had not strayed from his.

"Is what she says true?" JPL asked, waiting for Oşolu to regain his balance.

"Yes. Mama has told me this story too many times. I am the one with whom Mama was pregnant."

JPL took Oşolu's hand and stared at the ring. "This and Mama's testimony might be the key to securing the throne again," he said softly.

The old woman spoke. "But another whose hands are not clean is eager to take the throne," she whispered.

"We know, Mama—"

She held up her hand. "But did you know it will happen in ten days, not in a month as earlier announced? Now that the last living council member who selected Oṣiwoolu is dead, the one who has had his eyes on the throne can claim it. This is the reason my son has gone to Ake Palace in Abeokuta."

"What is Oriade's business with that?" JPL's voice shook the room.

The woman's eyes filled with tears. "He is deeply involved. Please forgive my son for his hand in all this." She sighed. "Oriade can hide his true nature when he is in his right mind, but when the palm wine takes control, he confesses all, and he has been drinking a lot of late." Her voice caught in her throat and she paused.

Oṣolu took her hand. "Forgive your son for what?"

"Forgive Oriade for his greed, and please believe that his business partner also bears the blame! If only they had not met that fateful night in the forest. The night that man with the clubbed foot sold his soul and began to steal his own people for riches!"

Oṣolu gasped as the revelation hit him. "So Sunmonu was behind the kidnappings in Abeokuta, and not just our capture? He was behind everything?" She nodded.

JPL whistled softly and signalled to Mr. Baidoo. "Thank you, Mama. Here, use this to buy something to eat."

He dug his hand into his pocket and dropped a shilling into her palm.

Her thanks followed them down the street, which was filling up with people.

"We go to Abeokuta now?" Oṣolu asked.

"Yes, but first I must send an urgent telegram to your parents, telling them what we've just learned. They must come as quickly as they can. I mean, they must drop everything and come!"

The message in the telegram was short:
CORONATION IN TEN DAYS-(STOP)-NEW INFORMATION TO STOP IT-(STOP)-MEET US IN AKE-(STOP)-

Chapter Eighteen

The Returnees
Abeokuta
Circa 1853

The journey to Abeokuta through Ota took two days. They rented a horse-drawn cart from Èkó to Ota, but from the look on JPL's face it would have been better and faster had they walked. The horse had a mind of its own, deciding to graze numerous times along the way, and their many attempts to make the owner beat the horse with his whip fell on deaf ears. He preferred to croon in its ear and coax it along. By the time they arrived Ota it was night, and Oşolu could hardly recognise recognise the small mud building or the gangly man running down the dusty road with flailing arms. The last time Oşolu had seen Demilade was 12 years ago, waving from the ship carrying missionaries and artisans on the first Niger expedition.

"Welcome home, dear son! We have been waiting!"

Demilade clasped Oşolu to his chest and cried tears of joy. He thanked JPL and gave Mr. Baidoo a cursory nod before ushering them in. The house was no more than a large room with a bench and bedding in a corner. There were no signs of a woman's touch.

Demilade went out and returned minutes later with three small bowls of water, which they gulped down their parched throats. "I am making some food in the back. It will soon be ready," he said as he sat on the mat.

"Thank you, Elder. You are cooking the food? You still live by yourself?" JPL asked, looking around the room.

Demilade shrugged. His face had filled out, but his eyes still darted about as though in search of something or someone, just as they used to in Salone.

"What do you expect? I have not lost hope that Labakẹ will one day return as I did."

Oṣolu glanced at JPL, who merely sighed and nodded. "I pray so," he said.

Demilade's face brightened. "I was surprised when JPL here told me you were coming first. I thought you were all travelling as a family. When will your parents arrive?"

"Soon, but..." Oṣolu looked to JPL again and refrained from speaking further.

"Elder, there has been a development," JPL said softly. Demilade looked quizzically at him.

"There was an accident and err, Oṣolu had to flee Freetown."

"What accident?!" Demilade cried. "Is the Kabiyesi all right?" His eyes widened as JPL told him what had occurred. When he finished, they sat in silence.

"Hmm," he finally said, shaking his head. "Why this? Why now?" he murmured, looking at Oṣolu. "Just when things were coming together."

"Nothing is lost, Elder. All plans are still in place," JPL said.

Demilade sighed. "You are right. Let us focus on what needs to be done: we leave for Iporo Ake village tomorrow, to Maami Wuraola's house. But first, let me tell you what has been happening in Abeokuta. We must be careful as we return."

Iporo Ake was a vast contrast to Hastings and Freetown. Clay huts littered the dusty, intertwining roads, and heads peeked from behind mat-covered doorways as they passed. The three of them followed Demilade, who walked with the confidence of one who knew where he was going.

"We are almost there!" Demilade called, pointing to a compound in the horizon. The moment he dropped his hand, dust began to rise from the ground. It swirled in the air, blowing debris in their faces and path as they ran.

"The compound is not far; can you see over there?" Demilade shouted above the howling wind, running towards the three huts about ten feet away. As they got closer, Oṣolu could see the weeds that had, in the distance, looked like hand painted designs on the walls of the huts. The worn thatched roofs shook from the force of the wind. The four of them paused at the entrance to the compound, marked by two banana trees that stood still, unaffected by the elements. They stepped into the compound and gasped at the stillness within. They had entered another world, free of the chaos they had just experienced.

Oṣolu blinked and looked around. His father had described this place many times. The middle hut would have been his grandmother's; the one to his left, his father's; and the largest to the right, his grandfather's.

"Do you know who that is?" JPL asked, nudging Demilade with his elbow.

A woman stood in the doorway of the middle hut with her hand shading her eyes.

"Of course! That is Idowu. She has been Şiwoolu's mother's caregiver for many years."

The woman's eyes widened as they fell on Oşolu. "Ehn? Who is this?" She took a step back, shouted, "Wuraola! Wuraola!" and ran back into the hut. Seconds passed and then they heard footsteps moving within.

"Welcome," a woman whispered. It was the same one in the doorway again. "Wuraola has been expecting you." Her eyes fell on Oşolu. She stepped out with hands on her waist. Patches of grey decorated her short hair.

JPL threw Demilade a questioning look.

"I have not been here to tell them anything!" he said, shaking his head.

"Wuraola has been expecting you. All of you." She pointed to each one. "The west winds have brought the four," she whispered.

Wood beat the ground within the hut. "Let them in!" The voice was firm. It reminded Oşolu of his mother's.

Idowu stepped away from the door. "She has waited too long," she murmured. "Go in!"

Ignoring JPL's advice to be cautious, Demilade grabbed Oşolu's hand and entered. The dark room smelled of herbs Oşolu recognised all too well. They sat in three pots lined on the side of the hut. Among them was agbo, the medicinal herb that his mother had made him and his siblings drink to cleanse their bodies once every quarter.

"Come closer, Şiwoolu," the figure on the stool called out. She held a cane in both hands between her feet.

Oşolu stopped, but Demilade gently pushed him forward.

"She doesn't know yet. Just go," he whispered.

Oşolu stepped over the steaming pot from which the smell of herbs emanated and took two more steps until he was inches from her. She held out her hands and the stick clattered to the floor. Oşolu knelt by her feet, and her hands found his face. She groaned as they moved over his eyes, nose, and head. The groans became increasingly louder as she massaged the contours of his face. Then he saw the tears that welled up in her still eyes.

"Is this a cruel joke? This is not my son. This is not my son," she repeated slowly.

Oşolu placed his hands over hers as the tears fell. "No, it's not Şiwoolu. It's Oşolu, your son's son," he said.

She grabbed his hands and squeezed them. "Şiwoolu's son?" She sighed. "So the oracle did not lie. The west winds brought you," she said, looking up with blank eyes, and pointed at each as though she could see as clearly as they did. "And you, you, and you."

The three men crouched and greeted her.

"Maami, I hope we meet you well," Demilade said.

Her hands touched Oşolu's face again.

"My son's son is here, but where is his father? I have waited too long. These bones are weary. It is time I lay them down to rest."

The tears fell down Oşolu's face as he patted her wrinkled hands. He turned to Demilade. "Nobody told me she was blind."

"Wuraola does not need eyes to see. She is the reader of hearts and seer of the unseen," Idowu said from the doorway.

Wuraola looked to the three men behind Oṣolu. "Did you not pass by the villagers? Did you not feel their warmth?" she asked with a dry chuckle. "They have made my life a misery here in Iporo Ake. But can I blame them? If they didn't, Sunmonu's henchmen would have destroyed them. The few that stood up against him have since grown cold in the grave, and the ones that appeared friendly only wanted to get close enough to kill me." She paused and took a deep breath. "That sorcerer, Makinde, spread rumours that my son was cursed and was the cause of the disappearances in the villages. Cursed! When he went missing in Èkó with my dear daughter-in-law and grandson, Ṣomide, it gave credence to the rumours. I begged the council to be patient and told them that my son would come back, that he would eventually return."

The tears fell in fat droplets down Wuraola's lined cheeks. "Then news reached us that they had all been captured – my own child! And Dotunu, I warned her not to go, especially when she was pregnant, but she argued that she still had one more moon before the baby came and she was sure to give birth late again. And my grandson Ṣomide, ah!" She hit her chest and raised a finger to the roof. "Betrayal from a friend, a kin, Sunmonu! Somehow, he pushed himself to be next in line to be king. That was when I knew it was he! If not for the oracle who said my son was not dead and the crown should not be given to another, that murderer would have been king long before now."

"Grandmother, please don't upset yourself," Oṣolu whispered as he lowered her finger.

"But even the voice of the oracle was not enough to stop Sunmonu's scheming ways," Wuraola continued. "It was Ṣodẹkẹ and Elemere Keṣi who stood by me. They were the ones who stopped Sunmonu from ascending to the throne. He had bought almost all the members of the council by giving them lands and goods. Even Sagbua Okukenu, the new council head who initially refused to take anything from him, has bowed to the pressure from the others." The ends of her buba flapped as she lifted her thin arms. "But now that they are both dead, I am once again deserted. No son, no kin ... until now."

Oṣolu wiped her tears with his hand.

"K'abọ ọmọ mi," she welcomed him, peering into his face, and for a moment he felt she could see him. "So the west winds have brought not my son, but my son's son."

"Yes, Maami," he said.

She held out her arms and drew Oṣolu into an embrace.

"Welcome home, son of my son. Welcome home." She looked behind him. "Thank you for bringing him. It appears the gods are truly not on Sunmonu's side. He moved the coronation date closer for fear of any interruption, but here we have the heir to throne. We must go to Ake tomorrow."

JPL shook his head. "Maami, but this is not Ṣiwoolu. He is on his way here."

"Hmm, Ṣiwoolu." Wuraola gave a wan smile and clasped Oṣolu's hand to her chest. Her heartbeat fluttered so lightly that he could hardly feel it.

"When the oracle told the ogboni council that my son was not dead, they also foretold that the west winds would bring the four and that one of them had the rightful claim to the throne. We always assumed it would be Oṣiwoolu; this is why the ogboni council would not allow Sunmonu to be crowned. But you are the four," she said pointing to each one of them. "Now that the west winds have brought the four, we must go to the palace in Ake."

She turned towards the doorway and called Idowu. "Prepare them something to eat. We leave for Ake tomorrow!"

Idowu bowed her head in Oṣolu's direction, turned on her heels, and disappeared amid protests that Ṣiwoolu was the true king.

Laughter rang out from the kitchen once again, and Dotunu looked up from folding the last piece of clothing beside her and smiled.

"Abby, Magdalene! I hope you've finished packing up those pots like I told you to at the crack of dawn! It's almost suppertime, and Ṣomide will soon be here to load the cart for tomorrow."

The two paused and then broke out in giggles. Dotunu shook her head as she got up and placed the last of Ṣiwoolu's shirts in the large metal trunk on the floor. She looked around the emptied parlour, surprised at the sadness she felt. She had always thought it would be a day of joy when she left Salone and returned to Abeokuta.

"Mama," Abigael said softly.

Dotunu turned to see Abby's and Magdalene's heads appear around the doorframe. Abby's eyes danced with excitement, and Magdalene, her face free of the red rouge on her lips, looked almost as young as Abby. Dotunu had to remind herself that Magdalene was in fact a few months older than Oṣolu.

"Are you finished?" Dotunu asked, walking towards them.

Magdalene giggled. "We finished a long time ago," she said, stepping into the room. "Well done here! So all we're waiting for is Harry and the cart to arrive tomorrow?"

"Yes. Two more days and Şiwoolu will be back."

Dotunu smiled at Magdalene as she was reminded once more why Oṣolu loved her. Her thick hair was plaited into braids and coiled into a bun at the nape of her neck. The dress that Dotunu had given her when she had fled the Quarters, a beige cotton dress with a cream lace overlay in front, fit her like a glove. The day Şomide had brought the news of Oṣolu hidden away in the *Voyager* was the very day he had brought Magdalene back to Hastings to stay with them. Her heart still bled at the thought of Godwin free in Freetown, though she had gone with a statement from Magdalene to report the years he had spent abusing his only daughter. She would never forget the look in his eyes when they stood face to face in the police station and she accused him. All he had said was, "Who will ever believe a prostitute over a respected man in this community?" She remembered shouting in his face, "Wait until your boss gets back! You will be disgraced!"

Magdalene ran her hands over the folded clothing and then reached forward to pull the top of the trunk down and latch it. Abby skipped around the room, humming a tune.

"Where is Daniel?" Dotunu asked, frowning.

Abby stopped and looked sheepishly, hands behind her. Magdalene looked out through the window.

"Abby, where is your brother? The last thing I told him to do was bring the rest of his belongings from his room.

Abigael scratched her head. "Hmm ... he told me to tell you he would be back really soon," she muttered.

Dotunu wagged her finger. "You children have started again, covering up for each other! Where did he go?"

A clatter of hooves sounded close to the house.

"Is that—" Dotunu began to say as the two girls ran to the window and looked out.

"It's Harry ... and Uncle Waltz!" Abigael shouted, hopping from one foot to the other. "He hasn't been here in ages, Mama!"

Dotunu got to the window just as Şomide and Waltz climbed off the horse-drawn cart, walked briskly into Waltz's house, and closed the door.

"What is going on?" she wondered.

Abigael shrugged and looked through the window again.

"Why is Şomide here a day earlier than planned, and why is he going into Waltz's house?" Dotunu asked, breaking out in a sweat.

Magdalene took her hand. "I'm sure it's nothing,"

she said. "They probably got a good deal on the cart and decided to come earlier."

Dotunu nodded as her eyes moved back to the house. It was nearing dusk, and across the street, several homes had lit their oil lamps, but the house next door stayed dark.

"Maybe I should go over there," she said, pulling her hand from Magdalene's.

"No, no," Magdalene responded. "Let me go. Abby, stay with your mother."

Abigael shrugged. "All right."

Magdalene nodded and walked to the door.

"Look, they are coming out!" Abigael shouted, pointing at the window.

Dotunu moved closer until her nose was pressed against the windowpane. Her chest began to beat as though it would jump out of her chest when Oşuntade appeared in the doorway.

"Why is she out of her bed? She knows better than to strain those legs!"

Dotunu's legs, though, were the ones that shook beneath her as Abigael ran to the door and Magdalene greeted the newcomers.

"Is Dotunu in?" Waltz's voice was soft. During their last discussion in Freetown, they had agreed that he would meet them at the harbour in two days to bid them farewell. Dotunu licked her suddenly dry lips and wiped her moist hands on her gown.

Magdalene opened the door wide for the three to enter, and Dotunu gasped at what she saw – drawn, tear-streaked faces and red eyes looked back at her.

"What has happened to my son?" she whispered.

Abigael grabbed Şomide's hand and shook it. "What? Where is James?!" she screamed.

Şomide touched her arm and shook his head, his eyes on Dotunu, who stood like a statue. Oşuntade, leaning on the cane in her hand, walked towards her.

"Dotunu." Her voice was croaky as she wiped at the tears racing down her cheek.

Dotunu rolled her hands into fists and gasped for breath.

"Dotunu, please." Waltz took two steps and was beside her. He placed his arm at her back and looked to Oşuntade. "There is no easy way to say this."

Şomide's shoulders began to shake uncontrollably and Abigael grabbed him around the waist. Oşuntade took another step and stood before Dotunu. Her eyes filled with fresh tears.

"It is not Oşolu. A telegram came and he is safe in Èkó. It is Şiwoolu."

Dotunu searched her face and knew. "He is dead."

It was difficult, but JPL was able to convince Wuraola that they would be able to bring the entire family from Èkó in enough time to stop the coronation. Based on his calculations, he was sure they were already on the ship and on their way. Wuraola agreed grudgingly, but only after JPL repeatedly answered her recurring question: "Are you sure Şiwoolu will come?"

JPL and Mr. Baidoo left the next day with a promise

to return with the family, while Demilade vowed to stay with Oşolu. Wuraola would not let him out of her sight. She found an excuse to take him around the compound. Her blindness did not stop her from pointing out places his father used to sit or eat. Years of living alone had made her familiar with her surroundings. Her hands would go up to his face many times during their conversations as she asked about his siblings and told him how she could not wait to meet them.

Oşolu felt close to his father when sleeping in his hut. He could tell that his belongings had been left untouched for too long. The moment he entered the building, his head was crowned with cobwebs and his nose assailed by the still, stale air. A sleeveless brown dashiki dangled on a nail on the wall; beneath it, a black calabash filled with hardened paste was covered in an intricate spider web design.

"What are you looking at?" Wuraola asked behind him.

"It's a calabash with some type of paste."

She smiled. "Ah, that. Do you see the dashiki on the wall? That was the attire your father wore to the emergency council meeting the day Alade was selected to be the Alake. That paste was used to paint his face like those of all the soldiers when they went into battle. I have so much to tell you! Come!"

And she did. From dawn till dusk, Wuraola told her grandson about her life and that of the family. First, she took him to the middle of the compound, where blue flowers sprouted from the ground, shaped in a perfect circle the size of two coconuts. She bent over them, calling to Idowu, "When last did you water these flowers?" Idowu ran out from the backyard with a large pot, apologizing profusely. Wuraola smiled as Idowu emptied the full pot of water on the flowers.

"Yes, thank you. Now, Alade, you can continue to flourish where you are," she said softly. Leaning on her cane again, she bent down and caressed the flowers. "This is where your grandfather is buried," she said as Oṣolu helped her to stand once more. "When I die, I will be laid next to him, right there."

Wuraola smiled and then began to tell stories about Ṣiwoolu: how he had been the only child of seven that had survived to adulthood, how he had been born with the umbilical cord around his neck and for that reason his second name was Aina, and especially how she had doted on him, taking him everywhere she went. When Oṣolu laid his head to sleep on the mat padded with wrappers at night, his mind wandered to these tales and he said a quick prayer for the family to hurry. With each day that passed, he could tell that his grandmother grew more impatient. Her cane tapped repeatedly on the ground as she sat on the bench outside her hut and looked out into the road, muttering to herself.

On the evening of the eighth day, while she, Demilade, and Oṣolu sat on the bench outside her hut, she spoke up.

"We must prepare to go tomorrow."

"Maami, it is not yet time!" Demilade insisted.

"Not yet time? Tell me, when will it be time? The time is now! For all we know, Sunmonu has already crowned himself king."

"Please, Maami, they will be here soon," Oşolu pleaded. "If by this time tomorrow they are not, we will leave at the crack of dawn on the day of the coronation."

"Swear it!" Wuraola demanded.

"Maami, I am a Christian. I cannot swear."

Wuraola chuckled. "I knew you would say that. You are one of those returned Saros who took on the white man's religion. All right, promise me then."

Oşolu gulped and looked away.

"I promise you, Maami," Demilade said.

She nodded and got up to retire for her siesta. Oşolu moved closer to Demilade on the bench and looked towards the road.

A lizard approached the entrance to the compound, stopping just before the two banana trees. It started and stopped many times while they watched in disbelief. It was as though an invisible line only it could see prevented it from advancing. After a few more attempts, it turned around and left. Demilade glanced at him.

"It seems your grandmother has fortified herself."

"Fortified?"

Demilade nodded and sat up on seeing a figure appear at the entrance. It was Idowu holding a trap with bush meat. She greeted them and walked to the backyard. Demilade looked knowingly at Oşolu and pressed his lips together. By the time the sun began to set, the aroma from Idowu's ila alasepo, soup made with okra, shrimp, fish and meat delicacies, was teasing their nostrils.

The next day did not bring the family and by evening, Wuraola was instructing Idowu to pack a few snacks for their short journey to Ake, which would only last a couple of hours. When she paused by the bench on which Demilade and Oṣolu sat, she said, "We have waited long enough for your parents to come. Sunmonu has taken from us twice – first my husband, then your father. No more. We must take back what is ours. Prepare to leave before daybreak tomorrow."

The wind whipped around the slight figure staring into the horizon at the bow of the naval ship. Her hands shook as she held on to the railing.

"Şiwoolu, this is not how we planned this. You were supposed to be here, beside me, when we returned to our home," Dotunu whispered, filled with sorrow. She closed her eyes and imagined him shipwrecked on an obscure island, his life ebbing away.

Footsteps echoed on the deck and paused. Dotunu wiped the tears away as the person drew closer. The figure stood behind her but said nothing, and she was grateful. The wind blew harder, whipping the folds of her dress up and around her. She pressed her hands on it until the gusts subsided.

"You should come back down. I don't want you catching a cold."

Dotunu turned and nodded at Waltz.

"We will be there in an hour or so," he added.

"Do you think we will have enough time to get from there to Abeokuta?" Dotunu asked. "JPL's telegram said we had only ten days; we have but one left now."

"Don't worry," Waltz reassured her. "Let's just thank

God this naval ship travels with such great speed."

"Yes, the governor gave it to us as thanks for Şiwoolu's service." The sob caught in Dotunu's throat and she looked away into the horizon just as the sun began to rise. "Will we make it?" she asked again, grabbing Waltz's shirt, her fingers grazing the buttons. He placed his hands over hers, his eyes burrowing into hers.

"I promise you, Dotunu, we will make it. But we will have to leave the children and Magdalene at Charlotte and James's house in Ebute Metta in order to make good time."

Dotunu sighed. "I wish all my children were with me."

"Şomide had to go and get his father's body, you know we couldn't leave that to Simon and Ireti, not with her expecting so soon. Come, let me take you down." He pulled her gently towards the stairs.

An hour later, a downcast JPL was waiting at the port with two carts and drivers – one to take Abigael, David, and Magdalene to Charlotte and James's house; the other to take JPL, Dotunu, Waltz, and Mr. Baidoo to Abeokuta. "We will ride all day and night until we get there," he said as the horse began to move.

Demilade's voice rose and fell in prayer all night as he knelt in the centre of the compound and called on God for protection. From inside the hut, Oşolu could also hear the low incantations and soft footsteps of Idowu and Wuraola and smell the incense from the backyard. He tossed and turned on the mat for hours but eventually fell into a sleep beset by a strange dream – the faces of his family members on board a ship, waving at him from the railings. Şiwoolu threw an object to him and Oşolu caught it without thinking. It was the scalloped ring, but it grew bigger and heavier in his hands and transformed into a white beaded crown.

"Papa, no!" he called out as his father's face disappeared and the ship faded. "Papa!" he screamed as he ran into the water. All he heard were his echoes.

"Oşolu!"

He startled awake.

"What ails you, king-to-be?" Wuraola asked, standing above him. She seemed to float in her white aşo oke wrapper and head tie with its fringed ends shaking as she moved her head. Cowries, wrapped around her wrists and ankles, tinkled as she took little steps around him.

"N ... Nothing. Are we leaving already?"

"We must. Idowu will bring you the outfit you will wear. Hurry, who knows if they have already conducted the coronation in secret?"

She stepped towards the doorway.

"Grandmother!" Oşolu shouted.

She paused and turned.

"I am not ready for this," he whispered.

Wuraola's chest heaved as she sighed. "I know, Oşolu. How could you have known this responsibility would fall upon your shoulders so early in life, just as it did on your father's?" She walked towards Oşolu with her hand outstretched and found his head with ease. She caressed it slowly.

"Do not fear what the enemy will do, rather, be more

afraid of your own conscience. It will haunt you forever if you do not rise to fight evil when you have the chance."

Oṣolu lifted his head to look at her. Wuraola's eyes blazed with a fire that kindled one in his soul, and finally his mind was made up.

Oṣolu's heart beat faster as he emerged from the hut, the coral beads weighed heavily on his neck and wrists. The heavily woven white agbada over his shoulders rolled down his arms and he held on to the carved stick Idowu pressed into his hands.

"How does he look?" Wuraola asked Demilade who was waiting for them.

Demilade's mouth was agape. "Like his father. Just like his father," he whispered.

Wuraola chuckled and held out her hand. Oṣolu placed it on his arm.

"Idowu!" Wuraola called out.

"I'm where you left me o!" Idowu shouted from where she sat on the ground behind them in the compound, grinding pepper with the stone. The rising sun shone on her face as she looked up at Oṣolu. "Look at how he resembles his father. He wore this very outfit on the day of his coronation," she said softly. "Take back what is yours!" She shook her two fists in the air.

Wuraola nodded and beat her cane on the ground. "Son, let us go!" she said, tugging on his arm. "Every moment we delay, we risk being too late."

Demilade made the sign of the cross as they followed him out of the compound.

"The gods go with you!" Idowu said and got up to watch them leave until they became specks in the distance. Whispering prayers, she returned to the grinding stone on the ground. Her head bobbed to the music in her head as she knelt over the stone and rolled the grinder over the small peppers repeatedly. Then she stopped abruptly, hearing shouts down the road. She jumped to her feet and ran to the entrance. Dust rose from the ground behind the advancing figures and Idowu stepped back into the compound.

"So these hateful villagers won't desist," she muttered, untying her wrapper and retying it firmly across her chest. She snapped her fingers at the four figures she could now make out and walked towards them.

"Maami!" The voice was distinctly a woman's. She repeated her calls for mother until she was upon Idowu, grabbing and shaking her shoulders.

"Where is Maami? Where is Oşolu? Are they here?"

Idowu pried the woman's hands off her and stared her down until she was quiet. By then three men were by her side, two of whom she recognised. Her face swung back to the woman before her and she gasped and grabbed her shoulders in return.

"Ah! Ah! It is you! Our queen! Dotunu, daughter of Elemere Keşi!"

Dotunu burst into tears. "Yes, Idowu! It is me!"

They hugged and then Idowu pushed her away.

"There is no time to waste! Wuraola and Oşolu have

gone to Ake. They have gone to stop that traitor from becoming king."

"Let us go then!" Dotunu shouted, pulling at her hand.

Idowu shook her head. "No. I must stay here and watch over you all with prayers. Wuraola has told me what I must do."

Dotunu looked at Waltz and JPL, who both nodded.

"I still know the way to the palace. Let's go!" she said, turning on her heels, and they followed, Idowu's incantations trailing them down the dusty path.

Half an hour into the journey, Oşolu and Demilade stopped for Wuraola to rest. Though she argued that she was fine, Oşolu saw her wince when she raised her left leg. Even Demilade had slowed his pace.

"Let's stop there!" Oşolu pointed to a dilapidated stall with sparse produce on its table a few feet in front of them. A girl who looked not a day older than Abigael ran from behind the stall and knelt before them as they approached.

"May we sit on your bench for some time to rest?" Oşolu asked.

The girl undid her head tie and dusted the bench. When they were seated, she asked if they wanted some water.

"What a well-trained child you are," Wuraola said as she looked in her direction.

The girl grinned. "I must be, knowing that it is you, Maami," she quipped.

Wuraola smiled. "Is that so? Who am I, then?"

"Hmm, Maami! You are the king's mother, mother of the true heir to the throne of Ẹgba Kingdom, of course!"

Her eyes wandered to Oṣolu and remained on the coral beads around his neck.

Wuraola nodded. "You are wise, dear child." She reached into the air in search of the girl. The latter moved closer and lowered her head until it touched Wuraola's hand. All were silent as the old woman prayed for the child.

"Get up now," Wuraola said.

The girl ran back behind the stall and returned with bowls filled with water, curtseying each time she handed a bowl to one of the travellers. When she finished and turned to leave, she looked out into the road and murmured to herself.

"What is it?" Oṣolu asked as he rose.

The girl pointed. "They are running. Four of them, very fast!"

He shaded his eyes with his hands and looked. It was hazy and difficult to see, but there was movement. Four figures advanced, shouting and waving.

"Who is that? Are our enemies after us?" Demilade asked, springing from the bench.

"Four of them. One is a woman," Oṣolu said as he strained to see.

"Ha!" Demilade shouted.

"Shh!" Wuraola said calmly and tapped her cane on the ground. She shook her head. "These are not enemies, you will see."

The figures drew closer – close enough that Oşolu could see the cut of their clothing. The woman's gown, which reminded him of the dresses women wore in Freetown, floated around her as she ran. Her long braids beat her shoulders as she waved her arms at them in a frantic manner. Her lips moved, but they were still too far away for the travellers to hear. Oşolu's breath caught in his throat when something flashed on the woman's neck.

"Mama?" he whispered.

"Who is that?" Wuraola asked as she too got up.

Oşolu took her hand. "I think it is Mama."

Demilade was beside them in seconds. "Mary? Mary is here?" He squinted. "Ha! Praise God! It is Mary!" he shouted and ran towards them.

"Who is Mary? Who is with her?" Wuraola asked in the same calm voice.

Oşolu squinted. "It's Uncle Waltz, and ... JPL and Mr. Baidoo." His lips trembled when he realised who was not with them.

Wuraola squeezed his hand. "Where is your father? Where is my son?" her voice was now frail.

"Come, sit here. I will return," Oşolu said, walking her back to the bench.

"Stay with her!" he shouted to the girl as he ran towards the moving figures.

Oşolu could tell his mother was crying before his arms wrapped around her. She had cried often in Hastings when she was homesick. She would bury her head in a pillow, hoping it would stifle her cries in the dead of night. Those were the days when he would sneak into his parents' room and slide in between her and his father, who was deep in sleep. She cried in the same long, heart-wrenching manner now.

"What happened?" He spoke into her hair. He looked at Waltz and was afraid for the first time. His eyes were red, his skin blotched. "Tell me!" he screamed. "Why are you not here with my father? We've been waiting for days!"

Dotunu's arms squeezed his waist as if life flowed from it.

"He's gone! He's gone!" she shouted.

Oşolu shuddered, remembering the dream. Everything began to spin around him.

"Oşolu!" Waltz yelled as he reached out to grab both Oşolu and Dotunu before they fell to the ground.

"What happened to him, Mama? What? You were both supposed to be here days ago!"

Dotunu grabbed Oşolu's face and pulled it close to hers. Her sleep-deprived eyes filled with tears again.

"There was an accident on the boat bringing him back to Hastings, a storm. He was found, but it was too late," she whispered. "Ireti begged him to wait for the British ship to bring him back to Freetown, but he wouldn't listen. He wanted to get back on time so we could begin packing."

Oşolu squeezed her quivering shoulders. "It cannot be," he whispered as the world spun.

Hands grabbed him from behind and pulled him away from his mother. "Your father is gone, Oşolu." Waltz's voice broke as he whispered in his ear. "I am so sorry."

Oşolu looked at a silent JPL and Mr. Baidoo. JPL took a step forward and squeezed his shoulder. "He is truly gone, Oşolu. It is hard to accept, but we must."

Dotunu looked towards the stall and gasped. "Maami! Maami!" She ran to Wuraola, who had turned towards the noise. Her head was buried in Wuraola's chest when the others got there.

"So this is the hand that life has dealt me?" Wuraola said softly as she held Dotunu and looked into the distance. "Indeed, Olokun took my Şiwoolu that day, never to return home."

Collecting herself, the old woman shook her head and shrugged. "So be it," she said firmly. Her eyes flashed as she looked over Dotunu's head at Oşolu, and in that moment, he felt again that she could see him. "The west winds have brought the one destined to take the throne. To Ake we go."

The woman hissed and kicked the stocky, dark-skinned man with the funny-looking red cloth tied around his neck. He grunted but did not move. She kicked him harder and he mumbled something and opened his eyes.

"Oya, start going! I left you here last night, drunk as ever, and here you still are." She clapped her hands over his head. "You're a disgrace! Can't you go home to your wife? Please, I am going to the coronation and must clean up before I go."

The man sat up and wiped his face, collecting the vomit that had hardened at the corners of his mouth. He recognised the plump woman, owner of the tavern where he had stopped for drinks when he arrived in Abeokuta the night before. The benches and tables packed with customers, in the wooden shack in the evening, spilled out on to the roadside. They were now neatly arranged on top of each other, but the ground was still littered with fish and goat heads from the pepper soup served with the palm wine.

"The coronation? I thought it was in a few days."

The woman grabbed the broom on the ground, her eyes flashing impatiently.

"It's been moved to today. Look, get up! I have to go home and get dressed before going; there's little time." She bent down and began sweeping up the debris around him.

"Ah! Ah! So Sunmonu wants to con everyone once more," the man said angrily and rose to his feet. "How far is the palace? It has been too long since I came here."

The woman straightened to her full height and eyed him from head to toe. "I can see you're not from here," she hissed and turned towards the road. "Take this road all the way down. You cannot miss it, you will see two pillars and an arched sign."

The man dusted off his trousers as he thanked her and began to run.

"Wait! Wait!" she shouted.

He stopped and turned around.

"Is this yours? I found it under a table." She waved a discoloured hardcover book in the air.

"Ah! Thank you!" He ran back and grabbed the book.

"I hope you're not thinking of attending the coronation like that!" she said, eyeing his tattered, dirty clothing.

"The coronation cannot happen," the man muttered to himself as he sprinted down the road, his mind plotting how to bring an end to Sunmonu's ultimate plan.

Now that the lucrative slave trade had gone sour in Èkó after the slave owners had lost the war to the abolitionists, things had gotten bad for Oriade. Sunmonu had turned his back on him, and his boss, Madame, as he used to call her, the wife of Oba Adele Ajosun, had been chased out of the palace in Èkó – she had run to Abeokuta to hide in shame.

Oriade shook his head. To think he had met that impostor, Sunmonu, in the Ẹgba forest the night most of the men in Abeokuta were at the emergency council meeting years ago, when the Ẹgba people were without a king. It had been a good night to catch villagers unaware, without the protective eyes of the ologun warriors. He and his close associate Makinde, the old recluse, had caught many young maidens and children that night – at least twenty if not more. Sunmonu had come upon them in the forest, visibly upset, on his way back from spying on his friend, Ṣiwoolu, at the meeting. He had told them he was angry that his friend had chosen to go with his father rather than with him for a final assignment to become a full-fledged trader. It made his blood boil to see the adoration and reverence Alade received at the council meeting and the attention Ṣiwoolu received just because of his father. He was also from a ruling house, but he knew that he would always be in his friend's shadow, never treated as a man with promise. The villagers looked down on him because of his clubbed foot. They never said it to his face, but their eyes screamed it. Sunmonu confessed that seeing Makinde and Oriade with the chained villagers sparked the crazy idea in his head: he would sell his kinsman and bosom friend into slavery and kill his father so that he would be next in line as king.

The plan to kill Alade was successful. Planting the poisoned bag of garri in Alade's hut, and Şiwoolu unknowingly feeding it to him when they returned from the emergency council meeting could not have been better planned. But Sunmonu was not able to capture his friend on his first attempt. Şiwoolu ran away after his father was murdered, spoiling Sunmonu's plan to bring him to the slave port in Badagry. The slave catcher he and Makinde had sent after him was murdered in the Ẹgba forest. The next attempt resulted in the same outcome – Şiwoolu and his family did not make it to Marina that first time. Oriade could tell Sunmonu was almost giving up on a third attempt to catch his kin when they met behind his house with Sigmund and the white man. He could hear the three talking as he cleaned out the small building. He should have known better than to ask why they wanted Şiwoolu so badly. Everyone knew the price for someone with royal blood was five times that of a common man. Şiwoolu always seemed to escape Sunmonu's claws as though guided by some higher power, so two years later, Sunmonu took matters into his own hands and invited Şiwoolu to his house in Èkó.

Oriade now licked his forefinger and raised it to the sky. "I swear, Sunmonu, that I, Oriade, will be the death of you. You and Madame Tinubu turned your backs on me when I needed you the most, so I will make sure nothing good comes to you."

He paused, took off his sandals, and began to sprint down the road, not stopping even when the girl-child at the roadside stall called on him to buy her goods.

The travellers approached the double pillars topped by an arched sign that identified the palace. Oşolu stood on Wuraola's left side and Dotunu on her right, while Waltz, JPL, and Mr. Baidoo marched behind them in silence through the opened doors leading to a large hall. The hallway was lined with sandals – so many that they had to be placed on top of one another.

"Who goes there?"

Two swords crossed over each other and interrupted their advance. At the end of the hall filled with people, a man in a flowing white agbada woven from aşọ oke stood before six elderly men dressed in red aşọ oke flung over their shoulders. Though middle-aged like Şiwoolu, the man's face looked fierce and aged from years of scheming and dark dealings. His eyes were small slits encircled by dark rings. Oşolu sucked in his breath when he saw the white beaded crown held delicately in the hands of one of the men. The elder holding the crown squinted at them and asked, "Who are you?"

Wuraola pulled her hand from Oşolu's, pushed aside the two soldiers in her way, and marched with her cane down the path made by the crowd. When she stood before the two, she raised her chin in defiance.

"As if you don't know, Sagbua Okukenu? You and everyone here ostracised me after my son was taken. Well, let me introduce myself again. I am Wuraola, reader of hearts and seer of the unseen. Today, Alade's grandson lays claim to the throne."

The elderly man took a step closer, shaking his head. "Alade's grandson? You are many years too late in trying to take the crown!"

Wuraola lifted her nose in the direction of white-clad Sunmonu. "And this man Sunmonu, whom my son Şiwoolu took as a brother and I as a son, wants to lay claim to the throne? No!" She banged her cane on the floor. The impact resounded in the deadly silent hall. With beads of sweat forming on his forehead, Sunmonu glanced from Wuraola's face to Oşolu and then Dotunu.

"Dotunu?" he whispered.

She shook her head. "How dare you call my name, you murderer! You killed Baami Alade and eventually Şiwoolu, but your plans to destroy his heirs will never happen! Look! Look! Here stands Şiwoolu's son, Oşolu, heir to the throne!"

The crowd stood and all began to talk at the same time.

"Silence!" Sunmonu ordered and raised a hand. The people fell silent. He began to walk towards Oşolu.

Waltz stepped in front of Oşolu and Sunmonu looked up in surprise at the mulatto man, whose eyes sparked with intense fury.

"I only want to look upon this man who claims to be Şiwoolu's son," Sunmonu said with a smirk on his face as he stepped back. He looked at the crowd. "My subjects, these women are lying. This woman Wuraola, as you know, is a witch! She killed her husband with the help of her son so she could control the kingdom through this same son, Şiwoolu. Why do you think she went blind? The gods were angry with her, of course!"

"No! It was you, Sunmonu! You murdered my husband and son!" Wuraola shouted, waving her cane in the air.

The traitor laughed deeply, enjoying the wave of distrust sweeping through the crowd. "As custom demands, I am next in line to be king as kinsman of the Jibodu Ruling House, and today I will be crowned!" He turned to the six elders and said, "Please continue."

"You cannot continue!" The manic shout rang from the entrance of the hall. A scuffle ensued at the doorway between a stocky dark man and the guards.

"Let me in!" he screamed. "My mother is from Abeokuta! I have every right to be here!"

"Let him in!" the crowd repeated, beating the benches and the walls in protest.

"Let the man in!" the elders shouted.

The guards released Oriade and he walked towards the group and paused beside JPL.

"Landlord? What are you doing here?" he asked.

JPL shook his head. "Oriade?"

"I am sure you have been searching for me in Èkó. It is this useless man, Sunmonu, who has made it impossible for me to pay my debt! My home has been taken over by debt collectors, and my mother has had to go and live in the storefront I rented from you."

Oriade walked up to stand beside Oşolu and looked

sideways at the two women. He wiped his face as though he had seen a ghost.

"Ha!" he exclaimed, pointing at Dotunu.

Sunmonu froze.

Oriade looked at him and chuckled. "You are finished, Sunmonu! Indeed, the gods are against you! Is this not the queen I deceived and helped entice onto the slave ship with your help? Today, I will stop you from becoming king!"

"Silence!" the guards shouted.

Oriade glared at them and turned back to Sunmonu, who was inching towards the doorway behind the throne. "I will reveal who you really are to these people!"

"Silence this man!" Sunmonu screamed.

"Let the stranger speak!" the crowd demanded.

"Thank you, good people!" Oriade shouted. He turned to Dotunu and bowed his head. "I know words are not enough to turn back time. I destroyed your family with my greed, and for that I am sorry. I have lived with this guilt since the day I orchestrated your kidnapping with this man and with a woman known to all as Madame Tinubu!"

"Is that what M.T. in M.T. Agents stands for? I thought she was just a rich trader and wife to Oba Adele Ajosun of Èkó?" JPL asked from behind Oṣolu.

Oriade smiled bitterly. "Yes, but M.T. Agents was just a cover for what we really did – the business of slave trade." He sighed. "Today I will make amends, not only because Sunmonu and Madame Tinubu left me in penury, but also to unburden myself of this guilt that has weighed on my conscience for so many years."

"Hmm!" the crowd murmured.

Oriade fell to his knees and looked up, first at Dotunu and then at Wuraola and Oṣolu. "I was the one who supplied the poison that Sunmonu mixed into the sack of garri given as a gift to Alade Okikilu to celebrate his selection as king. Ṣiwoolu gave him the poisoned food at the feast in Iporo Ake."

"Yeh!" the crowd shouted. "Treason!"

Oṣolu sobbed, feeling the weight of the revelation from the co-conspirator.

"Hold yourself, young king!" Wuraola said, grabbing his arm as his hand went up to wipe his face. Oriade pointed at his finger.

"My mother's ring. It laughed at me when your father wore it that day at the Marina, and it laughs at me again. I was never good enough for her."

"Continue!" the elder with the crown ordered.

"Makinde, Sunmonu, Madame Tinubu, and I kidnapped villagers from Abeokuta and brought them to Badagry and Èkó to sell to the white men. We sold many, too many to count, and in turn we became wealthy. Look! Here is one of our books with a list of the captured." Oriade pulled out the hardcover book from inside his shirt.

Dotunu shouted and reached for it with trembling hands, tears spilling down her face. "Yes, I remember this book in your room, Sunmonu. Ṣomide was playing with it, and you ... you grabbed it from him!"

"Treason! Death!" the crowd screamed as they rushed towards Sunmonu. The guards circled him, barely able to restrain them.

The man with the crown handed it to one of the

elders beside him and reached for the book. "Let me see." He looked around the hall and asked, "Is my son Adeyomi here? He is a student at the new missionary school."

A young man no older than Daniel stepped out and took the book. He scanned the first page and looked up with wide eyes.

"This man speaks the truth, Baami! These are names and ages of people, dates, and names of ships." He gave the book back to his father, who handed it to the next elder. They converged in a circle and talked in low tones, overshadowed by the crowd's demands for Sunmonu's head.

"Please, no! I beg of you!" Sunmonu shouted, falling to his knees. "Forgive me, Dotunu, Maami Wuraola! Forgive me!"

"There was nothing my son would not have done for you. He loved you!" Wuraola's voice broke.

Oṣolu's hand fell over Dotunu's as he and Wuraola held her on either side.

"Forgive me!" Sunmonu shouted as the elders signalled to the guards to grab him.

"Traitor!" the crowd screamed as the guards dragged him forward by the neckline of his agbada. It rode up his thigh, revealing his clubbed foot, and the crowd spat, cursed, and clawed at him.

One of the elders held out his hand to Oṣolu. "Come forward, Oṣolu, son of Oṣiwoolu, son of Alade Okikilu."

Chapter Nineteen

Fulfilment
Iporo Ake, Abeokuta
Southwestern Nigeria
Circa 1854

Dotunu stared down at the three headstones in the centre of the compound. She sighed and bent to pull out the dandelions that seemed to sprout the second she uprooted them. Satisfied after pulling out the last one, she caressed each headstone and stood upright.

"Olori Dotunu."

She turned and saw Idowu smiling at her.

"No more sorrow, starting today. These three are together, in a better place."

Dotunu nodded and looked down at the headstones of Alade, Wuraola, and Şiwoolu.

"I know. The joy on Maami Wuraola's face when she passed..." she whispered. Dotunu had found her swaddled in her wrapper with a soft smile on her face on the third morning after Sunmonu's coronation was stopped and he was hung in the forest.

As Idowu turned to leave, Dotunu touched her arm. "Thank you for staying with me through my year of mourning."

Idowu smiled. "Wuraola would not have wanted anything else. I will be here whenever you visit."

They heard footsteps approaching, and Idowu grinned when she saw who it was.

"Welcome back to our village, o Wali-zi!"

Waltz and Dotunu looked at each other and burst into laughter. They had tried many times to correct her without success.

"It's WA-L-T-Z, " he said.

"Wali-zi," she crooned back.

Today, they did not try as hard as they often had. Idowu ran forward and wrapped Waltz in a tight hug; he swept her up in a warm embrace.

"You look like a son of the soil already!" Idowu gushed as she pulled back and admired him in his buba and kembe.

"Ah, thank you. From you, that is a great compliment. Are you coming with us to the palace?" Waltz asked.

Idowu shook her head and frowned. "No, no. I stay here with Wuraola, you know that!" She walked away towards the backyard, looking almost offended.

Waltz looked at Dotunu in the first colourful buba and iro she had worn in over a year. As was customary when mourning, she had donned a black attire until now. The ankara material, like his, was light blue and yellow, the aṣo ẹbi every member of the family would be wearing today.

"Did I say something wrong?" he whispered, taking a step closer to her.

She smiled and looked up at him, and he could only marvel at how effortlessly she wound the blue head tie around her head.

"Don't worry about it. Idowu is ... Idowu. She and Maami Wuraola found each other years ago. She feels she owes her, even in death."

Waltz looked around the compound. "So the children and Magdalene are at the palace already?"

"Yes. Şomide took them there yesterday. If it were up to Abby and Daniel, they would have been there last week when school closed."

Waltz chuckled, then paused. "So Şomide enjoys being a schoolmaster."

Dotunu smiled. "Yes. He doesn't regret turning down the opportunity to be the king. He's always wanted to teach, he revels in it. The pupils call him Tişa!" They laughed together at the pronunciation of "teacher" by the pupils, and then were quiet. Dotunu studied him for a moment.

"Are the others on their way?" she asked as her heart skipped a beat, imagining the looks on their faces when they made their announcement.

"They should be arriving any minute now – Oşuntade, Ireti, Simon and the baby, Charlotte and James Senior and their family, and Demilade, not to mention the entire Ęgba Kingdom ... but does that matter?" he asked, holding out his hand.

She looked down at it and slowly placed hers in it. "No, it doesn't," she said softly.

"Good. Now let's go and find out the news that your uncannily wise son, Oşolu, has for us today. I am so proud that he made the decision to be a regent for a year. The elders were surprised, but I'm happy they accepted his choice."

Dotunu nodded with pride. "He needed that time to decide what was best for him, not what was expected of him," she said.

Waltz chuckled. "Oṣolu has many skills, particularly in managing competing and highly disparate tasks. Is this how kings behave – they just go off anytime to do whatever they want?" He arched a brow and Dotunu giggled.

"You know he's always enjoyed trade. The kingdom didn't come under attack the few times he was away, traveling with you and JPL, did it?" She sighed. "I can only guess that the reason he has put Sagbua Okukenu, the head of the council, in charge when he's been away has to do with his announcement today."

Waltz smiled. Dotunu looked thoughtfully into the distance.

"What is it?" he asked softly.

"Oh, nothing. I was just thinking how far we have come and remembering the things we have endured to come back here. And how happy I am that you came back with us, with me."

"It was a promise I had to fulfil."

A light breeze blew into the compound as they stood looking at each other.

"Shall we?" Waltz said.

"Let's," Dotunu said, and for a moment he gently stroked her fingers, which tightened around his as they walked out of the compound towards Ake.

Acknowledgements

I thank the Coker family for documenting our family history. As a young child, I was amazed at their dedication. I listened to their conversations when they met at my Grandpa Coker's house. They were proud of their lineage, and it rubbed off on me.

To my mother, Dr Olubusola Campbell, who painstakingly handwrote historical events of my forefathers, I will always be grateful.

To my dear friend, Anwuli Ojogwu, who always believed in this story when it was just an idea. You were the push I needed.

To my first readers: Tania Heller, Mariko Hewer and Yejide Kilanko, thank you for the feedback.

To my family and friends who have been listening ears and sturdy shoulders, you made it all worthwhile.

To my Saro family in Sierra Leone who opened their hearts and homes to me in 2016 – Uncle Saidu, Hassanatu, and Calypso – you are the epitome of African hospitality.

To Tooki and Jainaba, thank you for making the introductions to my Saro family.

To Narrative Landscape Press, it has been a journey. Thank you for taking the ride with me.

Saro was borne from a simple question of where I came from. I think we ask ourselves this question at least once in our lifetime. I'm not referring just to the physical location but the people – ancestors – we originated from. To my ancestors who made it possible to write this story, I hope you're proud of this work, *Saro*.

Glossary

Abaja Òró – Tribal marks distinctive of the Ẹgba people of Abeokuta

Abeokuta – Capital of Ogun state in southwest Nigeria and part of the Ègba Kingdom

Aké – Community of Egba people located in Abeokuta.

Aṣé – Yoruba response to a prayer

Badagry – Coastal town in Lagos Nigeria, once a slave port.

Dahomey – Kingdom in the Republic of Benin

Ègba – Yoruba tribe residing in Abeokuta

Ehn – A verbal expression emphasizing a comment

E kaabo – Yoruba for welcome back

Èkó – Lagos in southwest Nigeria

Ewé – Leaf or leaves

Gallinas – Country Region in present day Liberia

Garri – Processed cassava flour

Idanwo – Test of life

Ipekere – Fried unripe plantains

Iporo Aké – Village in subdivision of the Ègba Kingdom

Kabiyesi – King

Kokoro – Snack made from corn

Mawu-Lisa – Dahomey god and goddess of the sun and moon

Oba – King

Ogboni – Ruling council of judges and legislators in Yoruba land

Oja – Cloth material used to secure a child carried on the back

Olodumare/Olorun – God

Olokun – Goddess of all bodies of water.

Olori – Queen
Oriki – Praise or poetry that expresses hopes of a newborn's future
Orisha – Deity
Orisha Oko – Deity of the forest
Orunmila – Yoruba deity of wisdom
Ọya – Goddess of wind and lightning
Parakoyi – Professional trader
Pele – Sorry
Regla de ochá – African diaspora religion created in Cuba also called Santeria
Ṣango – God of iron and thunder
Sikar – Cigar
Ṣokoto – Trousers or pants
Tiṣa – Teacher
Yemoja – Deity of the ocean floor

About the Author

Nikẹ Campbell is a Nigerian-American, born in Lviv, Ukraine, and raised in Lagos, Nigeria. She was a finalist for the 2018 Red Hen Press Fiction Award for her historical fiction manuscript. A selection of her short stories from her collection, *Bury Me Come Sunday Afternoon*, have been adapted for film, which have won international awards. She is the author of the historical fiction, *Thread of Gold Beads*. *Saro* is her second work of historical fiction.

Nike is based in Florida, USA, with her family.

Narrative Landscape Press

Have you read?

www.narrativelandscape.com